Awakened by Spirits

Rita Borba

Book 1
The Guardian Trilogy

Silverthorne Press

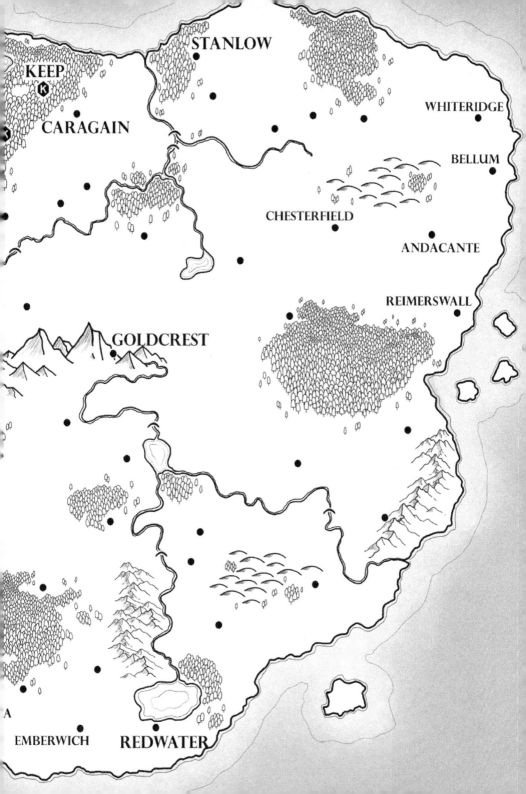

PROLOGUE

"If only I could go back to when I was six knowing what I know now..." Lane told herself on her way to the orphanage where she had lived since she was three. She kicked a rock, her gaze trailing its trajectory. "I would have done things differently."

The day her life began going downhill was engraved in her mind as if it had happened yesterday. She remembered it and the years that followed all too well.

She'd been six years old when it all started. It was the middle of a summer night. She woke up to go to the bathroom, leaving the dorm where all the girls slept and walking all the way to the other end of the building, where the restrooms were. On her way, three limbless creatures entered the orphanage through a window. About the length of her small arm and twice as thick, their black, slimy skin left no trail behind as they slithered towards her, at a much faster pace than she had ever expected.

Although scared, her legs somehow obeyed her. With her heart pounding against her ribs, she took off running, only to find herself on the floor the moment she rounded the corner. Miss Deleon, the orphanage's headmistress, stood before her. Lane had slammed against her.

The impact knocked the air from her lungs, causing panic to creep in as she tried to speak but couldn't. Brushing her brown hair out of her eyes, her gaze darted from wall to wall, searching for the three creatures. The corridor, however, was empty save for Miss Deleon and herself.

"Where? Where are they? The snakes. They were coming for me. They were…"

"Calm down, dear. It's dark, and you're tired. It was probably nothing. What are you doing up anyway?"

"I-I was going to the bathroom," she responded, eyes constantly scanning each corner of the corridor.

"Come." Miss Deleon extended a hand to help her stand, escorting Lane to her bed, staying by her side until she fell asleep again.

The following day, seeing the creatures at the forest's edge, Lane tried showing them to the other kids. She nicknamed them Shadow Crawlers since they had no limbs and disliked the sun. No matter how she described what she saw, the other kids didn't seem to see what she did, even with the Shadow Crawlers in front of them, right there in the open.

As the day went by, she began believing what Miss Deleon had told her. It was merely her imagination, though that did not ease her mind. Her fear was real. Sleeping in the large dormitory with the other girls didn't make it better. She felt exposed and vulnerable, especially with the lights off.

The lack of sleep made her jumpy. She barely ate, played, or spoke, and the headmistress quickly noticed. No answers came out of Lane, so after four days, Miss Deleon showed Lane a small, simple room on the third floor.

The space was tight, with a ceiling just high enough for the headmistress to stand. A bed was snugly encased between the walls by the window. To the right of the entrance, a small mirror hung on the wall at face height. To the left, a little closet with three drawers. Her three shirts and spare pair of pants could fit in the first, leaving the others to store the dust that would accumulate over the years.

That was it, and she loved it. It was farther from Miss Deleon's room, but here, Lane could leave the lights on whenever she pleased. Miss Deleon didn't have to ask twice. When Lane stepped inside the room, a wave of calm washed over her. She would stay in the room as long as Miss Deleon allowed it. With only two entry points—the window and the door across each other—and one too high for anything to crawl in from, the room offered a sense of security far more comforting than the freedom to leave the lights on at night.

It was perfect. From then on, she slept soundly, never again in the dormitory with the other girls. The new room became her sanctuary, quickly becoming an unexpected bonus when the other kids distanced themselves from her and started calling her weird and a freak.

In that room, she didn't have to hide or worry about side looks and whispers. She could be herself.

Outside, the whispers found her. They gained a life of their own when she moved to the room. The kids treated her as if she had a deadly disease, saying Miss Deleon had moved her farther from them because it was airborne.

From then on, everything she did was a result of that new 'disease' of hers. It didn't matter if it made sense. Her running faster than boys three to four years older? Abnormal. Her picking up movement in a heartbeat? Weird. Her seeing better, especially at night? Freaky.

As the differences became more apparent over the years, the distance between her and the other kids grew. The sentiment slowly grew past the orphanage and into the villagers of Stanlow. Within two years, everyone in Stanlow kept their distance from her.

Her talents were used against her to explain why they didn't want to interact with her. When she persisted, they turned to more hurtful comments, and the older kids became aggressive. They shoved her to the ground, punching her when she dared to stand up again. The small scar on her jawline left by a boy three years older reminded her to stay put until they left.

If she weren't driven by pride and stubbornness, the first time she was shoved would have also been the last. But she was. And so, she fell. Again and again. More times than she liked to admit before learning to stop coming near them. When she accepted the obvious and painful truth, they didn't seem bothered. If she didn't approach them, they didn't either.

Being rejected so often hurt and made her life at the orphanage lonely. She still had Miss Deleon, but it wasn't the same. The headmistress was closer to being a mother to her than a friend. She'd always been there, since her arrival at the orphanage when she was three. She was the only one who still treated her normally. Lane would have lost her mind long ago if it weren't for her.

And she almost did, if she was honest. It was a close call, but Miss Deleon's presence and the fact that she decided to find a place outside her room to play at age nine saved her from herself.

The idea came to her while enjoying the morning sun in her bedroom, seeing one of the older kids leave the orphanage to go to the village. That's when it hit her. The forest could be her playground. She loved being outside and would avoid others staring at her, coming too close, or starting a fight.

It was perfect, except Miss Deleon didn't allow children younger than fourteen to leave the premises. Asking wouldn't do it. Lane had heard many older kids try it before. Sneaking out was the only option, so one day, she came into the canteen at lunch and told the headmistress she wasn't feeling well. Without waiting for Miss Deleon to ask if she wanted soup in bed— an indulgence everyone was allowed when unwell—Lane turned around and left. In the corridor, she ran out of the orphanage, only slowing down when surrounded by trees.

Immediately, she felt at peace. A sigh of relief escaped her. She had broken the rules, but it was worth it if it meant she didn't have to be locked in her room, day in and day out, with nothing to do.

She skipped gleefully, delighted with herself for taking the risk.

That day, she played with pebbles, pretending they were dolls, she climbed trees, and played with sticks as if they were swords. She stayed out all day, going back only at sundown, hoping to be just in time for dinner.

If Miss Deleon is busy serving dinner, she won't be as mad, she snickered at her brilliant plan.

Her smug smile was clean off her face when a branch snapped to her left. As she turned to see who the culprit was, a Shadow Crawler jumped at her, biting her arm, its teeth carving into her skin and anchoring itself to her. It had moved so fast she hadn't had time to think or dodge the attack. She froze in place, the Shadow Crawler digging his teeth deeper into her skin, until the adrenaline subsided and pain kicked in.

It's real. She ripped it off her arm, the creature wriggling in her hand as it tried to escape, but she grabbed a rock and smashed its head.

"Oh..." She had expected to see a splash of blood and hear a sound from the impact, but instead, the creature disintegrated into ashes as if it had never existed. "How am I going to explain this to Miss Deleon?" she muttered as she paced back to the orphanage with her right hand covering the wound.

"Where the hell have you been? I came to your room to check on you, and you were gone," Miss Deleon yelled, clearly distressed, when Lane knocked on her bedroom door. The woman's blue eyes shifted to Lane's left shoulder. She gasped. "What happened? For crying out loud. I leave you alone for five seconds, and you hurt yourself. What did you do?"

"I..." Lane followed Miss Deleon into the kitchen and sat on one of the benches. "I... fell from a tree."

"A tree?" Miss Deleon raised her eyebrows as she examined the wound. She prodded for answers as she cleaned the wound, but no matter the question, Lane didn't tell her. She had learned the hard way when she was six that talking about the Shadow Crawlers would only make things worse.

"If you don't want to tell me, fine. Don't. We'll see how the wound heals. Until then, you're grounded and forbidden to leave the orphanage."

"What? No! Why?"

"Because those are the rules, and you know it."

"That's not fair. You know no one likes playing with me. What am I supposed to do? Wait in my room until I'm fourteen? That's five years. It's torture."

"Then make an effort with the other kids. They will warm up to you if you give them another chance."

"Yeah, right. Like I haven't tried. They'll warm up to me when the snow starts melting in the winter."

Without acknowledging her remark, Miss Deleon finished caring for the wound before letting her go her way. Each day after, Lane sat back on the bench, and Miss Deleon checked the wound, cleaned it, and changed the bandages.

After seven days, the wound was as good as closed. A big scar had taken over its place as proof that the creatures weren't a fabrication of her imagination. She wasn't crazy. They were real.

"You're still not allowed to go outside," Miss Deleon reminded her after the last check-up, throwing the used bandages in the trash. "I know you find it hard to believe, but I understand your point. I still think you could give the other kids a chance now you are all older, but that's on you to decide."

"Great, thanks for the pep talk," Lane said expressionless, as she walked away.

"I'm not done yet, Missy," Miss Deleon snapped. Lane sighed and turned around. "And I would advise you to think before you act. I have tolerated enough the last few days because I know you don't have it easy, but don't push it. I'm not your friend."

"Right, like everyone around here. Don't worry, I know. Everyone has made that loud and clear." Her eyes turned red.

"I'm sorry, I didn't mean it like that. What I wanted to say was that you need to be more respectful while talking to me," Miss Deleon corrected herself, her voice softer. "I'm here to help you. You know that. I care about you. I don't see half what happens out there, but I know it hasn't been easy."

The look on the headmistress' face, as if Lane were broken or weak, made her chest tighten. "Can I go?" she managed to ask, her voice trembling, barely holding back her tears. She didn't want to be weak.

Miss Deleon straightened her back. "Almost. I have one more question. Is there anything you need? Anything at all I can help you with?"

"No," Lane answered without thinking. "Can I go?"

"Sure."

Without another word, Lane turned on her heels and left the kitchen. Once out of Miss Deleon's sight, she sprinted to her room, slammed the door shut and buried her face into her pillow, letting her tears flow freely. No matter how well-intentioned, the headmistress' words stung like salt on an open wound. And simultaneously, she had a point. She always did.

She needed to find something meaningful and fulfilling to fill her days with. But what? The thought of facing Miss Deleon before knowing the answer filled her with dread. Skipping dinner was the easiest way to buy herself extra time to think.

Being outside had been the best experience she'd had in years. Even with the possibility of being attacked by Shadow Crawlers, she'd been free to do whatever she wanted without dirty looks. She craved more of it, but persuading Miss Deleon to let her go outside with the prospect of returning every day with a new wound for her to care for wouldn't do the trick. Her privileges would be revoked as fast as they were given.

"Can I talk to you?" Lane asked the following day after breakfast.

"Of course. Can you help me bring things to the kitchen while you do?"

Lane grabbed a pile of dirty glasses and followed Miss Deleon. "I've thought about what you said and want to train. I think it would help me get my mind off things."

"I agree," Miss Deleon said as they returned to the canteen.

"I also...want to learn how to fight."

"Fight? What for?"

An image of the Shadow Crawler with its teeth deep in her arm came to mind while she gathered the dirty cutlery into a stack of plates. "Who knows? It might come in handy someday. But..." She stared at the pile of dishes in front of her.

"Yes?" Miss Deleon asked, grabbing the plates Lane was staring at, and returned to the kitchen.

Come on, you can do this. She took a deep breath long after the water began running in the kitchen. "I don't know," she managed.

The headmistress stopped cleaning the plates, turning to face Lane, who stood awkwardly by the kitchen door. "What about from the beginning?" she suggested before restarting the scrubbing.

Lane rolled her eyes, but a shy smile pulled at her lips. The headmistress didn't say no. That meant there was a chance of her getting what she wanted.

"What about increasing your physical abilities first? You can run and work out your muscles. That's a good first step."

The smile vanished from her face. "That's not what I mean."

"You're nine, Lane. There's no need for a girl your age to start fighting.

Think of something else to pass your time."

"I can't go outside, I can't fight. What am I supposed to do then? Clean the floors? Watch paint dry?"

"We have talked about this. Those are the rules."

"But..."

"No, Lane. I'll have to say yes to the other kids if I say yes to you. I don't want to do that. So, the answer remains the same. I won't have it."

"I can be discreet."

"No."

"Seriously? You're always thinking about the others first. That's *so* unfair. I hate you," she screamed before storming off outside, passing by some of the kids, who looked surprised to see her.

Before Miss Deleon could come after her, she was in the forest and, this time, prepared. With a knife she'd stolen from the kitchen, if a Shadow Crawler appeared, she would easily kill it and show Miss Deleon she could be outside without hurting herself.

Only that day she didn't encounter any danger. After hiding the knife underneath a rock, she paced back to the orphanage, frustrated with the lack of action she encountered. Arriving just in time for dinner, the aroma of stew made her stomach rumble, clearing her mind of any thoughts about the trouble she was undoubtedly in. The relief was short-lived.

The nerves crashed back down as every orphan stared at her. Each step she took towards Miss Deleon felt like a burden, her shoes weighed down by the anxiety of the scolding that awaited her. The hundred eyes glued on her, eager to see how it would unfold, didn't help.

She stopped before the headmistress, knees shaking and heart pounding so fast she was sure the people all the way on the other side of the canteen could hear it. But Miss Deleon only offered her a bowl of stew in silence, her face blank and devoid of any emotion. Somehow, that felt worse than what she'd been preparing for.

When the orphans lost interest in her as fast as they had gained it, she realised how much this dinner felt like a regular one. Except for Miss Deleon's disappointment, breaking the rules hadn't changed anything.

Sure, what Miss Deleon thought of her was a thousand times more important than the kids who hadn't bothered to give her a second chance in years, but still. Miss Deleon would come around eventually. She was certain. So, from then onwards, she spent her days in the woods.

Training as best as she could, she ran, lifted rocks, and pretended to fight with imaginary enemies. Climbed trees, handled the knife she had stolen, and even tried to fight the Shadow Crawlers that came after her. Every time, she was either bitten or scratched badly before disintegrating them into nothing or running back into the safety of the orphanage.

Why do they only go after me? Me and no one else... And why do they disintegrate like ashes? If I could take one back, maybe Miss Deleon and the others could see them then. They would have to believe me then.

But each Shadow Crawler she managed to attack, no matter how soft or hard the blow, how slow or fast it was, they all disintegrated into dust.

Miss Deleon managed to ignore it all for a total of three afternoons, but seeing Lane's bloodied clothes every other day made her come around rather quickly. She made Lane promise that if worse things happened, for how ridiculous she thought it was or sounded, she would immediately come to Miss Deleon and tell her about it. In exchange, Miss Deleon would care for her wounds without asking for too many details about how and why.

After shaking hands, Miss Deleon gave Lane manuals on how to fish, hunt and build fires. She spent the years that came owning those skills. At thirteen, she begged for days to get books about combat. Eventually, Miss Deleon conceded, giving her all the ones she had, including a random book about weird but beautiful plants she had never seen before.

With everything she needed to survive the harsh winters of Stanlow for when she had to leave the orphanage after her eighteenth birthday, she trained every day to prepare.

CHAPTER 1

As she sprinted blindly through the streets, one thing was clear: she couldn't stop. Lane had hoped her trip to Caragain would offer a fresh start, but instead, it seemed it would end up killing her faster than Stanlow's harsh winter ever could. And it was all thanks to the Shadow Crawlers.

At first, Caragain was exactly what she'd been looking for. A big city filled with possibilities where her dream could become reality: a life away from the orphanage, without worries, judgement, and those damned creatures only she could see. Though never a possibility in her mind, the latest had been possible in this city. It had blown her mind, but it had been true.

For a while.

After travelling from Stanlow for fourteen days through forests and plains, she arrived exhausted and hungry. Caragain's broad streets, vibrant buildings towering over her, each a different colour from the neighbouring homes, all led her to a packed central square filled with tents, merchants, and buyers.

She'd never seen a place as beautiful. Granted, she'd never seen much of anything at all. Her life from age three had been spent in the orphanage of a town up north named Stanlow, where every structure was built of wood, a story high, and on the brink of falling apart. Its climate was harsh and cold, but here, it was warm and mild.

How? We're not that farther south.

The soft breeze at the beginning of spring coaxed the dormant plants out of their winter slumber. Never in all her years had she seen the first sprouts break through the ground this early in the year, just days after the first full moon of the season. In Stanlow, that would only happen somewhere halfway through spring's third and last moon cycle.

Her stomach growled at the air filled with spices, fresh produce, and the mouth-watering earthy scent of stew. She had never seen so much abundance of everything in one place.

The colours painting the city, the smells of every delicious dish being served, and the number of people gathered in the square were mesmerising. It buzzed with so much life that she missed the sun going down. In Stanlow, doors and windows would have been shut long before twilight, with only the moon and stars illuminating the streets. But here... It was as if those same stars had been plucked from the sky and hung on strings, casting a shimmer onto everything around them.

I shouldn't be here.

Night had fallen, and she was in the middle of a busy square. She tensed. Shadow Crawlers could come at any minute, and her attempts to live an ordinary life would die with them.

I'm not going to let what happened in Stanlow happen here.

She'd made the mistake when she was six to tell everyone at the orphanage about the creatures. She had insisted on it, pointing at them lurking in the shadows with their limbless bodies. Their black, slimy skin that somehow left no trail behind mocked her from a distance, taunting her as no one else saw what she did.

The orphans distanced themselves from her, and the sentiment eventually spread throughout the small village and before her eighth birthday arrived, everyone always mysteriously turned mute or blind whenever she was around.

Everyone, except for the headmistress. She never treated me differently. I can't have that here. This is my fresh start.

Eyes darting everywhere and ears tuned to any unusual sounds, she rushed out of the central square in search of a quiet area. With no money to rent a room, she would have to make do with a place on the streets.

Hours later, she found an alley in the back of a bakery whose walls were still warm from the ovens. Surprisingly, not a single Shadow Crawler had crossed her path. At first, she thought it was luck, but after searching for five days straight with no results, she dared to relax.

Are there really no Shadow Crawlers here? Is that even possible?

Now, looking back, she knew she hadn't found paradise. Hope had simply clouded her judgment.

On those blissfully naïve days, she caught up on her sleep, filling her stomach with bread tossed away in the bakery bins. Somewhat sure Shadow Crawlers wouldn't show up out of nowhere and freshened up from a bath in the pond nearby, she felt comfortable asking the baker for a job— any job.

With her history of being shut off by the Stanlow villagers, she was surprised the owner told her she could clean the floors before opening and after closing in exchange for the day's leftovers and a few coins.

She immediately accepted.

Wanting to save up money, she tried surviving with only the leftovers and the occasional piece of fruit her employer gave her. Not a day passed before her growling stomach made her sprint to the butcher next door. After buying all the beef jerky she could, the owner offered her the same deal as the baker.

With a full stomach and a place to sleep, she was happy. It wasn't luxury, but for the first time in years, she wasn't afraid to be outside the orphanage. Before finding Caragain, the orphanage had been the only place the Shadow Crawlers didn't enter. She didn't know why, but for whatever reason, they stayed outside. Whenever she'd left the gates, they made up for the time she'd been inside. They were to her like moths to light. They followed her around, attacking her whenever she found herself in the shade. Only her and no one else.

It had almost driven her insane, but the scars they left on her, scars everyone could see, made her cling to sanity. Imagination couldn't hurt you physically.

If the orphanage's headmistress, Miss Deleon, could see what she had found in Caragain, she would be proud of how much Lane had accomplished in such a short time.

Her day-to-day quickly developed into a simple routine. She began the day preparing the bakery and butchery for opening, followed by a run in the park nearby to stay fit. Halfway through, she often stopped at a more secluded area and practised with her knives—a small one she had stolen from Miss Deleon's kitchen years ago that she always carried in her jeans' back pocket, and three made from sharp rocks in her backpack.

Even without seeing a single Shadow Crawler, her body couldn't fully relax. She had been training almost every day for the past nine years. The last five, she had even added fighting to her scheme after begging Miss Deleon for her books about it. She'd gotten them, after several days of extra labour around the orphanage. She'd even gotten a few extra about hunting, fishing and weird plants.

Going without training after so many years of it being her main source of distraction felt wrong, especially when she had all the time in the world to incorporate her usual Stanlow training in her routine. So, she did.

When her workout was done, she took a shower—if you could call it that—in the park's public bathroom sink. If necessary, she cleaned her clothes in the same sink and hung them on a wire she'd tied between the bakery's alley walls.

On days she had time, she wandered to a new part of the city or went to the market to chat with the locals until she had to return for her closing shifts. Her bosses often stayed late, entertaining her with stories about their customers while she cleaned. It was funny to hear about what bothered them and what they found rude and entitled.

Most of the time, their stories were about people already having a lousy day letting their anger out on a slice of meat that had supposedly been cut wrong, having to wait too long, or being handed the wrong bread, which had been precisely what they'd asked for but for some reason, the baker should have known they meant the other loaf with a completely different name.

Even here, where everything looked perfect to her, people were angry and took it out on others for things beyond their control. It was no different than what she'd endured in Stanlow, but luckily, she didn't have to deal with it anymore.

Her routine ended with a last short walk around the block before tucking herself into the cardboard bed she had behind the bakery's garbage bin.

Typically, she fell asleep to the sounds of the leaves rustling with the wind, the water from the canal tapping against its walls, and the occasional person rushing home from a late shift or a party that had dragged on for too long. But on one of the colder evenings since her arrival twenty-eight days ago, none of those sounds comforted her to sleep. Instead, the world around her was too silent. It was unnatural.

She walked around the block, searching for anything unusual to confirm her suspicions. Part of her begged her to leave when it sensed something terrible was coming. She didn't know what, but her gut rumbled in defiance, warning her to enjoy the peace while it lasted.

Unfortunately, the following night, she understood what it meant. Four Shadow Crawlers attacked her. Not separately, but at once, which was strange. Even in Stanlow, no matter the circumstances, when she left the orphanage, they always came at her alone. She had encountered more than one on a single day before, but never together. Never in groups.

As adrenaline coursed through her veins, she couldn't help but smile. Her years of training had paid off. Within minutes, they were gone, and she was unhurt. At least three years had passed since a Shadow Crawler had last bitten or scratched her. With a job where she was expected to look decent, she needed to keep the streak going.

Unfortunately, whatever god was watching over her, they did not listen to her prayers. The night after, ten Shadow Crawlers came after her. On high alert, she responded immediately. Since they couldn't swim, she ran into the pond in the park near the bakery to separate them, thinking it would be easier to take them out that way. But she'd been wrong. After throwing a few pebbles and seeing them being dodged with ease, she stopped. It made too much noise, and the last thing she wanted was to bring anyone's attention to herself.

Enticing them to jump at her didn't work either, so she resorted to running. The trees in the park would make it easier to split them into smaller groups and would provide coverage. When she turned to face them at the edge of the park, three Shadow Crawlers lunged at her.

"Suckers!" she cackled, dodging the attack and sprinting away. The creatures hit a tree. Knowing they were too dumb to learn from their failures, she did it again, and two others fell for it. "I can do this all day, boys!"

The remaining five bolted at her, three jumping for her chest. She spun out of the way a second before the impact and dashed towards the two that had stayed behind. They attacked her, but she sliced them in two, disintegrating before reaching her.

Without skipping a beat, she turned around, stabbing each of the three Shadow Crawlers lunging at her in quick succession.

When the five who had stayed behind after hitting a tree caught up to her, she tried the trick again. "Idiots!" she yelled, seeing two taking the bait. But there was no time to gloat. From the corner of her eye, she sensed movement. Two Shadow Crawlers jumped, one towards each side of the tree. With no time to alter her trajectory, she leaned backwards to evade the attack, almost losing her balance. The fifth Shadow Crawler seized its opportunity, lashing at her and sinking its teeth into her leg.

She screamed in pain. "Enough!" Her hand tightened around the handle of her knife, the ashes of the five remaining creatures gone before touching the ground.

With her face still red from all the running and slicing, she limped to the public bathroom in the park and cleaned her wound the best she could. In the alley behind the bakery, she grabbed the emergency kit she'd gotten from Miss Deleon and spread lotion on her wounds. After wrapping it with gauze, she tried to sleep but was unsuccessful before her morning shift came around. An unsettling tightness in her stomach told her things would worsen before improving.

The wound felt less and less painful throughout the day, but the gut feeling persisted. Trying to get her mind off it, she went to the market, on a long walk through the city, and even cleaned the bakery's floors twice on her late shift. Time still passed by painfully slow.

When the streets fell silent, she waited, a tight knot in her throat. During the day, a thousand scenarios had played out in her mind, but never in her wildest dreams would she have guessed right.

A swarm of at least fifty Shadow Crawlers sprinted towards her. Probably more. No, *definitely* more.

In the chaos, she spotted other creatures she had never seen before. What they were, she didn't know. Getting a closer look wasn't exactly an option.

She had to run. Ten the previous day had been challenging enough. Surviving a herd this big was practically impossible. Running was the only alternative. Where to she didn't know, but she couldn't stop.

Luckily, she'd walked through most of the city and knew how the streets in the ten-kilometre radius around the bakery were connected. Winning in the middle of these narrow streets would be impossible.

She needed a plan. Fast. Running straight wouldn't work for long. The number of Shadow Crawlers and the full moon worked in her favour. The creatures kept to the shadows as much as possible to avoid the moon's light, but their numbers caused them to push each other out of the way, slowing the pack down.

But where could she go? To a park? Or the central square? It had open spaces, which were handy to split the herd into smaller groups.

"No... Too many people," she thought. Where else?

Shuutin.

"The Shuutin forest! Of course!"

Adjusting her trajectory, she sprinted with a purpose. The forest was about six kilometres away from where she was. It would be tough to fight afterwards, but it was the best solution she could come up with. With all the trees, the Shadow Crawlers wouldn't reach her all at once. And if she were lucky, there would be a pond or a lake she could get into until the sun came out. "Try and catch me in the water, suckers!" she shouted at the Shadow Crawlers following her.

If she could reach it, she would be fine. So, she raced until the treeline came into view.

Run faster. Faster!

She couldn't quite understand why the need to go faster came over her, but she resisted. If she pushed herself too hard, she'd be too exhausted to fight the creatures once inside the forest.

Faster!

The urge grew stronger, becoming almost painful. It had warned her about the Shadow Crawlers coming, perhaps it was right about this too.

Almost at the forest's edge, clouds covered the moon. A few creatures broke away from the pack, slithering towards her at lightning speed. One of them lashed at her leg, barely missing it. Two others leapt right after. Lane dodged one, but the other bit her right shoulder. She screamed as pain shot through her.

A few more steps and she'd be in the forest. Pushing herself to keep going, a wave of dizziness hit her, slowing her pace.

She stopped.

"Run! What are you doing? Run!" a male voice screamed.

She fell, crossing the edge of the forest.

Who was that? was her last thought before her vision blurred into darkness.

CHAPTER 2

Lane found herself inside a room, its memory familiar but distant. Most of it was blurred, but she'd been here before. A long time ago. This was...

My home, right?

Her childhood home.

She looked up and stared at two people sitting in front of her. A soft mist covered their faces as they had breakfast and discussed what they would do. Lane could choose.

Anything she liked. It was her birthday, after all.

"Park! Park! See fishes," she said with a big smile on her face.

The man before her had auburn hair with dark streaks and copper eyes. Though blurry, he looked familiar. The warm sound of his laughter fired up a memory deep in her mind, causing a wave of happiness to pour over her. In a split second, she knew who he was.

Her father.

"Great! It's decided then. You only need to put your shoes on. Then we can go."

She waddled into her bedroom, returning with her favourite shoes. "Here, Daddy. Put on! Fast!"

"I'm going to grab you a jacket in case you get cold." Another voice filled the room—her mother's. Another delightful wave washed over her.

She turned around. An elegant woman with a blue dress and silvery, wavy hair joined them.

"Is everyone ready?" her father asked. "Let's go, then."

They all stood up and walked to the park.

She screamed.

⋆⋅●⋅⋆

Lane woke up with a jolt, her head pounding. She couldn't remember what had happened before falling asleep, but the dream with her parents still resonated in her mind as if she were still in it. Why had it played again? The last time had been years ago.

Her surroundings sharpened. She was lying in a bed, but not her own. Her room at the orphanage was her little sanctuary where she could escape the side looks and whispers. This one was four times its size. The only similarity was the bed, closet, and mirror. Everything else was different. The desk where the mirror rested was a luxury she had never considered having. The walls weren't made of naked stones but painted white and smooth—at least, those that weren't made of glass. The one to her left and the one facing her bed were almost entirely windows, framed with intricate wood-carved sculptures of flowers and tiny animals, all painted by delicate and precise hands.

"You're awake!" Lane startled and looked to the right. There hadn't been anyone there a second ago, and she hadn't heard a sound, but somehow, a girl was smiling at her with her big, curious green eyes. Her straight, brown hair was pulled back and fixed in a bun, except for a little strand she kept playing with. "You've just been transferred to your room. We weren't expecting you to wake up this fast, but that can only be good. Since you're up, thanks for dropping all your little friends at our doorsteps. We've been working like crazy because of you."

Lane couldn't process what was happening. "Who are you?" she asked, taking the girl in. "And where am I?"

22

"Well, you're in *your* room, and I'm...Wow! What are you doing?" the girl asked as Lane tried to get out of bed. "Calm down. You've just spent three days knocked out in the infirmary. Take it easy. Don't stand up too fast. You need to eat first."

Three days? How? What happened? Try to remember! Her head was spinning. To hold her balance, she pressed her arms against the bed.

"Ouch!"

"Yeah, your shoulder will take a while to heal. You're lucky nothing else happened to you. They would have shredded you to pieces if we hadn't gotten there when we did. You just stood there, right in front of the barrier. It was weird."

"The barrier?" She didn't know what the girl was talking about, and the more she spoke, the dizzier Lane felt.

"You know, the barrier around Shuutin? The one keeping humans and demons away," the girl said mockingly, but when no signs of understanding followed, she added, "You don't remember, do you? That can't be good. I should get a healer to check on you." The girl hesitated before turning towards the door.

"Wait! I'm fine. Don't go." The girl happily obliged. "What...do you mean by demons?"

"You know... The things following you the other day." The girl's eyes narrowed, never leaving Lane. "You had a bunch of them coming after you, remember that?" A vivid memory came rushing back.

"I...I was running from them. There were like fifty of them..."

"More like ninety."

"Ninety?"

"Yeah." She grinned from ear to ear. "I got, like, ten of them, and there was still plenty left. I've never killed so many at once. It was kind of cool, actually. And a good practice."

23

Lane stopped hearing what the girl was saying, her hand lifting to her right shoulder. "I started feeling funny after the bite. I fainted, didn't I?"

"Eh... yeah... Gulgath do that to you. I'm surprised you're already up."

"The what now? You mean the worm-like creatures?"

"No..." The girl looked worried. "How hard did you hit your head? The worm-like ones are the Karazak. They are annoying but harmless, especially in larger groups since they become slow and predictable." Lane's gaze narrowed, and the girl continued, "But Gulgaths? Those with two sets of arms and legs? They are the ones to look out for. They're dangerous. They have poison that paralyses you." The last words sounded more like a question than a statement. "That's why you're still dizzy. The substance hasn't left your body completely yet." The girl waited, allowing Lane to process the information before asking, "Does it ring a bell?"

Lane shook her head. She recalled seeing other creatures than the Shadow Crawlers, or Karazak as the girl called it, but that wasn't the question. She wanted to know if any of it sounded familiar.

It didn't, and not for the reasons the girl thought.

"Well, no need to worry. We'll make you as good as new. Especially since demons normally don't gather around in such big groups and go after someone like they have a debt to pay. You're in luck! We want to know why they like you so much."

What was Lane meant to say? The girl was kind and helpful—traits that had never been directed at her by people younger than herself.

"Every five-year-old knows all this. You probably know it too. The poison mixed in with the impact of the fall is just messing with your head. You'll remember it in no time. Don't sweat it."

"I...I don't...I..."

The girl didn't know who Lane *actually* was. She thought she was one of them, whatever that was. But one thing was clear. The girl could also see the creatures and knew more about them than Lane. From what she could gather, there was at least one more type, one worse than what she was used to. How many more existed? She needed to learn as much as possible before they figured out she wasn't one of them and kicked her out like everyone always did. The information would be valuable for her to survive on her own.

"Diana, what did I tell you?"

Lane jolted at the sound of a male voice, sending another sharp wave of pain through her shoulder. At the entrance stood a young man, seemingly frozen in time. He wore the same black outfit as Diana, but on him... With his pale skin and dark hair... It only pronounced the emerald green of his eyes.

His gaze, stern and stoic, locked on Diana. "I told you she needs to rest." It shifted to Lane, sending shivers down her spine. Every inch of him exuded authority, from the stillness of his stance to the deliberate movements. No sign of hesitation or weakness.

She swallowed.

"Hi, I'm Kage Akuma. Welcome to the Keep. You have some clean clothes in the closet. Use them. Get dressed, then eat. I have some questions to ask you later today." Without waiting for an answer, he turned to leave.

"Wait, what? *You* have questions? For me?" Lane asked, surprised. Kage stopped just at the threshold of the room and turned around. "Sorry to disappoint, but I think you know more than I do. There's nothing I can say you don't already know."

"I don't know what happened before you got to our doorsteps. You'll tell us everything once you're feeling better."

"Seriously?" His tone didn't agree with her. Who did he think he was to order her around? He didn't know her. "I don't have anything to say." She tried to stand, but the dizziness returned, forcing her back down. "I just want to go my own way."

He would never fall for her lies. It was better to leave before they sent her away. At least that way, she'd go on her terms. She wouldn't be rejected.

"You can't even stand up. Eat and gain strength. Diana will show you around the place. I'll find you later to resume our talk." Kage turned to leave. Again.

"I'm fine," she snapped, staring at the back of his head.

His demeanour told her she was nothing more than a nuisance he wanted to be done with. The sooner, the better. That same look had been plastered on the faces of every villager from Stanlow, but for some reason, seeing it on someone who didn't even know her pissed her off.

"Sure. Stand up," he said after meeting her gaze.

"Kage..." Diana mumbled.

"No. She says she's fine, right? So, let her stand up." Without taking his eyes from Lane, he added, finger pointed at Diana, "without any help."

Eyes locked with his, she slid to the edge of the bed. The warm embrace of the afternoon sun provided the strength her muscles lacked. With a deep breath, the dizziness melted away. In one motion, she stood, proud she'd shown this Kage guy she wasn't as weak or pathetic as he made her sound.

"Perfect. Diana, give her a tour." Without saying another word, Kage turned around and left. This time, she was too baffled by the lack of warmth and sincerity in his voice to interrupt him again.

CHAPTER 3

"What's his problem?" Lane asked, ploughing back on the bed.

"Don't take it personally," Diana said. "I think he's just grumpy because of all the extra work you brought in. He's normally less stiff. Just give him some time."

If I stay long enough.

"You can only find answers to your questions if you stay."

"How did you... "

"Know?" Diana laughed. "It was all over your face."

Lane's mouth corner twitched. She quickly looked down to cover it up. What if she was mocking her? Pretending to be friendly only to make it hurt more when she kicked Lane out? There didn't seem to be a drop of malice from Diana, but Lane had been hurt too many times.

By those who can't see the monsters... She can.

"You don't have to if you don't want to, but you can stay here for as long as you'd like. Things have been weird lately. You have no reason to trust me. We just met, but it's not safe out there for our kind right now."

Our kind... Whatever that means. Lane wanted to say yes, her heart throbbed at the idea. She wanted to know what 'our kind' meant, she wanted to follow the girl, but... Her past anchored her down. Heavy and present with all the doubts that came with trusting someone who would later hurt her. "Thanks, but I've been fighting those things my whole life. I'll be fine."

"Just like you were 'fine' the other day? I get it. It's annoying to be stuck somewhere you don't want to be, but the moment you step outside the barrier, another swarm will be on you. For some reason, they like you." She shrugged, as if this was the most normal conversation ever. "Stay for a while. See if this Keep is the place for you. Get better. And if you still want to leave in, let's say a moon cycle, I'll escort you out myself. I promise."

Lane hesitated long enough for Diana to add, "It's twenty-eight days. If that's too much, at least wait until your memory is back. You'll need it out there. In the meantime, we can train together. We can help each other get better. I promise I'll make your time here count. I won't waste it. I'll even sweeten the deal. If you stay the whole twenty-eight days and still want to leave, I'll give you one of my knives. Let's be honest. Some of the things you had with you were sad," she chuckled. "I mean, real sad."

Lane couldn't hold in her laughter. "They were, but still better than my bare hands."

"You can say that again. I can't argue with that."

The girl made Lane feel at ease. She made Lane want to open up. Perhaps it was Diana's energy, or because Lane had never spoken this much to someone she'd just met. Most people never gave her the time of day, and even when they did—like her bosses in Caragain—Lane had always shared little about herself, and they had never asked. It wasn't their business, and odds were they wouldn't be part of her life long enough to care, so why bother?

But this... This felt different. Lane's gut told her Diana would understand and accept her instead of laughing. She would listen and help. If that same feeling hadn't told her to run from the Gulgath, she might have ignored it.

But it had been right in crucial moments. Twice. It was time to listen to it.

"I need to come clean, but I want you to promise not to say anything to Kage about it."

"I can't promise that. I can't put the others in danger. If you have information Kage should know, I'm sorry, but I won't keep it from him. I hope you understand."

It wasn't the answer Lane hoped for, but somehow, it further solidified her trust in Diana. The girl was impressive. Younger yet already so unwavering and confident. Lane couldn't help but smile.

I want to stay.

The worst that could happen was they'd demand she leave. In that case, she'd return to her old life in Caragain and pretend nothing had happened. She'd been through it enough times to know she would survive it. So, why was her heart racing? Why were her palms clammy?

Maybe they won't ask me to leave. Maybe I can stay and learn from them. With her heart in her throat, she took a deep breath and said, "I'm not one of you."

"I figured."

Lane's eyes widened. *You did?*

"I've been living in this Keep for a while. I know everyone."

"No, you don't get it. I'm not like you." Lane fidgeted with her fingers. "I'm not from a Keep or whatever that is. I haven't lost my memory, either. I remember everything."

"You're funny. That's a good one," Diana chuckled.

"I'm serious. I grew up north, in a little village, as an orphan. So, whatever you think I am, I'm sure I'm not it."

"Oh."

"Until today, I thought I was the only one who could see those things, the Kaza...Kara..."

"Karazak."

"That. You would've figured it out sooner or later, so..." She took a deep breath. "Do what you must. I'll go my own way if I have to. I won't come back here if you let me go. I just don't want any trouble. I won't even talk about it, I promise. Until now, I didn't know other people could see those things, so I can leave and pretend that's still the case."

Pressure built in her chest as she braced for the words coming her way. Though she had volunteered to go, it wasn't what she truly desired. She wanted to find out more about these people, but the rejection would hurt less this way.

Wouldn't it?

"Would you actually like that? I know *I* hate to be surrounded by people I don't get along with. It feels...lonely. I can't imagine what it's like if they also don't know a thing about demons. I'd go insane, to be honest. Don't you want to be around someone who understands it all?"

Lane was met with kind, hopeful eyes. Diana wanted this as much as she did. *Why? What could she possibly gain from it? Is she as lonely as I am? If everyone is like Kage, I get it.*

"If you do, I'm it. *We* are it," Diana went on. "Sure, maybe what you're saying is true. I didn't think they allowed orphans to be raised outside the Capital, but who knows?" She inspected Lane like she was a rare object. "Oh! Maybe you were kidnapped! Or maybe you were raised there as an experiment, to see what happens when you grow up in isolation." Lane raised her eyebrows. "Right, sorry. Never mind. But seriously, now that you know there are people like you, do you want to walk away and pretend we don't exist?"

Lane opened her mouth only to close it a moment later. She didn't. Of course she didn't. Whoever these people were, she already had more in common with them than anyone she'd ever met. They could see the same creatures. They wouldn't push her away because of that. For any other reason? Sure. But not that. Back in Stanlow, it was all she'd ever wanted. Why was she doubting staying now that her dream was being handed to her on a silver platter?

Is the possibility of being shunned down the line that scary? It wouldn't be the first time. Why not try and see where I land?

"Do you like living alone?" Diana asked.

"Does anyone?"

"I don't think so, but I also don't get why you're so hesitant. Nothing is stopping you, is there? You can stay and see how we live. See how it feels." Diana was locked on Lane like a hawk on its prey, registering every move. With the faintest twitch of Lane's lips, the girl lit up and added, "Who cares if you don't know what you are? I'll teach you. I'll teach you everything." Enthusiasm filled the girl's voice, and Lane found herself smiling. "And I can start by explaining what we are. Let me do the honours because you, my friend, just like me, are a guardian." Diana's chest lifted, and a proud smile spread across her face.

"A guardian?" Lane raised her eyebrows, the grin remaining. The contagious lightness with which Diana talked and carried herself infected Lane.

"Yes, a guardian! We're duty-bound to keep the streets safe from demons. There's more to it, but that's the short version. Good enough for now. The long version can wait until we get some food in your system. I don't want you fainting on me. I'd never stop hearing from Kage about it."

Talking to Diana felt effortless, as natural as with Miss Deleon. She wanted to tell her everything, ask her everything, and know more about this guardian world she'd encountered. She could if she stayed.

Not to mention the restful nights, warm baths, and food. A welcome shift in pace after almost two full moon cycles of travelling and surviving on the streets.

Lane sighed dramatically. "Okay, fine. I'm staying on one condition. I want you to show me all the possible exits right now. I want to know how to escape this place if I feel the need to do so. The moment I can't trust you anymore, I'm out of here."

"Anymore? I like that. I trust you too, so we got ourselves a deal..."

"Lane. My name is Lane. Nice to meet you," she said and extended her hand.

"Hi Lane, I'm Diana Slora. It's a pleasure to meet you, indeed." They shook hands. "I didn't catch your family name. What did you say it was?"

"I... I don't know. I don't remember anything about my parents, and the only thing the lady from the orphanage knew was Lane. So, I'm just Lane."

"Sorry, I completely forgot. My bad."

"Don't be. You couldn't have known."

Silence fell, and the awkwardness she'd expected at the beginning of their conversation settled in. Her mind was furiously searching for what to say, but at the same time, she couldn't formulate a single question to ask.

"Okay, then. Should we go for the tour?" Diana eventually asked, seemingly unbothered by the stillness.

"Yes, please," Lane said, relieved that the girl had taken the initiative.

They left the last room in a long corridor—her room for the following twenty-eight days—and walked towards the bright light about halfway down the hall.

"This is my room. If you're looking for me and can't find me in the canteen, where I'm at sixty percent of the time, you can find me here."

Two doors down to the right. She stared at the door illuminated by the flickering torches on the walls before resuming the walk down the corridor.

As they walked towards the bright light, a mixture of excitement and nervousness crept up on her as the noises became louder. What was happening there? Was it a trap? Would she have to sprint back to her room and barricade the door? It was the only place she was sure was safe. All the other doors could be traps or filled with people ready to pin her down. And if she made it to the room, would she have to break the beautiful windows to escape? Diana didn't emanate any animosity, but her brain worked overtime thinking of ways to flee.

They stopped just before reaching the light, her heart pounding hard and fast against her ribs.

"Here are the bathrooms." Diana pointed at a door to the left, calm and collected. "Everyone can use them, so don't forget to bring a towel and clothes when you shower."

"Just like in the orphanage, so I know the drill," she forced out, trying not to raise any suspicions.

"Perfect, then to the best part," Diana said excitedly as she turned to the right and into the light.

Lane couldn't believe her eyes. Any doubts melted away. It was as if the pages of the floral book Miss Deleon had given her had come to life. Opening it for the first time, she thought the headmistress had played a prank on her. She'd never seen most of the plants and flowers illustrated, and their descriptions sounded fabricated.

How could a plant shine?

But now... She stood in a beautiful, bright, open hall with extremely high glass walls. The forest extended into the building as if no glass separated them. The plants and flowers were so vibrant and alive it felt like stepping into another realm.

Her gaze immediately went up to the Fairydew Drapers, covering the ceiling with cascading pink and purple flowers, some almost reaching the ground. A beautiful Sunstalk Tree towered over her with its sturdy stem. Its broad leaves, each with its own intricate nerve patterns, were unique like fingerprints. It was mesmerising.

In the corner of her eye, small flames danced in a gentle breeze. Immediately, she knew what they were. Her favourite flower in Miss Deleon's book, the Sundrop Starflower, with its deep blue petals that slowly transitioned to a vibrant orange. She had seen them countless times in Miss Deleon's books, but the pictures didn't do them justice. They radiated with light even in the shadows of the Sunstalk Tree's leaves.

As her gaze unglued itself from the Sundrop flowers, she recognised the Moonlace Ferns as they gently illuminated their surroundings. Closing her eyes momentarily, she enjoyed the warmth of the sun on her skin, the sweet scent of the flowers in the air, and the sound of birds chirping and flying around. It was incredible. Magical.

The area had all kinds of people walking around. All in the same black outfits Kage and Diana wore. All busy and stressed, barely noticing the newcomer.

"Normally, things are quieter around here, but the demons you brought have put everyone on edge. Every day, a group of guardians patrols the border while other groups go to Caragain. Weirdly enough, we haven't found most of the demons following you. They just...vanished."

Lane frowned, and Diana added, "Don't worry. That's what we're trained to do. It's *literally* our job description. We'll find them." Diana pointed to the area on the left of the open hall. "Speaking of training. Here's our training area, my second favourite place at the Keep. If there's anything you want to learn, you name it, and we've got it. How cool is that?"

Lane was only half-listening, her eyes fixated on two girls training near the gym's entrance. The way they moved was beautiful—strong and fluid at the same time, as if they had combined fighting with dancing. It was hypnotising.

"What are they doing?"

"That's the guardian style. Thousands of years of fighting demons make you develop a style compatible with their movements. If you know which type of demon you're fighting, you can adapt to have better chances of winning. If you stay long enough, I can teach you the basics."

Lane lit up. "Really?"

"Of course! I promised I would make it worth your time, didn't I? And, besides, I always like teaching rookies how to fight."

"I might not know this style, but I've been training for nine years." *Well, only five of those were actual fighting, but that's irrelevant.*

"We'll see about that when we get in the ring. But first...the rest of the tour. As you can see, at the end there, behind the fighting rings, there's a door. That glass door in the back, right there. You see it? That door leads to the forest. That's exit number one. Next to it, the room in the back, there to the right, is the infirmary. Above it, the library, where you can find books about demons, poisons, antidotes, wounds, first aid, you name it."

Head held high, she went on. "If you turn around, you'll see our meeting area. We gather here when there are things we all need to know, like, you know, a bunch of demons heading our way." Diana winked. "A bell rings, meaning we must meet here as fast as possible. You drop what you're doing and come to get the instructions for what needs to be done. Most of the time, it's about one or two demons showing up in Caragain, so your little show was a welcome change. A bit of adrenaline now and then is good to keep you sharp, you know? Especially when no one dies. Although I shouldn't say that. Most people aren't happy with the extra work."

Lane's cheeks turned red, a knot forming in her throat. No words would make the situation better.

"I'm kidding. Don't worry about it," Diana chuckled. "Anyway. There, at the end of the meeting hall, where you see those five doors. Well, the big white one is the entrance. Or exit number two of the Keep. And with it, we can conclude the number of exits we have."

"That's all?"

"Unless you also want to count windows. But you can do that in your free time. We have enough of those. The other four brown doors are offices. One of them... Oh, that one where those people are coming out," she said as three guardians opened the door farthest to the right. "They were probably just briefed and are going on a mission. I can't wait to have my first one. You have to be sixteen to get one. The first three years on a Keep, you're trained. Afterwards, you start going on missions."

Lane's eyes grew. *Will they force me to go on missions right away? I have no idea what to do.*

"Don't sweat it. I'm sure Kage wants to see what you're capable of first. He needs to know before sending you out with others. He's strict about that. He wants everyone to come back alive, you know? But anyway, that was Kage's office."

Lane stared at the door for a second, already dreading her talk with the guy. Would he deem her unfit to stay? Was there anything she could do to show him she was worth betting on?

Am I? What can I do that they can't? I have no skills compared to them.

She had decided to take Diana up on her deal and stay, which meant she had to talk with Kage about what had happened before her arrival. She swallowed at the thought. There wasn't much to tell. Hopefully, he'd be satisfied with whatever little information she had to offer.

"And behind these doors, the most important part of this building: the canteen," Diana said with a big smile as they reached the end of the beautiful hall. "The food is good, and it's always ready to serve. Healers like me prepare it to help everyone regenerate faster after a long training. No matter when you're done working or practising, you can always pass by and get a nice hot meal to comfort your growling stomach and your tired muscles. Believe me, you'll feel the aches vanish as you chew."

"Seriously? That's insane."

"Well, I might have exaggerated a bit, but yes, that's how we can keep the high pace of missions and workouts that we do. Smart, right?"

"Yeah, sure. As long as those warm meals are there. There's nothing like a nice bowl of stew after a good practice."

"You can say that again. My thought exactly. That's why I decided to end our tour here. There weren't many other options, to be honest. As you might have realised by now, the Keep is not that big."

"Wait... Is this all?"

"Well, there are some other things underground, like jails and labs, but they haven't been used in centuries, and we aren't allowed there. So, yes, this is it, which is perfect because it means we can grab a meal. Then we relax until your arm is better. Once it is, we can train," Diana chirped.

"Yes, please. I need to move more and talk less. My arm is as good as new," Lane said, carefully rotating her arm, testing if her shoulder still hurt. To her surprise, she felt only a soft sting. "See? I barely feel it. So, after we get a nice, warm meal, we're fighting."

"What? How? That's impossible. Most people take at least a moon cycle to heal from a Gulgath's bite. Some never completely heal. Let me check it." Without permission, Diana rolled up Lane's sleeve and unwrapped the bandages. To her surprise, the wound was closed, the swelling as good as gone, no scar tissue in sight. Only an off-putting bruise remained, a reminder of the nasty bite.

"Damn, girl. I don't know what you've been eating, but let me know and give me some. You have mad healing skills. But you're right. Since your wounds are basically healed, we've got ourselves a fight after lunch. Fun!"

CHAPTER 4

The training area was amazing. The ceiling was three to four stories high, with platforms at different heights. The armoury had every imaginable fighting instrument. It had fighting areas, targets to practice with, and an enormous pool too deep for Lane's taste.

Everywhere she looked, someone was training. Even...

Is he flying? A guy floated from one platform to another, meters above her. Before she could process it, her attention was pulled to a girl by the pool. She created walls of water while a guy on the other side spat balls of fire at her. *How are they doing that?*

"Ready?" Diana asked.

Lane closed her mouth and focused on the girl. "To kick your ass? Definitely."

"You wish!"

In the blink of an eye, Lane was pinned to the ground. Three moves. After all her years of training, she'd expected more of herself. The memory of her being punched in the face by one of the orphans for standing up flashed before her eyes.

"Like I said, a rookie." Diana chuckled as she let go of Lane.

"Right..." Lane sat on the ground, annoyed.

"Don't worry. I'll teach you how to evade it." The girl's breathing became irregular when Lane didn't stand up or react. "Oh no... Did I go too hard? Are you hurt?"

The panic in her voice pulled Lane from her thoughts. "I'm fine. I'm fine."

The kids at the orphanage had always laughed after pushing her to the ground. Standing up too quickly was asking for a more brutal beating to ensure she stayed put. When Diana laughed, her instincts kicked in, but the reaction that followed as she remained seated, waiting for Diana to create distance between them... Lane hadn't expected it. She felt sorry for the girl, but mostly stupid for being brought back to when she was nine so easily. She'd seen the technique Diana had used on her before. Miss Deleon's books had taught her. She'd never tried it on someone before, but she did know how to evade it.

"I was only processing your move. I'll have it next time. You'll see," she said more to herself than to Diana as she adopted a fighting stance.

Diana struck immediately, aiming to pin Lane to the ground the same way, but she dodged it, twirling to the side just in time. A grin stretched wide across her face.

"You learn fast, but we're not done yet," Diana said, her tone still as joyful. She lunged forward, not giving Lane a moment to think, and pinned her to the ground. Again.

"Seriously?" Lane shouted in frustration.

"I guess my moves are just too advanced," Diana said smugly. "I'll take it easier on you."

"Don't you dare," Lane said firmly, her eyes fixed on Diana. "Don't treat me like I'm broken. I can take it."

Diana's head tilted. "A-are you sure?"

Lane's training usually consisted of fighting with imaginary enemies who did precisely what she expected. Or being attacked by Karazak, not exactly the sharpest tools in the box. All predictable. But this... Fighting with someone who thought during the fight was challenging and frustrating. But much, much more fun. Her heartbeat quickened, and her stomach tightened with the anticipation of what Diana would do. Would Lane dodge it or be pinned to the ground? Not knowing made her restless and excited. She wanted more of it.

Bouncing lightly on her toes to channel the newfound energy, she grinned and said, "Bring all you've got, Diana."

She had so much to learn. Whenever Diana taught her a movement or combination, questions about how to do related manoeuvres filled her mind. They practised for what felt like hours. Everything Lane learned felt strange but also familiar and comfortable. After a few tries, her body understood what it had to do, and it was all because of the books Miss Deleon had given her about fighting. The basis of the movements in the books was similar to what Diana was teaching her.

I'm glad the time I spent training wasn't a waste.

In the end, both girls were exhausted. Lane had fallen on one knee and couldn't stand up, as if glued to the ground. Diana was folded forward with her hands on her legs, a few steps away from Lane, but she didn't move. Another step would probably bring her down.

"I tell you she needs rest, and you bring her here, Diana?"

Where did he come from? Lane asked herself. She hadn't heard Kage approach them.

"I-I looked at her wound. It's healed, so I thought there was no harm in practising."

"Her wound is what?" A drop of emotion covered his face. Was he impressed? Confused? Lane didn't have time to work it out. He'd already pulled himself back together. "Show me," he barked.

Lane hesitated and looked at Diana first, who nodded. She rolled up her sleeve and took off her bandage. Turning to Kage, his face was still stone-cold.

As expected.

"It's even better than this morning. How is that possible?" Diana asked, eyes wide open.

"Better how?" he demanded, his gaze fixed on the wound.

"This morning, there was a big, ugly bruise on it. Now, it isn't even half its size." Diana grinned at Lane and said, "We're ability twins. That's so cool."

"What?" Lane glanced back and forth between the other two.

"What's your name?" Kage asked, letting her arm go and stepping back.

"Lane." Her voice was softer and more timid than she'd anticipated.

"Here," he said, handing them a protein bar each. "Eat. Then take a shower and put on some clean clothes. When you're ready, come to my office."

⋘•●•⋙

While taking a shower, she thought of her life back in Stanlow. All the training sessions and all the wounds from the Shadow Crawlers—Karazak. She often dreamed about getting rid of every last one of those pesky little creatures to roam the world without worries. Or even stay. Stay in Stanlow with Miss Deleon. If the Karazak hadn't existed, her life in Stanlow would have been tolerable. They were the reason it had always been doomed to fail, and she hated their gut for it.

Until now, she was under the assumption she was the only one who could see them. When she was younger, the other kids stared at her sceptically when she pointed at the Karazak before running away laughing. She learned to keep it to herself, but the damage had been done. People gossiped, and the news spread.

When she was eight, everyone had already distanced themselves from

41

her, whispering concerns as she passed. They tried to be discreet at first, but the whispers had turned to talk by the time she was ten. No one was worried about being cautious anymore. Those words still resonated in her head.

"Why does she even bother?"

"She's not the brightest."

"I heard she has no friends, so she talks to herself."

"I heard she hurts herself so others feel pity for her. Pathetic."

Even if false, her reputation preceded her throughout her time in Stanlow. No one was willing to associate with her, fearing what others would say. Even so, she went out to look for a job like any other orphan. Unsurprisingly, she came home empty-handed, which was a problem.

Living in Stanlow was harsh because of its winters. You needed two things to survive: food and a roof over your head. And you couldn't come across them without money.

It was almost impossible to stay warm in the winter, even with a shelter. Except for the orphanage, the houses were made of wood and poorly maintained. Most villagers had to store enough wood to keep their fireplaces burning throughout the winter since letting them go out made it almost impossible to relight them.

As if the cold wasn't enough, winter was even more brutal if you didn't have food. Hardly anything grew outside. Therefore, no money equalled no meals. You'd starve. So, yes, finding a job was a necessity.

With her gloomy future ahead, she tried for years to change the villagers' minds, but the results were always the same.

"I'll work twice as hard for half the pay!" she once screamed at a lady who made and sold clothes.

"I don't want your labour."

"Are you a bad businesswoman? I'm giving you a good deal. More work for less pay. I'll even work the wool like no one else has ever done. How can you refuse?"

"How can you not understand I don't want anything to do with you? Like clockwork, you come after every full moon, and we have the same conversation. I don't want you near me. Get that in your head."

For years, she'd clung to the hope of finding a job since the only alternative she could think of was to live on the streets with the Karazak. When her last conversation with a villager from Stanlow ended badly, she was desperate. To her knowledge, the orphanage was the only place the Karazak couldn't enter since that one time when she was six. But without a job, she couldn't afford to stay.

Never in a million years had she expected to find another sanctuary that would protect her from demons. Let alone one where people understood her. It was surreal to be where she now stood.

Maybe it will work out after all.

Back in her room, she put on one of the black suits everyone around here wore. The fabric was softer and more elastic than expected. She could move and breathe with ease given how tight it looked. Her eyes followed the curves of her body in the mirror, from her toes to her head. She could see the contours of her muscles through the fabric, the result of her hard work and years of practice. Smiling, she took a step closer to inspect her face.

Most would say she was closer to twenty-five than her actual age. Perhaps that had been another reason for not getting a job in Stanlow. Her mind immediately went to Bianca, the perfect example of what people in Stanlow adored. She had everything Lane didn't—curly black hair, beautiful blue eyes, and elegance. How could the straight brown hair, brown eyes, and all the fighting scars compete with her?

Girls like Bianca spent their days waltzing around the village, making a show for every family to see. They would drop things and hope a boy would come to their 'rescue'. More than one always did, fighting each other to win a sliver of her attention. It was pathetic.

Girls like Bianca seldom asked for a job, as most families hoped to turn them into family members by marrying their sons to them. If the girls agreed, which they always did, they could only hope to have pretty children like themselves. Then, they could try to get their children to marry someone from a higher class to get a better life. If they didn't, they still had a stable family and a job to fall to.

Part of Lane was happy she wasn't traditionally beautiful, as she couldn't see herself following that path. How dull and meaningless would such a life be? To have your only purpose be looking pleasing to the eye and procreating little clones. To push all your interests and dreams aside for the stability and security of a home.

The bitterness of the women in Stanlow when they talked, not only about her but to everyone who did the slightest thing wrong was enough proof to Lane that they were miserable. Compared to the ones selling goods in the market in Caragain, friendly and content, Lane knew giving yourself up completely for a guy would never be the way to go.

She would rather follow Miss Deleon's footsteps of being alone and taking care of forgotten children than sell herself out for so little. Still, a small part of her was jealous of those girls. Such a life would have been easier. No bites and scratches, no headaches or sleepless nights.

If everything went well at the Keep, she'd never have to envy such a life ever again. For that, she had to survive one conversation with Kage. One.

Diana had not cared that she wasn't an actual guardian, but what if Kage did? What if there were things Diana didn't know?

Her training with Diana had made her want to stay even more. Here, she could learn about this world of guardians. Here, she could have a life worth living. She could make friends.

If Kage allowed it.

CHAPTER 5

Lane and Diana stood before Kage's office door. To the side, a wooden tag engraved with *Kage Akuma* was drilled into the wall.

"I didn't expect his name to be written like this. Cage with a K?"

"His name is pronounced Ka-gey, but everyone always gets it wrong, so he goes by Cage. It's easier, and I think he's gotten used to it. He always introduces himself like that."

Silence fell between the two. Lane didn't want to enter the room, so instead, she simply stood, her heart pounding furiously as she stared at the name tag and traced it with her eyes.

"Are you ready?" Diana asked, and Lane responded by swallowing. "Don't worry. I'll be with you the whole time. I know Kage was pissed earlier, but I'm sure he's fine now. He had some time to cool down."

With my luck, he probably didn't. She took a deep breath and knocked on the door.

"Come in," they heard Kage say from the inside. When Lane remained frozen in place, Diana opened the door. "Welcome. Have a seat," Kage said, gesturing to the two red chairs to his left.

The office was modest but dark, unlike the beautiful hall behind her. Books filled the wall on Lane's left, where the red chairs they were supposed to sit on awaited them. Across from the bookshelf was a small red sofa in the same style as the chairs. Behind it were portraits of other people with black hair and light-coloured eyes. Underneath them, two tubes came out of the wall, each with a loose net blocking the exit.

In the middle of the room, right in front of her, a large table of dark wood with Kage sitting behind it. "Thank you for coming, Lane," he said after they sat down. "And thank you for bringing her, Diana. I will escort her to her room when we're done here."

"But... I thought..." Diana muttered, her voice no longer cheerful as her eyes shifted between Kage and Lane.

"Thank you, Diana," he repeated, gesturing with his right hand to the door.

No, please don't leave me, Lane's wide eyes said to Diana. The girl's face was flushed, avoiding Lane's gaze at all costs, as she stood up in silence and left her alone with Kage.

"Lane, thank you for taking the time to talk to me." She hadn't realised it had been an option. He'd made it sound like an order. "Tell me what you know."

"I already told Diana. It's not much."

"It doesn't matter. Tell me what you've been through. Everything you remember. With or without demons involved. Even if it happened long ago."

"Everything?" She swallowed. Kage nodded once and waited in silence.

They stayed like that for a while. Some part of her somehow warmed up to his cold, emotionless voice and told her it was okay to answer his questions.

Why?

Why was her gut feeling telling her to trust him? And why did she have to tell him everything? What difference did her life in Caragain make? What difference did her life in Stanlow make?

She wanted to know, so that was exactly what she asked him.

"Because I asked," was all he said.

She narrowed her eyes and pressed her lips. Diana might have his back, but she knew nothing about him. She owed him nothing. "I've told Diana what I know. Ask her."

"I already did while you were getting ready." Lane couldn't hide her surprise, even though Diana had told her she'd do just that. "I know you are an orphan from somewhere up north. You know little about guardians and what we are, but that can't be all. There's a lot you haven't told us. There must be. Why else would all those demons follow you? I need to know why, and I'm afraid I cannot let you leave until I do." The room felt heavier as he spoke. Darker.

So, it wasn't a choice to stay, after all.

"As surprising as it might be, there isn't more to tell. I lived in Stanlow most of my life before going to Caragain. Now, I'm here. End of story."

"No. Something must have triggered them. I'll know if what you tell me is relevant when I hear it." He nodded once.

His stone-cold demeanour telling her what to do annoyed her. She clenched her fists. "Like I said, besides the Karazak the other day, there isn't much to tell."

But no response came her way. He just sat, staring at her with his green eyes piercing through her, trying to find what else she wasn't saying. But there was nothing left to say. Her life was boring. Everything except for the last few days in Caragain was compliant with an ordinary life. Why couldn't he understand that? Why did he have to ask for what wasn't there?

He isn't listening. Why isn't he listening?

"Why don't you tell me what you want to hear so we can get this over with? I don't know what else to tell you. You might find it hard to believe, but not everyone has impressive or crazy pasts to share," she spat when his silence became unbearable.

The green eyes that had first hypnotised her were now getting on her nerves. She didn't want to talk about her boring past of spending years alone, practising against trees and bushes when a Karazak wasn't around. Or her mundane life of cleaning the bakery and butchery floors in exchange for scraps. Her life wasn't impressive. Why was that so hard to understand? She didn't want to talk about the past that had brought her so much misery. She wanted to focus on the future ahead and what this guardian thing meant for her.

"Just tell me. Tell me what you want to hear. I'll say it, I promise, because I don't know what you deem relevant." His green eyes were unmoving, staring at her without hardly ever blinking, building up the frustration inside her and getting her to ramble. "Maybe one of the relevant things you want to know is that I first saw one of those things when I was six. Or maybe what's relevant is that I was bitten by one for the first time when I was nine. No, wait. Can it be that what's relevant is that everyone around me thought I was a freak who cut herself for attention?"

"Were you?"

"No!" Lane stood up abruptly, pushing the chair back and walking towards the door. "We're done here."

"We are not. Sit down." The heaviness in his voice made her blood run cold. She pressed her teeth, took a deep breath and sat back down. "I need to ask. I can't assume things. I need to understand the whole picture."

"Sure. And do you have it?" Her eyes were red.

"Not yet. When did you arrive in Caragain?"

Lane raised her eyebrow, but Kage remained frozen, staring at her with his harsh gaze, waiting for an answer. She rolled her eyes and sighed. "About a moon cycle ago, with the beginning of spring."

"Something happened the other day." He paused, never taking his eyes from her. "Something strange. We haven't had any demons in Caragain in years. Then, just like that, demons started popping up in the city. Those same demons decided to go after you."

Her gaze drifted to the carvings on the sides of the desk. Its pattern lines blurred together by the lack of light in the room.

"By the look on your face, you know what I'm talking about. Tell me what you saw."

The words came out of her as a whisper, as if she feared the demons would find her again if she spoke too loudly. "Everything was fine until that one evening."

She told him about the first night and how, in the ones that followed, she was attacked by smaller groups of Karazak before the massive herd that led her to the forest. As she did, his eyes remained locked on her, his whole body rarely moving.

"The rest, you know. I woke up in one of your beds and found out those things are demons and that you are guardians."

Afraid her movement would trigger him, her gaze shifted to him as slowly as possible. She wanted to stay and hear what he had to say, and at the same time, she wanted to run out of his office as fast as she could. Her intentions for this conversation were to secure her place at the Keep to come to understand this new and exciting world of guardians better, but she might have just achieved the opposite.

And for what? To be difficult? To push back on his questions only to end up telling him what he wanted to know? Whether out of fear or trust—or both—she regurgitated it all faster than a Karazak disintegrated after being killed.

And now he's going to kick me out. Great. This is just great.

When their eyes met, his stare made her question her words. She'd told him everything, hadn't she? So, why was he still staring? Her heart pounded faster and faster as he held the silence. Did he know something she didn't? Was he testing her?

"Thank you." He said after what felt like hours of silence. "You lived in an orphanage. Where exactly?"

"Stanlow. Up north," she blurted before she could think about whether she wanted to answer.

"How old were you when you lost your parents?"

She froze. The one thing she couldn't talk about, would never talk about. That day was locked away so deep in her memory that she couldn't remember what had happened. Not that she wanted to. A few years after her arrival at the orphanage, Miss Deleon explained that her parents had died in an accident and that she'd been lucky to survive.

But had she?

"Lane," Kage said, snapping her out of her thoughts, "how old were you when you arrived at the orphanage?"

She blinked. "Three."

"How did you know about Shuutin being a safe place?"

"I..." She couldn't think straight. It always happened when her parents came to mind. "I-I didn't. I don't know why I chose it. I was thinking about a park or the central square when something inside me said..." Her gaze shifted to the floor as she remembered that night. "It was like a voice inside me told me to go to Shuutin. So, I did. The same voice told me to run faster when nearing the forest too. As if some part of me knew danger was coming and that getting inside the forest was enough to be safe."

She followed the lines carved on the desk with her eyes. When Kage didn't fill in the void, she met his gaze. To her surprise, his features were softer.

"That part of you was right. We have a barrier preventing demons and humans from entering the forest. You are safe inside it."

"Why?"

"The forest is our home. Keeps are spread throughout the border to patrol and protect the Capital. I think part of you did know. I assume because of the Sight."

"The what?"

"The Sight. A gift only a few guardians have. Most are bonded to a spirit but can hardly ever communicate with them. In some cases, it's because the spirit is in one of the first stages of her evolution and isn't strong enough to connect with your mind. However, during the last century, most spirits have evolved past the first stages of their evolution. Most cases nowadays that can't communicate with their spirit are due to a disconnection between the guardian and the spirit. The match might have been right when they bonded, but their bond has weakened over the years.

"Only a few guardians still have such a connection with their spirit. It's a precious talent that comes with advantages. Your spirit sees more than you do. She isn't confined to the tangible world we live in. She can see in every direction, giving the illusion that she knows what is coming before it comes, hence the name. Listening to her would be wise. She can guide you in the right direction."

Lane's eyebrows rose. "What do you mean by 'spirits'?"

"Diana didn't tell you that part? Spirits are magical creatures from a realm parallel to ours. They offer to bind with guardians, and if the guardian accepts, they become one until the guardian's life ends. With the binding, we get abilities that help us better navigate our lives in this realm."

"Like flying," she said, thinking about the guy at the gym.

"Yes," he said, his back straightening. "Initially, they weren't made to fight demons, but to make our lives easier. Spirits came to us able to do the bare minimum. Ruffle the terrain to plant seeds. Summon water on top of the dry fields. Shine light to improve crops' growth. Things like that. Now, the difference between spirits is more visible. Some are farther along with their evolution, making them more powerful and having more developed abilities. Take Diana, for example. She has a water spirit, but she can do more than sprinkle water. Her abilities are in the healing category. She can close wounds, stop infections, and revitalise plants. Spirits from a century ago could not."

Hearing Diana's name, a question popped into Lane's mind.

"My wound... Diana said I was her ability twin. Does it mean I'm also bonded with a water spirit?"

"No. It's more complicated than that."

"Oh..." Lane looked down, disappointed.

"Normally, you get the first signs when you are around eight. If you're strong, you attract spirits more easily, so you might get them earlier, at around six years old. The weaker ones get them later, at around ten or twelve. I don't feel any strong presence inside you. If you haven't noticed anything by now, I'm afraid it means you don't have one."

"But you just said... The Sight, it's..."

"I know. Spirits are extraordinary creatures. We still know little about how they operate and their capabilities. They use us as conduits to bring the spiritual realm into ours, but the possibilities of how they do it are limitless. We divide those manifestations in three categories. The first is a guardian. Those who are fully connected. Then you have Hollows."

Lane raised her eyebrow. She didn't like the sound of that. "Hollows are those without a spirit, making them more human than guardian. What your body does *is* a worldly manifestation of their power. You heal incredibly fast for a Hollow. So that's not what you are."

Her muscles relaxed hearing that. "Your profile aligns better with the third category, what we call Drifters. You are in tune with the spiritual realm but not fully connected to a spirit. It's a different type of bonding than Diana's or mine. One where the spirit doesn't reside in you and, therefore, only manifests partially. It's not unheard of."

"Can I...tune in to that connection? Can I use it when I want to instead of when it comes? Like during a fight? And can I gain more access to its abilities by working on this connection?" Her thoughts went miles per hour as she imagined what was possible with the Sight.

"Unfortunately, like I said, we know little about how spirits operate. We know such a connection is possible for those in tune with the spiritual realm whose bodies cannot contain the full force of a spirit. According to scholars, the abilities that manifest are mostly random. Strengthening the connection with your spirit might be possible. From your story, you only heard a few words from her, correct?"

She nodded, and he went on. "Well, you could potentially have full conversations. Although I do not know if this applies to people in your situation. The Sight is a rare gift, especially without a full binding. You might be the first one in this situation. You have to figure it out yourself."

No surprises there. That's just about how my luck works, she thought, feeling both content and frustrated. Why couldn't she have someone guide her for once? Why did she have to figure it out on her own again?

"The more you allow her to come to you, and the more you listen to her, the stronger the connection will become. Your spirit isn't the problem. She can hear you just fine. You're the one who needs to learn to listen better, which is attainable with practice. You don't need a teacher. From what I saw today, you will be fine without one."

Was he watching me? The corners of her lips twitched. *And why is he telling me all this?* It didn't go hand in hand with the stoic glare. He could have just told her no and been done with it. Instead, he tried to make her feel better by opening the doors to what she could and couldn't do with her

Sight.

He waited until their eyes met again. "Every guardian learns this before they're thirteen. If you're staying, Diana will bring you up to speed on everything." He paused. "Can you tell me more about the moment things changed in Caragain?"

"There isn't much to tell. At first, everything was normal. If you say there weren't demons in Caragain, I can vouch for that. I thought it was weird at first. In Stanlow, the longest I went without seeing a demon was probably a little over seven days, and I was sick and stuck in bed for five of them. If I don't count that one time, I think the longest I've gone without spotting one was three days. That's why Caragain was like a dream come true. Not a single one in sight for a whole moon cycle."

Kage showed no emotion again as she spoke. He sat still in his chair, back straightened, barely blinking, and eyes fixed on her.

"That one night was like the silence before the storm. I don't know how to explain it, but the streets were so quiet it felt unnatural. And then...something changed. I know it sounds weird, but...it was dark and distant," she realised as she spoke, her eyes scanning his face for any signs of understanding.

She found nothing.

"It made me want to run back to Stanlow for a second, but it also woke a part of me that wished to defy the change." She paused, hoping he'd comment on that. When he didn't, she went on, her shoulder slightly sagging. *I guess he's done talking.* "It sounds weird, but I can't tell you much more. I don't know how to put it into words. To be honest, I don't understand what happened."

After another long pause that sent Lane's heart through the roof, he spoke. "I have a request for you before you leave."

"Okay." She responded too fast.

"Keep this conversation between us. Don't tell others what you told me. Not even Diana. I'll let her know what I think she should know."

"Why?"

He didn't answer.

"If you want me to keep quiet, I want to know why."

Without breaking eye contact, he paced towards her and sat on the chair beside her. Her mouth dried as he approached her, his green eyes hypnotising her. "Just like you said, something changed. I believe due to guardians who decided to work for the enemy."

"Enemies as in demons?" He nodded. "They seemed pretty brainless when I fought them."

"You only fought Karazak in the past, and were bitten by a Gulgath on your first encounter." His answer wasn't mocking. He was only stating the facts, and still, it stung.

His next words were like adding salt to the wound. "There are stronger ones that think, plot and kill. Don't underestimate them." His jawline tensed.

That little twitch of a muscle, the stretched-out silence that came after, and the humiliation she felt after he indirectly called her weak were enough reasons for her not to ask any more about those other types.

He would've said more had he wanted her to know more, just like he did with the Sight. So instead, she asked, "Why would a guardian side with them if they are your enemies?"

"That's what I want to know. The change we felt was powerful, which means they summoned one of the stronger, if not the strongest, type of demons. That's not good, especially if they are feeding them information about our missions."

She stiffened. "What do I have to do with that? Why do I have to keep what I told you a secret?"

"Having so many demons after you isn't normal. They disappeared the moment you passed the Shuutin barrier, so we know they wanted you and you alone. They had a goal, a behaviour never seen in such low-levelled demons, which is worrying."

A nauseating feeling settled in Lane, but Kage continued, "I want to understand why before too many people find out and ask questions or before the information falls into the wrong hands. For now, only Diana and I are aware of what transpired. We completed the report about the demons but didn't mention anything regarding them following you specifically. That's why I wish you to keep your story to yourself. Even your past. We don't want others prying where they shouldn't. If demons have guardian allies, we don't want them to discover where you are."

"You're telling me all this, but how can I know I can trust you or Diana if you can't even trust the people you grew up with?"

"A bit late for that." He paused, his eyes narrowing slightly. "But you can't. You can only truly trust yourself. Trust your judgement. Trust your gut feeling, the Sight." He leaned forward. "Tell me, Lane, what does your gut feeling tell you about me?"

"That... Uh..." She swallowed, her cheeks turning red and eyes dropping to the floor. "Is still inconclusive." But that wasn't true. Somehow, she'd warmed up to the cold front he presented her and, at some points, had talked to him as easily as with Diana. Wasn't that trust? Or was she just naïve because a big part of her held tight to the idea of making this Keep her new home?

"That much I was expecting." He stood. "I hope to change your mind before the next full moon," he added nonchalantly as he paced towards the door.

The walk to her room couldn't have taken over five minutes, although it felt like ages. He didn't acknowledge her in any way, and she didn't force it.

The hall was now much quieter than during the day. The few guardians still working in the big hall would hear whatever they'd said, and she didn't want that.

"You'll have questions once all the information sinks in," he said as she opened the door to her room. "When I'm free again, I'll come find you. As a thank you for your cooperation, you can ask me anything."

"Really?" she blurted out with a smile and could swear his lips twitched slightly.

"I didn't say I was going to give you answers. I'll consider it when I hear your questions. But I'll listen," he said, again with his cold and monotone voice.

"Well, that's better than nothing, I guess. Do you have time tomorrow?"

"No, and I don't know what the coming days will look like due to the horde of demons delivered to our door. But you'll hear from me, Lane. Good night."

"Good night, Kage," she said, her cheeks blushing. She couldn't close the door fast enough.

CHAPTER 6

"Good, you're still alive," Diana said, grinning as she entered Lane's room.

"What happened to 'I'll be there the whole time'? You didn't even fight it." Lane giggled.

"You know how scary he can be. But you're still alive, and I believe you made a good impression since he escorted you to your room. Let's face it, even if this is your first day, it's not hard to find your way back. Literally, one corridor." Lane blushed, and Diana laughed. "But tell me, what happened in there?"

"Uh... Well... Kage said he would talk to you about it himself. But not much more than what I already told you. He said I should stay quiet about it all. And that I should only trust myself. Talk about a warm welcome."

"Of course, he did... He never trusts me. Everything always has to pass by him first. I know things have been weird lately. Even Kage is acting differently, not being the rules follower he normally is. But he could trust me a bit more. I know he must have his reasons. He always does," she said, rolling her eyes. "Don't get me wrong. If I had to choose someone to follow, it would be him. But it would be nice if he trusted me more and shared more with me."

"Right..." Lane fiddled with her hands before mumbling. "What...is your relationship with him?"

Diana raised her eyebrows. "Subtle change of subject." She chuckled. "But you're asking about me and Kage? Seriously? Can't you tell?" Lane stiffened, the redness returning to her cheeks, making Diana crack up. "Oh, you should see your face. That's hilarious, but don't worry, I'm just messing with you. He's my brother."

"Your what? No way!"

"Well, by marriage. My dad and his mom got together like five years ago."

"Oh, okay. I was about to say, you don't look that much alike. Are you close in age?"

"Not really. I'm fifteen. He's twenty-two."

"What? How? I'm turning eighteen tomorrow. I know I seem older, but he doesn't look a day past seventeen."

"Your birthday? Really?" She squealed. "By the spirits, that's great. I love birthdays! We have to celebrate it. I have the perfect present. It's going to be me kicking your ass a little less."

"You're so generous," Lane said sarcastically.

"You can say that again." Diana winked. "Don't mention it." She twirled the only strand of hair not tied in a bun between her fingers, a grin on her lips. "And about the age thing, I keep forgetting you know as much as a baby. We age slower than humans. Especially if we have abilities. If you don't, you age almost as fast as a normal human and live to around eighty. A hundred, tops. If you do, the stronger your spirit is, the slower you age. And the slower you age, the longer you live. The slowing down starts taking effect five years after you get your abilities, so Kage has been ageing slowly for a while now."

"That's so cool. What can he do?"

Diana scratched her head. "He doesn't like talking about it, so I think it's best to ask him yourself. He can decide what to tell you. But he definitely does, and he's crazy strong. You don't get to be commander of a Keep at twenty if you're not."

"You're making me curious. I'll ask him about it tomorrow."

"I wouldn't count on it. You probably won't see him. He always takes the day off. It's the day his father died. He likes to be alone."

"Oh... Sorry. Yeah... He told me he was going to be busy. I'll wait for another time."

"Yeah, you probably won't even find him. He always vanishes for the day, but don't worry, your birthday will still be amazing. So, rest because you'll have the beating of a lifetime tomorrow." Diana smirked.

"I thought you were going to take it easy on me."

"I never said that. I said I would kick your ass a little less. But I can still manage the beating of a lifetime within those boundaries. Don't worry," she winked.

"Can't wait."

❧•●•☙

Lane was in the room with her parents again. Her surroundings were sharper this time. She saw her mother's deep blue eyes and the smile that had always made her feel better, no matter the circumstance. She saw her father's soft expression—always present when speaking to her, even when she misbehaved—warmed her heart.

They were having breakfast and discussing what to do. Lane could choose. It was her birthday, after all. But before stepping out of the house towards the park, she woke up with a jolt, tears running down her cheeks. Not at the orphanage, but at the Keep.

Right... The Keep.

The sun wasn't out yet, but she didn't dare fall back asleep. Staring at nothing, she lay in bed and let the hours pass. The excitement of the

60

previous day that Diana had infused in her had expired. She didn't feel like doing anything or seeing anyone.

Hours later, she was pulled back to reality by a knock at her door.

"Go away, I don't want to talk to anyone," she whispered so they wouldn't hear her.

Another knock. "Lane? Are you in there?" It was Diana.

Gathering her strength to stand up, Lane slowly dragged herself to the door. When she opened it, Diana was already walking away.

"Hey Diana, sorry. I was still in bed."

With a soft smile on her face, Diana rushed back to Lane. "Still in bed? It's past lunchtime. That's no way to start your birthday."

My birthday... This wasn't any different from the previous ones. After celebrating the first two years at the orphanage and spending most of it crying, she decided to stop. When everyone pushed her away, she never tried again. What was the point without friends or family to commemorate with?

"I guess your body needed the rest after all. Sorry for waking you up."

"You didn't. I just didn't feel like getting out of bed. Didn't sleep well, that's all," she mumbled.

"That's a shame. Why? Do you miss things in your room?"

Lane didn't want to talk about it, but the worry in Diana's words touched her. "No, it's probably the new bed," she lied, forcing a smile. "Might need some getting used to."

The perky Diana was back, her whole face radiating. "Could be. But you know what always cheers me up? Some nice hot food and a good practice afterwards."

I just want to be alone, Lane thought, but said, "Sounds good. Let me get ready. I'll meet you in the canteen." Without waiting for an answer, she turned around and closed her door.

Not being in the talking mood, she was glad Diana wasn't pushing her to chat. But the girl was right. A meal did do her good. At the orphanage, breakfast was either oatmeal or bread with a choice between cheese, jam and butter. Here, the options were immense. The pancake with flowery honey and freshly cut fruits was divine. The one with the creamy nut spread was too. They hit all the right spots, especially with the watermelon juice Diana had grabbed for them.

"We don't have to train if you aren't feeling well yet, you know?"

"That's nice of you, but like you said, it'll be good for me. It'll let me clear my head." Diana tilted her head slightly, so Lane quickly added before she could ask anything else, "Unless you're afraid you're going to get your butt kicked and are looking for a way out."

"No way! I was waiting for your slow mouth to finish eating. But I guess we're done." Diana quickly cleaned their plates and sprinted to the fighting area, taking her stance. "You're sure you want to do this? You're moving way too slow for someone who wants to kick my butt."

Lane smirked, the first genuine smile of the day. Feeling better, she used that little spark of energy to attack Diana without warning. It still didn't help to get the upper hand.

The moves she'd learned the previous day helped her stay in the fight. She wasn't pinned to the floor immediately, and the longer they fought, the better she felt. Diana had been right about this too. It was like she was gaining energy from it, not getting tired. They fought for hours straight, with only a small break in between, before Diana asked to stop.

"Damn, I'm a good teacher. The practice is helping. You're moving faster already."

"Really? That's good. It means my Sight is probably working."

"You have the Sight?"

"Kage said he thought I did. I must say, it does feel like I can see what you're up to, even when I'm not looking. It could just be me compensating for knowing I should be able to do it, but still, I think I feel it."

"If Kage says so. He knows all about it. After all, he has it too."

"What?" Lane blinked. "He didn't tell me that."

"Yeah, I shouldn't have either. Like I said, he's private about those things."

"I'll pretend I don't know." Lane winked. "Want to go for another round? I'm ready," she said, jumping from one foot to another.

"I don't know how you can keep going, but I need to rest a bit longer."

She looked at Diana with pleading eyes. "But it's my birthday..." It was the first time in a long time she used her birthday to get what she wanted, and it felt weirdly satisfying.

The girl rolled her eyes. "Okay, okay. But can I teach you about demons instead? I need some rest. I don't have your stamina."

"As long as I'm learning, I'm not complaining."

"You will. *After* we get a snack."

Each got an apple from the canteen to satisfy their stomachs until dinner, as well as a shake filled with healing properties. Lane wasn't sure if it was her mind playing games or if she did actually feel the tiredness dissolve in her muscles. Either way, it was extremely cool.

As they ate, Diana explained about the different demon categories. Like Kage had mentioned, there were others besides Karazak and Gulgath.

Demons were divided into two groups: Greater Demons and Lesser Demons. The first, and luckily the scarcest, were the strongest and most intelligent demons. They could create and control the latter.

Within the Lesser Demons, there were five levels. The Karazak were at the bottom, with Gulgath on top. Both were too weak to be seen by humans—a fact Lane knew all too well—and too weak to possess anyone, unlike the three highest levels.

"So, from the bottom to the top, you have Karazak, Gulgath, Azrunol, Dregma and Ezraan. And the Greater Demons at the tip of the pyramid controlling everyone, right?" Lane asked.

"Yes, perfect. Tomorrow, we'll start with how to fight Karazak. Then, we'll move up the ladder once you have a good enough understanding of it. Karazak and Gulgath are the core of the business. We want to get that right."

"Really? I would think the stronger demons would be the priority."

"They would be if they existed. They haven't been seen in over a decade. I think the only one around here who has ever fought one is Mister Kohler, the librarian. He's the only one from this Keep who fought in the last demon war. He's over a century old, basically a book himself." She chuckled. "He's here to keep an eye on us and teach the newcomers for their first three years. He doesn't want the hustle of being the commander. Don't know why. But anyway, what I meant to say is that the other demons were all killed. Focusing on Karazak and Gulgath is better."

༄ ● ● ༄

Lane didn't like to admit it, but she was a creature of habit who quickly adapted to the situation ahead. Within a few days at the Keep, she developed a morning routine with Diana. They would get ready, have breakfast, and train together until lunch. Afterwards, they would train some more, with a snack break jammed somewhere in the middle. If the weather allowed it, they would go for a short walk outside before returning to either the canteen, the training area or one of their bedrooms.

During the training sessions, Diana would teach her about demons and how to fight them. Some of the movements in the guardian style were similar to how she practised in Stanlow, making it possible for her to keep up with Diana's teachings.

64

She had to repeat every movement until there was nothing left to improve. Diana picked apart everything, from how straight her back was to the angle of her elbows to the bend on her knees... She understood now why Diana got tired faster than she did when they fought. Maintaining those positions for so long was almost painful. She thought her training in Stanlow had been rigorous, but her shaking legs proved her wrong.

Nevertheless, she relished every second of it. Not quite as much as Diana did, or the guardians who, after witnessing her struggle for days, felt like intervening and offering advice on how to go lower or move faster.

She couldn't complain. She still enjoyed it. Not in a million years had she expected to be surrounded by people who talked to her, helped her, and showed interest in her.

"Lower, Lane. Go lower!" Jack, a red-headed, fiery boy, screamed from across the gym.

One morning, he sat with them during breakfast and asked a few questions about Lane's life. She answered vaguely, as Kage requested, and luckily, he got the hint and didn't push the subject. Instead, he commented on the amount of food they always ate and, from that day forward, decided it was perfectly fine to give her advice every chance he got. Advice she could do little with most of the time. How was she supposed to go lower when her knees couldn't bend any further?

"Don't be an idiot, Jack. She needs to go higher. How is she going to possibly stand up in that position?" Mary interjected, flipping her blond braid back. She walked up to Lane and rested a hand on her shoulder.

Her legs shook with the added weight. *Is she made of steel?*

"Don't listen to him. He doesn't know what he's saying."

Mary and Jack were the two guardians she'd seen fighting in the pool on her first day at the Keep. Whatever one said, the other was quick to contradict. Not always with words, just like the fireball Jack threw in their direction as retaliation for Mary's comment. Lane instinctively dropped to the ground. Mary, used to it, easily defended herself by forming a wall of water. It evaporated as the two collided, a burned smell filling the room.

"Guys, do that outside. We've talked about it. No one likes the smell of burned sweat," Phoebe, a girl with a voice too loud for the small body she had, screamed from the gym entrance. "It's disgusting."

"It's Jack's fault. I had to act quickly. Sweat was the closest thing to water I had."

"Do it outside," Phoebe repeated, not even turning to them as she approached the wall covered in weapons. "And Lane, don't listen to them. Your stance is fine height-wise. Just bring your left foot slightly closer to your core. You'll have more explosive power for the next move." She grabbed a sword almost as long as herself and went her way.

One or more guardians joined her and Diana during breakfast or lunch every day. In no time, she'd met almost everyone. It wasn't hard. Including herself, twenty-five people lived at the Keep, and most of them had come to introduce themselves out of curiosity. She didn't have to do much to get to know them.

Diana had instructed her not to lie about coming from other Keeps. It would raise questions since some guardians had worked in multiple over the years and would ask about certain people.

"It's a good way to bond. Especially when you can trash on someone together," Diana told her. "Nothing like a common enemy to bring people together."

Her best option was to say she'd lived outside the barrier most of her life to take care of her grandparents. Apparently, it was many did after the last demon war. This way, she would avoid questions she had no answers to. Most backed off from such sensitive subjects.

Lane's days were filled with fun and exciting new things. There was so much she'd already learned about fighting, as well as things she never thought she would, like swimming. The first time Diana offered to teach her, she refused. No inch of her body wanted to enter the cold water to splatter around like crazy in front of everyone. But when Diana found a few hours a day with little people around for them to practise, Lane reluctantly accepted and had to admit she'd had lots of fun.

Her new life was fantastic. She could enjoy it without being bitten by demons and having to worry about money and food. A moon cycle ago, she would have never thought it possible. Everything here was better than her previous life, except for the nights. She dreaded going to sleep.

Two reasons kept her from having restful nights. Firstly, the fear of dreaming about her parents again. She tried avoiding it by sleeping less, but the dream had recurred each evening, regardless of how brief her nights were.

Secondly, the fear of waking up in her bed at the orphanage and realising the Keep and the guardians had all been a dream, a fragment of her imagination helping her escape her situation back in Stanlow. She never expected to feel at home after leaving the orphanage. Sure, she thought her life would improve in Caragain, but she hadn't raised her hopes to protect herself from disappointment.

After less than a moon cycle in Caragain, the only thing missing were friends. No one filled the hole Miss Deleon left in her until, out of nothing, Diana came into her life. She had raised her expectations and now was afraid to lose it. She wanted to stay at the Keep, even when she felt like an outsider, pretending to understand a joke. Or when others talked about missions they had tackled together.

She had a whole life of catching up to do.

To minimise lying awake in bed as much as possible, she kept herself occupied for most of the day, exhausting herself to fall asleep the moment her head touched the pillow. Luckily, Diana didn't seem too bothered to keep her busy.

Back in Stanlow, she didn't have friends. Diana was her first. At least, she thought that was what they were becoming. She hadn't expected to talk so easily with someone, especially someone younger than herself. Not that age mattered, but it was funny to think her first friend was someone three years younger. She couldn't stand the kids in Stanlow who were sixteen or seventeen. A bubbly fifteen-year-old did the trick, apparently.

It was nice not to be alone for a change.

CHAPTER 7

The raindrops hitting the glass ceiling of the open hall were music to Lane's ears. The sound always calmed her, soothed her, and brought her back to herself. It was exactly what she needed after another night of having her parents in her dreams.

It had only rained three times since she arrived twenty-one days ago, much less than she had expected for spring. Still, every time it did, she made time to listen to its melodic sounds.

Her time at the Keep until now had passed by flying. Around her usual routine with Diana, she'd done a few chores to help out. It wasn't much, mostly cleaning halls and equipment that came back from missions, but she was happy to contribute back to the place that had taken her in.

Kage had told his sister to teach Lane about the guardian ways to prepare her for future missions. He would give her time to get used to her new life, but couldn't justify sending everyone besides Lane out to fight demons for too long. Not if they wanted to keep her background hidden from the others. And Kage wanted to do just that until he at least figured out why so many demons had come after her.

She was past the training age, and everyone would expect her to be trained enough to go on a mission. Kage could pin the delay on Lane being bitten by a Gulgath and being in recovery, but that would only work for so long. The healers had already expressed no concerns about her health.

To prepare for what would come, her time was mostly scheduled around learning to fight. With practices in the morning and practices in the afternoon, Lane was grateful for the meals filled with recovery energy that cleaned all the muscle aches and tiredness away.

This is awesome. I can go on forever like this.

Diana and Lane had improved greatly with their technique. They could train for three hours without interruptions or supplements, and still had energy for a walk in the forest afterwards. Today, since it rained, Lane stayed in after their first training session to watch others practise while Diana went to check if the kitchen needed her help.

Lane sat on the ground, mouth wide open, as Phoebe trained with a boy named Max. The two were on a whole different level than her. They weren't holding back because the area was relatively empty. Some Keepers were out on a task, while others had received their moon cycle off and had gone home to visit their families. They had the space and took full advantage of the situation.

They moved so fast she could barely follow them, needing to focus only on Phoebe to understand parts of what was happening. It took her a while, but when she finally picked up a couple of moves, she went to mimic them. As usual, it didn't take long for her body to understand what it had to do. Thrilled, she scanned the area, memorising how far each wall, pillar, object and person was from her. With her eyes closed, her body did as it pleased.

She'd done something like this in Stanlow before, but never with this much space. Here, her mind was present and relaxed. There were no threats, no possible surprise attacks from Karazak. She felt free. It didn't matter who or if anyone was watching. This was for her and her alone. Only her movements existed. And...

The warmth surrounding her, caressing her skin.

With a sharp turn, the same warmth followed her, encouraging her to keep going. Without hesitation, her body surrendered entirely to it. The sensation was so refreshing and light, it was intoxicating. It was like nothing she'd ever experienced. As long as her body moved, she wouldn't stop. She could go on forever.

Not a single thought crossed her mind. For the first time, she was just...her. She was simply being, and it was all thanks to the Keep. Here, she was safe. She didn't have to worry. Her body and mind could align and flow together, until a shiver went through her. All the warmth dissipated. Her arm had hit something.

How? Even back in Stanlow, with less space around her, she never hit a tree. Her perception of her surroundings was impeccable, with or without her eyes open. Someone must have walked into her space, but why?

Her body went rigid when Kage stood before her, their arms connected. She swallowed, unable to move any further. Why was he there?

"Follow me," Kage ordered, letting his arm down and walking away.

Her mind was still coming down from the high she'd just been in, but her legs followed him without her consent. What was happening? Max and Phoebe, whom she'd been observing earlier, were now watching her, along with the few others who had also been there.

For how long? She scanned the room, hoping to find clues as to why Kage was there, but was only met with wide eyes pinned on her.

I can't have done something wrong, can I?

She'd been minding her own business, going about her day. What was wrong with that? Her heart raced. Had she broken a rule due to her ignorance? If so, Kage wouldn't punish her for that, would he? Her palms grew clammy, and her breath quickened when she suddenly saw Diana. She wasn't supposed to be there. Why was she back so soon? And was she shocked? Worried? Scared?

Should I make a run for it? No... Kage would catch me in no time, for sure. Just go with him, yo-you'll be fine, she thought, not believing her own words.

He entered his office, waited for her to follow, and closed the door behind her.

"What in the world were you thinking?" he asked through his teeth, his voice cold, not waiting a second after closing the door. "Who the hell binds in the middle of the training area? Are you trying to kill someone?"

"What are you talking about?"

"I saw you." His voice raised, towering over her, blocking the exit and making her feel small and weak, like a mouse stuck in a trap.

"Saw what?" She took a step back, her hands shaking.

"Please don't lie."

"I'm not lying," she said as she tried her best to keep the shaking in her voice to a minimum. "I was doing my thing, then you ruined it."

"If I hadn't shown up, you could have hurt someone."

"I was well aware of my surroundings. There was no one near me. I wouldn't have touched a soul."

"Abilities can travel farther than where you stand."

Now, she was truly lost. What was he talking about? She was already connected to a spirit. Not fully, but connected, nonetheless. He told her himself. She didn't have a spirit that manifested to the outside, only one that healed her faster and talked to her.

"I've told you spirits are complicated. In the rarest of cases, one has a connection with the spiritual realm instead of with a spirit. You used to fall into that category. I didn't expect to have to explain the nuance of such rare cases back then." His gaze softened, though his voice remained as sharp. "One thing is certain: the uncertainty of what kind of guardian you are is gone. You are now bonded to a spirit. Fully."

"What?" The room felt hot all of a sudden. She couldn't think straight. Why was her body reacting like that? Her heart racing, her palms sweating. Wasn't she supposed to be happy? Then why was the room collapsing on her? "Wait, no... That's impossible. I... You... You said it yourself. I'm too old."

"I was wrong."

"No... I... I can't..."

You can, a voice resonated in her mind.

Her body warmed up. Her breaths shortened, and she could feel her heart hammering against her ribs.

"I... I..."

You can, the voice repeated.

Feeling dizzy and hot, her vision blurred.

You do.

"I can't be," she whispered, searching for something to hold on to.

I am here.

Lane wanted to throw up, run away, and scream. The room got hotter, too hot to breathe. She couldn't think. It was too much. But why? She dreamed about having a spirit the moment she heard about their existence. Flying around, throwing fireballs into the pool, healing wounds... It could be possible now. So why was her body reacting like this?

I am here.

"Please, stop," she whispered, tears falling down her face.

"You might not have known you were binding with a spirit, but you did." Kage's voice was close, soft. The room's temperature dropped slightly. "I'll help you figure it out. You have nothing to fear. I'm here." His hand rested on her back, firm but soft, and the temperature lowered.

She could breathe again.

"I know this is a shock, especially after being here for so long and thinking it was no longer an option," he added as he guided her towards the sofa, his hand never leaving her back. "The most plausible explanation is that your training made you stronger and susceptible to a spirit."

He was close enough that she could feel his cool breath on her skin. "Tomorrow, we're going to train outside. Alone and away from everyone. I'll teach you to control it. To get used to your spirit safely."

She stared at him, her eyes wide, and nodded. "But...aren't you supposed to bind at an early age?"

"Yes, you are." His hand left her back, and a cold rippling washed over her. "Your upbringing is a peculiar one. You were living with humans during your binding period. It might have closed you off to spirits. If you didn't know what they were, you could have partly repelled that option subconsciously." He leaned back, lips pressed together, and Lane found herself wanting to fill in the space. "Now that you are in an environment that encourages it, perhaps a spirit found a way to bind. I can't know for sure." He paused, his eyes drifting through the room as he thought. "It would explain the Sight." He turned to her, his eyes again distant and emotionless. "Is there anything you can remember from your childhood involving abilities?"

Lane searched her past, from her days at the orphanage to her encounters with demons. Nothing involving abilities stood out, not even when demons attacked. Her life at the orphanage had been ordinary, apart from seeing things humans couldn't.

She opened her mouth to answer but froze when an incomplete idea of a memory surfaced. Her body went rigid.

"You found something."

No, not that day. The room's temperature spiked again, faster this time. More suffocating. She paced the room, struggling to steady her ragged breath and pounding heart. *Anything but that day.* She would do anything but remember it. It was buried deep in her mind for a reason. She didn't want to find out why.

The heat of the room was crushing. Her vision blurred, and she gasped for air. Lost to where she was in the room, she reached out blindly for something to support herself, but her legs gave in.

"Lane." But she could barely hear him. "Lane, look at me. It's okay. You're safe." But she didn't move. He knelt, turning her to face him. "By the spirit." Her eyes were vacant and distant. "Come on, Lane. Come back to me. Focus on my voice and nothing else. You can do this."

His voice was far and dampened, and her attention was glued to one thought: the room was too hot. She was going to suffocate. There was no escaping it. She gasped, but her lungs didn't fill up with air.

I will leave, the voice resonated in her mind.

Instantaneously, the heat dropped, and she felt empty. Kage's voice became clear, and the room was no longer blurry. When her gaze met his, a tiny part of the emptiness filled with warmth and calmness due to the green emerald eyes pinned on her.

"Come back," she whispered.

"I'm here," Kage replied.

"She left. She's gone. I can't feel her anymore." Lane held back her tears as desperation sipped into her. "I made her leave. She's gone."

"Who? Your spirit? She can't leave you. She's still there."

"But I can't feel her, I can't..." The tears now flowed down her cheeks. "I can't hear her. I panicked and made her leave me. Didn't I?" She swallowed. "Didn't I? I lost my connection with her."

"No." He chuckled. But only for a moment. He quickly caught himself mid-laugh and turned it into a cough as his stoic expression returned. "It's not that simple. She connected your body to the spiritual realm but let it go because you weren't ready and panicked. But she's still with you."

"Really? That means she can come back, right? Because I'm ready, I really am now. I didn't know what to expect, but I do now. I can do this, so please, come back. I need you to come back."

"I don't think that's a go—"

Are you sure?

"You're still here! Yes! A thousand percent, yes, I'm sure."

Okay.

In a flash, the room got brighter. Lane looked down to where the brightness came from and couldn't believe her eyes. There was a ball of light between her and Kage. To the best of her effort, she controlled her breathing and suppressed the anxiety trying to creep inside her.

She stood up, and the ball of light reacted by getting bigger and hotter.

"Relax, Lane. Your spirit knows what she's doing."

She wanted to believe him but sweat ran down his face. The temperature of the light affected him too. It wasn't only inside her. He would be cooked alive if she panicked, just like she would. How could he tell her to relax? How did she think this was a good idea?

You didn't think, like usual.

How could she turn it off? Make the light go away?

"Let the ball go. I'll catch it. No one will get hurt."

"Let go? How?" she asked between ragged breaths.

"The ball is connected to you. Your stress is making it grow. If you relax, your connection with your spirit strengthens, and she'll let the light dissipate. If you stress with the connection activated, the light reacts to it and pulls on your energy because it thinks it needs to protect you. The spirit can't break it."

As he talked, the ball of light pulled at her as if her belly had a string attached to it like a feeding tube, and she understood what he meant. She, too, pulled at the string, trying to break it, but the light only saw that as a request to act. It sucked back at the string even harder, growing bigger.

"No, don't fight it. You need to let go."

Let go? How was she supposed to do that? Nothing worked. If she pushed the light away from her, the ball took it as an invitation to suck more energy out of her. If she pulled at it, it did the same. The bigger it got, the thicker their connection became and the more energy it sucked out of her. Panicking, she pulled the string again to make it smaller, but it didn't work.

Listen.

How could she when she was about to die from her own stupidity? How could she think she could control it right away? As if an ability were like a knife, tangible and easy to drop when she was done with it. With those thoughts, the ball of light grew again, now big enough to blind her.

"Let go, Lane," Kage ordered.

"How? I can't."

"Just take a deep breath and relax. It's that easy."

"It's not working."

Relax.

"I'm trying."

"Just breathe, Lane. Breathe with me." Somehow, Kage placed his hand on her back. "In... And out... Come on. You got this. In... And out...Yes, that's it, well done. In... And out... Great."

They breathed together in silence for what felt like hours. At some point, for some reason, the connection with the ball faded, and a wave of relief washed over her. But the wave was short-lived. When the connection disappeared, the ball of light expanded, and it did so rapidly. Before she could act, her body sank to the floor, her eyes heavy.

"Kage..." she whispered as the room went white. And then black.

CHAPTER 8

She woke up in her bedroom, groaning. Her body ached all over.

"Finally, you're awake! I was so worried!" Diana said, pulling the chair closer to the bed. Despite her pounding headache, Lane forced herself to smile. She didn't want to trouble Diana too much.

"I don't know what Kage did to you, but when I saw you come out of the room in his arms, I thought you were dead! What happened?"

Hearing his name caused the memories of what happened to come back flooding in.

"How's he doing?"

"Who? Kage? He's fine. He comes by every five minutes to see if you're awake, but apart from that, he's like himself." The door opened. "Speaking of the devil. I assume you want some time alone with her?"

Kage nodded. Diana sighed and left the room without another word. Lane tried to sit up, but her body didn't listen.

"Don't force it. This is the effect of using your ability too much. The first few times, you're going to be inefficient with your energy. It will drain you faster," he said as he approached the bed. Her gaze was fixed on him, her face pale as she thought of the ball forming between them. "Don't worry. No one got hurt."

Her shoulders relaxed, and colour returned to her cheeks. "That's a relief."

"The good news is, now we know why so many demons were after you the night we met." Her head tilted in response. "They most likely sensed a light spirit wanting to connect with you and wanted to get rid of it while it was still unbound. It's easier that way, and that's the kind they fear the most since it can destroy them the easiest. All the other types need more effort to destroy them. For example, fire. It's not enough to burn them. You need daggers of fire piercing through them to do the job."

"Really? I would imagine them burning to ashes before disappearing."

"They are more resistant than you would imagine. Only light kills them straight away like that."

He took a few steps closer to her. "You remembered something in my office, and it triggered a response from your spirit. You panicked. Twice."

Her gaze fell to her fidgeting hands. *You don't have to remind me of that.*

"It wasn't wise to ask for her to come a second time. My office is too small to attempt that."

"I'm sorry."

"We need to figure out what you're so afraid of remembering. Its connection with your ability is so strong that it's probably stopping you from using it properly. We can't leave it as is. It's too dangerous. I've heard of guardians in similar situations due to traumas, and they all eventually died, their abilities consuming them."

"I can't."

"I'm afraid you'll have to."

"I can't," she repeated firmly, her eyes meeting his briefly before drifting back to her fingers.

"If not for you, do it for Diana and the others. Our bodies aren't made to suppress abilities. You'll kill yourself if you suppress it for too long."

She shrugged, but when she spoke again, her voice was dull. "That's great, but I don't care. I can live with the idea of having a short life. I accepted it years ago, so don't worry. I'll be fine."

"That's not good enough. I don't know how strong your spirit is, and I can't take any chances. Your body will give in to the pressure sooner rather than later. As the commander of the Keep, I can't let it happen."

"I. Can't," she answered, her jaw tight. *Is he not listening?*

You listen, a voice resonated in her head.

"It's not up to you. As the commander, I'll handle this based on the worst possible outcome, which means the spirit inside you is fully developed and, therefore, strong. Your body isn't used to being connected to a spirit and will probably show signs. And fast. What happened in my office is an excellent example of a mild outburst. More will come if we don't tackle this properly."

"I don't care. I'm not doing it," she repeated, still avoiding eye contact and adding some conviction to her words to make Kage—and herself— believe them.

"Stubbornness might have led you to where you are now, but you must learn when to stop fighting against things. It's turning to recklessness. This isn't only about you. If you give in to it, you could have an outburst as big as Caragain."

"Great. That makes it all much better. But the fact remains. I. Can. Not. Do. It. It's impossible. I don't want to hurt anyone else, but I can't."

He didn't speak, only stared at her, so she added, "I'm not being stubborn. It's just what it is. I couldn't even control it in your office, and that was me thinking about facing the memory. Not even the memory itself. I can't do it. I'll just take this time to get as far away from everyone as possible until it eventually happens. No one will be hurt. It's that simple."

"How can you put out a fire?" he asked.

Her eyebrows rose, clearly annoyed with the change of topic.

"Amuse me."

She rolled her eyes, facing him. "With water?"

"Exactly. The same applies to abilities. Some people control fire. They have the biggest trouble fighting people who control water. And you..." He took a step closer. "You can control light. I control the darkness."

The light coming into her room disappeared. A wall of shadows covered each corner of the room, leaving her speechless.

"I can help you. But you need to want it. I can't force you into it." He took a step towards her. "You are a guardian. You have an ability. A rare one, if I might add. Don't let it go to waste."

With those words, her mind began processing what had happened in the office. As surreal as it sounded, she had used an ability. Her ability.

Light.

Yes, a voice resonated in her mind, and a warmth blossomed in her stomach.

Hi.

She touched her stomach.

Finally.

Her eyes shifted towards her stomach.

"She's talking to me. It's so strange and so familiar at the same time." Her words came out faster with each sentence, eyes sparkling with excitement.

"It takes time to get used to it. As I told you, most people call it the Sight, but it sometimes feels more like a strong gut feeling. Listen to it."

"You have it, too, right? You can teach me to use it."

His eyes locked on her, unblinking and intense. "How do you know?"

"Right... I'd like to say I can feel it, but unfortunately, Diana told me." She faked a smile. "I did tell her I wouldn't tell you about it. So, can you pretend

I asked you instead? She didn't mean to. We were talking after practice, and it came out."

He snorted.

Was that the first genuine expression from him? Could she even call it a smile? It softened his features briefly, bringing out a warmth she hadn't seen before.

That's more inviting.

"In her defence, she did say if I wanted to know about your ability, I'd have to ask you. So... she did keep some things to herself." She faked another smile.

"I'll remember congratulating her," he said, again as neutral and monotonous as ever.

Silence fell for a second, interrupted by her cough as she realised she had been staring. "What do we do now?"

"If you still have questions, you can ask them now. Otherwise, we'll meet tomorrow morning after breakfast to train. I have some things to take care of."

She tried sitting up, and her body responded to her request. Not without aching, but at least she managed to sit upright.

Finding a question she couldn't ask Diana was hard. Her mind raced but came up empty. When the awkwardness grew as he waited, frozen as a statue, she asked the first thing that popped up.

"You talked about demons being summoned. Did you mean Greater Demons?" She sighed internally. *Diana could have answered that.*

"Yes. Karazak and Gulgath are the weakest of the Lesser Demons and can be summoned by simple vengeful actions or thoughts. They don't need a lot of energy to be pulled out of their realm and into this one. On the other hand, Azrunol, Dregma, Ezraan, and Greater Demons do. Someone must summon them on purpose. Greater Demons control all Lesser Demons under them. The summoning of one would explain Karazak's and Gulgath's odd behaviour."

"You think someone summoned one?"

"I do. The stronger the demon, the more energy it needs to cross over. The energy gathered on that day was too strong to have been for a Dregma or Ezraan."

"Why?"

"There are fanatics for everything, but even among them, most guardians would never do it. Whoever did this must have been manipulated. Demons can be persuasive." His gaze was heavy on her. "They feed into a guardian's insecurities to make them do anything they want." He took a step closer to her. "Imagine having someone constantly whisper lies in your head. If they do it long enough, you won't be the same afterwards."

She swallowed. "Is the Capital doing anything about it?"

"They are trying to devise a plan before they spread the news. It would instil chaos otherwise, and that would do us more harm than good."

She frowned. "Why would they have to? Didn't everyone feel it?"

"No. Only those with the Sight did. You didn't sense it. Your spirit did and then alerted you to it. Most can't hear those warnings. The Capital know exactly who those people are, except for you. They communicated with them to keep quiet for now."

"How did they do that?"

Kage mentioned the tubes coming out of the wall underneath the paintings in his office. One of the tubes went all the way to the Capital, the other to the Keep adjacent to this one. The tubes were created to communicate swiftly between places. An Air Wielder would blast a message from one end to another, having a message arrive in hours instead of days.

"That's smart. Will guardians be able to stop whatever is brewing? Did the Capital say something about it?"

"We will, and they didn't. Not yet," he said, straightening his back.

"How can you be so sure then?"

"It has happened before. We survived it. We'll do it again."

"Really? When?"

His jaw tightened. "There have been three Demon Wars in our history. The last one, the Third Demon War, was fifteen years ago."

A knot formed in her stomach with that answer. She looked down, embarrassed. "Diana told me what happened. I should have known. I'm sorry for your loss." He didn't reply, and the knot pulled at the ends. With a dry mouth, she asked, "What happens if guardians don't win?"

"We will." Before she could ask anything else, he said, "That's enough for today. I'll see you tomorrow."

Without waiting for an answer, he was gone, leaving her alone to ruminate on the wasted questions. Once done beating herself up, she twisted and turned all night, processing the day.

How insane was it that she now had a spirit inside her? One that could one day destroy a demon in a heartbeat, but simultaneously made her life outside the forest harder. Would her life in Stanlow have been easier if she'd connected sooner? Would it have turned up differently if she had never had it? Perhaps Karazak wouldn't have come after her, and she would have had a normal life. Would she have preferred that to this?

Never. This is way cooler.

With all the unanswered questions swimming in her mind, she managed only a few scattered hours of sleep and an exhausted Lane. At least it led to a dreamless night. No memories of her parents for a change. She would eventually have to face what blocked her ability. Probably sooner than she desired, but that would not be today.

Today, she would enjoy training with Kage.

Although it was still dark outside, she was done waiting in bed. Normally, she would eat a pancake or bread with honey and fruit and a spoonful of eggs on the side. But today, she couldn't finish half of it.

"Good morning," Kage said, looking at the fork filled with egg she was forcing herself to eat. She smiled awkwardly and blushed. "Don't force it down. Your body has obtained a new source of energy. You don't need to eat as much. Once you start learning how to use your ability, you'll go back to eating more to replenish. At some point, it'll switch again. Your ability will energise you more than deplete you," he said, leaving her to grab his breakfast.

"Do you mind if I sit here?" someone said, startling her.

A guy with blond hair and blue eyes, skinny and about a head taller than her, stood on the other side of the table.

The flying guy, she thought, nodding to him.

"Hi, I'm Luke. You're new here, right? From which Keep were you transferred?"

"I'm Lane. And sort of, yeah. But I have almost a full moon cycle under my belt. That must count for something," she said, purposefully avoiding the last question.

"Nah, that still counts as new. We don't get fresh meat often, so welcome. I hope you're enjoying yourself. I must say, your ability is sick. You don't need to hide it from the rest. Everyone respects each other's abilities, especially ones we haven't seen in a while."

"I'll keep that in mind," she said, picking at the fruit on her plate.

"I'm serious. I've never seen a Light Wielder in action. I wish I had a cool ability like yours."

"What do you mean? I saw you *flying* the other day."

He laughed. "Sure, I can do that. But what good is that in battle? Fly away? Blow wind in the enemies' faces? Cool them off and give them a shiver? Real handy, indeed."

She chuckled. "You don't really believe that, do you? You can slash them into pieces from above. You can slow them down with a tornado to give your allies time to kill them. You can..." Lane drifted off at Luke's growing smirk. "You can already do all that, can't you?" He nodded, and she rolled her eyes. "Well, I still think it's all really cool."

"I am, aren't I?" He smirked. "Joking, but anyway. Those ideas are indeed good ones. I haven't tried them in a while, I'll do that. Although that doesn't take the fact that there's still you. You can come in with your badass light and be like... Pew! Pew!" he said as he gestured with his hands. "Or you can blast some sunballs around, and demons die immediately. Crispy like bacon."

If only he knew she couldn't do any of that. She laughed, partly at what he said and partly at the irony of the situation. "I still think you're more valuable in battle. You're more skilled, I can guarantee you that."

"I guess we'll have to put it to the test one of these days." He winked.

She snorted. "Sure. I'll be ready in a year or two."

"Great. I'll wait five if I have to," he said between chuckles, stopping abruptly when Kage arrived at the table and sat close to her. Too close. They were almost touching.

"Luke. What are you doing up so early?" he asked, his voice sharper than usual.

"Getting ready to train. I like an empty gym. No need for restrictions."

"Sounds good. Good luck," Kage said, staring at Luke without saying another word until he left. The tension between the two of them could cut.

What was that all about? she thought, but decided not to get into it. Kage's gaze stayed glued to the canteen door for the remainder of the meal.

⚜ • ● • ⚜

They walked about three kilometres to find a place to practice. Just as the sun rose, they found the perfect place. A clearing of a reasonable size, far enough from the Keep no one could hear them or get hurt if something went wrong.

"Here is good. I want you to stand in the middle, over there. Close your eyes and feel the sun. Feel it until it's a part of you."

"Okay..." Lane was sceptical but stood in the middle of the clearing, eyes closed. Feeling. Waiting.

Maybe this ability is why I love being outside so much. Maybe this is why I always felt depressed in those dark winter days.

"Focus," he reminded her.

Keeping her thoughts from drifting away every few minutes was difficult. Her mind couldn't relax, unlike the previous day when she was moving freely and enjoying the moment.

"I don't think this is working," she said after what felt like hours of standing in the sun doing nothing.

"It is. This is your first try. Focus and give it time. Keep going."

She sighed but did as he directed until her legs shook uncontrollably from standing still too long. The sun was past its highest point, and whatever she was doing, she was doing it wrong. Usually, her body knew what to do on its own. She didn't have to think this much. But now... She was lost, and Kage's only suggestion was to *feel the sun,* which annoyed the hell out of her.

"Forget it. This isn't working. I need a break," she said and dropped to the ground. "My legs can't take it anymore."

Without a word, Kage stood up and left.

Seriously? Is this what he calls training together? I can't believe I was excited about this. She kicked a rock. *You can be done with me, but I'm not with you.*

87

"Are you serious?" she yelled, running after him.

He turned around. "Your legs work just fine, after all."

"Was that what you wanted to test? Are you happy now? I was an idiot to be excited about today. I thought I would learn something, but maybe I should have trained with Diana instead." *Nothing? Really?* So she added, "Or maybe with Luke. I think I'll do that tomorrow."

He stiffened, which was the only hint of emotion he showed before saying, "You do what you want, but you'll lose my help if you start training with Luke."

"Help? You call this help?" she screamed, unable to contain her frustration. "What do I need that kind of help for? The demons looking for me? Oh, right, they can't get through the barrier. So, tell me, why do I need it here? And how is what you did today protecting me? You sit in the shade all day doing nothing. You must have had such a tough time back there. Such stressful and arduous work. Poor you."

He didn't blink or speak, only remained motionless, staring at her without a hint of compassion in his eyes. Seeing him stand without a care triggered her. She wanted to scream at him until her lungs couldn't take it anymore. Until he gave even the slightest sign of understanding.

Why spare his feelings when he doesn't care for mine?

"My whole world turned upside down in seconds. I have no idea what is happening or what I have inside me, and you tell me to stand in the middle of a clearing for hours to feel the sun? How is that helping me?"

Am I crying? She swore she was but felt no tears running down her cheeks, only steamy frustration.

"Lane, relax."

"So, he talks *and* comes in with another great tip. Why didn't I think of that? Relax? Thank you for the wonderful advice. I'll keep that in mind for when I feel the sun again," she shouted. "You don't get it, do you? But why should I be surprised? I'm the stupid one here. I'm stupid for actually believing we would do something out here. Stupid for actually believing you were going to teach me."

"Lane, look at me."

"Yeah, I know, I know. Relax, right? I just need to relax and feel the sun while you sit down and use me as a break from your work. Don't worry, I won't bother you again."

"Look at me!" His voice was tense and urgent, freezing her in place. Was he worried about her? "Let it go," he said softly, nodding and moving closer to her. "It's okay."

Listen, a voice told her.

"You're right." He went on. "I should have explained why we were doing what we were doing. I shouldn't have left you behind, but you must relax. I know you can."

Why was he looking at her like she was a wounded animal? Why couldn't he take her seriously and treat her like an equal? Why was he here if he despised it so much?

"Lane."

Look, the same voice told her.

Look where? She didn't want to look. She wanted to scream at him some more. To tell him how much of an ass he was for leaving her behind for no reason.

"Lane..."

The softness with which he spoke her name broke some of the bitterness she was feeling towards him. As her gaze shifted towards him, a shimmer caught her eye.

"Lane, don't."

The urgency was still present in his voice, but she didn't care.

"Look at me. Don't look down."

She did. His eyes sparkled back at her with an intensity she had never seen before. Was he crying? No... That couldn't be it. He was too good at keeping his emotional wall up to cry in front of her.

Then what is it? Why is he looking like th—

Her thoughts halted as she understood where the spark in his eye came from.

"Lane, don't."

But he was too late. Her eyes had gone down, expecting to see a bright ball of light like the one she'd created in his office, but instead, she was met with her body covered in a light so bright and red it was painful to look at it for too long.

"No, no, no, no, no, no, no. Not again," she whispered to herself.

"Focus on my voice. Look at me." Could she? Her breathing was shallow, her vision turning blurry. "You can do this. You've done it before, remember? Just breathe with me. Take a deep breath in." She did. "Now, breathe out slowly." She hesitated, thinking of what had happened the day before.

Trust him.

She wanted to but couldn't. A knot tightened her throat, preventing her from breathing. She squeezed her eyes shut, clenching her fists until her knuckles turned white.

"Lane, look at me." His voice was closer and still as firm. "Open your eyes, Lane. Come on. I'm here."

His hand rested on her shoulder, gliding down to his hand, relaxing her body. She opened her eyes, and as if he'd unlocked a valve in her, she breathed out again.

"My shadows will catch the light. It won't go through it, I promise. Just let go, okay?" She nodded, and a wall of shadows surrounded them. He placed her hand on his chest and said, "Now, focus on my breath"

The rising and falling of his chest pulled her into a hypnotic rhythm. She breathed with him, feeling the stored tension dissipate into thin air. With it, the light expanded, and it, too, vanished when it met with the shadows.

She fell to the ground, exhausted and cold.

CHAPTER 9

Lane looked out of the window at the darkness outside. Everyone was probably still asleep, and she should've been doing the same, but her mind wouldn't shut down. The events from the clearing played repeatedly in her head, trying to understand why she'd gotten so mad so fast.

He left me.

It might have been a test, but she'd felt lost and alone, just like when she woke up at the orphanage for the first time. All she'd known was gone, forcing her to start anew. That same fear crept inside her unannounced when he left her on the ground. The difference was that this time, she could do something about it. She sprinted after him to fight for her place at the Keep, to tell him he couldn't run away from her, but when he showed no signs of caring... It infuriated her, and she lost control.

If he hadn't been there...

It was clear she'd have to confront the memory as soon as possible, as painful as it would be. Waiting for another outburst wasn't an option. Her body protested when she tried to stand up, every muscle sore from the outburst and unwilling to cooperate.

"Just push through it, damn it. What's muscle ache compared to what you've been through?"

She gave it another try and managed to sit on the edge of the bed. With a few deep breaths, energy filled her body, and she stood up with the help of the bed frame. When the dizziness stopped, she crossed the room to the mirror. A black shirt hung over her chair. On her, it looked more like a dress. Its scent hit her nose, one she'd recognise anywhere—a mixture of pine wood and metal.

The memory of why she had his shirt made her blush. Her light had been so intense it had burned her clothes to a crisp. Kage immediately removed his shirt and handed it to her while looking away. After the longest and most awkward walk back to the Keep, he didn't ask for it back. He simply told her to come to him when she felt better before leaving her alone.

She'd had enough time to rest and think. Now, it was time to act and learn to control her ability. Not waiting for her mind to change, she knocked on his office door. When the door didn't open, she waited a while longer, thinking he was making himself decent after being woken up earlier than expected. But nothing happened.

Did he even sleep in his office?

When the silence prolonged, she tried the handle. To her surprise, it.

"Kage? Are you there? It's Lane."

No one replied.

She hesitated to go any further. He wasn't the type to be pleased about having people in his space without him present. Sighing, she closed the door and headed to the canteen to pass the time. She took small bites of her cheese and jam-filled bread. If Miss Deleon saw her eating like this, she would have asked if she was all right. She finished her breakfast so slowly that the last sip of her tea had gone cold and tasteless.

Feeling bored, she headed to the training area, but no one was training there yet. Her only companions were the plants in the hall. They shone brighter at night, illuminating the path she walked at least ten times while waiting for Kage and wondering what they would do at the clearing this time. They were as beautiful during the night as the day.

When she couldn't think of anything else to do, she sprinted to the still-empty office. This time, she barged in, grabbed a piece of paper and wrote, "Meet me at the same spot as yesterday. I want to remember."

෬•●•෬

"Focus," she told herself in the middle of the clearing after her attention drifted for the third time.

She readjusted her stance and took a deep breath. Her skin tingled in response. Excited, she opened her eyes to see if she was glowing, but the sensation disappeared.

Sick of standing, she sat down with her eyes closed. In silence, she stayed put until the first rays of sunshine radiated through the branches. The tingling sensation returned when the golden strings kissed her skin. Holding back her excitement so as not to scare it away, she cursed when it still did. This time, not because of her but the sound of someone approaching.

Annoyed and alert, Lane was back on her feet. "I heard you already. There's no need to hide," she yelled while scanning the area for the threat and doing her best not to show how fast her heartbeat was racing.

Out of the blue, a sharp object flew in from the left towards her, too fast for her to register what it was. But not fast enough that she couldn't dodge it. She rolled under it and away from its source. Before she could stand, another blade flew at her, now from the right. This time, instead of dodging it and creating distance, she slid underneath it and sprinted towards the attacker. She swallowed a curse when no one was where the attacker was supposed to be.

Being surrounded by trees when she didn't know where her opponents were was dangerous. It diminished her visibility and gave them an advantage. Turning around to go back to the clearing, she found herself being lifted from the ground and pinned against her opponent's body with a knife to her throat. It happened so fast she didn't have time to react.

Where had he come from?

"Don't come outside alone again. Especially not this early and far from the Keep."

It was... Diana? Lane had expected the attacker to be Kage. She was sure she'd smelled his scent in the wind. How was she picking her up like that? She was too baffled to speak.

Diana let go of Lane and walked to the clearing. "Kage told me you were here. Not happy to see me?"

Before Lane could answer, Diana transformed into Kage. She instinctively jumped back. "What was that?"

"I can use my shadows to change people's perception of me. I'm not the only one. That's why, next time, wait for me. Even inside the barrier can be dangerous."

"Like being attacked by flying disks without warning?" Her tone was sharp, but her smile told him she wasn't serious.

"I rustled the leaves. I didn't have to. I did it to get you ready."

"You could have killed me!"

"I had enough faith in your capabilities. I've seen you train with Diana."

You have? Her cheeks turned red, but she said, "The Diana thing was smart, but you should hide your scent better. I knew it was you after the first attack." She smiled, feeling good about herself for picking that up. "Otherwise, I wouldn't have sprinted to the trees like a fool."

"Even if you did, you were at a disadvantage. I easily got to you. It was still the wrong choice."

"You were always at an advantage because I couldn't see you, but I knew it was you. That defeats the purpose of being sneaky."

Another disk flew towards her. It was high enough she didn't have to dodge it, but the scent that hit her made her heart skip a beat. It was sweet and flowery, just like Diana's.

"How?"

He lifted a little jar with a pink liquid inside.

"Okay. If you can manipulate what I see and smell, I still don't know if you're the real Kage." A shadow figure formed beside him. "Is that enough for me to know? I mean, for all I know, you can also fake that. I wouldn't know how, but that's beside the point. You could still be someone else."

"Sharp. You would be surprised how many people think this *is* enough proof." He took a step towards her. "I can tell you a piece of information you haven't told anyone else." He took another step. "Something you only told me." One more step. Now, so close she could touch him if she extended her arm. "I know you were three when you woke up in Stanlow."

"You remember that?" she blurted. "I guess that means you're the real Kage," she quickly added, realising she had said the first part aloud. She hadn't expected him to remember half of what she'd told him, much less something as insignificant.

He smiled briefly before all emotion left his face again. "You shouldn't let me come this close until you know for sure, either." He paused, his eyes going from her mouth to her eyes. "I read your letter. Do you want to do it now?"

"I-I do, but I have a few questions first." He stepped back and pointed at a fallen tree nearby. "I was thinking about it, and I don't understand how my memory has anything to do with my ability," she said after sitting down. "The memory is about..." She took a deep breath. "My parents. But I was three back then. How can that influence my ability now?"

"Trauma works differently with everyone and can leave long-lasting effects behind. You might have witnessed something that made you unconsciously afraid of having an ability. Using it now might be triggering that fear. We can try to get to the memory and see if it influences how you connect with your spirit. If it does, we'll keep going. If it doesn't, we'll know the two are unrelated. We'll move on to the next memory until we find the reason behind the block."

"Sure, it makes sense, but can I ask you something else?" He nodded. "I know...that it's hard for you, but can you..." She peeled pieces of bark from the tree trunk they were sitting on. "Can you tell me about the last Demon War?"

"Why?"

"My parents died when I was three. That was fifteen years ago... So was the war." She paused. "If they have anything to do with one another, it might help with my memory."

He took a breath. "It was a terrible war. It lasted for two seasons. We lost a third of our men fighting the summoned demons. I was seven, and even though I'd already bonded with my spirit, I didn't fight. But my father did. He died at the end of it with his squat. Demons were summoned inside the barrier and stormed the Capital, so most of the soldiers resting or recovering from the fight didn't have a chance. My dad was there with his squad, preparing to leave for another mission when it happened. They tried to save as many people as they could. But..."

His gaze was distant as he talked. He was so close she could reach for his hand if she wanted, but somehow, he felt distant and inaccessible.

"As they sprinted to the swarm of Dregma and Ezraan, a blast of energy took them out. The Council thinks a man used his ability to protect his family and the people around him, but he miscalculated. He must have been hurt and angry because his reaction was too powerful for the situation. In the end, he didn't just kill the demons and himself but everyone within a five-hundred-meter radius, which included his family. And my dad."

Lane felt dizzy. "I'm sorry."

"The war ended that day. Most demons were in that kill zone. The few outside it were easily defeated." Without looking at her, he asked, "Did it help?"

Tears ran down her cheeks. "I'm sorry," she whispered before looking the other way.

"For what?"

She didn't know but felt the urge to say it anyway. Did people say that when someone died? She wasn't sure. It was the first time she found herself in such a situation.

"Did it help?" he asked again when she didn't reply.

Not daring to look at him, she wiped her tears and stared at the ground. "The memory has played in my dreams almost every night since I've been here. I know something bad happens because I always wake up screaming. I just don't know what, so I don't know yet."

"Can you tell me what you remember?"

Her throat felt dry. She grabbed the water bag they had brought and drank the whole thing. It didn't help.

"In the dream, I'm home with my parents. It's my birthday, and I can choose what we will do, so I choose to go to the park. We get ready and head there, but we don't get far. I always scream for my parents to stop and wake up." She paused, feeling her tears fill up her eyes. "If I could go back, I would've just asked them to stay home."

"Do you want to remember?"

"I don't, but I have to, don't I? I don't have a choice. I don't want to hurt anyone else."

"You haven't hurt anyone yet, and as long as I'm here..." His hand rested awkwardly on hers. "You're not going to."

The corners of her mouth twitched. "How am I supposed to remember when my mind refuses to?"

"I'll cover you with my shadows." He pulled gently at her hand to guide her to the middle of the clearing. "It will help you reach a deeper state of mind. When you think of the memory, you can visualise it as if it is happening right now. My shadows will help you. You won't see me, but I'll be by your side the whole time."

She nodded, and the darkness enveloped her. It was cold, like plunging into a pool, yet soft and airy.

"Breathe. It isn't water."

She hadn't realised she was holding her breath. Hearing him, her body relaxed, and air filled her lungs.

"I'll be here the whole time. You won't see or feel me," he said as he let go of her, a chill filling its place. "But I'm here. Now, think of your memory."

Slowly, the shadows changed into different colours and shapes, and the place of her dreams materialised before her. Her body remained in the clearing, but her mind had been teleported to her house. Just like in the dream, her parents were having breakfast and discussing what they were going to do.

She could choose. It was her birthday, after all.

When they went to the park, she hesitated at the edge of the door.

"You got this," Kage whispered.

She braced herself. Not knowing what would come after was nerve-racking. With a deep breath, she stepped forward.

"What the—?" She hit her face, but against what she didn't know. There was nothing in front of her besides her parents, who were a few steps away, looking puzzled and calling her name.

With her arms extended, she tried again. But her hands met an invisible wall keeping her from going further. She pushed against it carefully, but the wall didn't budge.

The sky turned darker, and her parents' voices became muffled. She stepped back, but somehow, another wall had formed behind her. She was glued in place, unable to move. Her parents and surroundings turned greyer, and fear began bubbling inside of her. Her heart pounded, and her breaths shortened.

"You're fine. You got this." Kage's voice grounded her. It was the reminder she needed that it was all a dream. She was at the clearing, not the house. The walls weren't real.

With a deep breath, her parents returned to normal. She could hear them calling for her, giving her the confidence to stand up straight. The barrier would break one way or another. She would only leave once it did.

Pushing against the invisible wall, each time harder than the previous attempt, the layer keeping her in place eventually snapped. She stumbled out of the house, again as the three-year-old Lane, and ran to catch up with her parents.

At the park, she fed the fish with some bread while her parents sat on a bench behind her. She couldn't believe her mind wanted to block this from her. The sun shone bright, her parents were alive, and she was overjoyed. If every birthday had felt like this, she would have wanted to celebrate every last one.

Little Lane turned around and called her dad to see the fish with her.

She couldn't remember a moment when she felt this happy. Her father's features sharpened as he walked towards her. She showed him the fish she'd fed and told him a story about them. Her father laughed with her, and Lane's whole body warmed up.

She could stay in this moment forever. The happiness she felt was almost overwhelming.

Wanting to share her story about the fish with her mother, too, she turned to call her. As she did, a new invisible wall held her in place. She pushed against it with the same confidence as the first one, but it didn't budge. This one was thicker. Heavier.

When she pulled back, the wall moved, but not how she'd expected. Hands wrapped around each of her limbs, turning her away from her mother and tightening more around her with every movement she made. Fixating her. Suffocating her.

Panic crashed over her, blurring her vision and constricting her lungs. She wanted to go to the fountain, away from whatever her mind wished to conceal from her, but the wall pressed harder against her ribs. Slowly, its hands moved towards her throat. She squirmed to free herself, only making the hands move faster. What else could she do? She was stuck. No amount of force could push the wall away from her.

She was going to suffocate. She was going to–

Stop, the warmth in her stomach told her.

I can't. I need to get out of here.

Stop!

She did. Her muscles twitched, but to her relief, the wall also stopped, inches away from her throat.

"Breathe, Lane. Just breathe."

"I can't! Get me out of here!" she screamed, and the wall moved again. "Get m—"

The hand wrapped tightly around her throat, suppressing her scream for help. She tried to squirm out of her confinement, but every limb of hers was pinned in place.

This is it, she thought, just before the darkness disappeared, and she was back in the clearing, gulping for air.

"It's okay. You're okay," Kage said, rubbing her back to help her calm down.

Feeling the sun on her face, even though it was no longer as strong as she expected, helped her relax. To her, minutes had passed inside the shadows, not hours. But the orange and red sky didn't lie.

"What happened?" he asked when her breath returned to normal.

"I tried to move, but I couldn't. I thought I was going to die in there, trapped in an invisible wall," she said, realising she was soaked in sweat. Her shirt was drenched, and Kage was... She stiffened. He was touching her back. She leaned forward immediately and rested her arms on her knees. Fortunately, his hand didn't follow.

"Is the park you were in in Stanlow?"

She turned to him and frowned. "No... It's not."

"How did you end up there?"

"I-I don't know." She paused, surprised she'd never thought of it herself. "I just woke up in a bed there. Miss Deleon never talked about it. She always said that what's in the past is in the past. And if I didn't remember, it was probably for the best," she chuckled at the irony.

"It must have been in one of the other Keeps. Can you describe it for me?"

"Not really. I know there were fish in a fountain, and some benches around it, but the rest is a big blur."

"Most Keeps are simple with just the necessary, like this one. I'll search for their plans once I have the time."

She suppressed a chuckle. If he'd been to Stanlow, he would never call the Keep simple. Every villager would see the Keep as a palace worthy of kings. Simple wouldn't be on the list of things they would call it.

"Can we try it again tomorrow?" she asked.

"Of course." She could swear she heard a glimpse of excitement in his voice. "But you have to listen to your body. If it is too much, you have to rest. That's non-negotiable. Your body isn't used to using your ability yet, and you can't break the barriers too fast. You need to give it some time."

"Barriers? Plural?"

He nodded. "You made great progress today. You overcame the first barrier. The weakest one. It's a warning sign telling you to go back. You can't unconsciously break it, like in a dream, but it'll open if you put some effort into it." He paused. "You got stuck in the second barrier, which is normal. Most people can't break more than one per session. It's too taxing for the mind. Hope you don't have many more to go through. The deeper you dig, the stronger they get."

She sighed at the thought. "I'm already looking forward to it," she said sarcastically.

But Kage didn't laugh. He was back to his serious and cold demeanour. Instead, he asked, "Can you try summoning light again?"

"Are you sure you want that?" She looked worried.

"You passed the first barrier. If the memory has anything to do with your ability, it should be slightly easier now."

She'd momentarily forgotten why they were doing this. "Of course." A wave of excitement overtook the exhaustion caused by breaking the first barrier. She quickly closed her eyes and focused on the last bit of sun left. Almost immediately, her skin began tingling.

"Open your eyes."

He didn't have to tell her twice. She did, although slowly, afraid that moving too fast would make the sensation disappear. But it didn't. She was glowing as if she were wearing a coat made of sun. It was beautiful. She smiled from ear to ear and felt a tear escape her eye. As soon as the droplet touched the light, it evaporated.

When the disaster from the previous day came to mind, her eyes darted to her body, prepared for the worst, but her clothes... They were still intact. She was ecstatic, unable to contain herself. She squealed and jumped, all the while holding the light against her body.

Kage was right. It worked. She did it. They did it. Not only could she now summon light, but she could hold it in place without feeling like she was burning. What would breaking the second barrier mean if the first helped this much with controlling her ability already?

She turned to Kage, her eyes immediately glued to his lips. He was smiling—a proper smile—and his whole being lit up with it.

Beautiful.

"Now, the hard part. Let it go, but gently," he said, returning to his usual demeanour.

It didn't matter. That smile was now engraved in her memory.

Without taking her eyes off him, she held the air in her lungs, not from fear but to enjoy the light against her skin a while longer. When her lungs complained, she slowly expelled the air, and her body relaxed.

Just like that, the warm light dissipated into the sky. She shivered, glad that her legs held their own. She didn't collapse or feel the effort of what she'd just done. No exhaustion, no...

Yeah, there's the headache.

"Good control. Well done. Tomorrow morning, we'll start with testing your limit. Afterwards, we go back to tackling your memory."

"Sounds good. I'm still bringing extra clothes and a jacket. Just in case, you know?" She joked, thinking about his shirt still hanging over the chair in her room.

CHAPTER 10

After a long, awkward silence on their way back to the Keep, Lane's headache gone and distant as if it never happened, Kage asked her about the orphanage and how she survived all those years outside Shuutin.

"How did you manage? Without the support?"

"I had the headmistress on my side. She never asked what I did in the forest, but she also never sent me away without tending to my wounds." She smiled, counting how often she'd knocked on Miss Deleon's bedroom door. It must have been at least a hundred times.

"It might not seem much, but it meant more to me than anyone could ever understand. It showed she cared, and it felt like I had a safety net I could fall back onto if things went wrong." She locked eyes with him. "A bit like you...helping me control my ability."

He coughed. "I'm the commander of the Keep. Keeping you safe is part of my job."

"Aren't you too young to be a commander?" she asked without first thinking about how rude the question sounded. "I mean, aren't commanders normally older?" she added to try to make it sound better.

"They are. But due to the Third Demon War..." His gaze drifted away. "The people who were supposed to be commanders became Council members, and those who were supposed to be warriors became commanders. Younger generations had to step in. It will take a while for the balance to be restored."

"Did you want this position, or was it shoved onto you?" Her eyes scanned him, hoping he'd give away any hint of what he was feeling.

"I asked for it."

He didn't say anything else, making her feel awkward. "Oh, okay." Was she supposed to ask why? Wasn't that implied in her questions? Her gaze shifted to the ground.

"It brings me closer to my father," he added after a short silence.

"Do you miss him?" she asked again before thinking. His knuckles turned white, and she swallowed. This was it. She'd gone too far. It was too personal. He would rebuild the emotional wall she'd been breaking down slowly.

"Don't you miss yours?"

Her shoulders dropped, relieved he hadn't stopped talking but also annoyed that he hadn't answered. She wanted to know him, but this was as clear a boundary as he would give her. So, instead, she focused on his question.

"Maybe. Can I? I don't remember him or my mother. I have no memories of them." She blinked. "If I could choose, I would one hundred percent choose a life with them. But does that mean I miss them? Or just the idea of having them? I don't know."

"You have memories of them, like the birthday one."

"That's true." She smiled. He was right. Their time together was cut short, but she did remember the heartwarming effect they had on her.

"I don't think that memory would be locked away if you didn't miss them," he went on.

"Unless it shows how terrible they were."

"Do you think that's the case?"

Her back straightened. "No. Not at all," she said with unwavering certainty, thinking of her father laughing at her fish story. A smile crept onto her lips, but it quickly vanished when the realisation of the situation sank in. The control of her ability was indeed connected to the memory of her parents.

There was only one way forward.

ཙ⚬●⚬ผ

The following day, they decided to practice with Lane's ability to give her mind an extra day to recover from the broken barrier. Standing in the middle of the clearing, eyes closed, she summoned the light. In a heartbeat, a coat of light wrapped around her. No fancy tricks, but that didn't matter. The light listened to her calls, and she couldn't be more thrilled.

After summoning and letting the light go a few more times, she repelled it slightly out of her body, holding it in place for a few seconds before repelling it completely.

Well, at least, she tried to.

In her mind, it would be as easy as summoning the light. But after two full days of training with Kage, she could barely do it, which was reason enough to give herself a break and try passing the second barrier again. Unfortunately, they always came to the same point as the first attempt.

Exhausted after only two tries, they called it a day. Kage left to sign off on missions, check on any updates from the Capital, and write reports on the area he supervised.

Lane, now with a free afternoon, went to look for Diana to see if she wanted to do something together. She found her in her room.

"Did you get enough of me now that you have a better teacher?" Diana asked, annoyed. "I don't get it. He never has time for me, but he can be with you, what? Four days in a row. How is that fair?"

Five...

Feeling guilty for leaving Diana behind, but especially for only thinking about her after saying goodbye to Kage, she apologised and explained why they'd gone to the clearing. Five days too late. She'd been so excited that Diana hadn't even crossed her mind. She was a terrible friend.

"It's just frustrating, you know? It hurts to be left behind."

"I know. I'm sorry. I didn't think it through. I'll be more mindful about it."

"It would be nice to practice again together. I've missed it. But the good news is, while you were out with Kage, I trained with Luke. He even picked me up a few times and flew me around. He's so strong. It's amazing," she radiated as she said it, back to her bubbly self.

"I'm glad to hear you had fun." But for some reason, Lane wasn't pleased to hear about Luke. He was probably the same age as Kage—somewhere in his twenties. What did he want with a fifteen-year-old girl?

Her protective instincts kicked in. If Luke had been there, she'd try, and probably fail, to kick his ass. She couldn't read him, especially not after Kage's weird reaction towards him. There was something fishy about it all, and she needed to understand it before Diana got herself too deep into things she wasn't supposed to. Talking to Luke alone would clear things out, but until that happened, having him around Diana like that could be troublesome.

Her attention returned to Diana. "You stay here." She left the room, only to return with various sweets. "The perfect dinner," she chuckled, handing Diana the plate to pick first. As they ate, Lane suggested practising together the following day after lunch.

Morning with him, afternoon with her. It would be perfect.

Luckily, Diana agreed.

❧•●•❧

While Lane admired the sky shifting from dark oranges to blue as they walked to the clearing, she told Kage about her promise to Diana. Knowing they didn't have all day, they tackled the barrier first. With each attempt, the amount of time in the memory shortened, as did the amount of energy she spent. That morning alone, she went into her memory four times, but the outcome remained the same. It didn't matter how fast or slow she got to the barrier. She always got stuck in the exact same spot.

"Let's call it a day," Kage suggested as he sat on a fallen tree with the bread and cheese they had brought for lunch in hand.

"This is so annoying." She joined him, dropping to the ground and resting against the tree trunk. "I can't imagine anything bad happening behind the barrier. And still, I can't even nudge it. Everything is so perfect and calm..."

"Things can change in a matter of seconds. You might not have grown up as a guardian, but here, every time someone leaves for a mission, we learn that the mission could be their last one. We go to the arrival room when we know they are returning." His eyes lowered, meeting hers. "The minutes you wait there feel like a lifetime, waiting and hoping, as the ignorance of whether they are alive or dead consumes you."

His gaze drifted away, his voice lowering. "When a group of soldiers come through those doors, you scan the room for that one person. You don't stop until the doors close." He blinked slowly, as if he were in the room himself. "That sound alone has broken more hearts than everything else put together. You know, at that moment, they aren't coming back. In a matter of seconds, your life changes forever."

Looking up at him, his eyes were red and damp. Hers immediately filled with tears. She wanted to comfort and hug him, but she didn't know how. Would he like that? Or would he push her away? Should she say something? If so, what?

"I hope there's nothing bad behind the barrier, but I don't want you to bring your hopes up too much. There's a reason it's there, unfortunately."

"I know," she whispered. "It's just..."

"It makes it easier to accept it if you think it won't be bad, I know. But sometimes, it only makes it hurt more in the end."

"Right..." But couldn't she dream for a bit longer that nothing terrible would happen once she broke the barrier? Or dream for one more day that her life had been perfect on her third birthday?

❧ ● ● ● ☙

Diana was again with Luke. They were on the second-highest platform, talking away from everyone. Diana's arm was wrapped around Luke's, giggling too much, and Luke seemed to be enjoying the attention.

Wanting them to come down, she screamed and waved to get their attention. Luke smiled and told her they would be down in a second. Surprisingly, even though he wasn't yelling, she heard him as if he were beside her.

After taking their sweet time to finish their conversation, laughing at each other's jokes as much as possible, they flew down to meet her. Acting like nothing had just happened, Lane grew suspicious about it all. To make matters worse, her gut feeling heightened her unease by telling her to stay alert.

"Are you ready to practice?" she asked Diana.

"Actually, I'm good. Thanks anyway. Luke was about to show me some cool moves, so you can continue your training with Kage."

"Can't it wait? We haven't practised together in days."

"And whose fault is that?" Diana snapped, raising her eyebrows.

"Right, it's mine. But we talked about it yesterday. I thought you understood?"

"Oh, but I do. Really."

110

"Yeah, so..." Luke interjected. "It sounds like you two need to talk. I'll leave you to it," he added before flying away, giving neither of them the chance to disagree.

The moment he was gone, Lane's bad gut feeling was too, putting her even more on edge about him. But why was the Sight reacting like that? Sure, she'd like it more if he kept to himself, but training with Diana wasn't wrong on its own. She hadn't actually seen him do anything to her, had she?

Not that I've been here to keep an eye. She immediately felt guilty.

"See what you did?" Diana asked, visibly annoyed. "Don't get me wrong, I understand. I do. I understand it all too well. I thought coming here would force him to get to know me. I thought we could bond as brother and sister. But I was wrong. I'm too boring for my brother's attention. I was before he turned commander, and I'm still now." She crossed her arms. "You were, too, just a few days ago, remember? But you became interesting when you almost exploded on everyone, and now he has time for you."

"That's not... He didn't..."

"I know, the truth hurts. I've gotten used to it, you better too, cause as soon as he sees you aren't as interesting as he thinks, you're back to being invisible."

Lane was shocked at Diana's words. Sure, she had the right to be mad. It sucked to be left out. She knew that better than anyone, and that's why she'd been so disgusted at her own behaviour. She'd done exactly what she'd shamed the people of Stanlow for. But Diana should also understand that Lane couldn't skip on Kage. She was doing her best to fulfil her promise without running the risk of having an outburst with her ability. That had to count for something.

"Again, don't take it the wrong way." Diana raised her arms beside her face. "I love my brother, but he's a workaholic. Everything he does is aligned with being a commander. If it's not, it has no value to him."

Lane didn't know what to say. If this had been bothering Diana for so long, she should have come to her earlier. It wasn't an excuse for Lane's actions. She had done plenty wrong, but letting one's emotions boil over like that didn't help anyone. If she'd known Diana was this annoyed three days ago, she could have done something about it. Now, it was too late to fix it. Diana was furious and wouldn't listen.

"That's just how he is, Lane. If you're not one of his projects to improve this Keep, you're not interesting to him. You'll get used to it."

Lane wanted to ask her why she was saying all this. Her mouth was wide open, but no sound came out. What was she supposed to say? Diana had the right to be mad. Sure, Lane understood why she was, but all the rest was unnecessary. Lane wasn't just a project to Kage. He was helping her as a friend.

"I'm not the only one who sees it. Luke pointed it out to me, and I think he's right."

Luke, of course...

"I've known him for a while now. He's a good person. He's only looking out for me. And for you, too, believe it or not. Besides, he's known Kage the longest. They used to be best friends, you know? Just like I'm trying to be yours."

Those last words dissolved the knot that had been keeping Lane from speaking. "A friend? I'm walking around, almost exploding because of my ability, and you're worried about us practising less together? Kage is the only one who can help me right now, so I need to spend more time with him. It's not a want but a need. A *good* friend would see this for what it is and be happy I'm getting the help I need instead of being butt hurt about hanging out a little less."

"A little less? I haven't seen you in days. We haven't talked in days!"

"You could have told me how you felt days ago before letting it get to this. You could have knocked on my door."

"Sure. *I* needed to do that. *I* needed to come to you, right? What about you? You could've knocked on my door, too, you know? I haven't moved. You know where I live. But sure, tell yourself whatever makes you sleep better at night. Go and have fun with Kage. You two were made for each other."

And with that, Diana left.

CHAPTER 11

The villagers of Redwater fled when the darkness came at the end of the first spring moon cycle, but Druzon had expected nothing else after being summoned. Being twice the height of an average human and so muscular one could discern each muscle from one another... It was a sight to behold and fear, especially with his black eyes and deep, dark red body covered in scars.

After being summoned, Druzon feasted on some villagers and kept others prisoner. He knew exactly what to do with each of them. He'd waited for this for decades, after all. Guardians failed him during the last summoning, leaving the Third Demon War to the Lesser Demons. No wonder it failed.

Druzon was still impressed by how quickly he figured out how to make the war useful. He turned his guardians' failure to his advantage, creating a new opportunity for himself. He wouldn't waste it. He would rule over this world and make it his. He would enslave all guardians and make them pay for sending him to the hellhole the spiritual realm was for centuries.

To do that, he needed to be summoned.

After the war, he found a hopeless guardian who could easily be manipulated: a warrior who had lost everything. For fifteen years, Druzon whispered in his ears, slowly making him believe summoning a Greater Demon was the only right choice.

Unfortunately, after a decade of mental torture, the guardian met a woman who softened his heart, rendering the whispers less effective. Nevertheless, Druzon persisted. He knew better. He only had to wait until the man believed to be free from his mind hellhole—the moment the man was happy again. Then, and only then, would Druzon strike to ensure the descent back into despair was as magnificent as possible.

The moment came after fourteen years of whispers.

The day after their wedding, the happily married man was strolling in the woods with his wife when Druzon ordered a swarm of Gulgath to kill her. Just like that, the last bit of the guardian's hope died with his wife. From then on, it was as if Druzon was the man himself. Whatever he said, the man did.

He led the man south, as far from any Keep as possible. When he came across Redwater, it was clear it was the perfect place. It was remote and a place no one would go unless needed, but its most striking feature was the lake around the village. Its water's orange-red hue came from the high concentration of iron, which was an essential component in Druzon's plan.

He made the man gather every child from the village. By sacrificing them before their parents, their blood, mixed with the grief, anger, and despair of the adults, would surely make the summoning work. Bringing such a powerful demon from the spiritual realm was strenuous. The more negative emotions were concentrated in one place, the greater the chance of success. Since another failed rising wasn't an option, Druzon did all he could to ensure it worked.

And it did. He was summoned, and once in this world, he feasted on the drained bodies and set his plan in motion.

✦•●•✦

Summoning the light when it was still dark outside was far more challenging than when the sun bathed her. After hours of focusing, she felt the slightest tingling sensation cover her body, too soft to make her glow.

"Are you ready?" Kage asked as the first rays of sunlight appeared.

"I'll never be, so we better just start."

As soon as the shadows surrounded her, she was in the house with her parents. Only now, she made it all go slower to enjoy the good moments longer before getting stuck in the invisible wall and starting all over again.

She was content at home with her parents. She didn't want it to end. Staying there forever would be a dream. After calling her father to see the fish for the fifth time, she returned to the house, again getting ready to go to the park, never touching the barrier that awaited her.

"Is everything all right?"

She almost jumped at the sound of Kage's voice. She'd forgotten where she actually was.

"Yeah, sorry. You can lower your shadows."

"I didn't sense any tension."

"I just...wanted to savour the good parts a bit longer. I'm sorry."

"That's part of the process." He threw her an apple and sat on the fallen tree. "It brings you one step closer to doing it. We'll try again tomorrow."

⚜ ● ● ⚜

Lane was lying on her bed, staring at the sky outside turning darker. To break the barrier, she needed all the energy she could gather. A good night's sleep was important, but her mind wouldn't shut off. Afraid of what she'd find, she didn't want to see what was on the other side of her memory. But simultaneously, she wished to understand her past and see how breaking another barrier would improve her ability.

It was still hard to grasp that she was capable of controlling light. How weird was it that there was a spirit inside her that could make her life much easier, as well as much harder? If she left Shuutin, demons would be easier to kill, but the more barriers she broke down, the more demons would come after her. If a partial connection with a spirit made ninety Karazak and Gulgath follow her, what would a full connection do?

Still, she longed to use her ability. She would have run to the clearing if she hadn't promised Kage not to use it when he wasn't around. Her body felt more alive than ever, and she could feel it vibrating, begging her to use it. Ignoring such an urge was challenging.

Her hand rested on her stomach. *I guess you've been waiting for this for a while.*

Yes. Her stomach warmed up, and she got goosebumps all over her body.

Her mind needed a stimulus. Lying in bed wouldn't cut it. She marched to the training area to observe other guardians. Focusing on their movements would keep her from listening to her body telling her to run to the clearing.

Before entering the gym, dread filled her stomach. Diana and Luke were talking in the middle of the training area. With a deep breath, she embraced herself for the mouthful she was about to receive from Diana.

"Hey! How are you?" she asked, her gut feeling twisting harder and harder as she approached them. She eyed Luke up and down, unable to understand which part of him was setting her on edge. They were at an appropriate distance from each other, and there was no touching involved.

"Lane," Diana almost squealed with enthusiasm. "I was starting to wonder where you were at."

"Oh…" Lane was taken aback. She'd expected a lot, but not that. "I went with Kage outside to train. We lost track of time, sorry. I didn't know you were expecting me."

"I wasn't, but of course you did. Did he at least teach you something new?" Lane nodded slowly as she tried to justify the reason for Diana's enthusiasm. "I'm glad. It's good to hear he at least spends time with a real person instead of only his paperwork. I sometimes worry about the amount of time he spends closed up in his office. It can't be healthy, you know?"

Lane remained speechless. She had prepared for another fight or outburst, not this.

"I need to apologise for yesterday. I was just annoyed and not in a good mood," Diana added as if reading Lane's mind. "Shouldn't have dumped it on you."

"No, you were right about me ditching you. You had the right to be mad. I'm also sorry."

"So, we're good?" Diana asked, opening her arms.

"Always," Lane said and went in for the hug.

"Great." Diana let go of Lane and turned to Luke. "Anyway... Sorry about that, Luke. Where were we before she came along?" She paused shortly, pretending to think about it, before saying, "Oh yeah, we were talking about which moves you could teach me."

"Show me what you've got, girl, and we can take it from there," Luke said with a grin.

Though the grin and the word 'girl' towards Diana had brought a shiver down Lane's spine, his demeanour was different from usual. He was more distant, less touchy and... Something else she couldn't quite put her finger on.

"Sure. Where do you want to do that?" Diana asked, stepping closer and caressing his arm.

Was she flirting with him? Had Lane just become the third wheel? This was the last thing she wanted to be right now. Or ever, for that matter, if it involved Diana.

Her gaze darted to Luke, trying to find the slightest hint of malicious intent in him. To her surprise, he stepped back and scratched his head. Lane

118

couldn't allow him to answer the question. She couldn't let Diana go through with whatever she was thinking.

The tension that had just melted away after Diana's pleasant reaction to seeing her came back tenfold. What could she say to stop whatever was going to happen from happening? Her mind raced, drifting away from the conversation, thinking of what she could best do to end it.

She was pulled back to reality when she heard Diana say, "I mean, I know there's plenty you can teach me. So maybe we could take Lane's example and train outside. Alone."

Diana almost whispered the last word in Luke's ears. Lane was shocked by her behaviour. They couldn't have been hanging out that much while she was training with Kage, could they? Diana was way too young to act or think like this. Where was this coming from?

She stared daggers at Luke. He was the oldest here, for at least five years, and should know better than to lead Diana on. He must have said or done something for Diana to act this way. What other reason did she have to think a man—not a boy, but a man—was interested in her? Or was this her fault? Did her relationship with Diana make her believe seeking comfort in older people was okay?

I don't like this. Her gut feeling agreed. It screamed at her not to let Diana go outside with Luke.

Think, the gut feeling told her.

"Oh, wait. I just thought of something."

Really?

Luke and Diana turned to her, Diana visibly annoyed.

Think!

"Right... I... You know..."

For crying out loud, make something up.

"I want to fight you, Luke. I want to know who's the strongest. You owe

119

me one, remember?" Luke's gaze shifted between the two girls, uncertain of what to do. Lane couldn't allow him to refuse. He had to take the bait, so she added, "Unless you're afraid, of course."

He smirked. "Bring it on."

Yes! Her stomach warmed up.

Lane avoided Diana's gaze like the plague by focusing on Luke. If looks could kill, she'd already be six feet under. Diana was probably listing all the ways to rain down revenge on Lane. That was okay. She could make a list longer than the distance between Stanlow and Caragain for all Lane cared. None of it mattered as long as Diana was safe and not outside alone with someone at least five years older than her.

⋐•●•⋑

Luke was skilled, that much Lane knew, but she wasn't aware he was *that* good. She had not been prepared for his speed and accuracy. Sparing with Diana looked like child's play in comparison. They usually gave it their all, and their fights lasted for hours, but with Luke... After an incredible, meagre ten minutes, Lane had to stop to catch her breath. Even so, her knees hadn't yet touched the ground, which was a small victory in her eyes.

Learning from him while fighting was nearly impossible. She picked parts of movements here and there, but he gave her no time to process and implement them or to think of ways to dodge them. Therefore, using his moves against him to see how he reacted wasn't an option, which was unfortunate since that was her best learning method. At least, it would be if her stubbornness didn't make her try anyway.

Half-understood movements were used back on him. They were too poorly executed to need proper dodging. After several failed attempts where she learned nothing besides how ridiculous she looked performing them, she resorted to using what she'd already learned from Diana.

Ten more minutes passed before she asked for another time-out, confused by how she was already gasping for air. This wasn't like her.

"Done already? Too tired to go on? Wondering why you're already out of breath? The answer is simple. I've also been practising new things. On what, you ask? On the tips you gave me," he said, his chest pushed out to go with the smirk on his face.

"Which tips?" was all she could say before taking another deep breath.

"Like how I could use my ability to slow down my enemies. I thought of a less flashy version. Blowing air on someone's face was a bit too obvious, you know? But I must say, it works quite well." He chuckled. "I slightly increase your traction with air. Just a bit at first, but as the fight progresses, I increase it more and more. It's subtle enough you don't notice it until you're so tired you can't go on. Cool, right?" He leaned towards her and smiled, clearly proud of himself. "But it gets better. I also reduce traction on myself."

His tendency to chat was a blessing. It allowed Lane to regain her breath. "I go slower, and you go faster. Clever. Thanks for letting me know."

She adjusted her stand to be lighter on her feet, a style she wielded better—her own from back in Stanlow. He took the shift as an invitation and attacked her again, even faster this time.

Left. Back. Left. She couldn't lose focus. *Right. Right. Back. Left.* The only thing she could do was dodge his attacks. He didn't give her any room to think beyond that.

Her legs ached, slowing her down even more than Luke already did. But she wasn't done yet. Winning was no longer an option... *If it had ever been one...* So instead, she focused on attaining as many insights as possible from him. Biting through the pain, she kept going. The only way to learn more was by prolonging the fight. She had to stay focused.

Where is he? She'd blinked, and he disappeared.

Above!

The Sight was a blessing. She wouldn't have lasted five minutes without it. Luke was too fast.

Now you!

She saw an opening and didn't waste any time, going right for the liver.

Too slow.

Damn it. The Sight was right. He dodged it easily and gracefully, circling and pushing her to the ground. She fell to her knees, her lungs begging for air. It couldn't have been longer than thirty minutes. Her new all-time lowest score.

"You aren't the only one who can change tactics mid-fight," he gloated as she caught her breath. "I increased your traction even more. I think by now it's the equivalent of you fighting with about five extra kilograms on each limb, so I must say, I'm impressed you lasted this long."

"You're amazing, Luke!" Diana cheered from the side.

"Well played," Lane said.

"You too. I haven't had such a great fight in a while. Most give up too quickly. Let's do this again soon."

"I was about to say the same. I need a rematch. I can't leave it at this." She smiled.

"You'll get it. But for now, ladies, if you'll excuse me, I'm going to bed. Early morning tomorrow." He bowed lightly to them and left.

Turning, Lane prayed her struggle against Luke had made Diana less annoyed at having her attempts be interrupted. Alas, it did not. Her frown said as much. Lane ignored it and kept a positive mindset by asking, "Want to have dinner together?"

"Why did you have to say that? I was making a move."

"Sorry, I didn't want you outside alone with him, especially this late. It's not safe."

"Is that your excuse? Luke is harmless. He wouldn't hurt a fly. Besides, we're inside the barrier. Nothing would happen." Every word was sharp, but Lane had expected that much. She would have been pissed, too, if someone had interfered with her plans. So, she ignored the tone and focused on Diana's words alone.

"Maybe you're right. Maybe Luke is harmless, but that doesn't take away from the fact that you shouldn't be going out this late. I must say I like him more now that we fought."

She wondered why Kage had such an aversion to him. Was it because of how Diana acted around Luke? They never talked during Lane's first twenty or so days at the Keep. It had to be something else. Perhaps Luke was getting back at Kage? It'd be a messed-up thing to do, but if it were the case, why act less flirty now?

"But that's beside the point, Diana. Demons aren't the only unsafe things out there. You never know what can happen when you're alone with someone. You might cross boundaries you don't want to cross and regret it."

Diana sighed and rolled her eyes. "We weren't going to do anything weird."

"It sure sounded like it."

Diana paced around the fighting ring. "Okay, sure. Maybe you're right." Her voice was still too sharp for the words coming out of her mouth. "I might have pushed it a bit too far. I wasn't thinking. I got carried away. It won't happen again, okay? You can stop mothering me now."

"That's all I wanted to hear," Lane smirked. She wrapped her arm around Diana and pulled her towards the canteen. "Now, let's eat. I'm starving!"

Talking to Luke, alone and with no distractions, was a priority now. She had to figure him out. Kage's reaction to him was strange, but it went hand in hand with how the Sight reacted to him. Most of the time, it told her to run and take Diana with her.

But the way he fought... He wasn't mean or cocky. He could've been done with her in seconds and even landed a few nasty punches with all the holes in her defence. Instead, he gave her time to think and catch her breath. He paced himself and made sure she learned as they went along.

It didn't make sense. The signs from others told her he was rotten, but the fight didn't align with that view. She'd been beaten by bad people before. Some of the orphans from Stanlow wanted nothing more than to find excuses to knock her down. She knew rotten, and Luke wasn't it. He couldn't be. She begged the spirits he wasn't, but as much as she believed in the good within people—especially those in this new, otherwise perfect life—she couldn't ignore how her guts curled every time she thought about Luke and Diana flirting.

CHAPTER 12

Luke hadn't been joking about waking up early. Lane saw him eating breakfast in the canteen a few hours before sunrise. She greeted him from a distance and sat at a table alone.

Those shakes are a lifesaver. The healing energy infused in the food worked its magic fast. Her body felt as good as new. She hadn't expected it after having her butt kicked so hard. But she had no muscle ache. She wasn't tired at all. She could train with Kage as if nothing had happened.

She waited for him on their usual meeting spot while wondering how far they would come with the second barrier. She'd seen her parents again. Now that the first barrier was gone, her dreams were often more terrifying. The wall would wrap around her neck, making her wake up wheezing. But not last night. Last night, it had been wholesome. Only the beautiful and joyous moments greeted her, which made it harder for her to believe something bad would happen once she crossed the second barrier. Nothing did after the first. Everything was perfect and peaceful. The same could happen again.

You can't consider any other possibilities. Doing so would delay facing whatever trauma was keeping her from connecting to her spirit. She couldn't have that. This was the only way to get there without hurting anyone again. Dwelling on the negatives wouldn't help.

Although her life had changed entirely since her arrival at the Keep, her time here felt longer and more realistic than her life at the orphanage. Part of her still believed she would one day wake up in Stanlow, only to find out she'd hit her head and go into a coma, dreaming of a world of guardians. Every night, she prayed that wasn't the case. Going back to her old life would destroy her. Something had always been missing. Now, at the Keep, she'd found a home, a place where she belonged.

Where is he?

She picked at the last three blueberries on her plate. He usually was up before she was, so why was he taking so long?

"Come in," he said from his office after she knocked.

"Good morning. Are you busy?" she asked, trying to keep her annoyance in check as she saw him working at his desk. "I've been waiting for you in the canteen. I thought we were going to train again today."

"I told you if you trained with Luke, I would be done with you," he answered, his nonchalant tone popping the bubble inside her, letting irritation seep into her voice.

"What? Are you serious? I've been waiting for hours." She glared at him, but his attention remained glued to the paperwork before him. He signed something and sent it off in one of the tubes coming out of the wall. The paper was sucked away, and Lane couldn't help but wonder if someone's job at the Capital was to spend the day pulling and pushing messages through those tubes.

Diana's words about her being his 'project' echoed in her mind. "Just so you know, I did it to protect your sister. I had to think of something. Otherwise, she would've gone to the woods with Luke alone to do who knows what."

His head shot up, eyes wide in disbelief. For the first time, he looked like he didn't know what to say.

"Maybe you should pay more attention to her instead of me. If getting with a guy you, for some reason, hate is what it takes to make you notice her, then believe me, she'll do it."

His gaze turned distant as he processed her words.

"Go talk to her," she said, turning on her heels and slamming the door on her way out. "What a jerk," she muttered under her breath.

He could've told her he was done with her. Having her wait for him like a girl who had just been stood up on a date was rude. Who did he think he was? Being the commander of the Keep didn't allow him to treat her like that.

She screamed and punched a tree, immediately regretting it as pain shot through her hand.

Smart.

"Shut up," she growled at her spirit, realising she was at the clearing. "I guess I can train on my own."

❧ • ● • ☙

Kage couldn't wrap his head around what Lane was telling him. Would Diana do that to get to him?

He didn't know how long it had passed, but Lane was no longer in the room when he snapped out of it. His shoulders dropped, relieved he didn't have to ask her to wait for him longer while he went to talk with Diana.

After searching her room and the canteen, he found Diana at the back of the training area on her way to meet Luke. "Diana," he barked.

Her bothered face softened when she realised it was Kage calling her. "Hey, what's up?" she asked after sprinting to him.

"I was wondering if you wanted to train with me today. I've got some time off."

"Did Lane talk to you? I was joking, okay? I'm used to you not having

127

time for me. So, I'm making new friends. I was about to go talk to Luke."

"Let's go for a walk. He'll still be here when we come back."

Diana sighed. "If you insist." She smiled and said, "But then I want that training too."

꧁•●•꧂

Alone at the clearing, Lane pondered what to do. Breaking the barrier wouldn't be wise. Not that she could get in the right state of mind without his shadows. Summoning light was also out of the question. She could lose control or get overwhelmed, although she doubted that would happen with how heavily it was raining. The dark clouds blocking the sun had the same effect on her ability as the night. She couldn't glow, much less play with her light. Still, risking it was dumb.

"Come on. There's plenty you can do. Back to the basics!"

In Stanlow, she trained by herself all day, every day. Nothing was stopping her from doing that here. She wouldn't be as efficient alone, but there was plenty to learn. Doing it alone was better than not at all. Her fight with Luke made it abundantly clear she still had a long way to go. Focusing on her skills instead of her ability wouldn't be a waste.

Tossing her jacket to the side, she grabbed two rocks weighing about the same and began punching the air. The rain poured heavily, but Lane welcomed it and wished it would worsen. No one would bother her in this weather. Besides, the sound of the drops hitting the ground and leaves around her calmed her. It always had. The refreshing wall of white noise surrounding her was peaceful and freeing.

With the rain easing in, she dropped the rocks and practised what she'd learned from practising with Diana and Luke, as well as from watching others. She integrated them into her fighting style to make it more her own, repeating them until her body operated intuitively. Or until her body gave up, although when the first rays of sunshine peeped through the clouds and caressed her skin, this last option would only happen at sundown.

With each passing hour, the sky turned bluer, and the clearing warmed up. The sun on her skin called for her. It begged her to use it. She fought the urge by trying more complicated combinations of movements, but the light...

One thought was all it took. One tiny string connected them. Before she could stop herself, she was glowing, and the tingling sensation spread throughout her body. A sigh of relief left her mouth, and she embraced the light with every cell in her body. This feeling was fantastic. Her body came alive, feeling faster, stronger and more agile. Her temperature rose, evaporating the water in her clothes, and still, she didn't panic or hyperventilate.

I've got it, she thought, feeling proud of herself. *What should I try?*

An image of the slicing objects Kage had thrown at her came to mind. Practising with light beyond summoning and letting it go without Kage was risky. Glowing already was, but there was no turning back. She was covered in light, and her body pushed her to do more.

"Screw it!" she said, pacing to the middle of the clearing. They came here because it was far enough from the Keep, right? The other guardians would be safe in case things went wrong.

Standing tall, she swung her arms in sharp, slicing motions toward a nearby tree. As expected, nothing happened. Feeling like an idiot, she grabbed a stick. Covering its end in light, she sliced the sky with it another hundred times, but the results remained the same. Frustrated, she tossed the stick away. That wasn't the way.

Being more visually oriented, she imagined her coat of light detaching from her arm and sprinting to the tree in incredible detail. She replayed it until her body asked her to move again.

With the sun no longer at its highest point, she sliced the air in two.

"Yes!" To a spectator, nothing had changed. But to her... The light had done as she asked. It had only been a centimetre, but who cared? She jumped and screamed, "Take that, Kage!"

It was nowhere near what Kage did, but it was a start in the right direction.

The movement had to be faster, stronger, more confident. She had to trust herself and her ability even more, but mostly, she had to make sure she aimed it right. Once it detached from her—if it ever did—it would be hard to make the light go in the desired direction. The farther it had to go, the less control she would have over it, making this technique unpredictable—even dangerous.

Knowing the light would thin out once detached, she positioned herself closer to the trees and slashed. With each failed attempt, the layer thickened. She sliced at the air over and over until her arm ached too much to continue.

One last try. Giving all she had, her arm ripped through the air.

Light travelled half a meter before disappearing. Immediately, a surge of energy came over her, the ache gone. But before she could summon the layer again, her ability reacted independently, enveloping her whole body and warning her someone was nearby.

"Calm down, Lane. It's just us." Kage came out into the clearing. "You could have hurt someone if it wasn't, though. I thought I told you not to practice without me."

The light dissipated, leaving her feeling naked and cold. What else was she supposed to do if he rejected her like he did this morning?

"What are you doing here?" she asked.

"We went for a walk." Diana came from behind Kage, replying before he could. "We're going to train together. Since Kage doesn't like doing it inside, we came here. But don't worry, I'll be fine even though I'm alone with him," she winked. "He's my brother, after all."

"You shouldn't be practising on your own. You know it's too dangerous." Kage repeated.

She ignored him. "Right. You can practice here, Diana," she said, grabbing her jacket. "It's all yours. I was about to leave anyway."

Without looking at Kage, she left. At the Keep, she filled a bowl with stew, a plate with bread and cheese, and a mug with tea—enough food to survive the rest of the day in her room. The last thing she wanted was to bump into Kage because she was hungry.

"Someone had a good practice," Luke said as he eyed her plate on his way to the buffet. "This stew is the best. You made the right choice."

Feeling embarrassed and not knowing what to say, she smiled awkwardly and marched to her room. In the comforts of her bed, she went through her memory. Starting at her house and all the way to where the second barrier was, but nothing happened. She paced to her mother's blurred face and back, and still...nothing.

After going through it several times, she sighed.

What would she say to Kage when she saw him? As much as she hated it, she had to be the bigger person and ask him for another chance. Without him, entering the deep state of mind would be impossible.

Tomorrow, she would go to his office and ask him, beg him if needed, to return to the clearing together. With that settled, she daydreamed about what she would do with full access to her ability. Being able to disintegrate a demon in the blink of an eye, her life outside the Keep would be much easier. She could travel, meet new people, and see new places. There would be no restrictions.

Images of magical places she had no idea if they existed floated in her mind. Given the chance, she would visit every corner of the world. Hopefully, Diana would want to go with her. Perhaps even Kage and Luke, if they could resolve whatever reason they had to hate each other. It seemed far-fetched, but then again, so had the idea of meeting others who could see Karazak.

Her thoughts were interrupted, the smell of sweat pulling her back to reality. In the rush to get to her room, she'd forgotten to shower after her training. With a grunt, she undressed and wrapped a towel around herself. Exiting her room, the door to her left opened, and she froze.

Kage stood beside her at the threshold of his bedroom, with only a towel around his waist. Her eyes couldn't help but gaze at the tattoo on his left arm and chest, and the chain with a name tag around his neck.

She used all her willpower not to swallow or stare at his bare body for too long. Or not to run back into her room and scream.

"Hi." She passed him by, trying her hardest not to walk too quickly.

The bathroom door opened just as she closed the curtain to her stall. The one next to her stall slid open and shut, and she swallowed. The water on the other side of the wall started running. Kage groaned.

"Everything all right?" Her hand flew straight to her mouth, eyes wide open. Why couldn't she think before talking?

"Nothing like a warm shower after a long day of work. Are you going to start yours?"

She hadn't turned her water on yet. She quickly did.

"Have you decided on whether you're staying for good?"

Her mind froze. Why was he making small talk while showering?

"Diana said you made a deal with her on your first day here. You were going to stay for a moon cycle before deciding. If I'm not mistaken, that's around now."

"Right. It is. But I... I don't know yet."

Does he want me to go?

"Let me know when you do, but if I have a say in it, I would like for you to stay." She blushed and smiled. "At least until you can control your ability, of course. Since I'm probably the only one you'll meet who can counter you, I feel obligated to ensure you aren't a danger to others."

"Right... Thanks," she said softly, her smile gone. "I'll keep that in mind."

Silence fell for the rest of their shower. Eventually, she heard him close the tap and open the curtain. He wished her a good night and left. She waited a while, and then a while longer to ensure he was gone.

CHAPTER 13

Lane didn't have to broadcast her decision. In her mind, she had already decided to stay, and the period she'd agreed on with Diana had already passed. She was three days overdue. But when Kage asked, she didn't want to tell him. She wanted to know his thoughts, hear him ask her to stay, and tell her that the Keep was where she belonged.

She should've known not to expect so much from him. Diana had warned her about it. He was the commander of the Keep and had to put his people first. It made sense, but knowing how low of a priority she was still stung. She thought they were on the track of becoming friends. He had been opening up—slowly but surely. But now, it felt like they were back to square one, which somehow hurt more than being rejected by all of Stanlow.

Enough. Nothing good came from sulking all day. Taking steps towards her goal was the only way to change things, and the first thing on the list was to meet up with Kage.

No matter how awkward it will be after last night.

Before leaving her room, she glued her ear against her bedroom door to ensure the coast was clear. At the canteen, she scanned the area but found no signs of Kage. Perfect. Her shoulders relaxed, and she grabbed some bread, cheese and jam—her all-time favourite breakfast. She had to talk to him but wanted to avoid him until she knew exactly what to say.

"Do you mind if I sit?"

She jumped, her heart racing, unprepared for someone to talk to her. It was Luke. "Sure. How are you?"

"I'm working on air daggers today. I condense the air particles as tightly as I can so they feel like metal. That's easy. The tricky part is always throwing them without them losing their shape. Same principle of slowing my opponent down, but at a smaller and harder scale," he said.

"Is it really that tricky?"

"Not if you're as good as I am, but I like to keep myself humble around others, otherwise they expect too much from me, you know?"

"Yeah, you are so humble, it's crazy. But that's actually an excellent idea. Do you mind if I try that too?"

"Maybe... What will I get for it? I was thinking about monetary compensation, you know? You can't buy food with friendship."

She laughed. He was growing on her, which made her even more curious about why Kage hated him. As well as why her spirit reacted weirdly every time she saw him.

You haven't yet, she realised.

"Wanna train together?" he asked.

"Thanks, but I shouldn't. I'm not that good with my ability yet. I'm still learning to control it, and I don't want to hurt you in the process."

"That's so kind of you." He winked. "Is that why you're practising outside with Kage?" He didn't wait for her to answer. "I mean, it makes sense, right? He can stop your light, and even if he's too slow, you're at a safe distance from the Keep."

"Right..."

"Don't get me wrong. There's nothing to be ashamed of. When I tested my ability for the first few times, I almost blew up the place." He laughed. "I had to clean the Keep *every day* for twenty-five days as punishment."

"Seriously?" she asked, leaning forward.

"Yeah. Twenty-five days! Almost a full moon cycle. On the bright side, if you want to know the dirtiest spots around here, I'm your guy."

"I'll let you know when I need that kind of information," she replied between chuckles.

"Highly confidential, so you're lucky to know me. But seriously. Jokes aside, it was a great punishment. I used my ability to pick up trash I didn't want to touch, which made me understand and control it better. Maybe there's a similar exercise you can do with your light."

"*Another* good idea?"

"You seem surprised, but two cost extra. There are no friend discounts at this establishment, I'm sorry. Not even for a pretty lady."

"Sure," she said awkwardly, shifting her gaze back to her food.

"I understand the hesitation. You have no idea if these ideas are any good, so the price might seem too steep. But you're in luck. Since this is the first time we're doing business, you need to know I'm legitimate. So, I'll concede. You tell me how you can put my ideas into practice, and you can have them for free, on the house, *if* I like what I hear. How about that?"

She stared at him with a grin, her arm stretched. "Deal."

They shook hands, and he asked, "Tell me. How will you tackle this?"

She paused to think for a second. "I would start by making the shadows of objects disappear and play with the natural contour of things. I think it would be a good start."

Her mind formed an image of what it would look like, and her excitement grew. "Oh, and afterwards, I could make the light appear farther away from me, in places where it wouldn't naturally appear. Or... I could try the daggers, although that's probably much harder." Not running to the clearing to try all the ideas popping in her head was an enormous act of self-restriction.

"A deal is a deal. You got yourself some free ideas, although it seems like that's not something you have to worry about. But..." He paused, and Lane raised her eyebrows. "Yeah, there's a third butt in this conversation, and it isn't yours or mine. As much as I hate to say it, add a fourth to the conversation. Take Kage with you. I've learned the hard way, you can miscalculate. For me, it meant I had to clean the ceilings instead of the ground, but for you..."

Luke had just opened a window for her to ask about his relationship with Kage, but should she?

He can always say no, right? But if I'm lucky...

"What's the deal between you and Kage?"

Luke's smile vanished. "That's a long story."

"You don't have to tell me, but I'm trying to understand you guys better. I thought I couldn't trust you at first because of his reaction," *and because of my spirit,* "but the more I talk to you, the more I feel like you're a good guy, which makes me wonder why Kage reacted like he did. I don't know what to think."

"You think I'm a good guy, he?" He smirked.

"Changing the subject that fast? Is it so bad?"

Luke sighed.

"I know it's not my business, but it also kind of is. You say you hate him, and at the same time, you tell me to train alone with him in the woods. It's kind of a mixed message, don't you think? I don't have time to play games like these. If I should keep my distance from him, I want to know, and I want to know why."

"I know how it sounds, but I still stand by it. I suggest you train with him until you control your ability. Kage can help you get there faster because you can push your boundaries more easily when he's around. But sure, I get it." He rubbed his forehead. "I'm not the best person to tell you about how great Kage is. We have a past. I don't like talking about it. We…"

Lane kept quiet, staring hopefully at Luke. He sighed when he realised she wouldn't fill in the silence.

"We used to be friends, okay? But seven years ago, a girl arrived. We both liked her. Kage and I discussed it to make sure we'd still be friends, no matter the outcome. At a certain point, I started dating her.

"Five years ago, we went on a mission. It was two guys, her and me, but it was an ambush. One of the guys went rogue and lured us into a trap." His gaze drifted, caught in the haunting memory. "Eight Dregma surprised us in an alley. We had to fight our way out through them, but in the process, she died. When I returned, Kage distanced himself from me after making abundantly clear I should've protected her, no matter what." His voice was raspy, and his eyes watery.

"How could he say that?"

"He was right. I should've protected her. I should've seen the demons coming from behind. I should have done everything I could that day. Even if it meant my death, I should have saved her." He clenched his fists so hard his knuckles turned white. "When I came back with only one other guy, I needed Kage to be there for me, as my friend, but he shut me off and went his own way. We've barely spoken since. I was impressed he mustered so many words the other day."

"You can't still be beating yourself about what happened." She leaned forward and reached for his hand. "Like you said, it was an ambush. You weren't prepared for it. It happens. Things don't always go as planned. I know it must have hurt, but look around you. You're alive. You have friends. You're improving yourself, so what happened in the past won't happen again. I'm sure the girl would be proud of you."

Her ability responded to Luke. Rather than glowing, a soft blanket-like warmth replaced the familiar tingling sensation. It flowed towards Luke and gently melted into his body. Surprisingly, she relaxed and let her ability do its work, allowing him to process whatever was happening in his mind. His distant gaze softened, tears falling down his cheeks, lips moving but making no sound.

Eventually, his body pushed her ability out. It was a sign that the warmth was finished doing whatever it had done. Without hesitation, her ability listened. It faded away softly and quietly, without Lane's need to intervene. She withdrew her hand and waited for him to return at his own pace and speak on his own terms.

"I have no idea what happened there, but thank you," he said at some point. "I feel better. Lighter."

"I'm glad to hear that."

"I hope you stay. Kage is probably the only one who can help you with your ability. Especially if you're scared of it."

"I'm not scared," she said, her tone sharper than she'd intended.

"You're afraid you're going to hurt someone, right? That means you're scared of it, and unfortunately," he said as he stood up, "that won't help you control it."

He is right, her spirit said as Luke left.

Shut up, she thought to her stomach, even though they were both right. With a sigh, she went to Kage's office. When no one answered, she headed to his room.

What is it with him and shirts?

"Hi." He leaned against the door frame with his chest bare.

"Hi." Her voice half failed her as her eyes went from his chest to his face, only now grasping how small she was in comparison.

"Is everything all right?"

"Yeah…" She coughed to clear her throat. "I just wanted to ask you if…" Her heart was beating so fast she was sure he could hear it. "If you wanted to train together again?"

"Sure, I'll meet you at the entrance in five minutes." He said, closing the door behind him.

That went well, she thought sarcastically.

ਦੇ•●•ੴ

Focusing on the space between her hands while Kage stood beside her, prepared to raise a wall of shadows in case it went wrong, was supposed to make it easier and more enjoyable. Still, her thoughts kept circling back to doom scenarios. When she felt a spark between her hands, she hesitated.

The speck of light flickered and disappeared.

"I'll stop it. Don't hesitate," he said, his voice firm, laced with an edge of impatience. "Your body will tell you when to stop. I'll catch it when you let go."

Taking a deep breath, light gathered between her hands, a tiny ball no bigger than a grape.

That's the easy part. She'd done it before. Her hesitation wasn't in this part of the process, but on Kage wanting her to make the tiny ball grow.

"How big?" she had asked him. To which he replied, "As far as it lets you." And that's what scared her. How far would that be? Both extremes were bad. If it didn't pass a few centimetres, it would devastate her. But the opposite frightened her even more.

I don't want to hurt anyone else.

"I'm here. I'll catch it. Trust me," he said, his confidence influencing and grounding her.

With each breath, she let the ball grow. It increased its size until her arms couldn't go any further apart. Her back stiffened.

I knew it. She shouldn't have done it. Her ability tugged at her, showing no signs it was ready to stop. It wanted to grow more. *This isn't good. It's going to reach the Keep.* Each inhale was shallow and shaky.

"Relax, Lane. I'm here," he said, and she could swear she heard a crack in his voice. But she couldn't confirm her suspicions. The light before her blinded her.

The temperature around her rose. *I knew it, I knew it.* How was she supposed to let the monstrosity she'd created go without hurting anyone?

"Kage", she said—or thought—she wasn't sure. Her heart drummed in her ears as she gasped for air. She didn't want to hold on to the light anymore, but how would she get rid of it? "Kage!"

For a brief moment, the room went dark. When she could see again, the ball of light was gone, and the temperature had returned to normal. She fell to her knees, exhausted and relieved.

"You did well," he said, "but you have to trust me. You weren't at your limit yet. You should have kept going."

"That's exactly the problem. It didn't even feel like I was near my limit. It's too much. I can barely control it now." She glanced away, feeling small and weak, frustrated with herself. "How will I control it once we pass through the barriers in my head? It'll become too much to handle. I can't do it. We shouldn't have broken the first barrier. It was there for a reason."

"You will control it eventually. Have some patience. Breaking barriers also strengthens your bond with your spirits. It will become easier. Give yourself time to learn and credit for the progress you've made. Most guardians take years to do what you've done in a few days. Your achievements are impressive."

The words coming out of his mouth were fine, but they still rubbed Lane the wrong way. His encouraging speech would have worked were it not for the monotonous delivery. He regurgitated it to calm her down, not because he believed it.

Diana's words echoed in her mind. She was a project. He didn't have to care as long as it was dealt with, right? Seeing him stand there, his stoic demeanour hovering over her after everything that happened, after she swallowed her pride to ask him for help... It annoyed her.

"And how am I supposed to know what's normal? I'm not like you. I wasn't raised by demon-fighting parents who taught me how to be myself." She stood up. "I grew up in an orphanage, thinking I was crazy for seeing things no one else could."

Her voice wavered, and she wiped a tear from her cheek. "Look at this." She rolled her sleeves, revealing scar-covered arms. He didn't flinch. She didn't know why she was showing them to him, but she couldn't stop.

"These are all the mistakes I made. Every wrong decision was awarded with a bite, a scratch, or a tear from a demon. I didn't have a fancy training area. I had to learn on the spot. Alone. Only to find out my life could have been so much different if I had been raised like a guardian."

Her voice grew louder. "To make it all better, I find out there is this thing inside me that could have helped me survive all these years. But no, instead, it might actually kill me." She took a deep breath, her hands trembling. "You tell me to trust you. Which I have been trying to do, but do you have any idea how hard that is with someone like you? You're like an impenetrable wall. I get nothing from you. Nothing. You go around making ultimatums about who I can and cannot talk to, and then turn your back on me when things don't go your way. But sure, *I* don't trust you."

Her chest tightened, frustration breaking through. "But wait, we aren't done yet. On top of it all, you tell me to *just* let go of all my fears, like it's that simple. But it's not. I have no idea what I'm doing. I'm not afraid, I'm terrified. I've been terrified since the moment I woke up in that room. Terrified this is some big joke that will vanish. Terrified of dreaming about my parents. Terrified of how big this ability is and what the barriers in my head will show me."

Tears streamed down her cheeks. "Part of me tells me I should listen to you, that I can trust you, that it's okay to let go. So, show me. Show me I can because, most of all, I'm terrified I'll hurt someone else. I won't survive if I do."

"You won't."

She scoffed. "Because you know that, is that it? You said it yourself. I could destroy Caragain if I let it all go. By that logic, I'm not nearly far enough from the Keep. I could kill everyone."

"I know what I said." A hint of emotion coated his voice. "I should have added that my power is strong enough to stop you from doing that. If I'm here, none of those things will happen." He paused, his gaze fixed on her. "Give me your hand. I want to show you something."

She stared at him, puzzled. Was he serious? Had he listened to anything she said? She didn't want to do what he told her right now. Not until he opened up to her. It was his turn to show her he could let go too.

When she didn't do as he asked, he paced towards her. Not wanting him to close, she stepped back, but he covered them both in darkness, using his shadows to pull her to him. All but the two of them disappeared.

"I want you to see how much power I have," he said, gently pulling her closer and wrapping his arms around her.

The boundaries between them dissolved into a burst of energy, an overwhelming sensation taking over her. His ability flooded her, as if she were an extension of him, revealing the vastness of his power. It stretched on inside him, with no end in sight. Even after he stopped her giant ball of light, it was filled to the brim.

She closed her eyes, her arms around his waist, her head resting on his chest. Light and shadow flowed together, in and out of both bodies. Twirling and twisting together as if reconnecting with a long-lost friend.

She let her ability do as it pleased, just like it had done with Luke. As light and shadow danced, the other side of her ability, her warmth, navigated through Kage's body until it was pushed out. When the warmth retreated, so did the light and shadow, each going into their hosts' bodies. Lane couldn't help but feel sad and cold. They were back in the forest, the sky turning dark shades of blue.

Slowly, they let go of each other. "Are you okay?" She looked up at him.

"I am." The corner of his lips twitched.

"Thank you for trusting me. I'm sorry for what I said."

"Do not. You were right. I was asking you to do what I wasn't doing myself. I'm sorry." They held each other's gaze until he added, "About all this going away... If you don't want that, I'll make sure it doesn't happen. I'll be by your side every step of the way. No more running away without explanation. You're one of us, and we take care of our own."

She saw it in his eyes that he meant it. Not knowing what to say in return, she hugged him.

⋐•●•⋑

Kage paced in his office after welcoming Phoebe and her team back from their mission. They had been gone for four days, travelling past Caragain and checking the land around it for threats.

He thought of the events of the day. The last time someone had kindled his protective instincts had been five years ago with Maya when he was seventeen. He wouldn't let things go down the same way.

Surprisingly, he didn't feel as sad remembering Maya as he usually did. The negative thoughts that normally followed didn't come. Somehow, neither did the anger when Luke crossed his mind. All the poisonous thoughts that usually filled him whenever he saw, talked or heard Luke were nowhere to be found. This time, his mind was empty, at peace. Any animosity from the last five years was gone. He even longed to...

I should speak to him again and see how he's doing. A knot formed in his stomach. He could already predict how the conversation would go. *That frightens you, but what happened with Lane doesn't?*

He'd never shared with anyone what he'd shown her. Neither had he ever put himself in such a vulnerable position. It was the easiest way to make her trust him with the training, but he'd assumed he would regret it afterwards. It was, after all, an intimate practice, mainly because of how their spirits came together. He hadn't expected that.

You enjoyed it more than I did, didn't you?

You have no idea, she replied.

He'd never seen his spirit respond like that before. That alone confirmed it was the right thing to do. If it also resulted in Lane no longer hesitating to use her ability around him, it would turn out to be the perfect decision. The process of breaking the barriers would undoubtedly go faster, and the chances of another outburst would decrease. It ensured the safety of everyone around her. He stood firmly behind his choice.

It was the right move, he grinned to himself. *Now, she trusts me.*

CHAPTER 14

Kage's feelings about wanting to talk with Luke hadn't changed overnight. After getting ready, he immediately went to the canteen. As expected, Luke was already having breakfast.

"Do you mind if I sit?" Kage asked after grabbing an apple. Luke looked up. Frowning, with his mouth half open, he nodded. They sat quietly for a while until Kage broke the silence. "How are you?"

"Fine," Luke replied, eyes never leaving his food.

Kage waited for him to elaborate as an awkward silence crept again between them. Pondering what to say, his mouth opened and closed a few times. He wasn't used to being speechless or not in control of the situation. Seeing a few guardians pass them with curious glances, he asked, "Can we talk in my office?"

"If this is about Lane, you don't need to worry. She's all yours. I was just being nice. I've got no feelings for her."

Why was he bringing her into this? It wasn't about her. He had found it extremely irritating seeing her talk to him, but that was because he had been mad at Luke. He had been angry for the same reason for the past five years. It was a sensitive topic, not one he wanted to discuss in the open.

Kage sighed and stood up. "It's not, neither is it about a mission. It's personal. I'll be in my office if you change your mind."

Luke's reaction was expected, but Kage had hoped for more. It was a long shot—five years too late—but he couldn't go without trying. If Luke didn't come, he'd deem it a lost cause. They ignored and avoided each other as much as possible since Maya's death, only barely communicating when necessary. Kage couldn't blame Luke for wanting nothing else to do with him.

Focusing on his work was pointless. Every little sound he heard outside his office made his gaze shoot to the door. He read the same document several times. Waiting. Hoping. When Luke showed up an hour later, his heart skipped a beat.

"I'm here. So, tell me, what's so important and personal that I must follow you? Why must it happen on your terms?" Luke's annoyance was palpable. He paced around in the office as he talked, unable to look the man sitting in his office chair in the eyes.

Before Kage could answer, Luke added, "Why do you think you can decide where and when we'll talk? I don't know what you want from me, but you couldn't be more wrong if you think I'm forgetting everything just because you decided to start a conversation. I needed you back then. I needed you, and instead of being there for me, you blamed me for her death. Who does that?"

Kage clenched his fists underneath his desk, his jaw tightening. Luke's words cut deep, but he suppressed the rising frustration. He had to take those words in. They were long overdue. This started way before he was the commander of the Keep. He would resolve this in the same role he had when it started, as Luke's friend—if he would take him back—not as his superior.

"I loved her too. I lost her too. I needed you by my side, and you discarded me like I was a piece of garbage." Luke screamed.

"I know."

Images of Maya's funeral flashed in Kage's mind. A bitter reminder of the days when the clove he created between them formed. Unable to stop the shattering wave of emotions crashing over him, tears ran down his face.

"Losing her hurt, but losing you at the same time made it all worse." Luke looked up and felt silent. He'd never seen Kage cry, not even when Maya died. He assumed he did, but never in front of anyone.

"I'm sorry. I know I have no right to come to you after five years and ask you to meet me in my office, but I've been in pain since I heard the news. A cloud of grief fogged my sight, mingling with the memories of my father, pulling me down like a dead weight. I fell into a pit of pain and misery, dark voices feeding into my insecurities. They never stilled but were less intrusive when I was alone and focusing on my work. So, I retreated. I retreated from you. From everyone. It was easier that way, less painful."

Kage swallowed and wiped his tears. "I've tried to approach you before, but anger took the best of me every time. I saw red whenever I thought of her or you until... Until yesterday. For some reason, I didn't feel angry anymore. Not a single drop of hate or disgust passed through me. It still hasn't. I know how I felt all those years, but I can't reproduce the feeling."

Luke was speechless. The Kage he knew always sat tall or spoke with strength, but the guy before him slouched and sounded defeated.

"I reread the reports. Something I should have done ages ago." Kage lifted the papers on his desk. "There's nothing you could have done to save her. It was an impossible situation, and you did the best you could. I was hurt and couldn't see that, but I should have. I'm sorry."

Their gazes met, and for a split second, their breaths synchronised. Luke's body loosened, the tension in his muscles dissipating as he said, "How do you think I felt? I've dreamed of that day almost every night for five years. For me, it was as if Maya died a million times." He scoffed. "Seeing you wander around the Keep like it was nothing, day in and day out, made it all worse. I knew you blamed me. You thought it was my fault, and because of that, at a certain point, I was killing her in my dreams."

Luke ran his hands through his hair. "You broke me into even smaller pieces than Maya's death left me, and then you walked away. I have been putting myself back together and am almost whole again." His hand rose to his heart as he said, "It's like you can feel it. What do you want? To break me again so we can stay broken together forever?"

Kage's eyes widened, his head shaking. "I wanted to apologise. I don't expect you to forgive me, but I had to tell you what I should have told you five years ago. I know it's selfish, but you must know I'm sorry for what I did and how I acted."

Kage paced carefully to the other side of his desk. "I've also dreamed about Maya every night. That is until yesterday. For the first time in five years, I slept. I slept long and peacefully." Kage swallowed, feeling guilty as he uttered those words. "Not only that, but I wanted to talk to you about everything and nothing. I wanted to train with you, tell you about my practices with Lane, and how managing the Keep is going." He paused, scanning Luke for any sign of understanding. "I hoped you had the same. I know it's selfish, but I had to ask."

"I..." Luke paced around the room again. "This is so annoying! I..." He screamed, making the air in the room twirl. "I want to be mad at you. Angry at you! And I should be able to. I deserve it after all this time." His shoulders dropped. "But I can't. The fight in me is gone. The bitterness, too, somehow. Just like you said. It vanished, and I can't summon it anymore." They locked eyes, and Luke sighed. "My dreams changed too. I didn't dream of Maya and didn't want to punch you in the face like I normally do." He chuckled. "I just wanted to come to talk with you. Like before..."

"I'm glad you did." Kage smiled lightly.

"No, don't get any ideas. This doesn't mean we're best friends again.

We're far from that. I still need to process this properly later. We can tolerate each other for now, but I can't promise we'll go back to where we were five years ago."

Kage nodded. The air stilled momentarily as if time had stopped to register what had taken place in that small room.

"But I'm glad we're talking again," Luke said, making time tick again.

"Me too." Kage took a deep breath. "And, of course, I understand. Take your time. We both need to."

"Yeah. This will at least make meetings much easier from now on," Luke said, the corner of his lips twitching. "You know, with us being able to talk without immediately wanting to punch each other in the face. Phoebe will be happy to hear about it."

"She definitely will, but about the punching part. We can still do that."

"You mean... I can beat your ass to let go of some of that pent-up anger?"

"I thought you said it was gone."

"I think we should make sure." Luke grinned. "I've been wanting to do that for years. Let's go." Luke flashed to the door, stopping just before turning the handle. "By the way, if you're thinking I'll go easy on you because you're the commander now, you're in for an awakening."

"I'd be disappointed if you did."

"Good. Just want to make sure we're on the same page. Outside?"

"Where else?"

Luke opened the door, and Kage followed.

"Kage, wait up!" Diana shouted as she ran after them.

"Hey, Diana, what's up?"

"I wanted to thank you for yesterday. I enjoyed it." She went in for a hug, surprising Kage. They usually never hugged, so after a brief hesitation, he hugged her back, and Luke, seeing his discomfort, pressed his lips to muffle his laughter.

"We'll do it again sometime soon, okay? You're getting better, so keep up the good work."

"Will do. I'm going for a run outside to get some cardio in," Diana said proudly, bouncing in place. "Luke, care to join?"

He smiled. "I'm good, thanks. Have fun."

"Oh, okay. No need for rescue? Are you two okay? I don't think I've ever seen you talk without going at each other's throats."

"We were about to fight it out." Luke winked.

"Fantastic. No better way to resolve things. Have fun."

❧●●●❧

Lane's embrace with Kage in the forest left her feeling a mixture of emotions she couldn't quite articulate. She'd opened up to him in her anger, and to her surprise, he reciprocated by being vulnerable in a way she had never expected from him.

Feeling good about the day ahead, she headed to the canteen. The sun was already a quarter of its way up in the sky, illuminating the glassy hall into the magical appearance it was. Not seeing Luke, Diana or Kage, she ate alone before going to the training area.

Two girls she didn't know well were fighting with daggers, their fast movements hypnotising. With effort, she memorised a few moves to practise with Diana later.

I should try those weapons out.

The two daggers in her hand weren't half the weight of her kitchen knife, much less than those she had handmade from glass or stone scraps. Her old weapons, although a thousand times better than fighting Karazak with only your bare hands, were heavy and dull.

She walked to a target and threw one of her daggers. Missed. She threw the second one, missing again. Her whole body stiffened, waiting for the giggle to come, like they always did back in Stanlow when she tripped or let things fall. But the giggles never came.

This isn't Stanlow, remember?

Never in her time here had anyone laughed at her for being unable to do something. They were all encouraging and helpful, and it wasn't because of Diana's or Kage's presence. It was how they were. Like Kage had told her, they took care of their own.

Am I really one of them?

She could not help feeling like an intruder. The area was the same as when Diana, Luke, or Jack and Mary were present, but the sensation that she didn't belong crept further into her. What was she supposed to do with the daggers? She'd never used ones like this before.

As if in response to her lack of action, the two girls who had been practising came to ask if she wanted some tips. A smile grew on her face, washing away all her worries.

They told Lane to feel the weight of the daggers in her hand and try to balance them on the tip of each finger. To properly throw them, she'd first have to understand the blades' imperfections.

"Also, you're holding it incorrectly. To throw it, you should grab the blade, not the handle. Like this," one of the girls said.

"And then you only have to learn to time the release perfectly," the other girl said. "Too early, and it goes flying. Too late, and you might lose a toe." She chuckled. "Give it a try."

The dagger flew.

"Well done," the second girl encouraged her, tapping Lane on the shoulder.

She hit a target. Not the one she'd been aiming for, and nowhere near the bullseyes, but still a huge improvement. Her toes were all still attached.

It was incredible what a few good tips could do. After a few more guided throws, the girls wished her good luck and returned to the mat where they'd been training. Lane practised until her wrists were sore. The bullseyes were still intact, and although her pride refused to leave it be, she decided it was a fight for another day. Only after she promised herself she wasn't done training did her stubbornness allow her to move on to a fighting mat.

A swarm of ninety imaginary Karazak and Gulgath surrounded her. She positioned herself in the middle of the mat and prepared for their attacks.

All her movements were precise and deliberate, faster and stronger than ten days ago, even without summoning the light. All thanks to all she'd learned from her friends. It made her smoother and more efficient.

Others noticed, gathering around her even from outside the training area, yet she didn't stop. She was in her world. For her, nothing else aside from the imaginary Karazak and Gulgath existed. After killing the last demon of the swarm, another ninety re-spawned. The cycle repeated until she was pulled away back to reality by a slow clap.

"Well done. Impressive."

"Hey, what's up, Di? Where have you been?"

"Outside, but the important thing here is that, apparently, you were pretending not to know how to fight this whole time. You don't move like that when we train. Are you underestimating me?"

"Of course not. I just—"

"It doesn't matter," Diana cut her off. "Let's do it now. Fight properly. I won't hold back if you don't do it either," Diana said with a daring smile.

"Just to be sure. You mean the usual, don't you?" Diana only raised one eyebrow, so Lane added, "Sure, sounds fun." She tossed the daggers into a corner. "Just give me a second."

But Diana didn't. She attacked Lane, hoping to catch her off guard, but Lane dodged it thanks to the Sight.

"What the—?" she blurted, shock all over her face. Her mouth opened to tell her friend to relax, but the look on the girl's face told her the request would be ignored.

Lane would have to take this fight seriously because, for some reason, Diana wasn't joking around. She was sure she'd break a bone or two if Diana landed a blow. With that thought, her skin glowed.

"Your half-awake ability won't help you. I'm winning today. I'll show you how a real guardian fights. You'll learn Kage isn't the only one who can teach you things," Diana said through her clenched jaw before striking again.

⋅≫•●•≪⋅

Luke had made the clearing almost twelve years ago. Kage had just arrived at the Keep and didn't want to practice inside, so one day, Luke cut all the trees in the area to surprise him with an outside training space. Since that day, for seven years, they were inseparable. The clearing had been their designated fighting spot.

"It's refreshing to give someone all I've got," Luke breathed.

"You're giving your all?"

"Everything I can not to kill you, yes. I could suck the air out of your lungs, but that wouldn't be fun, now would it? And what about you? You haven't done anything fancy with your shadows yet. Afraid of seeing who's actually the strongest?"

"One cannot reveal all its cards to the enemy at once. I'm saving the best for later." Kage smirked.

"Sure thing, honey. Keep telling yourself that."

"Are you saying we should take it up a notch?"

"That's exactly what I—" Luke snapped his face to the Keep.

"What?"

"We need to go back. Now!"

Kage didn't hesitate.

CHAPTER 15

Diana struck repeatedly, giving Lane little time to dodge. Keeping up with her pace was difficult. Lane was slowing down, even with the help of her spirit.

"Getting tired? Yeah, I haven't told you what I've been working on while you were playing pretend with Kage. I've developed a new technique with my ability." Diana smirked. "I thought about it after seeing you fight with Luke."

Lane didn't reply, using the brief break to catch her breath. Diana was in a foul mood. Lane had never seen her this angry before and prayed she would never again. It was frightening.

"Healing abilities go both ways, you know? I can give you the energy to heal you, or I can take it." The smile on Diana's face turned more wicked by the second. "You think you can just come in here and steal everyone's attention, don't you? First Kage. Then Luke. Who's next? I hope it's me because, whether you like it or not, you've got it."

Lane could have sworn Diana's voice became sharper and lower, but she had no time to analyse it. Her full attention had to be on dodging Diana's attacks.

Duck!

It was too late. Diana took advantage of her interrupted concentration, landing a punch to the stomach. Lane flung against the wall five meters behind her, falling to the ground, baffled as to how she hadn't lost consciousness.

Focus.

Diana was already charging. The light layer that had formed behind her to soften the blow slid to the front in anticipation of the incoming blow.

Use me!

She couldn't. Lane didn't want to hurt the people around her, especially not Diana. It didn't matter that her friend didn't seem to mind hurting her.

What else?

I don't know. She might not survive the attack if she didn't. Diana's eyes said as much. But Lane couldn't. She really couldn't. Hurting others only because Diana was in a weird, vengeful mood wasn't right.

Use me!

Before Lane could protest, the spirit intervened, and a ball of light appeared. Diana hesitated briefly, only to resume sprinting even faster.

Is she not going to stop? Lane closed her eyes, preparing for whatever was about to happen.

"Stop!" Kage roared from the entrance of the training area as he engulfed the room with his shadows.

Diana's attack didn't reach Lane. Instead, she was picked up by a soft, cold and familiar hand. When she could see again, she was sitting on one of the chairs in Kage's office. He stood before his desk, and Diana sat on the sofa.

"What in the world was that, Diana?"

"What? We were training."

"Are you sure? Because to me, it looked like you wanted to hurt her."

"It's called fighting for a reason, but sure, protect your beloved Lane and put all the blame on me, your terrible half-sister. It's always my fault. Miss Perfect here can't do anything wrong."

The spite in Diana's voice froze Lane in place.

She wasn't joking. The last shred of hope that Diana had been playing a part was gone.

"Are you serious? You were out for blood. I've never seen you like that."

"Maybe if you'd spent more time with me instead of running around with Miss Perfect there, you'd know more about me," Diana screamed, standing up.

Where did all that hate towards Lane come from? They'd talked about being left out and even hugged it out. Had Lane misread the situation? Was Diana still mad about it? It looked like it, but if that was the case, her reaction was still out of proportion.

"If that bothers you so much, you should have told me instead of going around and picking a fight with someone."

"As if you'd listen. You haven't been yourself since Maya. Boohoo, you couldn't save her. Get over it. She's dead," Diana screamed those last words at Kage. "The least you could've done was replace her with someone more stable. But no, you have to go around and look for the most damaged person. Again. Didn't you learn anything from Maya? Or are you trying to save her to redeem yourself? It's not like it's going to bring your first love back. She'll still be as dead as she is now, and it's all your fault! You didn't ask to go on that mission with her. You knew it was dangerous and did nothing about it." Diana's voice turned to a whisper. "You killed her. Her blood is on your hands, and no amount of voluntary work will make it go away. But hey... It's not like she was your first, right? You weren't able to save your dad either."

How could Diana say that? Lane turned to Kage. The pain in his eyes broke her. She wanted to go to him and tell him not to listen, that Diana was only speaking out of anger. But she couldn't. A stabbing pain radiating from her chest bound her to the chair.

Luke barged into the room. Behind him, Lane caught a glimpse of other guardians, like Jack and Phoebe, following to see what was happening. However, as he stepped inside, Kage screamed, and shadows burst out of him. The force threw Luke against the wall and slammed the door shut.

In seconds, Kage and Diana were, together with the door and bookshelf's side of the room, engulfed by darkness. The shadows missed Lane by a hair. Dark, thick and violent, they were different from those Kage used for her memory.

She screamed for Kage, her voice lost in the darkness before her. This couldn't escalate any further. She'd lose at least one of them—maybe both—and she wasn't prepared for either. With all the strength she had left, she stood up. Ready to take a first step into the shadows, Luke stopped her.

"What's happening? What's wrong with him?" he asked.

"Diana is talking about his dad and Maya. I think she's provoking him into a fight."

"By the spirit! We have to do something."

"Diana is near the sofa. You go to her. I'll get Kage."

Luke nodded, and they both fought their way through the darkness.

Every limb of her body was five times heavier. Walking through the heavy shadows was painful, but she had no choice. Kage wasn't being himself. She had to help him.

"She never loved you, you know?" Lane heard Diana's voice through the shadows. "She gave you attention to string you along, but she only had eyes for Luke. I bet Lane's the same. Did you see how they fought? How close they got to each other?"

The shadows pushed down on her harder.

Use me.

She had to, or she wouldn't get to Kage in time. But how? The shadows were darker than a cloudy night, not a hint of light around her to be called.

Use me.

If the light weren't inside the shadows, she'd have to bring it from outside. It was there, even if she couldn't feel it. Taking a deep breath, she imagined the light coming to her, gliding underneath the shadows and meeting her.

Faster.

How? She couldn't use her ability underneath the moon and stars to lighten the darkness yet. How was she supposed to do it here?

Does it matter? I have no choice. He needed her, and she wasn't going to let him down.

She pulled at the tingling sensation her ability came with. She pulled as hard as she could until the shadows recoiled. Slightly, but they recoiled.

More.

The first specks of light were in her hands, forming a path through the shadows for more to come. In response to the threat, the shadows pressed down on her. She screamed, pain radiating from her chest, but the light remained in her grip. If she were in any other situation, she'd jump with excitement.

Use me.

I am, aren't I? she snapped at her spirit as she took another strenuous step towards Kage.

Properly.

I don't know how to do that, she thought.

You do.

Right, cause I was just playing around just now. She rolled her eyes. She didn't have time to argue. She had to light up the room. With thick shadows surrounding her, her chances of blowing past the room walls were slim.

The light expanded against the shadows, pushing them away. Lane screamed as her arms too pushed against the heavy wall.

The shadows didn't budge.

"No one will ever love you, Kage. Even your dad preferred to die instead of being with you," Diana's voice echoed in the shadows.

Hurry, dammit.

Instead of pushing in all directions, she focused the light forward, towards where she was sure Kage stood. Illuminating the whole room was a waste of energy. A tunnel to Kage was enough.

With another step, she called for him, begging him to come to her. She could feel she was close, but the shadows made it all ten times harder. Her breaths were short and sharp from the four steps she'd taken so far.

A lunatic laughter resonated through the darkness, and Lane lost focus. The shadows came crashing down again, the pain so agonising it blinded her and brought her to her knees.

Crap.

She forced herself not to think about the warm, metallic slime she coughed out.

The light wasn't enough. Her attempts ate at the precious time she didn't have. She had to focus on one task at a time. The pain blurring her sight warned her this was most likely her last chance to get it right.

She gathered more light, pulling at the faintest hint of it from outside the shadows. As the light poured in, she pressed her teeth, fighting the pain as she stood up. Lifting her arms like she had at the clearing wasn't an option due to how tired she was and the shadows pressing against her.

I don't need that. She took a deep breath and focused on her hands by her thighs.

A ball grew between her hands as more light poured in from outside the darkness. When it was about twice as wide as her shoulders, she took a deep breath and released it. The room lit up, allowing her to see where Kage stood. A jolt of energy surged through her, and she leapt to him. Her hand wrapped around his wrist seconds before the shadows closed back in on her.

"Kage, it's me, Lane. You have to stop. That's not Diana." But Kage wasn't listening.

"Are you going to let your little sister get in your way? How can you save the world if you can't even keep her in place?" Diana went on.

Kage took a heavy step towards his sister, his body visibly tense. Lane pulled herself closer to him and wrapped her arms around him. "Kage," she screamed. "Look at me!"

He took another step without acknowledging her, his gaze fixed forward.

"I'm sorry," she said before summoning her ability. The warmth answered her call and melted into his body. His gaze didn't flinch, but his hand clawed around Lane's right arm, trying to jerk her off him. She held him tighter, making the warmth flow faster and deeper into his body.

He roared, his gaze shifting to her.

"Do I deserve your attention now?" she asked with a faint smile.

Kage's eyes were completely black and filled with rage. His free hand shot to her neck, and she gasped as he yanked her away from him, lifting her off the floor.

She couldn't breathe, but it didn't matter. There was only one thing to focus on: the warmth flowing. It was the only way to save him. She cleared her mind, pushing the pain aside, and let the warmth pour from her neck to his hand.

Kage roared again and tightened his grip, the corners of her vision blurring again.

With her last breath of strength, she lifted her hands to his arm, providing her warmth with extra entry points into his body. The warmth rushed in as her consciousness slipped away. Her arms, exhausted, fell back down, and she whispered to him, "It's not your fault."

⋯•●•⋯

Luke dragged himself as fast as he could through the darkness, hoping he was going in the right direction. With the help of his ability, he could repel some of the shadows, but it wasn't enough. He hadn't registered where Diana was when he entered the office. Before he could do anything, he'd been propelled against the wall, and she had disappeared in a sea of violent shadows. He only knew where to go from what Lane had told him.

With the darkness pressing him down and making each step heavy and slow, the area to cover felt enormous. He had taken five steps in total and was already gasping for air. Finding Diana would take forever. He needed another strategy.

"No one will ever love you, Kage. Even your dad preferred to die instead of being with you."

Diana couldn't possibly believe that. He'd sensed at the clearing someone was out for blood. He suspected an outsider had barged in and was holding people hostage. It never crossed his mind that Diana was behind the bloodthirsty feeling. It couldn't be, could it?

He had to get to her. There had to be a better explanation.

A high-pitched laughter resonated through the shadows, freezing Luke in place. The source was close, somewhere left of him. Holding his breath not to make a sound, he turned as slowly as he could. To his dismay, the shadows didn't allow him to see whoever stood near him.

He found himself hoping they couldn't see him either. With his fists clenched, he braced himself for what would happen once he stepped towards the one who had laughed so dramatically.

The room lit up. *Thank the spirits for Lane.* Diana was just three steps away from him. He rushed to her, calling her name, only to freeze when she turned to face him. Whoever was in front of him wasn't Diana. It was her face, sure, but her features were so twisted she looked demonic.

The shadows came down on him and blinded him again. He shook his head. Whatever he saw had to be a figment of his imagination, probably from the lack of oxygen in the darkness. At least now, he knew she was an arm's length away. He could touch her if he wanted to. One simple movement of his arm before she moved out of his reach.

He had to do it. But his body didn't react.

"Are you going to let your little sister get in your way? How can you save the world if you can't even keep her in her place?"

For crying out loud, Lane is counting on me.

The words clearly coming out of Diana pulled him out of his daze. It wasn't the time to think about why she was screaming obscenities at Kage. Not yet, at least. First, he had to pull her out of the crushing shadows.

He stretched his arm, his hands wrapping around Diana's arm. She was so cold he almost immediately let go of her. Pushing any thoughts away, he focused on his ability, creating a tunnel towards the office door.

Once they were out of the shadows, he let go of her, falling to the floor exhausted.

"Oh, dear Luke. You did such a good job. You finally saved the damsel in distress, didn't you? Better late than never, am I right?"

Her voice sent a shiver down his spine. Her face did too. He hadn't imagined it. Her blood-seeking eyes stared at him like he was filth.

"I'm impressed, but I think you saved the wrong person. You should have helped Lane, but that's too late now. Kage is probably just about done taking care of her." Luke stared at the shadows, at where he suspected they were. "Poetic, isn't it? They haven't yet professed their love for each other, and now they are too late. One killed by the other." She screeched.

Luke crawled towards the shadows, but Diana stepped in front of him.

"No. That's not how this will play out. I won't let you get to her. I've worked too long to get here. I've promised my Master I would destroy her, and I will. She's too dangerous for him. She must die for his plan to go as he envisioned."

Luke wanted to run, scream and fight, but his body froze. He was back in the abandoned warehouse with Maya and the other guys. The traitor had talked of a Master. Why was Diana doing the same?

How could she?

Diana crouched and whispered, "But don't worry, I won't let you suffer. I'll be quick for the sake of your pretty face." She leaned in, her fingertips hovering just above his cheek.

He pulled away before they could make contact, and annoyance filled her face. She straightened back up and kicked him in the stomach hard enough to send him sliding against the wall. "It's a shame. I was hoping to possess you and take you with me to Redwater. We would have had that date Lane so rudely interrupted." Diana laughed. "The best part would be that this time, no one would be around to miss you. I could devour you whole." Diana sighed dramatically. "Pity. What a feast it would've been."

She'd fooled them all. She'd been helping demons, but for how many moon cycles? How did they not see it coming? He had brushed the anger outburst aside as typical teenage behaviour. He used to be angry and frustrated at her age. Every little thing annoyed him, and he didn't always know why.

He should have been more careful.

She stepped towards him, her hand raising for her final blow. In response, Luke drew his dagger. The only thing left for him to do was to take her with him when she killed him, even if a tiny part of the Diana he knew remained inside. He wouldn't let her get away. He wouldn't let her kill more guardians.

Diana laughed at the sight of his trembling hands. "What are you going to do with that? Do you believe you can kill me? Oh, Luke... That's hilarious."

She kicked it so fast out of his grip that he only registered what had happened when the pain reached his hand.

In the blink of an eye, his dagger was lost in the sea of shadows.

"What will you do now? How will yo—"

Diana stiffened as the darkness vanished and the door to the office burst open, now free from the pressure the shadows had been exerting on it. Phoebe and the other guardians barged in, all gasping at the same.

"No!" Luke screamed. His eyes were fixed on Lane, who was being held by the neck, hanging lifeless. His gaze darted to Kage, fast enough to see his eyes shifting from black to green before he collapsed.

"Well, that's another way of getting things done. As long as she's dead, I'm not complaining."

Scraping at the bottom of his energy pool, Luke created a wall of air to separate Kage, Lane and himself from Diana.

"It's pointless to fight me. I thought I had made that clear." She walked right through his wall.

"What in the spirits is happening?" Phoebe screamed, her eyes frantically scanning the room.

Diana's predatory eyes snapped to Phoebe. "It's your lucky day. I'll get you next time," she said to Luke before vanishing out of the room.

CHAPTER 16

Druzon screamed, feeling another demon from his future army die far away. He didn't like it. His plan was running smoothly until now. No one would ruin it for him. "Who knows what has happened?" he yelled at all his subordinates.

I do, Master, a demon replied in his mind.

"Tell me everything, Gadmerad."

It's the Light Wielder, Master. I sent one of your demons to possess a boy to kill her like you ordered, Master. She killed the demon, but not before he did his job. She is no longer a threat, Master. She exchanged her life to save the boy, Master.

"That is a valuable exchange. Have you been seen?"

Unfortunately, I have, Master. I had to retreat.

"Come home. I will reward you for your efforts."

Thank you, Master. You are too kind, Master. I'm on my way, Master.

"Prepare three humans for Gadmerad when he returns. He will feast on their blood and bathe in the red lake to evolve. He has earned it."

It had been a great choice to create his base at Redwater. The iron in human blood was essential to evolving Lesser Demons, but its high concentrations in the lake's water accelerated the process even more. This would cut his preparation time. Druzon was pleased.

❧•●•❧

Kage woke up on the floor of his office with a headache, pushing himself off the ground and into a sitting position. When his eyes focused, he realised he wasn't alone. His office was overflowing with people. Some were cleaning the floor or putting books away, while others discussed what to do next.

"How are you feeling?" Luke asked, resting his hand on Kage's shoulder.

"What happened?" He didn't remember leaving the clearing. How had he ended up in his office?

"Well... How can I put this? Does anything about Diana ring a bell? Anything about Lane?"

His eyes widened. At the sound of her name, the memories flooded back in. His gaze fell on his trembling hand in disbelief. He fought the demon when Diana spoke of his father and Maya, but not hard enough. The damn thing took over and...and... If he had been stronger, she wouldn't be...

He couldn't finish his thoughts. Uttering those words would solidify things, and he wasn't ready to face that reality yet. His hands covered his face as tears poured down his cheeks, unable to hold them in, even with so many guardians around.

"It wasn't your fault. You were possessed. Your eyes were black."

"It *was* my fault. I was too weak to protect her. To protect them."

"Diana is still alive, but she isn't...herself," Luke corrected him, hesitant to say more.

"You know what happens to possessed people. There isn't a chance she's coming out of it alive. She's gone. It's *my* fault."

"You were possessed to. Somehow, you're not anymore. I have no idea how that happened, but if we figure it out, we could try it on her."

Kage's back straightened. With the hopeful option for Diana's future, his

167

attention fell back on Lane. "Where is she?"

"You should rest first. Maybe even take a day off."

But Kage wasn't listening. He stood and repeated, "Where is she?"

"Kage, that can wait until tomorrow."

"Where is she?" he barked, everyone around them stopping in their tracks.

"Take it easy, okay? Everyone is on edge because of what happened. She's in the infirmary. They are doing all they can," Luke said, but Kage was already walking out the door. "You'll only be in their way. Wait for them to call for you."

Kage had to see her. He had to make sure, to see it for himself. He wouldn't believe it otherwise.

Marching through the training area, he stopped in front of the infirmary. A slender woman with long, black hair and dark eyes stood at the entrance and said, "Kage, you need to wait outside."

"To hell I do. I want to see her, Althea. Now."

"I'm afraid that's not possible. You need to rest, and we need all the space in there to help her."

"Althea, let me through."

"I'm sorry, Kage," Althea said, touching his shoulder.

"Althea, what are you..." Kage fell asleep before he could finish.

Luke caught him before he hit the ground and said, "Thank you."

"Likewise. Now, take him to his room so he can rest properly. I need to go back in."

❧•●•❧

I guess I didn't make it.

Lane floated on nothing, surrounded by an endless pitch-black plane. Summoning the light to brighten the space didn't work. Neither did any of her senses. No smell, touch, light, or sound—only darkness.

168

I hope he's free. The image of Kage's black eyes was plastered on her mind. If he wasn't, her death had been for absolutely nothing.

She wished into the darkness for Diana's well-being, even though, deep down, she knew her friend was being manipulated by something far worse than what Kage had. The person who attacked her wasn't Diana. Lane was ashamed to think for even a second that it could have been.

"Maybe this is my punishment for failing them."

She not only let Diana and Kage down but also Miss Deleon, herself, and especially her spirit, who had started coming through. Her promise to return to Stanlow, to show Miss Deleon what she'd done with the opportunity she'd gotten, was now broken. She was supposed to pass the barriers and see what was on the other side, but that would now be impossible. Whatever happened was forever forgotten, meaning she'd also failed her parents.

So much had hung on to her success, and now, she was stuck here, whatever this place was, not allowed to join her parents in the afterlife. No wonder... She failed at everything she'd set to accomplish.

Becoming a working member of the Keep, instead of one leeching off their kindness, would never come to fruition. She'd never repay the debt to everyone who'd been kind to her. Kage had been helping her cross the barriers in her mind to prevent an outburst and turn her into a valuable asset in his arsenal of guardians. Even Luke had told her something along those lines. Her ability could kill a demon with a single shot, but only if she could control it.

I guess they got to me before I could get to them. Demons got rid of her before she could find her power. *I was supposed to be safe in the Keep.*

During every step in her life, she'd missed information to act accordingly. First, in Stanlow, not knowing who she was made her an outsider. Then, in Caragain, not knowing about her connection to the spiritual realm made Karazak come for her. And now, at the Keep, not knowing which threats lurked around her, made demons decide when her life would end.

It had to happen eventually. My luck ran out.

❧•●•☙

Angered for being knocked out, Kage rushed to the infirmary, ready to rip someone's head off. The sky had shifted to a dusky blue as the twilight settled in, meaning hours had passed since the disaster.

He found Luke and Althea chatting by the infirmary door.

"Kage, hi. I was telling Luke how Lane is. The broken right arm and seven ribs are being taken care of." Althea informed them. Seeing the worry on Kage's face, she added, "Those were probably caused by the fight with Diana. I heard from Phoebe that Diana threw Lane pretty hard against the wall. It's amazing she held on for as long as she did. One of the ribs perforated her lung. Breathing must have been painful. The damage done by the lack of oxygen, due to her lungs filling with blood and the..." Althea's gaze shifted from Kage to Luke. "The choking. They...caused the most problems. We're still working on that."

Althea looked down for a second. "Her body took a beating and went into a coma to protect itself. She's still critical, and we can't force her to heal too fast. She's not going to wake up any time soon. I'd give her at least half a moon cycle, if not a whole one." She paused, letting the information sink in. "She'll be constantly monitored by a healer to ensure she remains stable. They'll rotate every sixty to ninety minutes so they don't deplete themselves too much."

Kage's gaze was fixed on the wall, his jaw and fists clenched.

Luke sighed. "We transferred her to her room."

Without a word or a thank you, Kage turned on his heels and rushed to her. He knocked on her bedroom door but didn't wait for an answer. When

170

he saw her, he froze. She lay in bed, too pale for someone sleeping, her chest barely moving.

He swallowed, stopping himself from leaving the room and waiting until he heard from Althea that Lane had woken up. He couldn't. He had failed her once already. Being weak would never be an option again. Leaving her sight wasn't either, not for anything.

He trudged towards the bed, pulled up the chair and sat down. The healer encouraged him to hold Lane's hand. Cautiously, afraid to move too fast and break her, he did as the healer instructed. His heart cracked, feeling her cold, hanging hand.

He didn't know how long he remained frozen, staring at his thumb caressing her hand. Long enough for the night to paint the sky black and a new healer to stand at the bedside across from him.

He pondered going to the clearing to see if his ability had anything to do with him coming out of the possession. To save Diana, he had to know how he'd managed. But that could wait. Diana was gone for now. Lane wasn't. She was fighting for her life because he had been too weak and pathetic.

How did a few words trigger so much in me? He was embarrassed by his actions. An Azrunol had bested him. *An Azrunol... Not even a Dregma. How worthless am I?*

When the first rays of sunshine entered the room, he muttered to the healer without lifting his head to see who it was, "Thank you. Thank you all for what you're doing."

His stiff body begged for him to move, but he couldn't let go of her. He wouldn't leave her, not until she opened her eyes. But he couldn't let the rest of the Keep down either. With the piles of paper forming in his office, he ordered Luke to bring them to him. He sat at the desk in her room, slowly working through the stack.

The days blended into one another. He lost track of how much time had passed. The pile with the signed-off missions vanished on its own, replaced by new ones about successfully concluded tasks and Capital reports that he, too, had to sign. Occasionally, a meal materialised before him as he refused to leave her side.

"Kage, go shower and eat. I'll keep an eye on her," Luke said, but Kage shook his head. "You haven't left the room in days. You need to shower. I promise I'll come running if anything changes, but you need to take care of yourself to be able to take care of her."

He lifted his head, his eyes red. "I can't let go of her. She needs me."

"It'll be all right, I promise." Luke paced to Kage, Althea in tow. "Come on," he said as the two helped Kage stand up. "Althea will supervise while you shower, and I'll keep your seat warm."

Slowly, Kage dragged his feet to his room, got a towel, and went to the bathroom. He used the same cabin from when he showered next to her, now wishing he'd told her to stay, not because he could help her with her ability, but because she could help him start living again.

When his dad died, he closed himself off. He didn't want to talk to or play with anyone, so he focused on his training. During the following year, his mother tried to get him to open up, but nothing worked. Worried about his decline in health, she decided to send him to a new environment. She requested his transfer to the Keep five years before the mandatory relocation.

There, he met Luke, someone who understood his pain. Both their dads had died on the same day due to the same explosion. They bonded over a shared grief. The load of negative thoughts and grief Kage had been carrying became slightly lighter with Luke by his side.

That was the first time since his father's death that his heart opened up to the idea of caring again. The second time was with Maya. Kage's heart had almost stopped when she entered the Keep for the first time seven years ago. The negative thoughts cleared some more with her, and he began seeing the bright side of things.

He had never been in love with someone before and didn't know what to do. By the time he decided to make a move, Luke had already won her heart over. What they didn't know was that Kage had already given her his. It had belonged to her the moment he saw her, and Maya had taken it with her to her grave.

After her death, he returned to his old habit of focusing on his training. The negative and poisonous thoughts that had been subsiding for the past seven years swallowed him again, returning ten times stronger. The only thing that damped them the slightest was to become stronger.

Time with others was a waste. It would only slow his progress down and eventually cause him even more pain when he began caring for them too much. He didn't need that, especially when he became Commander. It was easier to make decisions when not attached. He managed to be impartial in his decisions of who to send on missions. That was until Lane came along.

He knew she was different when she first collapsed a step away from the Shuutin barrier. It was the first time in five years that seeing someone in danger had shaken him to the core. Stupidly, he dismissed it as a reaction to seeing a swarm of demons behind her. Deep down, he knew better. That's why he had avoided her as much as possible. And he succeeded for twenty-two whole days. He'd counted. It could have been more if she hadn't bonded with her spirit in the middle of the training area. He wouldn't have interfered if it had happened to anyone else, but his body reacted before his mind could stop him. In a heartbeat, he went from observing her at a distance to standing before her, blocking her arm and demanding she follow him. His anger towards her carelessness for her well-being vanished when she panicked in his office.

After the first outburst, the urge to take her to his bedroom and not let anyone near her until he was sure she was okay almost consumed him, and still, he pretended she was nothing special to him. Even after sharing his training spot with her... Something he never did. Or letting her see the depths of his ability... Something else he never did. He ignored his feelings for her.

How blind can one be? She had to be on the verge of dying for him to see it. He wouldn't forgive himself if she didn't wake up.

She made all the negative and poisonous thoughts go away. After their embrace at the clearing, he felt free and light. He never thought it to be possible. For the first time since his father's death, he slept peacefully.

I let my guard down.

Diana's words had cut so deep that the negative thoughts about his father and Maya, as well as the poisonous thoughts about Luke, came back crashing down on him. They drowned him in sorrow, and a demon took hold of him. He suffocated in his pain while the demon manipulated him into killing her.

How naïve was he to think those thoughts would vanish like smoke and let him be? If he hadn't loosened up, their return wouldn't have ripped his heart open, making him vulnerable to the demon. When the possession took over, he was so enraged he saw red. He was unable to stop himself. All the while, she gave everything to help him.

I almost... He was unable to finish the sentence. He didn't deserve her. The least he could now do was to reciprocate her sacrifice. It would never be enough, but he had to try to come close.

৳৩৽•●•৶৶

After hours in the dark, a small light appeared in the distance. Lane immediately thought her summoning had worked, only taking longer to react in this new realm.

Somehow, she knew the answer. It hadn't. The light wasn't floating towards her. The opposite was true. Although she didn't feel it, she was the one gliding.

The dot grew bigger, slowly transforming into her childhood home. She stopped a few meters away from it, not daring to get closer, not yet ready to face her memory. Instead, she floated in the darkness.

I'm not in a hurry, now am I? I'm dead. She had all the time in the world.

Days passed with her staring at her childhood home, feeling increasingly anxious instead of relieved that she didn't have to face the barriers anymore. With a sigh, she floated towards the light until she became the little three-year-old Lane. Instantaneously, she was happy. It was her birthday, after all.

Soon after, she was at the park. "Daddy, look! Blue fish!"

"You're right. It's so beautiful. Want to show it to Mummy?"

Little Lane nodded and called for her mother, but her body froze before she could face her. She pushed against it, feeling the invisible hands from the wall creep up her leg to pin her down.

"I'm dead, right?" she screamed. "So why do I still have these barriers? Let me see what all the fuss is about!"

Her temperature rose, which usually meant her ability was reacting to her emotions, and she was seconds away from panicking. But she wasn't glowing here. Her breaths didn't become ragged, and her body didn't freeze with fear. Instead, a surge of energy washed over her, allowing her to fight against her mind and push the invisible wall until it gave in. It wasn't much, only a few inches, but enough to boost her to try again.

From the top of her lungs, she screamed as she pushed the wall. The invisible hands wrapped around her stomach, and the temperature became suffocating. If she were alive, she would've been frantic by now.

"I guess that's one of the perks of being dead, right? I can't die a second time," she snorted. "Besides, this is my light. It's about time I embrace it," she added, even though her skin still wasn't glowing.

The temperature kept rising, and the wall kept giving in little by little. With each successful push, the hands retracted, encouraging her to keep going.

Now halfway turned, she wasn't stopping.

At the Keep, she learned a lot from everyone, except the one thing she wanted to know the most. Sure, it was also the knowledge she feared the most. Uncovering the truth would be devastating, but she would never forgive herself if she didn't. Peace would never come without it.

She had to know. "I want to know," she screamed, pushing as hard as she could. The wall gave in entirely, and she stumbled, now facing her mother.

"Mummy! Look," she said as if the barrier had never been there. Her body felt normal again. All the heat had dissipated.

The joy she felt was welcoming. Why did she have to struggle to get to this, to feel this? This was the second barrier she passed where nothing happened. The happiness and excitement were intoxicating. She could stay in it forever. Why did the barriers have to protect her from this? From the most pleasant moment in her life.

Her mother walked towards her. "Did you see a pretty fish, honey?"

"Yes, look," she said, turning to the fountain and pointing at the fish. "Blue fish!" She swung back around to see if her mother was looking. "No! No! Mum!" she screamed, eighteen again.

Why did they go to the park? Why did they listen to her?

"Mum!" she screamed, tears pouring down her face as she tried but couldn't reach her mother. "No, not another one." She fell to her knees, helpless, defeated, and suffocating from the heat her body was producing. "Mum..." she whispered.

A demon had its teeth carved on her mother's shoulder. One set of claws going through her neck, the other through her back. Its nails were so long Lane could see them sticking out of her mother's chest. The light blue dress was soaked in blood.

Lane had not been prepared for this. She'd been wrong. She didn't want to see this. She wanted to go back. Back to when she was happy and having breakfast with her parents. Back to before breaking both barriers. Or even just the last one. Anything. Anything was better than this.

For some twisted reason, the situation remained frozen. She was stuck, pinned by a new invisible wall, forced to face her dying mother.

"If I can't go back, take me out of here. I want to leave," she screamed. "Get me out!"

Something listened to her request, and she fell back into the darkness. The fountain became smaller and smaller, and her temperature returned to normal. There was nothing left to do. Her parents were killed trying to protect her from demons, but they still got to her through Kage and Diana.

Nothing mattered anymore. She was dead. What else could she do?

⟫•●•⟪

Kage dropped the plate of food when Luke exited Lane's room, a bright light shining behind him.

"She just started glowing out of nowhere. No warning or anything. I was about to call you."

Kage rushed past him and entered the room. To his disappointment, she wasn't awake. Her chest barely moved, but she glowed bright, and the room's temperature rose dangerously fast.

"We need to dampen the light. Otherwise, we can't get close enough to heal and stabilise her," Althea said. "Do something, Kage."

She didn't have to say it twice. Kage summoned his shadows and coated Lane's body, leaving only her face untouched. The healers went back to healing Lane through the shadows. Two were needed to keep her stable.

177

The shadows worked as a conductor, so they didn't get burned.

For a moment, their efforts worked. The room's temperature decreased, and her glow softened, only to ramp back up. Lane burned even hotter and brighter than before. It was so intense that parts of the shadows tore open. Kage quickly patched the holes, making the layer thicker.

"Luke, go get another healer. Now!" Althea ordered, and Luke sprinted out of the room, but as fast as her temperature rose, so did it drop. Before Luke was back, Lane was stable again. The only question was, for how long?

CHAPTER 17

Since leaving the memory of her parents, everything around her was black, except for her mother. She was in the middle of the darkness, far enough that Lane couldn't reach her but close enough to see every detail of what the demon had left behind.

The creature was not there, nor was anything else. It was just the two of them. Lane didn't want to look, but she couldn't stop. Whenever she turned, her mother followed. Even with her eyes closed, the woman remained before her with her light blue dress covered in blood, her silver wavy hair flying in the non-existent wind, and her ocean blue eyes staring back at her.

"Is this the real punishment? Is this what I get for not surviving the demon attack? What else could I have done to prevent it? Tell me." But her mother didn't move. "I was still learning to understand the world you were born in. How could I have known this would happen?"

Her mother smiled.

Being attacked by a demon like that must have hurt.

The holes where the demon's nails had been were visible from where she floated. Still, with all the pain she was probably in, she smiled. Even in death, her mother tried to pretend all was okay to protect her. She smiled so Lane would look, not at the holes or the blood but at her face.

And she did. She lost herself in her mother's soft smile. It was one without anger or ulterior motives. A smile that radiated love and warmth, and that used to make her feel better. But today, it did not. Nothing could make her feel better after learning her parents had died at the hands of demons.

Her mother shook her head, her gaze shifting slightly to Lane's right. Now, it was Lane who froze. Seeing her mother like that was enough. She didn't want to see her father dying too.

Her mother shook her head again.

Was this the second part of her punishment? Did she have to see both her parents die before she could move on? It was fitting if she looked at it in some sort of poetic way. They died at the hands of demons to save her, only for Lane to delay her death by fifteen years. They saw her being raised like a pig for slaughter. Now, she had to face her past before being allowed to move on.

Her mother shook her head more violently.

"But I don't want to. This hurts enough already. I know the pain isn't real," she whispered. "I know I'm dead, but... I don't want to... I..." She sighed. "I guess I owe you this much, don't I? To know what happened. To see it through until the end. Maybe I'll get to meet with you if I do."

Lane took a deep breath and turned to her right. As expected, she saw her dad. His eyes were wide open and filled with grief, fixed on his wife. By the position of his mouth, he was screaming, even though no sound came out of it.

When she turned to her mother, her mother's eyebrows were raised. She stared at Lane with a tilted head as if asking what else was there. Lane scanned her father one more time. He was screaming and running towards her mother. What else was there to see? She had to be missing an essential

180

piece of information. It couldn't be her surroundings since everything else had vanished. What was it? She didn't know what to look for. There were no demons or blood on him yet. There was...

"Nothing wrong with him! He was still alive here," she exclaimed, turning to her mother, who was again smiling. "He didn't die at the hands of demons!"

Hope reignited in her. She had to return to the memory and break the third barrier to know what had become of her father. For all she knew, she could be running out of time and would soon fall into permanent darkness, never again allowed to see how the memory developed.

She screamed at the darkness, demanding to be returned to the memory, hoping whatever had taken it away would listen to her again. But nothing happened. She remained where she was, floating in the darkness for what felt like years. Her gaze shifted between staring into nothing and at her mother's bloodied face.

Eventually, she remembered what she had done the last time to get to the memory. Besides floating in the air, she had called for the light. If she did the same now, she would probably return to the memory.

"Come," she spoke to the darkness. "Light, come." But nothing happened. *Am I doing it wrong?*

She knew she was supposed to do something but couldn't recall how to make herself do it. With each passing day in this darkness, she felt more and more like the Lane from the orphanage.

A distant memory, something to do with warmth, scratched at her before being pushed aside by a thought.

Did I ever leave Stanlow?

Perhaps this blackness was the transition back to her normal and simple life. One where her parents, just like Miss Deleon once told her, had died in an accident. One that didn't involve demons and abilities, nor this magical world she had fantasised about. A world she could barely remember after so long in the darkness.

A light came to her, and before long, she found herself on the threshold of her room at the orphanage. Even though the image was blurry and painted in grey tones, she could see two people in her room: one lying down in her bed and one kneeling before it, holding the hand of the first.

Had Miss Deleon given her room to someone?

I haven't even left yet. Why did she give my room away?

Her eighteenth birthday hadn't yet passed, and she was already getting rid of the remnants of her existence. Lane had expected Miss Deleon to let her stay until the end and even leave the room empty, at least for a while, in case she couldn't survive alone. She thought herself to be special in Miss Deleon's eyes.

Who else had earned themselves a soft spot in her heart? Lane wanted to know. Was it a new orphan?

She took a few steps forward, avoiding the wood plank she knew would crack, and the image sharpened. With it, she realised the person kneeling was Miss Deleon. How didn't she recognise her silhouette faster? Probably because the woman didn't have her blond hair tied in her usual tight bun.

But the most important question was...who was so important to the headmistress that she hadn't only given them Lane's room but also had her kneeling next to them?

She leaned to the side to see if she recognised whoever had taken her little sanctuary from her.

Her back straightened, her eyes narrowing and eyebrows wrinkling. She turned to the right to face the mirror, but it wasn't in its usual place. Had Miss Deleon reorganised her room too?

There. On the left wall.

Inspecting her face, she touched it to ensure she was real. How could she be in two places at once? She took a few extra steps towards Miss Deleon. The image brightened slightly and became more defined. She could now also hear Miss Deleon pleading for Lane to wake up. Her body told her to put a hand on Miss Deleon's shoulder to let her know she was okay and on her way home. To let her know there was no reason to worry. But was that the truth? Was this an out-of-body experience? Perhaps she was on the verge of dying, and her soul had left her body, wondering what to do. If that was the case, was she the soul? The ghost? How could she be sure?

Going outside to look for clues could help, not that she knew what to look for. Maybe seeing it would be enough? She didn't know, but a subtle force pulling her towards her bed came as an answer. Maybe she only had to go back into her body. She wasn't sure, but the comfort exuding from Miss Deleon made her believe it was the right choice.

She was no longer in the darkness, where she'd been lost for many moon cycles. Or was it years already? Did it even matter? She was no longer alone and could go back to her life.

With another step, she heard Miss Deleon promise Lane she wouldn't have to leave the orphanage when she turned eighteen. She could stay as long as she wanted and help Miss Deleon with daily chores.

In her dream life, she had already turned eighteen. She had learned something. Something important. She had also met someone. Someone important. But it had apparently all been in her head. In reality, she hadn't had her eighteenth birthday yet. She was still in Stanlow, lying in her room, dying from something. And now, Miss Deleon was allowing her to stay instead of having to survive the harsh winters without food or warmth.

Warmth? Wasn't that important too?

If it were, it wouldn't have to be anymore. What Miss Deleon offered was a blessing. She wished to hear those words for years during the countless sleepless nights. Now, she could stop worrying and settle at the orphanage.

She could help Miss Deleon with chores, meals, and the children. She wouldn't disappoint the only person who had ever believed in her.

Crouching down beside Miss Deleon, the image sharpened, its natural colours restored. The pulling sensation towards the other Lane intensified. She only needed to reach her other self to return to reality. She was one arm's stretch away from escaping the darkness.

⊱•●•⊰

Kage woke up abruptly to the healers screaming. Since the light outburst seven days ago, two had always stayed at the bedside—one healing and the other standing by in case an extra hand was necessary. Lane's body had remained stable with little signs of progress. They checked and adjusted fluctuations daily while repairing broken bones, bruises and scars. The progression was slow so as not to ask too much of her. It was going well until, out of nothing, her vitals dropped, free-diving into dangerously low levels.

He sprinted to the infirmary while screaming for Althea. Halfway through the training area, she met him, and both rushed back to the room. Lane's vitals were dropping fast, and the healers couldn't explain why. Althea scanned Lane but could also not understand what was wrong. She ordered one of the healers to use all they had to pull the vitals back to normal levels and the other to get all the fully rested healers. They would need all the manpower if the problem weren't resolved fast.

Kage nested himself near the bed's corner before Althea could throw him out. He went down to one knee, his face close to Lane's, and held her arm as he whispered in her ear that everything would be all right.

CHAPTER 18

Lane was yanked back just as she reached her arm towards the version of herself lying down. She crashed to the ground, her tailbone slamming against the wooden floor. With her eyes narrowed, she snapped around, anticipating the presence of the person who had tugged at her, but instead found an empty room behind her.

She stood up, lightly massaging her lower back. Giving it a second try, another forceful tug disturbed her balance.

Two forces pulled at her. One to her body and one to the door. She thought she understood what the world wanted from her, but now she was confused again. Which way to get back to reality? To get out of this place, out of the dark, the fastest?

The logical option was before her: her body. The air around it was warm and peaceful, while the door felt wrong. The air was dark, cold and twisted. How more straightforward could it get?

But the force pulling her to the door kept yanking at her every time she stepped towards the bed. She crashed on the floor a third time and couldn't help but snort.

"Of course, it's not going to be that easy. What was I thinking? There's always something. I can't just go in peace, can I?" She gritted her teeth, fighting the two forces disturbing her balance. "No... I have to... Fight through every..." She stumbled, barely crashing back down. "Step... Of the way."

Once she found her balance, she noticed Miss Deleon was facing the Lane standing up. The headmistress' eyes were puffed and red, but the sadness slowly shifted to happiness as she recognised Lane.

"You... You can see me?" Lane asked, and Miss Deleon nodded while extending her hands towards Lane. "I'm coming back home, Miss Deleon. Don't worry. I'm on my way." Lane tried lifting her arms, but the force pulling her back glued them to her body. No matter how much she fought against it, they didn't budge. Miss Deleon's head tilted. "I'm coming, don't worry."

She screamed, frustrated at the forces deciding for her. "I've had enough of this. For crying out loud, just let me go the way I want. Let me make my own choices." But her arms didn't budge. "Let me decide which way I want to go," she growled at the forces.

If her arms weren't going to move, her body would. Gritting her teeth, all her energy was focused on bringing her foot a few centimetres closer to Miss Deleon. The moment it hit the floor, a shiver ran down her spine. She froze.

How? I don't get it.

None of it made sense. Seconds ago, her body told her to go to the other Lane because that was the safest route. But now, it screamed at her to go the opposite way. Every inch of her body begged her not to go any further. It was convinced home wasn't before her but behind her. How was that possible? How could a single step change so much? For all she knew, it was all a mind trick from Death to get her to follow the darkness, a test to see if she would choose the wrong path. The easy path.

"Ignore it," she told herself.

However, the force pulled at her twice as hard after her remark, ensuring she wouldn't brush it off. The intense and primal reaction to it made her pause again, not because of how hard it had tugged at her but because of the scent of pine trees and metal that came with it.

That's home, she asked more than she affirmed. Doubts crept in. What if it was another trick from Death? Using what she desired the most against her to tempt her to choose wrong.

What am I supposed to do? She'd fought so hard to get near the bed. Something that hard to get couldn't be a trick, could it? How could walking to one's death be so taxing?

Not knowing what to do, she turned to Miss Deleon for guidance. She was the person whom Lane always sought for wise words. A vivid memory came to mind of Miss Deleon leaning against the kitchen top, cleaning her glasses and preaching about how tough life outside the orphanage was and how decisions were not to be taken lightly.

Lane chuckled. Those damned glasses were always dirty when the conversation became serious. The headmistress had to keep her hands busy by putting things away or cleaning the dishes, the floor or her glasses when nothing else was available. They were probably the cleanest thing at the orphanage.

Where are they? Miss Deleon wasn't wearing them.

She scanned the room but couldn't find them anywhere, which was odd since Miss Deleon never walked around without them. Not once in all the years Lane had lived at the orphanage had she ever seen Miss Deleon without them on.

Maybe she took them off because she was crying?

A plausible explanation, yet it felt off. Revisiting the room, a nagging sensation tugged at her. The window was missing, and the other Lane was sleeping with her head on the wrong side of the bed. Even if Miss Deleon had brought her to bed, her pillow was always on the left side. She couldn't have gotten it wrong.

The mirror. She glanced to the left. It also wasn't where it was supposed to be.

That wasn't all. The room itself was much longer than the real one. How many steps had she taken from the door to the bed? In the real version, she could barely take three.

How could it look so different from reality if it *were* reality?

Without thinking, she stepped back. A horrid scream filled the room, and her blood went cold.

Miss Deleon's face turned horrid. The other Lane opened her eyes and screeched, "No! Don't go." The voice coming out of it was hers but filled with fear and pain. The Lane in bed sat down, screaming non-stop, not even to catch her breath. "Don't leave me!"

Lane took another step back, and the familiar faces melted away, exposing two weirdly pale faces with bright red eyes. They crept towards her, twitching and cracking as if their bones and muscles were too weak to hold their weight.

"Come back!" the thing that had once been Miss Deleon screamed.

Lane took another step back with her hands behind her, searching for the door handle. The pleas turned into threats, and the twitches and cracks disappeared as the two creatures stood.

With her heart in her throat, Lane found the handle and quickly went through the door. The creatures sprinted in response, but they weren't fast enough. The door slammed shut, Lane's hands firm around the handle, preventing it from turning.

After hours without a single sound coming from the doors, she felt comfortable letting go to follow the soft scent of pine trees and metal.

꽃••●••꽃

Two days had passed since her vitals returned to normal. Lane was still lying in bed, and Kage, afraid something else would happen, didn't dare leave her sight or fall asleep for too long. During that time, he mostly sat close to her, holding her hand and continuously asking her not to give up. His responsibilities as commander were set aside. He couldn't focus. So, after reading the same text several times without understanding a word, he asked Luke to appoint Mister Kohler as his temporary replacement.

Maybe I should stretch my legs for a second. If I'm fast enough, I...

He didn't get to finish his thoughts. Lane was pulsating. At first, the bursts were soft and slow but steadily increased in frequency and intensity. His eyes shot at the healers in the room, both as shocked as he was.

"Carl, what's happening?" Kage barked at the young man in front of him.

"I-I don't know," he stuttered. "Her vitals are stable, I-I don't get it."

Kage's gaze shifted between Lane and the healer. Janet, the other healer in the room, a girl who had been at the Keep almost as long as he had, took a hesitant step back before sprinting out of the room.

No matter what Carl did, Lane kept going. With each pulse, the light turned hotter and brighter, and the healer could barely keep his hands near her. Seeing him struggle, Kage snapped out of his daze and covered Lane with his shadows.

"Don't stop, Carl." He turned to Lane. "I'm here. I've got you," he whispered.

"What's happening?" Althea asked after rushing into the room with Luke and four other healers, including Janet, in tow. "Let me check her."

Carl moved aside, and Althea dipped her hands inside Kage's shadows to protect herself from the intensity of the light. The air around Lane turned a light green as Althea's ability searched for symptoms to explain the sudden change. She scanned Lane twice but couldn't find a reason. Her vitals were stable, so why?

"Let her pulse, Kage."

"What? Are you insane?"

"I can't stop this. Her body has to do whatever it has to do. Raise your shadows and let her pulse. If anything changes, I'll be right here. You put the walls down, and I'll stabilise her."

"No, that's too risky. Do something."

"I'll be hurting her if I do. Trust me."

Hesitantly, Kage obeyed. He closed Lane and himself off from the others, fell to his knees beside her and started whispering to her, calling her to him. He had to trust Althea on this, much to his discomfort.

⟨◦•●•◦⟩

Knowing which direction to go in the darkness was challenging. The scent came and went, never with the same intensity as the previous wave. When she began doubting if she'd made the right call leaving Miss Deleon and the other Lane behind, a whisper assured her she had. It carried her name and helped her find which way to go. Alternating between following the voice and the scent, depending on which one presented itself to her, she floated with purpose in the darkness. Bit by bit, the whisper turned into a call, and the waves of pine trees and metal became a permanent scent in the air. They told her to come home, and she didn't hesitate.

⟨◦•●•◦⟩

Kage heard faint noises from the other side of his shadows but ignored them. He focused on calling Lane to him and letting her pulsate faster and faster like Althea had ordered. Eventually, she was a constant beam of light. The intense light tore right through his shadows, turning the room white. Luke, Althea, and the other healers covered their eyes and fought the painful heat that overtook them. They pleaded with Kage to use his shadows, but he only had eyes for Lane.

190

Light replaced the darkness. Lane squinted, her eyes stinging with the overwhelming change. It didn't matter what had made it possible, but she was grateful to be out of the void. Anything was better than the dark.

Slowly, her senses returned. She was lying, no longer floating. A sea of voices replaced the silence she'd gotten accustomed to. The pine tree and metal scent wrapped around her, and a figure loomed over her as her eyes adjusted to the light.

Is this another memory? Another trick to make me choose Death?

Kage had never been this close to her, but neither had Miss Deleon knelt before her or walked around without her glasses, and she'd still seen it happen in the darkness. Needing to make sure, she raised her hand, never taking her eyes away from his beautiful green eyes.

Green, not black.

Her hand gently rested on his warm neck, his heartbeat slow and steady. The wall of shadows surrounding them, or what was left of it, disappeared. The bright light subsided with it, replaced by familiar furniture and faces. Still, her eyes were fixed on Kage.

His heartbeat... I didn't feel mine in the darkness.

Do you feel it now? Her stomach warmed up. She took a deep breath, not knowing whether to scream or laugh. She'd forgotten about her spirit, her heartbeat, and Kage. She'd forgotten about the Keep and everything she'd gone through. But now, her memories flowed back in. Every good and bad memory, the times spent in the clearing with Kage, chatting with Luke and training with Diana. Her life in Stanlow, Caragain, and now at the Keep.

She couldn't believe she almost forgot it all.

"Hi," she said to Kage.

"Hi," he replied.

CHAPTER 19

While the healers checked Lane's vitals to ensure she was all right, she noticed most of her scars were gone. She stared at her arms for a while, visualising where each scar used to be, but the more she tried, the less she could remember. She waited for her breath to quicken and a knot to form in her stomach, but neither came. Instead, a calm rushed over her. Her skin looked like blank paper, ready for a new chapter to be written on. She could live with that. Except for...

With a trembling hand, she touched her left shoulder where her first scar was supposed to be. A sigh left her mouth when she felt a bump. It was not as prominent as it used to be, but still present. A reminder that the past fifteen years had happened. Not her fondest moments, but they'd shaped her into who she was today, and she didn't want to forget it.

After being checked by the healers four times on Kage's orders, she was allowed to stand up. He helped her stand, telling her to be careful since she'd been sleeping for fourteen days. But that was the last thing she wanted. She wanted to move. She *needed* to move. The darkness had felt like an eternity, not fourteen days. She had to go outside to feel the sun on her skin and use her ability. She was about to explode.

"You passed the second barrier, didn't you?" Kage asked.

"I did," she replied and stiffened at the thought of her mother.

"You don't have to talk about it. Let's go outside first."

"No, I don't think so," Althea interrupted as they walked to the door. Lane stared at Althea, puzzled. Who was she? Was she new to the Keep? Why was she ordering her around?

"Lane, this is Althea. She's the best healer in the Keep. You might not have survived if it weren't for her," Luke said proudly.

"Thank you," she said, and Althea bowed slightly, "but Kage is right. I can't hold it in much longer. I *need* to go outside."

Althea sighed. "Fine... You'll probably do it anyway if I take my eyes off you, so why bother? Besides, I don't want you dying on us and having our work be for nothing. But I'm coming with you to supervise. That's not up for negotiation."

Without hesitation, Lane agreed, and the four walked to the clearing. Kage put up a wall of shadows around her and himself while Luke and Althea waited outside.

"Are you ready?" she asked him.

"I am. You?"

"As ready as I'll ever be. Just be prepared for what might come out. I'll try to point it up as much as possible."

This time, she didn't have to close her eyes or focus for too long. The waves of light hung in the air all around her, making calling for the light more palpable and much easier.

Effortlessly, she glowed. Holding the light momentarily, she thought about how to make it pour in a controlled way. It was preferable to be there for two hours and let it come out slowly rather than going too fast and being incapable of stopping if needed.

I am here and will control it. Do not worry. Just relax and enjoy the show.

Hey, you're talking to me! Like really talking, Lane thought.

I have been the whole time. Her stomach warmed up.

Right... Sorry about that.

You listened when it mattered.

Yeah, thank you for looking out for me...

Bhaskara.

Thank you, Bhaskara. Now, let's do this together.

The light left her body in every direction. It expanded towards the ground, burning the grass. It expanded towards the shadows, stretching them out. Unsure they would hold, she pulled her arms in before putting it to the test. The light retracted, disappearing into her body.

Taking a deep breath, she raised her arms to the sky, a ball of light appearing between her hands. She took a moment to enjoy how easily it responded to her requests, eyes beaming with excitement.

With a simple flick of her head, a beam shot into the sky. The excess energy flowed through and out of her. Pulling her hands further apart allowed the beam to grow thicker.

The electrifying sensation coursing through her was exhilarating. It was ten times stronger than before she broke the second barrier and felt ten times better. The thicker the beam, the more her body responded to it. What she had to see to get to this point was awful, but this sensation made it all slightly more bearable, and could she dare say, worth it.

Thank you, Bhaskara, for waiting for me.

Thank you, too, for allowing me in.

Ten minutes later, she felt like she could go on, but the pressure in her body had returned to normal. She pressed her hands together to stop, and the beam disappeared. Mirroring her actions, Kage took down his shadows.

"That was awesome! I've never seen anyone expel that much energy at once. That's going to be a hell of a headache," Luke said as he got close.

"I don't think so. I just took the edge off. It was too much pressure."

"Only the edge?" Luke raised his eyebrows as he smiled. "Damn girl, you're strong. We'll need that rematch soon. I have a feeling it'll be much more fun this time."

"Not yet," Althea said, eyeing Luke, before Lane could agree. "But I'm glad I didn't stop you," she added. "You were right."

"How did it feel?" Kage asked as he joined them.

"Different from the other times, but much, much better. I feel stronger and more in control."

"You also look younger. It's like you lost a couple of years, you know?" Luke said. "Now you look, what? Twenty? Twenty-two, max."

Lane frowned. "That's not as big a compliment as you think. I'm eighteen."

"Oh..." Luke's face went red. "I didn't mean it in a bad way, you know? I mean, like... You know."

Lane burst into laughter, and the rest joined in.

"You need to think before you speak, Luke," Althea said, patting his shoulder. "But now this is handled, let's return to the Keep. You're not allowed to train for a few days, so this clearing is off-limits."

"What? You just said I'm fine. What am I going to do inside all day?"

"I don't know. Maybe you can read some books or start a new hobby," Luke answered. "Or you can go on a romantic date with Kage," he teased.

Lane wanted to make Luke feel embarrassed again for overstepping with his comments, but she couldn't contain her smile, much less the blush spreading across her cheeks. Embarrassed and unsure what to say, she bit her tongue and avoided glancing at Kage.

"But..." Luke added, faking a smile to ease the awkward silence that had been instilled between the four of them. "We need to talk about the demon first. Everyone is on edge about how one got inside the barrier."

❦•●•❦

Gadmerad sensed a wave of rage from Druzon and immediately knew the light girl had survived. He was almost at Redwater but now doubted if he should continue. Perhaps, laying low in a nearby city for a while was wiser. He was in the body of the guardian girl, Diana, after all. He could easily blend in with humans and see how his Master's plan unfolded. If Druzon failed, he could stay behind, hidden among humans and arrange his Master's next arrival. After that, Druzon would undoubtedly forgive him for his insolence.

Gadmerad, are you almost in Redwater?

"Master. I am, Master. Is there anything I can do for you, Master?"

You told me the girl was dead.

"I thought she was, Master. When I left, she hung by her throat, lifeless, Master."

I underestimated her and overestimated you. Return at once to evolve. You must finish what you have started.

"Yes, Master. I appreciate your kindness, Master."

Not wanting Druzon to change his mind about his evolution—and unable to go against his orders this close to him—Gadmerad sprinted back to Redwater. As a Dregma, he could control about seventy percent of the body he was in, but the girl was tough and fought constantly. He'd shoved her to a corner and tried to break her spirit but could rarely control her effortlessly. He'd often avoided other guardians at the Keep for that exact reason, only appearing when necessary. It was exhausting to fight her all the time.

Luckily for him, seeing her friend die had been her breaking point. After, Gadmerad could do as he pleased within the limits of his own strength. Evolving into an Ezraan meant he'd have complete control over the body. He would not fail Druzon again.

The trip to Redwater took a total of fifteen days. An unpossessed guardian would have needed well over three times that time to do the same, but since he was controlling the girl, he could skip sleep and meals most days. He couldn't go fully without. The girl's body would fall apart otherwise. Only once he was fully evolved would her body become a shell for him to manipulate until his time to shed came. She would survive half a moon cycle without food as her body would become a cold-blooded organism that could survive with the smallest amount of warmth.

When in Redwater, he was happily surprised by the state of the village. Near the red lake, humans were putting cages together, and others were building a throne worthy of Druzon at the village square.

On his way to his Master, Gadmerad's gaze landed on seven humans locked in cages made of bones from the remains of the humans used to ascend Druzon. Each had its cage.

Excessive, Gadmerad thought, until he came closer to one.

The human chewed at the bone and growled, shaking and hitting his prison more violently than a human would normally act.

Their black eyes made everything fall into place. Druzon had possessed them with Azrunol, the third level of Lesser Demons, and let them do as they pleased.

"Master," Gadmerad said with a bow.

"Gadmerad, what are your thoughts about my experiment?"

"Impressive, Master, like always. Although I do wonder why an Azrunol, Master? And not a Dregma like myself, Master."

"Of course you do. At first sight, it might seem counter-productive, but they are easier to introduce in a body, especially one unwilling to cooperate. With an Azrunol, the host offers less resistance. You should know that from your last adventures. The host doesn't even notice it if properly distracted."

Gadmerad swallowed as he was reminded of his failure.

"I must evaluate which conditions allow my Lesser Demons to evolve the fastest. As you can see, I have two environments. The three on this side have been subjected to as much fear, panic and pain as I could subject their feeble minds to. I diminished the intensity when one of them died." Druzon spoke with no emotion. "On this side, these four have been subjected to some degree of fear but have also been given what humans call hope. I told them they could survive if they did as I told them. They seem to be doing slightly better since none have died yet. If a Dregma hatches faster in one of these groups, I will know which direction to take."

"Impressive work, Master." Gadmerad bowed again.

"It is. Every second towards my goal counts, especially if that girl is still alive."

Gadmerad stiffened. Druzon had now mentioned his shortcomings twice. He hoped his Master hadn't changed his mind. The last thing he wanted was to be punished back into the spiritual realm for failing.

Nothing was worse than being crushed by the overwhelming gravity forced upon demons by the spirits floating above them in that realm. The only time it had been okay to go back was when he had to hide his presence from the Light Wielder at the Keep. It had been temporary, and when inside a host with a spirit, the gravity had been bearable. The spirit's positive charge had cancelled his negative one, creating a pleasant atmosphere similar to that of the guardian world. That was the only way the spiritual realm was manageable. Going back without the spirit's buffer because Druzon decided to kill him for his failure would be hell.

Gadmerad would do everything in his power to prevent his return to his realm. This one was better, comfortable, painless. If it were up to him, he would never leave.

"You are much too wise, Master. As expected from someone as great as yourself, Master. Thank you for sharing your thoughts with someone as simple as me, Master."

"Yes, yes." Druzon waved his hand at Gadmerad. "Feast on the three humans and bathe in the lake. Once you have evolved, return to your quest and finish it."

"Yes, Master. Of course, Master. Thank you, Master." Gadmerad bowed repeatedly as he retreated, careful never to show Druzon his back.

Far enough from his Master's grip, his shoulders sagged, and he ordered a handful of Azrunol, who roamed around the village in their natural form, to bring the humans to the lake. The faster he got this over with, the better. He disliked the process of evolving. Being vulnerable made him uneasy. Unfortunately, fulfilling his duty was imperative. It was that or die at the hands of his Master for disobeying him, and Gadmerad preferred to stay alive.

CHAPTER 20

The bells echoed throughout the Keep, and everyone rushed to the central area. In less than thirty seconds, the room was filled with all twenty-five stationed guardians who were not on a mission.

"Thank you all for coming." Kage's voice resonated across the walls. "First of all, this is not an emergency. No demons are attacking Caragain or the surrounding area. Be at ease."

Kage waited, scanning the room as the tight shoulders sagged and stern faces relaxed in the crowd. "Secondly, I heard you are worried about what happened with Diana and me. I should have addressed it at once, but fear not. I assure you, I am not possessed or infected."

"Lies," someone screamed from the crowd.

"You have to understand, Kage. We saw your eyes," Phoebe interjected, demanding the murmurs to stop.

"I know you have, but I am clean. It is hard to believe, but it's the truth."

"Impossible," someone else in the crowd screamed.

"Would a possessed guardian be as distraught with what happened as I was? Would he help the healers with Lane's process like I did? He would not, not after you found him out. He would have escaped with Diana. He would have fought back because demons know what we do when they possess us." He paused and scanned the area. "We've always done that because we thought there was no cure." He paused, scanning the room. "We were wrong."

"How?" a male voice asked.

"I do not know if it's my ability or something else, but I will not rest until I find the answer. When I do, you will all be tested and, if necessary, cleansed."

"So what? Are we just supposed to wait and hope nothing is growing inside us or influencing our moods and choices?" Jack asked from the crowd.

"You all know the risks that come with our job. Going on a mission means you might come back infected or possessed. I understand that having demons inside the barrier is frightening. Seeing it first-hand can be daunting, but not unheard of. We know they use us to get inside. We know they manipulate and lie."

He straightened. "I'm suspending missions until we better understand the situation at hand. We need to remain alert. If you wish to isolate, for your safety or that of others, you can request to be put in a cell in the basement." He locked eyes with Phoebe. When she nodded, he moved on to Luke and Mister Kohler. They, too, nodded.

Mister Kohler is nothing like I had imagined. She had expected to see a hunchbacked man falling apart with age, but Mister Kohler was anything but. His slightly wrinkling skin and white hair were the only signs of age. He stood straighter than most around him and looked like he could run a marathon.

"Mister Kohler, Phoebe and Luke will assist you with that. Otherwise, I urge you to go about your normal life the best way you can. It's no easy task what I ask of you, but I'm positive we can surpass this together."

The room fell silent as everyone ruminated on Kage's words. They had all, by default, signed up for this at birth by being born a guardian. Then, a second time, when accepting the bond with their spirit. They were likely unaware of the real dangers they would eventually face.

Had anyone ever told them what they had to give up if they accepted this life? Was it even a choice? They were sold on the idea of spirits and abilities before learning the dangers that came with it and the sacrifices they would have to make. They were influenced to choose an ideal, not a lifestyle, and forced to answer before they could make an educated choice.

After less than two moon cycles at the Keep, she already felt the world's weight on her shoulders. How did the others feel after being here since they were thirteen? The difference between those with years of experience and the energetic and bubbly Diana, who had yet to go on a mission, before the possession was astonishing. This job shouldn't be for everyone born a guardian, but for those made for it. Or for the few like herself who fought demons her whole life without knowing better.

Maybe in another life, she wouldn't be a fighter. Perhaps she'd be a fisherman, seamstress, shepherd, or painter. Who knew? If she had been given the time to think of anything other than surviving and killing demons while in Stanlow, she could have had another future.

In another lifetime.

"If you have questions, please feel free to pass by my office," he said, ending the meeting.

He went to his office, signalling Lane to follow him. "I know you want to return to the clearing as soon as Althea allows it, but I need to figure this out first," he said on his way to his desk. "I can't have them wait any longer."

"Right, about that. I can help. It's not your ability that defeated the demon. It was mine." His gaze snapped to her. "I want to tell you everything," she said. "But first, I want to know what happened that day."

You won't talk about it otherwise, will you? His gaze left her, a darkness settling under his eyes as he began pacing the room.

The silence stretched until she walked to him. "Should we go for a walk?" she asked, touching his arm and turning him to her. The dark room brought her back to the limbo. The shorter they stayed there, the better. "I'm mostly curious about what happened to Diana. I remember the rest and don't blame you for a single part."

His jaw tensed, his voice low. "You should."

"Why? I didn't blame you for a second. No matter what you tell me, I won't start doing that now. You couldn't have known what would happen. They caught you off guard."

"That's exactly the problem. I let my guard down and ended up hurting the Keep and you." He gritted his teeth and stepped away from her soft touch.

"Kage, look at me, please." She waited. "Please," she whispered, and after a painful couple of minutes, he turned to her. "No one expected those words to come out of Diana. The demon inside you took advantage of the situation, but as my ability fought, I felt you fighting it alongside me. You didn't stop until the end. If you had, I don't think I would have killed it."

She wanted to close the gap between them but didn't dare.

"So, you *did* help. That I'm not dead is enough proof because, believe me, I would be otherwise. If not by the hands of the demon, by my own. You pulled me back from the darkness. I followed your scent and voice. I'd still be in that bed if it hadn't been for you. You saved me. Twice."

He stared at her briefly. "Follow me."

He guided her out of the office, out of the Keep. To where, she didn't know, but it didn't matter as long as she wasn't crammed in the office. Outside, she could think straight. She could breathe again.

After walking for fifteen minutes without aim and hoping for him to start the conversation, she asked, "What happened to Diana?"

"She vanished after she thought you were dead."

"She's possessed, isn't she? I felt it when we touched each other during the fighting, but I couldn't quite grasp what it was. When I touched you in the office, it clicked. She didn't want me dead. The demon did." She paused as Kage's black eyes flashed through her mind. "But her eyes... They weren't black. How is that possible?"

"Dregma and Ezraan can do that. Only Azrunol turn your eyes black when they possess you."

"But...Diana said they were destroyed during the war."

"Demons aren't created as one thing and stay like that forever. They can evolve like spirits do, which means that even if we got rid of every last Dregma and Ezraan fifteen years ago, Azrunol and Gulgath have had enough time to evolve into them."

"So, they will never stop existing. And you said they can pass the barrier inside a guardian, which means everyone in this Keep could be possessed."

"That's unlikely. You saw how reactive Diana was. If everyone were that way, we would have noticed it. Most of us are infected, though. It comes with the job. We can't prevent it, so we learn to deal with it. From our first day at the Keep, we're told to fight off the negative thoughts," he said, his gaze turning distant. "We learn that becoming possessed is most likely a matter of when, not if. When we turn, we either lock the guardian in a cell or, if they signed a form beforehand, we kill them along with the demon."

"That's awful."

"Is it? I believe it's the most humane thing we can do. There's no cure for it. Or at least, there wasn't one until now. I'm the first guardian in history to go back to normal after a possession. How did you do it?"

"I...am not completely sure. I think my ability has this warmth side that detects the demon in someone when I touch them. It streams into their body and cleans it from the inside."

Bhaskara warmed Lane's stomach in agreement. "When I grabbed your hand, my light warned me to be careful. When I saw your eyes, I put two and two together and knew a demon was controlling you. I used my ability to defeat it, but..." She paused, thinking of the moment they had at the clearing. "Have you been outside the barrier since we hugged at the clearing?"

"No. Why?"

"That's weird. How did you get infected again?" Kage tilted his head, and she added, "I'm sure I cleansed you the day you showed me your power. My warmth reacted to your body, just like in the office when I helped you and..." She hesitated. *Will he be mad to know I know?* It didn't matter, he had the right to. "And in the canteen, when I talked about Maya with Luke."

"What?" His eyes widened.

"I-I know about her." She swallowed, preparing herself for the rage outburst. "I asked Luke why you didn't like each other, and he told me. I should have asked you, I know. I'm sorry, but you were mad because I trained with him, and I had to know why."

"I would have done the same in your situation. I shouldn't have lashed out, especially without an explanation. It was wrong of me," he calmly said, resuming their walk, and her shoulders relaxed, glad that he understood why she'd done it. "Only the thought of Luke used to make my blood boil. I tried fighting the poison but ended up drowning in it. The demons inside us fed on our grief for long enough. Now that they are gone, so is that feeling. We're talking thanks to your ability."

She smiled. "I was surprised he came with us without you objecting, but I figured you'd talked. I'm happy for you. Also, for Luke, especially since he found someone in the process."

"Luke?"

She raised her eyebrows. "Don't tell me you didn't see all the looks and touches between him and Althea."

"I had other things on my mind." There was no hesitation in his voice.

She blushed, glancing at his lips. "Right..."

They walked side by side, not close enough to brush his hand 'by accident' and see how he reacted. She wanted to be as close to him as when she woke up, but didn't know how to make it happen. An awkward silence filled the space between them as her mind ran through all the questions and thoughts that wouldn't materialise.

How can he walk so unfazed by the uncomfortable silence?

Luckily, salvation appeared after a short distance. A lake filled with lilies hidden between the trees came into view, delivering the distraction her mind needed.

A willow on the other side of the lake called to her. Without asking, she darted to it, getting there first to see what he'd do when he sat down. A smile escaped her when he relaxed his legs, and his thigh rested against hers. If she dared, she could rest her head on his shoulder. But she didn't. For all she knew, she was seeing things that weren't there, and he hadn't even noticed their legs were touching.

She forced her focus to shift to the lake and the lilies. The blue, pink, white, purple and yellow flowers created beautiful patterns in the water. She could stare at them for hours.

Are there fish in there?

With that thought, her mind automatically connected to the painful memory of her parents. She stiffened, making Kage pull his leg away from hers as he sat up straight. Now, a visible gap between them.

"I just thought of my father," she blurted out before giving herself time to think about what to say.

His gaze met hers, revealing a hint of worry within him she'd never seen before. It invited her to open up. With a deep breath, she told him about the darkness and the thoughts of being dead. She told him about the memory and the barrier, how she crossed it and how there was another one. At least one more wall to understand how her father had died.

While she talked, tears streamed down her face. He listened, letting her gather her thoughts and say what she wanted.

"It can't have been easy to go through it alone."

"It wasn't. After, I wanted to give up in the darkness. I almost did. I almost chose wrong."

Their eyes locked, and he hesitated. His hand moved towards her, stopping a few times on the way. She leaned in to meet his touch, but his hand was back on his lap, and his gaze fixed on the lake.

"We should go back," she eventually said, seeing the dark clouds forming in the sky.

The first drops fell just as they entered the Keep. After battling through her life's longest and most awkward walk, she wished him a good night without meeting his eyes and ran to her room.

She stood by the window, admiring the rain. The drops falling against the glass calmed her. The irregular patterns captivated her, and she realised she had also missed that sound in the darkness.

Her mind wandered back to their walk to the lake, imagining what would have happened had she dared to brush his hand. Or if she'd had rested her head on his shoulder under the willow.

Not that I was going to. She couldn't. Not until most barriers had come down. Those in her head and those between them. Kage would have to open up more before she dared take a step like that.

CHAPTER 21

Mister Kohler welcomed Lane and Kage into the library. The space was bigger than it looked from the outside but also gloomier than one would expect. The dark wood of the bookshelves covered every inch of the walls, and the torches illuminating the area weren't enough for a place where people came to read.

After explaining Lane's situation, Kage asked Mister Kohler to keep the information to himself until Lane's mind barriers were gone and she could control her ability without restraints.

"I know you must report whatever you deem worthy to the Capital…"

"Do not worry, Commander. I want the best for this Keep and its residents. I have nothing to tell the Council. I haven't in years." He winked. "I'm of the opinion that things can be best resolved locally."

"I appreciate it, Mister Kohler. If you change your mind, I will not hold it against you, but please inform me so I have time to prepare." Mister Kohler nodded, and Kage added, "I need to get some work done, but if you could bring her up to speed on Guardian history in the meantime, it would be a great help."

"Of course. It would be my pleasure." He picked up a few books. "Come, my child. Sit. Sit." Mister Kohler pointed at a table.

"Let me help you," she offered.

"No, no. I know I seem old, but I'm perfectly capable. Sit. I'll be right back."

He dropped three books at the table only to grab four others. With the pile balanced on the table, Mister Kohler sat beside Lane.

"Let's see. We can best start with demons. That's the core of the business, after all."

He pulled a book from the middle of the pile and opened it on a page with illustrations of all five types of demons. On the left corner, Lane recognised the Karazak that had agonised her for years. Little, black, worm-like creatures the size of her underarm but twice as thick. The Gulgath next to it wasn't new either. They were similar to the previous, only twice as long and with four limbs.

But she barely gave them any attention. In the middle, a drawing of an Azrunol brought a shiver down her neck. It was more human-like than the other two, with a head and longer limb, but it stood on all fours and slightly tilted to one side, crooked as if unsure of how to stand properly.

"Is this what was inside Kage? How didn't he feel it?" she asked, her eyes glued to the page.

"Demons, like spirits, do not follow the same laws of physics as we do. When a demon possesses someone, they aren't this shape," Mister Kohler pointed at the image in the book. "Inside the host, their solid form compacts to fit the available space."

"How?"

"They live in two realms. When they roam in this world like Karazak do, they are fully in ours. When they are what we call "dead", they are sent back to the spiritual realm. But when they possess or infect someone, they are in both realms simultaneously. How that works remains a mystery, but we know they can decide how much of themselves they have on each side."

"Why?"

"It's the same process with your spirit. You can't use your ability when she isn't connecting to the spiritual realm. The more she comes in contact with it, the more of her power she allows you to use."

"I thought the energy needed came from me, not her."

"It does, and it doesn't. It's a combination of both. You see, the stronger the spirit, the stronger its connection with the spiritual realm. But an ability can only manifest in our world with the help of what is created on this side."

"My energy?"

"Exactly. The limiting factor of a guardian's strength is either their energy source or the spirit's strength. The same goes for demons. The stronger they are, the better they can connect to their world, allowing them to control more of their host."

"Okay, that sort of makes sense. Is that the reason why Karazak and Gulgath can't possess us?"

"Yes, that's exactly why. They are so weak that even humans can't see them. Azrunol normally don't possess us either, but that's because of the black eyes. They've learned from the past. As soon as someone's eyes turn, they are killed or incarcerated."

"Why not save them?" she asked, inspecting her hands.

"The Council tried for years, but the demon never left the host and only became more erratic. They never found a solution, not even with the strongest healers. Eventually, they gave up and decided it was best, given the guardian's permission, to end their suffering as fast and humanely as possible."

Lane swallowed. She could change that if she passed her mental barriers.

"But times are changing. Hopefully, for the better." Lane met Mister Kohler's gaze, and he smiled. "Guardians have learned a few things about spirits in the last few centuries. For example, what we thought was a limitation to their strength turned out to be a threshold they had to surpass to evolve. Though powerful enough to kill a human not equipped for bonding, the first spirits were nothing compared to those we now know. You are the perfect example." Lane tilted her face. "You are the first Light Wielder who can do what you do."

"Really? That's cool. Are there more out there?"

"It is extremely difficult to say with precision how many spirits of each type there are. Firstly, there isn't an equal number of each type. Water and fire are the most common elements. Air and earth follow in second place, while light and shadow rank last. Secondly, some spirits like to take their time finding their host. Some wait decades in the spiritual realm for the right person, making it impossible to know for sure how many are waiting."

"Maybe there are Light Wielders at other Keeps or the Capital. It would be nice to talk with them and see how they use their ability."

"It would, but the chances are slim. The number of spirits, and therefore that of guardians too, has been decreasing for at least a hundred years. The only way a spirit can evolve is by merging with others of its kind. They combine to become more. So, the stronger a spirit is, the fewer of its kind exist. Why, I cannot tell you. It's just what scholars have discovered in the last decades."

"How many spirits do you need to evolve?"

"Who knows?"

"Then how do you know which stage your spirit is in? How do you know how many more you have to go?"

"You don't. And don't bother asking her. Your spirit can't tell you either. Many have tried, but there are things they cannot disclose simply because they don't know themselves. With each evolution, they become wiser. The first spirits were like toddlers, barely spoke at all. We've come to learn some things, but where their limits lie isn't one. You can only make assumptions based on your spirit's ability. Yours, for example, has an impressive one. Evolution-wise, I would say she's in the later stages, if not the last one. The chances are your light spirit is one of the last ones, if not the last."

"Does that mean soon there will be more demons than spirits in this world?" Her eyes shifted to the drawing of the Dregma and the Ezraan, both too human for her taste. Unlike Azrunol, they both stood straight. Dregma had dark, red skin and long, claw-like fingers.

"It might already be so."

The memory of her bloodied mother and the demon around her flashed before her eyes. A Dregma had attacked her.

Ezraan were even more eerie. If she came across one, she'd never look at them twice if not for their twisted features. The malice they carried was etched on their faces.

"The Ezraan are bigger and stronger than the Dregma," Mister Kohler said, seeing that her eyes wouldn't leave the paper. "They can fully control their host. A Dregma does it for about sixty to seventy percent. With both types of possession, the eyes of the host don't turn black, making them harder to spot."

Let's hope Diana has a Dregma inside her.

"They are also more intelligent and can manipulate those around them into thinking they are the ones going crazy. Still, they are nothing compared to Greater Demons," Mister Kohler added, turning the page. An enormous, dark-red-skinned man stared at her. Its muscles filled with protruding veins, his skin covered with scars—just like hers used to be. "They are the masterminds. They control every Lesser Demon they create. None can disobey them."

"Have they always existed?"

"Not according to our records." Mister Kohler explained how, over three thousand years ago, the first spirit asked a human to bind with them in exchange for a longer life and power. The human accepted but died in the process. The spirit, eager to bind, moved on to another human with the same request, but failed once more.

She repeated the process countless times to no avail, creating a trail of death behind her. Eventually, she found a human strong enough to bind with. Not a big, strong man but a young girl determined not to use the power of the spirit for herself but for her family, to protect them from the neighbouring stronger villages.

Seeing that they needed to find righteous people to bind, other spirits followed suit. Many bonded with good and kind humans whose intentions were pure. With that, the first group of guardians was created. Year zero on their calendar, compared to the year 1045 of humans.

As time passed, guardians isolated themselves, thinking themselves better than their spiritless brothers and sisters. By only mating with each other, they created children susceptible to spirits who weren't necessarily pure of heart.

"Guardians have become humans with abilities, in my opinion. Many see us as better or superior, but what initially made guardians great was bred out of us. You see, now, everyone can have a spirit if their body is strong enough to manage the surge of energy. The heart was taken out of the equation." He sighed, his eyes filled with sorrow. "I am sorry, my child. I'm rambling instead of answering your question. In the beginning, there were only guardians. The first Greater Demon appeared around two thousand years ago. How? We don't know. What we do know is that he created an army of Lesser Demons and attacked. Since guardians had no idea what they were and how to fight them, many died."

"That's awful."

"Awful indeed, but we were bestowed this gift to help humans flourish. We did the opposite. We shoved them aside like they were inferior. We sought power instead of integrity, and we believed we could get it by ignoring our responsibilities. Unfortunately, if things come too easily, it usually means they have a hidden price attached to them."

Mister Kohler went back to the previous page. "Since that day, demons have roamed the world. The few guardians who survived the massacre rebuilt and learned from their mistakes. They learned to fight and were prepared when the Second Demon War came about 750 years ago. The damages were minimal, which, unfortunately, made the Capital arrogant and complacent. The Third Demon War showed us just how much we had truly fallen from our grace. It happened only fifteen years ago, and many died. Too many, if you ask me. More than necessary if the Capital had taken the necessary precautions."

Lane swallowed. Her mother came to mind. She opened her mouth but was interrupted by approaching footsteps.

"Mister Mallory, what do we owe the pleasure?" Mister Kohler asked.

"Hi, Mister Kohler, how are you? I saw Kage and Lane coming up earlier today. I thought I'd come to investigate after my practice. Giving Lane a history lesson?" Luke asked as he strolled to the table and grabbed one of the books on the pile. "I see we're going back to the basics. I remember reading this when I was still living at home. 'The Capital: A History', perfect as a bedtime story." He turned to Lane and winked. "Nothing like reading about the Second Demon War to fall asleep like a baby."

The three turned to the library entrance as another pair of footsteps echoed through the dark walls. Not long after, Althea showed up next to Luke.

"Hi, what are you up to?"

Mister Kohler turned to Lane, allowing her to choose how to answer the question, but before she could, yet another voice joined them. "What's going on here?"

They all jumped. None had heard Kage's footsteps, but somehow, he stood behind Luke and Althea, two books in his hand.

"Talk about light feet, man. You scared the demons out of me," Luke said.

"What's going on here?" Kage reiterated.

"Nothing much. I came to see if you guys needed help with anything, but I see Lane is in good hands."

"Actually...you came right on time," Lane said, eyeing Kage. "There's something you need to know."

In the morning, she'd convinced Kage to tell Luke and Althea about her past. There were risks in doing so, but they'd saved her life. If that didn't mean something, she didn't know what did. Besides, Bhaskara had also agreed.

With Diana gone, Luke was closest to her in this Keep. He came with Althea, so now she was too. It could mean little to them, and they probably didn't reciprocate the thought, but lying felt wrong. If they knew, she wouldn't have to pretend as hard. She could be herself, and they could teach her things as they searched for information on how to help Diana.

To her surprise, the only thing Luke said after she'd explained her situation was, "I can't imagine being raised like that, but now I understand why you're so weird." He grinned and winked at her.

"That's why I get along with you. Kindred spirits gravitate towards one another," she replied, playfully bowing her head to Luke. "But yeah, now you know."

"Why are you telling us this?" Althea asked.

"Diana needs us. Lying won't help our situation. We need all hands on deck. I can't go sneaking around with Mister Kohler so he can teach me about the guardian history without you noticing. It's a waste of time, and we don't have much of it."

"And has Mister Kohler been helpful?" Luke grinned.

Mister Kohler raised one eyebrow, whipping the grin off Luke's face. "I was talking with Miss Lane about our history before you showed up and interrupted us. If you want to help, grab a book and read in silence. You can explain its content to everyone once you're done."

"What? I didn't know I'd have to prepare a presentation. Can I still opt out?" Luke asked.

"Read these first," Kage said, ignoring his comment and handing him the books he'd brought. "I found them in my office. I'll come back later to see what else you found. I'll help tomorrow if we still have books to read."

Lane gave Luke and Althea each a piece of paper and told them to write all the information they came across, even what they thought was common knowledge. It was easy to overlook what they already knew when connecting the dots. Writing it down could help prevent it, and Lane would understand it better with the background information added to it.

Mister Kohler mumbled under his breath before resuming his teaching on how little they knew about how demons came to be.

Scholars had theories, but they couldn't say for sure if demons were created together with spirits as their counterparts—their negative side— or if they were something else altogether. Had they lived for over a century in the spiritual realm until the first Greater Demon crossed over to this one? Had they formed as a by-product of spirits bonding with humans? Had they emerged inside the realm gradually for an inexplicable reason? Spirits had no answer to those questions, and therefore, neither did scholars.

What guardians did know was that demons could possess and manipulate. Killing them meant they would disintegrate back into their realm. Karazak and Gulgath needed little to cross into this world. A vengeful thought was enough to pull them out of their realm. But the stronger demons were more difficult to summon. A ritual had to be performed if the

Greater Demon wasn't present.

"Who in their right mind would do that?" Lane asked.

"Crazy people. People who worship them," Luke answered before Mister Kohler could. "And I'm assuming this author is one of them. He has this theory about how demons were created, especially Greater Demons. I've never read anything like this before. It's kind of disturbing, actually."

"Let me see that." Mister Kohler snatched the book off Luke's hands before he could give it to him. One glance at the cover, and he tensed up, eyes wide. "Where did you get this?"

"Don't look at me. Kage brought it."

Mister Kohler abruptly stormed off, book in hand, without saying another word.

"I can't be the only one who thinks that was weird, can I? I mean, what's his problem? It's just a book," Luke said after a few seconds of silence.

"I kind of want to know what's in it now," Lane said.

"Luckily for you, I did listen and took notes."

Luke proceeded to tell them what he'd read. In the first chapter, the author explained how he thought guardians, by distancing themselves from humans and only mating with each other, had created children susceptible to spirits from birth. The conditions to bind with a spirit faded, and even those without pure intentions were allowed to bind just because their parents were powerful guardians.

"Mister Kohler said something along those lines," Lane added to Luke's monologue.

The second chapter explained the author's thoughts about how the first Greater Demon was created. He hypothesised it happened when guardians without the initial moral compass killed other guardians.

To prove it, he experimented.

For the first test, he had guardians kill other guardians with the same,

217

different, and opposing abilities. When all failed, he thought perhaps the host's intentions were crucial to creating a Greater Demon. So, he brainwashed guardians into believing they had to kill someone to survive, which also didn't work.

The author almost lost hope of finding the answer when he realised some guardians had stronger connections between them than others. He went on to interview different couples to understand the reason behind it. He found out that the strength of the connection depended not only on the bond between guardians but also that between spirits.

Soulmates.

Each spirit had its other half, but it wasn't just any other spirit with the opposing ability. A fire spirit had water as its counterpart, but the author couldn't have any fire spirit kill any water spirit. He'd tried that already. He needed a specific fire spirit to kill a specific water spirit.

Wanting to test his theory, he kidnapped three of the interviewed couples. One for each of the three formulated hypotheses. Firstly, he wanted to know if killing one's soulmate was enough, even if the guardians were sedated and not conscious. If that didn't work, he wanted to know if killing one's soulmate while awake was enough, even without the intention to kill. And if that also failed, he would brainwash a guardian into wanting to kill the other to see if doing it with intention would do the trick.

A shiver ran down Lane's spine as she imagined how the prisoners felt. She couldn't believe someone would experiment on others. They must have had so little regard for life to even think of doing this, much less plan it and take action.

The first experiment, to Lane's horror, failed. It meant the author would keep going. He had killed a guardian with the unconscious hands of their soulmate, but nothing changed. No Greater Demon was born when the soulmate realised what they had done either.

Displeased with the results, the author went on to his second experiment. To his frustration, the second experiment ended much like the first one, so the author brainwashed one of the last two subjects into wanting to kill their soulmate. Once his subject was prepared, he proceeded with his final experiment.

"And?" Lane asked.

"I don't know. The other pages were empty. The book ended there."

"Seriously?"

"My exact thought, but I don't think we can ask Mister Kohler about it. We hit a nerve there."

The information lingered in Lane's mind, but the word *soulmates* resonated harder than the rest. Immediately, when Luke told her about it, she thought of Kage. But more specifically, she thought about the day he showed her how far his ability went at the clearing. She remembered how her spirit reacted to his and how happy they were to come together. It felt like she was reconnecting with a long-lost friend. Perhaps she was. One very special friend. Her soulmate.

Her belly warmed in agreement as Mister Kohler's words connected to what Luke said.

"There were two Demon Wars with Greater Demons present, which means that at least twice in our history, a guardian wanted to kill their soulmate and succeeded." She paused, letting the words sink in. "I can't imagine ever wanting to kill someone, much less the one I love the most."

"Did you write down the name of the author?" Althea asked.

"No, I didn't think it was relevant since I assumed we would have the book with us."

"Shame," Althea said. "Having this talk inside this old, dark library is giving me the creeps. I'm going to get some fresh air. I'll be right back."

With Althea gone, Lane took the opportunity to talk with Luke about them. She waited long enough to ensure they were alone. "Althea is nice. I like her. When did you start hanging out together?"

"Trying to steal her from me?" He grinned. "But she is, isn't she? She's so patient and helpful." His eyes glowed in the gloomy library. "When she took care of you while you were... You know. We talked for the first time, as in an actual talk and not like a work-stuff talk. It's been great."

"I'm glad my almost death made that happen." Luke scratched his head, and Lane laughed at his discomfort. "I'm joking, but seriously, you two look good together."

"Well, I haven't made any moves yet. We're just hanging out."

"What? Why? What are you waiting for? There's at least one demon trying to kill us. You never know what tomorrow will bring."

"I know, and honestly, I don't know why I haven't asked her out yet. I normally don't have any trouble making the first move. But with her, I've been waiting for the right moment to make it perfect, you know? But I keep making excuses as to why the moment isn't right yet."

"Well, almost dying does the trick, apparently." The image of Kage close to her when she woke up came to mind.

"I hope we don't need to go that far," Althea said behind them. Luke and Lane jumped from their seats. They hadn't heard her approach them.

"Althea, what..." Luke paced towards her, his face bright red. "How much did you hear?"

"Enough," she smiled, closing the gap between them and kissing him. He blushed brighter, hesitating for a second as his brain realised he wasn't dreaming. He kissed her back.

"So, Althea," Lane said after they sat back down with her. "Tell me about you. Where do you come from? What do you like doing? Why did you come to this Keep? I want to know everything. This situation needs to be assessed and approved before you can continue seeing each other," Lane teased, leaning back on her chair.

Althea laughed. "I was raised in the Capital but went to a village south of here, in the human part of the world, when I was thirteen instead of going to a Keep. My grandparents live there, and I went to take care of them. My mother needed to stay in the Capital for her work. My father, just like many, died during the war." Her voice was calm and controlled. Lane couldn't hear any pain behind such heavy words.

"When I turned twenty, my grandparents told me to go to a Keep for proper training. I refused and stayed until they threatened to kick me out if I didn't." She chuckled. "That's how I ended up here. I had decided to go from one Keep to another until I found a place to stay, but since there was a shortage of healers, I got a room on my first try," she chuckled. "That was four years ago, and since I love it here," she glanced at Luke with a smile, "I decided to stay. Besides, I get a lot of freedom to do what I love. I have tons of time to read about medicinal herbs and experiment with mixing powders, fluids, roots, or whatever else I come across." Her eyes sparkled as she spoke. "I have crafted healing potions and ointments that accelerate the healing process."

"Really? Can I order some of it to go? I'll definitely need some once I adventure out of the barrier on my first mission. I have a way of finding demon teeth stuck in my skin. Don't ask about it. It's a talent of mine."

They laughed, "I doubt that'll happen again with your ability. But sure, I'll save a jar ready for the occasion."

"Great. I appreciate it."

"But that's me in a nutshell. I love being here and have loved it even more since I met Luke." She grabbed his arm and hugged it. "So, thank you for almost dying." Althea winked.

Lane laughed. "Glad to have been of service."

"And? Do you have your verdict?" Luke asked.

"I do. I must say, when you forbade me from going outside yesterday, I wasn't sure. But now I see it. You're approved." She turned to Luke. "I like her. You have good taste."

"Was that even a question?" he asked, gesturing to his body. "But I'm glad. What a relief," Luke replied sarcastically. "I don't know what I would have done otherwise." He turned to Althea. "So, now that Lane approves of you, would you like to look for more books about demons?"

"Just leave," Lane interjected. "You don't need to make an excuse to be alone with each other. I get it. Just go."

"You're an angel, thank you," Luke said, his back already turned.

CHAPTER 22

"Where did you get this?" Mister Kohler barged into Kage's office.

"Hello to you too, Mister Kohler. Please, do come in," Kage said without looking away from the papers on his desk.

"Do not play games with me, boy. Where did you get this book?"

Kage finished writing his sentence before standing up and slowly walking to Mister Kohler. He grabbed the book and examined it.

"This is one of the books I found in here." Kage gestured at the bookshelf. "All I did was search for books that had information about demons, and that one, along with the other book I brought to the library, seemed relevant. Why?"

"That's impossible. I know all the books in this Keep. I filled and organised your shelves, and I've never seen this book. How could I? The Council has banned it. They don't want guardians reading this nonsense, much less impressionable ones like your friends."

"Who read it?"

Mister Kohler snatched the book back from Kage. "Luke, but I assume he already told Lane and Althea by now. You need to make them understand that what's inside this book is nothing but the crazy ideas of a fanatic from centuries ago. There is no reason to pursue this any further." Kage raised his eyebrows, so Mister Kohler added, "If you do, I'll report Lane's recent bonding to the Council."

Lying in bed alone was hard. Lane either thought of her parents or Kage. Both made her heart race for entirely different reasons. Not wanting to face the dread that came with thinking of the barrier and what lay behind it, she focused on Kage.

She'd noticed him on her first day. Who wouldn't? She wasn't blind. He was one of the most handsome men she'd ever seen. But she hadn't been immediately struck by him. Had she been curious? Of course. She'd wanted to get to know him, but she'd done her best not to spend her whole day talking or thinking about him.

He didn't know how to open up, but his actions had told her he cared. He'd been by her side when she was in limbo. Even if duty-bound, he gave up his time to help her pass the barrier and understand her memory.

She swallowed.

The image of her mother, bloodied and claws sticking out of her body, came to mind. If her mother died like that, how did her father? Going back to see him being impaled the same way was the last thing she wanted. Seeing him fight for his life and die wasn't on her list of 'things to do' either. And still, she couldn't stop imagining how he died. The different angles. The number of demons charging at him. The duration of the attacks. The endless number of options took over her mind.

"Yes?" Kage's voice brought her back.

She was standing in the corridor, in front of his bedroom door, with him leaning against it shirtless.

When had she left her room and knocked on his door? She couldn't remember. He stared at her, head slightly tilted, waiting for her to speak. Her eyes lingered on his tattoo before meeting his.

"I can't sleep. Can I come in?" she asked before processing who she was talking to.

He straightened and, without a word, went to sit on his bed. She took it as an invitation, closing the door behind her. She paced his room, surprised to see its layout was the same as hers, except for his one window compared to her two. Being the commander of the Keep didn't come with many perks. She'd expected his room to be bigger or have more furniture, but they were interchangeable.

I still prefer mine. This one is too dark.

"Anything on your mind?" he asked.

"Right. Sorry," she stopped and turned to him. "I can't sleep. My mind keeps circling back to my parents. I can't shake it off."

"Do you want to go back to Stanlow?"

She frowned. What did that have to do with anything? "What?"

"Do you want to go back to Stanlow?" he repeated.

"Yeah, sure. I do."

"Why?"

"Because..." She didn't understand why he was asking her that, but thought of an answer anyway. "I want to see Miss Deleon again and show her how far I've come. I want her to know I'm alive and well and that she was right about Caragain. I want to thank her for pushing me to go south. But I only want to visit. I don't think I'd ever want to live in Stanlow again."

"Where do you want to live once you can control your ability?"

She smiled.

He was distracting her, forcing her mind to change subjects. She went with it. "I don't know, but if Karazak aren't a threat, I'd like to see as much as possible. Travel to all the villages and cities I can find on a map and see how things are done there. Get to know the locals, learn from them, and help them. And you?"

"I'm already where I want to be."

She eyed his tattoo as she waited for more to come, but nothing did. With all her courage, knowing he would shut her off anyway, she asked if it had any meaning.

"It does."

That's more than I was expecting. But he surprised her further by walking towards the mirror and saying, "It's about my father, my ability and my life as a guardian." His hand brushed over the black and white images, and she joined him. "The smoke symbolises the shadows. You see them everywhere because they are a big part of who I am and have influenced everything I've done. This on my chest is about my father and how I remember him, a strong-minded man who knew what he stood for."

It was a bird with a body of black flames. Shadows surrounded it, but it effortlessly claimed the space in Kage's body. It exuded strength and determination. "He controlled fire, hence the flames, and he is the closest to my heart because he was the first loved one I've ever lost."

The longer she observed it, the more it took on the shape of a heart, and the more the flames appeared to bleed.

"The rest, the part on my arm, is about my life since he died." He pointed at his shoulder. "This one is one of the flowers from the hall and symbolises my move to the Keep. It was the first thing I noticed when I arrived."

"Me too. It's a beautiful hall."

"This part with the wind is about meeting Luke." The wind swirled alone before fusing with water and carrying a couple of flower petals. "And about Maya. She was a Water Wielder." The water was encapsulated in the wind, away from the shadows. A knot formed in her stomach when, at some point, the wind disappeared, and the water twirled with the shadows lurking in the background.

"And this one is about Diana." It was a little plant, small and fragile, like he probably saw his sister. The roots were long and faded into the shadows, barely visible in that part of his body.

"It's beautiful," she said, not being completely honest. What else was she supposed to say? Some parts of the tattoo fascinated her, like the bird and the wind. However, the parts concerning Maya and Diana...

The section designated for Maya had a mixture of water, wind and shadow. From the way the petals and water were drawn, it was clear they moved towards the shadows. Somehow, the softness of the shadows around them brought a romantic tone to it. Was she reading into things? Or did he still think of Maya in that way?

The shadows and details were less prominent in the area reserved for Diana. What was the meaning behind this difference? Was it deliberate, revealing Kage's true feelings towards Diana? Or was it to continue the natural fading that started with Maya's section and extended to Diana's? A way to make the tattoo seem more like a whole?

Lane couldn't shake off the feeling it brought up.

"Soon, I'd like to add one about you," he said as he turned to her, their gazes locking.

What would his symbol for her look like? Would it find its place close to his heart? Would it be filled with as much passion as the symbol for Maya? Or would it be an afterthought, away from his shadows, just like the symbol for Diana?

You could ask him, you know, Bhaskara said.

I guess I could, but... She hesitated. The last thing she wanted was to be rejected for asking something too personal.

"Do you have any ideas?" he asked, his voice lower, softer.

Her eyes shifted to his lips. An image of them under the willow, her head resting on his shoulders, crossed her mind. She shook her head, her heart pounding as she stared at his emerald green eyes.

The side of his lips twitched, and he leaned forward. Too surprised by his closeness, she froze, only blinking as he came closer still. Her heart raced with anticipation. She wanted nothing more than to feel his lips against hers. To have his arms wrapped around her. Not giving herself time to second-guess her decision, she tilted her head upwards, closing the gap between them and kissing him.

In response, he wrapped his arms around her, kissing her back with an intensity she wasn't expecting from him.

She'd fantasised before about being intimate with someone, especially on her long trip from Stanlow to Caragain. But all the scenarios had happened in her mind, where she had the narrative and could take the lead or stop whenever she wanted. But now, two people were playing the game.

She'd had a short-lived boyfriend back at the orphanage. If you could even call it that, since she had been five and just before everyone turned their back on her. They had only held hands and eaten every meal together. It was safe to say she didn't know much about relationships and how they were supposed to feel. But what she was feeling right now with him... It had to be how it felt when things were right.

Right? She didn't actually know. Her mind clung to what he was doing. Every movement, every stroke of his hand on her skin, every breath. She couldn't turn it off, not even as his gentle touch tempted her to relax and enjoy the moment.

He guided them towards his bed, but was she prepared to take the next step? Some parts of her wanted to, but others didn't feel comfortable enough yet. She didn't want to regret going too fast. They would have plenty of time to get more intimate. There was no need to rush things. Other things had priority. Things that would heal her from within and allow her to open up completely.

I want to be myself for that, which means I need to know what happened to my father first.

With her father now floating in her mind, she suddenly needed space.

She pulled him away. Seeing the worry on his face, she quickly added, "Sorry, the memory came back again."

CHAPTER 23

"The thing about soulmates is still so messed up. I can't stop thinking about it," Luke said after they gathered in Kage's office and told him about what they'd read the previous day.

"Right? I can't believe Mister Kohler took the book from us. I want to know who the author is," Lane added.

"About that. Mister Kohler came to me with it." Kage sat on the edge of his table. "He forbade us from searching any further on the matter."

"That's crazy! Why not? Saying that just makes me want to do it even more," Luke said.

"The Council banned the information. I understand why after hearing about what was in it. The last thing they want is to have guardians experimenting on each other."

"Oh, now there's really nothing that can stop me. Banned? Banned! Are you serious? Now I know for sure we're on the right track. I'm definitely searching for the author's name."

"Luke, I don't think that's wise," Kage said.

"To the demons with being wise. We have the right to know. Where's the book?"

"Mister Kohler took it."

"Do you know the name of the author?" Kage stared at Luke in silence. "I'm sneaking into his room if I have to. So, you either tell me, or I'm finding out on my own."

"Luke, that's reckless," Althea responded.

"I don't care. If what the book says is true, you know what it implies, don't you? So, what I don't understand is why you're all so okay about this. Especially you, Kage. Why don't you want to know? Why would Mister Kohler stop you so easily? This information is insane."

Silence fell, and everyone turned to Kage to wait for his response. "Just drop it, okay? He has his reasons."

"I told you already, I'm not going to. I don't care about the reason behind Mister Kohler's behaviour. It's weird that the Council has banned this information. I'm finding out more one way or another."

Kage stood up and paced the room. "Rafael Tirich."

"What?"

"The name of the author. Rafael Tirich."

"That sounds familiar," Luke said.

"The only Tirich I know is the Tirich's Children," Althea added.

"Oh yeah! My mum used to tell me stories about them when she didn't want me to do something. She was always like, 'Don't go outside alone at night, or the Tirich's Children will take you away forever." Luke laughed. "It was crazy. I was so afraid of these 'children' that I had trust issues with kids I didn't know."

"Mine used to tell me not to go up the mountains near my grandparents' house because that's where the Tirich's Children lived. One time, I asked why that was so bad, and my grandfather told me these children were friends with demons, so I shouldn't want to play with them," Althea snorted. "I'm still a bit afraid of going near that mountain, honestly."

"Kind of twisted to give them this man's name," Lane said.

"Not if he's behind the book. The kidnapping and demon-loving parts fit the memo."

"Luke's right. Kids' stories often have roots in truth," Kage said. "Or they want to teach you some life lessons. The question is, which one is this one? If it's true, do these Tirich's Children truly exist?"

"Do we know when he was alive?" Althea asked.

Kage shook his head, but Luke jumped excitedly, grabbing the paper where he'd written down the information. "I knew it was handy writing about the guy. At the moment, I thought it was a waste of paper, so I jotted it in a corner. He...began writing the book in the year 2516."

Althea went pale. "That's around seven—"

"Seven hundred and fifty years ago. The Second Demon War!" Luke gasped as he connected the dots. "What if he made the war happen? He could have created a Greater Demon with his experiment and been killed in the process. One can't finish his book if he's dead."

"This guy died centuries ago," Lane added. "If he were important, you would have learned about it besides a name on a bedtime story, right?"

"There are some things people prefer to forget," Kage said. "Books disappear, names vanish, and reports are stored in the darkest corner of the archives. It's not hard to pull when people are mourning the deaths of their loved ones."

"We should look for other books by him. This might have been his last, but it could not have been his first. Those who experiment on people normally start smaller," Althea said.

"You're right. We need to find more of his work," Luke said, turning towards the shelves.

"I checked every book after talking with Mister Kohler yesterday. I found nothing," Kage interjected. "I don't know if he has anything to do with that, but we shouldn't give Mister Kohler too many reasons to think we're still working on this."

"Then we go to the Capital. We might find answers there," Luke said without a second thought.

"That's a good idea, but we need to focus on Diana too." Kage's back straightened. "If she's out there and we can save her, we must work on that."

"I was about to say the same. We don't need to know who the Tirich's Children are. Not right now. For all we know, they are just a scary kids' story to keep you from wandering away," Lane said.

"But what if they're not? What if they're responsible for how Diana is now? Or for the Third Demon War," Luke replied. "If any of that is the case, I want to know. It means they are responsible for the death of hundreds of guardians, including our parents." Luke gestured to Kage, who nodded in agreement.

"Right... I forgot. My parents, too." With Luke's puzzled face, she added, "Long story, I'll tell you later. But you're right. They could be behind more than we think. We need to make sure, but we also need to help Diana. And I must say, I think Diana should be our priority right now."

"Or we can do both. I can leave for the Capital tomorrow. With my ability, I'll arrive in five days. My mother lives there, so I have a place to stay, and we can tell Mister Kohler I'm going for a visit. It'll probably take a while to access the good parts of the library and go through all the books and records, but it's our best shot," Luke suggested. "I'm our best shot." He winked.

With a chuckle, everyone agreed, which meant Lane still had time left in the day to focus on practising with her ability. From experience, she could kill an Azrunol. What about a Dregma or an Ezraan? Even if she did, there was a bigger problem to solve. For her to kill a demon, she had to touch the possessed person. Doing so with Diana while the demon inside her wanted her dead wasn't an option.

Not if I want to leave with my life. "I have to see if I can use my light on someone from a distance."

"We would need an infected guardian for that. How do you expect to find one?" Althea wondered.

Lane smiled awkwardly. "Well, Kage and Luke were infected without knowing, so..."

"I was what?" Luke blurted.

If Althea was infected, Lane could practise on her. It wasn't the same as being possessed, but it was a start that would no doubt help her understand her ability better.

"Althea, can I check if you're..."

Althea sighed but nodded, and Lane immediately rested her hand on her shoulder. "I assume that smile means I'm going to be your lab rat, right?"

Lane's smile grew.

"Should we try it outside?" Kage suggested.

Lane nodded and was by the office door in a heartbeat.

"Wait a minute. You're still recovering. You can't use your ability yet. I won't allow it," Althea said firmly.

"It's okay. I heal fast and feel better now than before the accident."

"Give it one more day. We still have time." Lane frowned, so Althea added, "You need me, and I won't help you today."

"We have no idea where Diana is. She probably saw my light beam, which means she knows I'm alive. The chances are she'll come back to finish what she started. We don't know when that'll happen, so no, we don't have time. Check my vitals if you must. I'm good to go."

Althea sighed, dragging her feet towards Lane to check her vitals. To her surprise, Lane's vitals had improved since the last time. She couldn't compare them to before the accident, but couldn't deny Lane was in good enough shape to train.

She reluctantly agreed.

Lane stood on one end of the clearing and Althea on the other, eight meters away. They had to assess how far she could be from someone to heal them. Kage stood near Althea, ready with his shadows in case she lost control.

Since breaking the second barrier, light and warmth came much more effortlessly. Due to Althea's restrictions, she hadn't tried anything new but knew she had improved. The light waves and warmth she detected around her were proof. If she made an effort, she could extend her perception at least double the distance between her and Althea. Sensing it made it all much easier. It wasn't magic anymore. The warmth didn't appear from nothing but was pulled out of the air and the organisms around her.

With one thought, warmth gathered around her hands. With another, it poured towards Althea. Or at least, it was supposed to. The warmth flickered, strands detaching and dissolving into thin air, while the largest chunk remained stubbornly glued to her palms.

Why? Everything was going so well.

You are not going to hurt her, her spirit told her.

How can you be so sure? I still can't control it completely.

Kage is here. He is strong. Trust he will do his job, Bhaskara said.

I know, but...

You have me. I will pull the connection the moment I sense it going badly. But it will not. You have done this before. You know how the warmth feels and works. Embrace it.

Bhaskara was right. She had done it before and not panicked. Three times. Once in the canteen surrounded by people, once in this clearing with Kage, and a third time in his office. She'd done it before breaking the second barrier.

The only difference was, she wasn't touching Althea.

I got this.

With a deep breath, she closed her eyes and envisioned the warmth gathering around her hand. She imagined it as extension blocks, adding a few to her arms to make them longer.

"Yes! Keep going!" Luke cheered, and she obeyed. Gathering more handfuls of warmth, she attached them to her arm, one after the other, until, in her mind, she had reached Althea. Opening her eyes, she was disappointed that the warmth had only travelled about a meter away.

It vanished.

"Why did you stop? You were doing great," Luke said.

"In my head, I was already there."

"You can't expect to do it on your first try. Do you think I made the air daggers right away? Of course not! And I've been practising for way longer than you have. It's normal. Try again."

"I know. I just thought..." Luke's eyebrows rose. "Never mind."

She closed her eyes and tried several more times, but the results didn't change considerably enough. Defeated that she'd only added half a meter more to the rope of warmth she'd been creating, they called it a day and returned to the Keep to have dinner. Afterwards, they split up.

"By the way," Kage said when she opened her bedroom door, "I looked up the blueprints of the other Keeps, but none of them have a park with a fountain. I think you were in the Capital on the day of your memory."

"Really? That would mean..."

"It must have happened around the same time my father died. Although it raises the question of how you ended up in Stanlow."

She shrugged. "Something else to figure out. But we'll have to worry about it another time." She didn't want to go down that rabbit hole. "There's more important stuff right now. After I heal Althea from a distance, we can try to break the barrier again. Once that's taken care of, we can think about Stanlow."

᭞᭞•●•᭞᭞

The following day, after breakfast, Luke headed out for the Capital. After seeing him off, Althea, Kage and Lane went to the clearing. Hours later, when the sun passed its highest point and the best moment for Lane to cleanse Althea went with it, Lane was beyond discouraged.

We could try something else, Bhaskara resonated in her mind.

If you have any suggestions, I'm all ears. This isn't working.

There are different ways to do this. Better ways, in my opinion.

And you're only telling me this now? Lane almost shouted.

Close your eyes.

Lane sighed, annoyed at someone else telling her to close her eyes without first explaining why.

I will get there, child. Be patient, Bhaskara said, and Lane chuckled. She sounded like a mother. *Well, I am thousands of years older than you. Now, listen to your elders without an attitude and close your eyes.*

Lane did.

Focus on the warmth around you. Notice how everything radiates warmth, how it floats in the air, how it is everywhere.

Yeah, okay... I know that already. So what?

You are not focusing enough. You are seeing but a small part of what I mean. Sit down and feel properly.

Lane did, swallowing a sigh as she rested her palms on the ground. With a deep breath, she sensed the warmth of the bird resting on a tree nearby, the worm on the ground crawling through the grass, and the warmth radiating from Althea and Kage. It was everywhere, even in the air.

See? You do not have to use or create your warmth. That costs too much energy. Use what is around you to your advantage.

Won't we hurt them? Lane asked.

We will not. We will use what is around them. If we borrow from them, it will be but a tiny portion. They will feel a cold breeze, nothing more.

Right... she thought, not entirely convinced.

We will work together to control it, do not worry.

She nodded and felt the warmth in her belly rise. *Take it easy.*

Do not worry. I always am.

With those words, warmth reappeared around her hands. The layer was thicker this time, and instead of imagining adding blocks to her arms, she thought of asking the surrounding warmth to join her and help her reach Althea. With her request, the air around her got colder, the warmth concentrating around her hand. Little bits sipped out of every living thing around her to help.

Together, Bhaskara and Lane managed to cover about six of the eight metres. Knowing this was the farthest she'd come before breaking down all the barriers, she asked Althea to meet the warmth.

A force inside the girl pushed the warmth away, fighting it not to come close. Lane nudged at the warmth. Less than two minutes later, whatever was resisting stopped, and the warmth left Althea's body.

"How do you feel?" Kage asked.

"Lighter, I think."

"Lane, check her again."

Sprinting to Althea, Lane touched her shoulder. A smile tugged on her lips when she felt nothing pushing against the light. "The easy part is done. Now for the hard part."

"I'll leave you to it. Just don't overdo it, okay?" Althea asked, leaving Lane and Kage behind.

The two sat on one of the chopped tree logs at the edge of the clearing and ate dried meat and an apple while mentally preparing for the next task.

They tried to break the third barrier in Lane's mind for the rest of the day, going precisely as Lane expected. She fought against the invisible wall for hours, but nothing worked. The wall didn't budge, and she had to see her mother die a dozen times. When the sun was so low that only a few rays reached her through the foliage, she fell to the ground in desperation.

How would she help Diana, and maybe even more guardians, if she couldn't help herself? All the barriers had to come down before Diana showed up. Without Bhaskara's full power, she'd risk coming up short. That couldn't be an option. The demon wouldn't leave without undeniable proof of her death this time. He wouldn't make the same mistake twice.

Do you want to know what is behind the barrier?

Why was Bhaskara asking that? Of course, she did. She wanted answers about how her parents died. She wanted to know what she could do with her ability afterwards.

It did not seem like you were trying as hard as you could. Do not take me the wrong way. I do not blame you. I would not want to see how someone I love died, either.

After returning from the darkness, she felt like six-year-old Lane, who didn't dare sleep with the lights out. Afraid of the nightmares she was sure would come, she barely slept. And the nightmare didn't greet her, not at night, at least. Since going through the second barrier, she saw her mother about four or five times a day. A reminder that she had to finish what she had started.

It was hard to admit, but Bhaskara was right. She hadn't given her all. She had avoided looking at her mother, and part of her didn't want to see what would happen to her father. She wished she could return to when she felt the happiest, just before breaking the second barrier. But she couldn't. She had to face what was coming or stay in this state of half-knowing forever.

I'm not ready.

When she took in her surroundings again, she found herself in Kage's room, sitting on his bed. He took her shoes and socks off and helped her into his bed. The next thing she remembered was Kage beside her with a plate of food. He held it to her, but she wasn't hungry. She didn't feel tired either, or much of anything, to be honest. She just wanted to lie in bed and not talk, to close her eyes and look at her mother.

CHAPTER 24

The process of evolving was shorter than Gadmerad had expected. Immediately, he felt stronger and faster. Although four days ago, he had thought about using the girl's body to hide from Druzon, he now couldn't wait to get rid of it. The last step of his evolution was shedding the host's skin. He could only imagine how freeing it would be.

After cleaning up the girl's body, Gadmerad told Druzon how he planned to kill the light girl this time. He promised to bring Druzon her head and offered his own in case he failed his Master again. When he was doing so, Gadmerad noticed the humans in the cages had been replaced by a new set. He wanted to ask what had happened but didn't dare to upset his Master by asking the wrong questions.

Gadmerad bowed to leave, but Druzon interrupted him to gloat about how his first experiment to evolve the Azrunol to Dregma had come with promising conclusions. Bestowing humans with hope wasn't more efficient than soaking them in fear. Three of the four hopeful subjects hatched a Dregma a day after all the fear-induced ones. The one who had done it before all others was likely the only one to believe he'd be free once he fulfilled his role. His desperate cries as he was about to die said as much.

Analysing humans to know which were hopeful and which were not was a tedious and nauseating job, especially if it didn't yield results far exceeding the fear-inducing experiment. Druzon, therefore, concluded fear to be the better option, even if it had killed a human in the process. Now, he had to assess which amount of fear yielded the best results, hence the second batch of humans.

Eight prisoners weren't enough to test all the gradations of fear Druzon had in mind. He needed at least four groups, each with four people, in case some died. The first was the control group. Nothing was done to them besides being in cages. The second group was tortured physically. The third, physically and mentally. And the fourth group, on top of everything, was possessed at random moments and forced to do the torturing of others.

As Gadmerad heard Druzon's plan, he noticed the floor was still soaked in the blood of the subjects of the previous experiment. He smiled. His Master was truly the most frightening and vile demon he knew. No other could ever surpass his viciousness, which was precisely why Gadmerad would always serve Druzon and no one else. He wouldn't let his Master down again. As soon as Druzon released him, he'd run back to the Keep to finish the job he had started.

⁂

Lane was still in bed, not wanting to talk, eat, or move. A day passed since she froze in the forest, and Kage carried her to his bedroom. He tried to give her space, but he became increasingly worried and didn't know what to do. He called for Althea in the morning, but she found nothing unusual with Lane. It was a mental block, and Lane would come out of it on her own.

When two full days passed, Kage sat beside her, forcing himself to open up about his childhood. He didn't find it easy, but she needed it more than he needed to be quiet.

"I love my dad. I still remember playing hide and seek with him. I remember him teaching me his favourite fighting moves. I remember him putting me to bed every night when he wasn't on a mission. He would spend all his free time with me." He took a deep breath. "Every time he went on a mission, he'd tell me how much he loved me and how proud he was of me. I'd always tell him I loved him back and was lucky to have him as my dad. I..." He coughed. "I always told him to come home safe. And he always did."

"But on that day, he was home, not on a mission." He clenched his hands. "We didn't get to say I love you one last time." His gaze turned distant. "I waited days for him to come back. I didn't want to believe he was dead."

Lane slid an inch towards him.

"His funeral came, and I still hoped it was a mistake. Only when I received his name tag did I accept reality." His hand gravitated to the chain around his neck. "I thought at first it was best not to know how he died. When the nightmares came, I assumed it was the universe telling me I deserved it.

"I saw him die in countless different ways in my dreams. Gruesome deaths. Whatever I could imagine...because I didn't know the truth." He straightened. "Looking back now, I know it was my mind telling me I needed to face it, that knowing was better than the abyss of ignorance I was stuck in."

Lane moved again, her arm now touching his.

"I only dared ask my mother after multiple nights of nightmares, and was relieved to know he died quickly. Once I knew, the nightmares disappeared." He looked at her. "The pain I felt didn't go away. Only the uncertainty did. Everything around me reminded me of him. I trained day and night to feel it as little as I could."

Lane shifted, her body now pressing against his.

"My mother saw I wasn't healing in the Capital, so she brought me to the Keep when I was eight. I didn't care. I was too numb from grieving. But now, I couldn't be more grateful for what she did." He smiled softly. "I met

Luke here. He understood my pain because he'd gone through the same."

He wrapped his arm around her, allowing her to come closer. "I want to be that person for you, even if I don't understand the depth of your pain. I know you won't get over it in a day. But if you can take anything from my past mistakes... Knowing is better than being in the dark. For as painful as the truth may be, it's better to know."

"I know," she murmured. She put her shoes on, grabbed her jacket and headed to the door. Before leaving, she turned around and said, "I'm going to break the barrier."

৯•●•৶

She didn't have to look back to know Kage was following her, even with the rain concealing his footsteps behind her. It was fitting that the last day of spring came with the heaviest rain of the year. Tomorrow, the red full moon would signal the start of summer with warmer and less wet days. The land was being soaked one last time in preparation for the harsher weather ahead. She was thankful for it. The sounds of the rain calmed and prepared her for the barrier she was about to cross.

She positioned herself in the middle of the clearing and closed her eyes. Kage didn't ask. She was ready. The shadow lifted over her and brought her to her memory.

For the past two days, she'd stared at her mother's bloodied face, sometimes with the demon attached, sometimes without. But the longer she looked, the more her mother's smile overshadowed the demon and the blood. That and Kage's story made her realise that staying in her daydream forever wouldn't bring her parents back. Nothing would.

Going back in time wasn't an option, just like remaining stuck in the state she was in wasn't either. Her parents' deaths would otherwise have been for nothing. They died protecting her so she could have a life, and she was wasting it lying in bed and feeling sorry for herself because she didn't want to face what she'd already seen.

To honour her parents properly, to mourn for them properly, she had to know how they died. Her mind took that option away from her when she was three. Kage was giving her back control. Instead of accepting the opportunity with open arms, she froze.

Enough was enough. She'd cross the third barrier. And the fourth. And the fifth. She'd go through as many as she needed to in order to understand her past.

The rain stopped the moment Kage's shadows enveloped her. She opened her eyes, and there, right in front of her, was her mother. No more blurred spaces or faces. She could see her surroundings as they were.

With the demon buried in her mother, her father ran in slow motion to rescue her. But the image froze. The barrier held her in place again. The cold, invisible walls pressed against her, but she didn't panic. Not this time. Instead, she took a deep breath and pushed the barrier open like a door. She passed through it effortlessly, and the memory resumed playing at normal speed.

Her mother stumbled, and for a second, the world froze again as her frail mother collapsed. In a heartbeat, her father was by her mother's side, guiding her gently to the gravel while killing the demon in the process.

Little Lane followed him, her legs too short to keep up. Her father's lips moved, but the sound never reached her. The screams around them were deafening. Her mother shook her head, and his wide eyes began frantically scanning the area. Afraid, Lane's little legs moved faster. Every fibre in her told her to keep running to her parents, where she'd be safe, but a bone-chilling scream cut through the noise around her. The petrifying panic in her mother's voice froze Lane in place.

Her father stopped searching, his gaze fixed on Lane as he gestured for her to come to him. But his eyes betrayed him. They wandered to something behind her. Little Lane, not knowing what to do, looked back.

Her blood went cold. After deciding to go to the park, this was the second decision she regretted most. A demon was on top of the fountain, readying himself to jump at her. His body was dark and twisted, claws dripping with blood.

A Dregma, her eighteen-year-old version thought.

Her body begged her to run, to get out of the way, but nothing happened. Her eyes were glued to the horrific creature now lunging at her. Even at three, she knew she was too late to escape his sharp claws. Frozen in place, she waited for the excruciating pain to take over her tiny body.

Seconds away from agony, fear was replaced by calm and the demon by a beautiful, shiny creature. Mesmerised by its beauty, Lane forgot about the demon. The screams were gone, a soft wind caressed her steaming cheeks, the smell of blood transformed into that of flowers, and the darkness was replaced by light.

She felt safe here, with the spirit floating before her.

Seeing the grace with which it glided towards her, her mouth felt open. The spirit reached her hand out, requesting Lane to join her. With no hesitation, Little Lane accepted the invitation.

The light disappeared in the blink of an eye, and she was back in the park. A rush of senses and emotions flooded her ten times more potent. The metallic smell of blood hit her nose. The demon was still coming her way, and her mother was still screaming her name. The fear and panic that had disappeared with the light returned and drowned her in despair.

A pressure grew inside her in response. It pushed against her skin, wanting to come out. She tried holding it in, but pain rushed throughout her body.

Lost and afraid, she turned to her parents for help.

Her mother was no longer screaming, her father no longer running towards her. Both stared, fear wiped from their faces. Lane didn't understand why. How could they stop fighting? How could they stand while a Dregma was seconds away from killing her?

Thinking of the impending doom, a waterfall streamed down her cheeks. Why was she holding in whatever it was that wanted to come out? Why suffer when everything was about to end?

Let go, a warm voice resonated inside her, relaxing her.

She let go of the pressure, and fear went with it. A light shone around her, tickling her stomach. She laughed, trying to grab one of the rays as the light got brighter and brighter.

Her mother called her, her voice again calm and angelic as always.

"Mommy, look." She giggled, turning to her parents just before they, and everything around her turned white. Feeling safe in the light and knowing it was better than returning to where the demons were, she didn't worry.

The eighteen-year-old Lane didn't ask Kage to pull the shadows down. Instead, she got the urge to lie down on the ground. Not long after, her body was back to being the three-year-old Lane. In her memory, she wasn't lying on grass but in a moving wooden carriage. Panic rushed over her when she tried to stand but couldn't.

"It's okay," a lady told her. "You're okay, Lane."

It was a familiar voice. She couldn't place who it belonged to, and her eyes felt heavy when she tried to look up to find out.

"Are we almost there, Theoden?" the familiar voice asked.

"Five minutes away, Agatha."

"Perfect, she's starting to wake up. We need to hurry."

The image vanished, and she found herself back in the clearing. Knowing nothing else would come, she stood up and said, "I've seen enough."

The shadows were replaced by rain. Drops caressed her skin, calming her and the perfect camouflage for the tears she felt coming.

"You did it, didn't you? But how? I didn't feel any tension." A hint of pride and admiration coated his voice.

"The barrier must have felt I was ready. I passed right through it."

"I didn't know that was possible. Are there any other barriers? What did you see?"

"No other barriers. This was it. I saw how I killed my parents." She told him without a hint of emotion in her voice. He frowned, and she elaborated. "I think that's why I kept saying I didn't want to hurt anyone else. Not because I thought I'd hurt you, but because *deep down*, I did know what was behind those invisible walls. I knew I had hurt people in the past. I knew I had killed my parents. And your father."

Her eyes scanned him as she spoke. She had decided to tell him before the shadows lowered, giving herself no opportunity to think of how to soften the blow. He had the right to know.

Once the words were out, she waited, bracing herself for whatever he made of it. She told herself she could handle any reaction, but that was a lie. She hoped he wouldn't abandon her, wouldn't ask her to leave the Keep. She wouldn't blame him either if he came to hate her for it, but it would sting worse than a Karazak bite.

All the details of what happened were carved in her mind, but she still had to process them properly. After the devastating truth, no energy was left for emotions. But that was for the best. She could give him the space and time to process it first, and after, she would run to her room and see what she made of it herself.

｛❦•●•❧｝

Kage heard the words that left her mouth, but none made sense. His father died in an explosion of energy created by a grown man trying to save his family.

The man's family... Her family. It could fit.

248

While Lane was unresponsive, he needed to keep himself busy. He analysed the blueprints of every Keep, finding none with a fountain. He'd expected that much since they were designed to be simple and efficient. Still, he revised them again, postponing the truth he already knew.

The only place like what Lane had described was close to where his father had died. The Capital. But nothing had survived the explosion. Bodies had turned to ash, leaving only the name tags of the dead soldiers behind. The only green spot had been the patch of grass where the one who had caused the sea of fire stood. All else was burned.

After hearing what Lane had to say when she crossed the second barrier, Kage knew her parents had died the same way his father did. The only probable option on how she had survived while no one else did was that one of her parents had created the explosion while protecting her.

Believing that to be the only possible truth, he presumed she wouldn't be too devastated to learn how her parents had died. It was, after all, a good way for a parent to go. Or anyone, for that matter. Dying to save their loved ones... It was also how he wanted to go.

Confident of his discovery, he told her about his past.

Or a version of it.

He'd twisted it slightly, but he had to. Saying he'd asked her mother what had happened the day after his father didn't come home wouldn't have resonated with her. Saying he'd poured himself into training partially because of his death, but partially because he wanted to become as strong as whoever had created the explosion wouldn't either. He knew how it sounded. It wasn't about the explosion, but the sheer strength and power required to accomplish such a feat...

He wanted that. He'd wanted it ever since his father died. He'd wanted it even more when Maya died. To be strong enough to protect those he loved. No one he loved would have to be afraid ever again if he achieved it.

But those words wouldn't have resonated with her. So, he told her what she had to hear to cross the barrier. He'd mixed his experience with Luke's, and it had worked. She pushed past her mental block with ease, but her explanation didn't make sense.

If what she said was true, a three-year-old created the explosion that killed hundreds of guardians and demons. It meant she was the idol he'd been trying to beat for over a decade. But how? How could someone bind with a spirit at such an age? It was unheard of.

The youngest recorded binding was of a five-year-old, and the story was closer to a myth than the truth. People that young died, their bodies too small and fragile for the surge of power. Even children strong enough to bind at six years old had trouble controlling the change. Often, they'd lash out. Even he did when he bonded at that age, and he'd trained to prepare. He'd been ready for a spirit and still lashed out. How could her body have survived at three?

Maybe the outburst was the only way to save her.

In any case, the explosion hadn't been her fault. It was a side effect of binding with the spirit. She didn't know it would happen. Not at three, at least. She was in an impossible situation and was given a way to protect herself. Who wouldn't accept it? Especially if you didn't know the consequences it would have.

His vision refocused. Lane stood before him, small and wet from the rain, waiting for him to speak. He wanted to hold her and console her for her loss, but at the same time, he wanted to walk away and avoid her until he'd wrapped his head around it all.

"I don't blame you for my father's death. That much I can tell you already," he said, monotonous and distant. "You were a kid and didn't know what was happening. Most lash out after binding with spirits. You were too young to know. Still, I need time to process...alone."

CHAPTER 25

Lane observed Kage leaving her behind in the rain. He needed time away from her. She did too. Still, it hurt. He was abandoning her. Again. A crack formed inside her, separating them, and she prayed to the spirits he wouldn't take too long to rush back to her.

The days following the passage of the last barrier were a blur. Passing by Diana's room made her miss the friend she desperately needed. Kage's bedroom door only intensified her pain. She stayed in her bedroom, except for the occasional run to the canteen or the bathroom.

It didn't matter how often she played the memory in her mind or how hard she pulled at her emotions. What she'd learned and Kage's reaction had made her numb.

Althea came over once, just like Phoebe, Mary and Jack. Each time, she told them not to worry and let her be before closing her bedroom door.

The first emotions surfaced on the morning of the third day in isolation. She was in the canteen, grabbing a piece of bread with cheese and jam, when her mind drifted to Miss Deleon giving her a pot of jam for her journey to Caragain.

Miss Deleon...

It was her, she thought, remembering the voice in the carriage. *Agatha...*

The realisation hit hard, and the first tears came so effortlessly she couldn't hold them in before returning to her room. Staring at the bread with cheese and jam, she felt betrayed. This wasn't the first time she realised Miss Deleon was more than a headmistress. After seeing the books gifted to her come to life in the hall plants and the guardian's fighting style, deep down, she knew. Still, she shoved that reality aside, pretending it was just a coincidence Miss Deleon had such books. Perhaps she'd given her the botanical ones as a prank, not knowing it was real.

It was unlikely, but the alternative—the betrayal of the one person she had trusted the most in her life—was too much to process at the same time as she discovered this new world she somehow belonged to. So, she avoided thinking about it.

Now, the truth had caught up to her. There was no denying it.

The last few days in Stanlow came to mind. The idea of talking to Miss Deleon about leaving had haunted her. Although she didn't want to upset the headmistress or come off as ungrateful, she had decided to put herself and her future first. To her surprise, Miss Deleon had been prepared. She'd set aside food and a little emergency kit. She suggested Caragain. She told her to take all the books with her in case she needed them. The same ones that had told Lane she wasn't a normal human.

Their conversation the morning of her departure now made more sense too. Lane had hesitated to go, feeling the weight of what she was leaving behind. Miss Deleon was the closest thing to family. She remembered thinking about staying, but Miss Deleon insisted she'd go.

"Don't get cold feet now. You're going, and that's final. I'll miss you, Lane. But there's nothing for you in Stanlow. I've known for years, and I'm glad you came to the same conclusion. There's a better life waiting for you outside this town of small-minded people. Go somewhere no one knows you and start anew. You deserve it."

Thinking about it still brought tears to her eyes. She'd lived with Miss Deleon for almost fifteen years.

"You'll be fine, my dear," Miss Deleon had told her, putting her hand on Lane's shoulder. "I can't give you whatever it is you're looking for, and I hope you can forgive me for not pushing you in the right direction earlier. But for now, think only about all the possibilities coming your way. You know deep down this is the right choice. And yes, it's scary, but everything worth fighting for is. We want them so badly that the idea of failing frightens us.

"But honey, I'm not afraid for you. I've watched you all these years and know you'll do whatever it takes to reach your goals. I've seen you come back from the forest with all kinds of wounds, wondering if it would be the last time you'd adventure into those woods. But no. You stood back up the following day and tried again. So, grab your stuff and go. The world is waiting for you."

She hugged Miss Deleon, thanked her for the past fifteen years and left. Now, those words made more sense. The hidden message behind them was now as clear as the blue sky after a storm.

"I hope you can forgive me," she'd said.

Lane could. It was a hard pill to swallow, but she could forgive Miss Deleon for that. Unfortunately, there was more to it. Miss Deleon had carried her out of the Capital...

Her heart ached with that truth. Never had she thought Miss Deleon was behind it. At best, after seeing the Keep, she imagined Miss Deleon to be stationed in Stanlow, with no ties to her before she arrived at the orphanage. But no. Miss Deleon had brought her there.

She must have known how my parents died all along.

Being lied to about such an important detail by the person she trusted most felt like a dagger to her heart. It was the first thing she felt in days.

When she opened herself to it, she couldn't stop it from pouring out.

Memories of her life at the orphanage popped into her mind, and things began making sense, like how the Karazak only entered the orphanage once. Miss Deleon must have lifted a protection around the orphanage after the first invasion. Or how Miss Deleon never saw her as weird or crazy. It was easy not to when you could see the same demons lurking around.

And then there was their last conversation. Miss Deleon had asked Lane to forgive her for not pushing her to go in the right direction earlier. She thought it was because Miss Deleon wanted her to find a job, not because she would discover who she was near Caragain. What she truly meant was that she hoped Lane wouldn't think less of her for keeping the guardian world from her.

But why shouldn't she? She lied for years.

She sacrificed her life as a guardian to protect you, Bhaskara said.

"Right... But why keep it from me? Why not tell me the truth from the start? We could have gotten over the past together, and I could have felt less alone. But instead, she kept me in the dark. Why?" she asked Bhaskara between sobs, but Bhaskara didn't have an answer.

Miss Deleon must have had her reasons, but by doing so, she deprived Lane of a part of herself for years. If she'd known at an earlier age she had been responsible for the explosion, she might not have had the barriers to cross and would've been able to control her ability earlier and faster.

Or maybe you would have hated yourself for it and would end up blaming yourself. You would never touch your ability again, making the thing that saved you in the first place the thing that killed you in the long run.

"Maybe..." She couldn't disagree with Bhaskara, but part of her still hurt when thinking about Miss Deleon. She knew, deep down, the headmistress had done what she thought was best. "Or was it all a lie? Just part of the role she had to play?"

Do not say that. You know she was not lying about who she is. No one can keep up an act like that for fifteen years. She did so much for you and protected you the best way she could. She loves you.

In her heart, Lane knew it to be true. Why protect her from the Karazak for fifteen years if she didn't? Why help her with her wounds, learn to fight, or give her a room for herself? It all came from love, but that didn't take away the pain. She was lied to for years. The reason behind it didn't matter. It made her question what else Miss Deleon had kept from her.

Returning to Stanlow, knowing what she now knew would be different. And awkward. But now, she had even more reasons to go back. The sooner, the better, so she could interrogate Miss Deleon.

Once that part of the memory was dealt with, she made room to think about her bond with Bhaskara. It was the reason why her parents died, as well as Kage's and Luke's fathers. Maybe even Althea's and many more.

It was not your fault. If you have to blame anyone for what happened, blame me. I knew the light would most likely burst out of you if I asked you to bind with me, but you must understand. I saw you grow for three years while I waited for the right moment to bind with you. When the demon came for you, I did not hesitate. I knew you could die from us binding too early, but I had to try. I have had many hosts over the centuries, but never have I been so certain about one as I have been with you. We were meant for each other. Letting you die without trying was not an option.

Tears rolled again down her cheeks as she felt the warmth in her stomach and the truth in Bhaskara's words.

"But... Wait a minute, this means... You were there when it all happened. You could have warned me about it before I went through the barriers. I could have been prepared."

No. I could not. My memories are only returning to me now. Before the last barrier, I knew as much as you did. I am sorry. If I could have prevented this pain, I would have.

"Right... Sorry." She coughed. "I keep thinking about the moment just before the chaos. My father is by my side, and my mother is behind me. They are both smiling, and I couldn't be happier." She sniffled. "I want to go back and savour that moment one more time. But I also see my parents just before the light outburst." She walked to the window left of her bed. Her reflection in the dark mirror looked back at her.

"One second, they were drenched in fear. The next, relief washed over them. They were calm and content when they left because of you." Her left hand went to her stomach, right where she felt the warmth from Bhaskara.

"They died in peace, not terror, because you came to my aid. They died happy, not worried because they realised with their last breath that I was going to survive, even if they weren't. They realised a spirit had come to my rescue. So no, I don't blame you for what happened. On the contrary, I thank you because you allowed my parents to die peacefully. And you saved me. You gave me a second chance in life."

She stared at her reflection for a while. "And I don't blame myself either. I was a kid and didn't know what binding to you meant. I was scared and felt safe with you, so I went to you. But none of it takes away from the fact that I'm sad about what happened. They died that day. Too many people did. I would do anything to go back and save them."

I know. I would too.

She curled into the sheet, and Bhaskara told her what she remembered from the three years she spent observing Lane and her family from the spiritual realm. She talked about Lane's mother, Anivia, who was bonded with one of the most powerful water spirits the Capital had ever encountered. No other healer surpassed her. Arduous injuries were nothing for Anivia. She would close them without a trace of the initial damage.

She could reverse time on wounds. Only the strongest healers can do it. It is their version of our warmth to destroy demons. Every time a spirit evolves, they gain new knowledge about themselves and learn new techniques. If I had not evolved with my previous host, you would not have been able to kill the demon inside Kage the other day.

After talking about Anivia, Bhaskara told her about her father, Keegan. He could control fire and was as powerful as her mother. His version of Lane's warmth was that Keegan could make people warm up to him with his ability and manipulate them into doing what he wanted. Handy, but morally incorrect, so he used it sparingly.

Bhaskara also told her how Anivia and Keegan had been soulmates as spirits and guardians.

Spirits in the spiritual realm searching for a host could see which guardians had already been taken. While Bhaskara waited for Lane to grow older and stronger, she saw how her parents' spirits danced and sang when they came in contact. Every time her parents touched, their spirits did too. Just like Bhaskara and Kage's spirit had done when he showed Lane his power.

"That never happened again."

Due to the barrier, I was not entirely present. That one occasion required everything I had. Now, I am confident I could effortlessly sense her presence.

The warm feeling in her stomach intensified, and she smiled. Bhaskara's anticipation was contagious. Lane wished she could feel her soulmate again now that she was free from all boundaries.

CHAPTER 26

Lane dreamed about her parents. This time, outside the park and without demons. A dream where they met by the lake near the Keep. They emerged from the lake completely dry, hand in hand, to a picnic that Lane had been preparing with food from the canteen.

Seeing they were slightly translucent, she hesitated. They didn't. With open arms, they approached her and embraced her, feeling surprisingly solid and warm. Overjoyed, Lane wrapped her arms around them and held them tight. With anyone else, she would have felt awkward hugging for so long. But this was right and long overdue.

She told them what had happened in the past fifteen years. No memory was left untold. She shared her perspective so they knew she was happy and safe. It didn't matter that it wasn't real and that her parents said little in return. Talking with them lifted a weight from her shoulders she hadn't realised she was carrying. Sharing what she went through, as well as her thoughts, feelings and frustrations without a filter, was freeing.

Although she couldn't tell by looking around her, they sat for hours. The sun remained in the same position the whole dream. No matter how much they ate, the amount of food never changed. The birds chirping and flying from tree to tree repeated a pattern every so often. Still, the dream was wonderful. The following day, she woke up rested and happier than she'd felt in years. She woke up light and free.

Lying in bed, her hand on her stomach, she contemplated the sunrise. Only when a door opened and closed in the corridor was her mind pulled back into reality. Her thoughts shifted towards Kage. She longed to talk with him, to tell him about her parents and her dream, and ask him how he was. But she also wanted to give him time. She didn't want to push too fast and make the crack between them bigger.

ঌ•●•঳

When her stomach growled, Lane stood up. Now, besides food, there was only one other thing on her mind: experimenting with her fully awakened ability. She could feel it singing through her body, begging her to use it.

From the corner of her eye, she caught a glimpse of gold in her mirror. She could barely believe her eyes. People would now probably guess she was sixteen or seventeen instead of somewhere in her mid-twenties, like they did before she arrived at the Keep. She hadn't looked this young in ages. To make things weirder, her eyes and hair had turned golden, glowing as if showcasing the light inside her.

I like it.

With a stomach full of bread, cheese, and jam, she sprinted out of the Keep after apologising for being rude to everyone who had come to check on her. Her mind raced on what she should try first.

Working on my defence is a priority, I guess.

Within fifteen minutes, she stood at the centre of the clearing, ready to create an armour of light so hot anything attempting to pass through would melt and burn. She wanted to visualise it in her mind, but before the image formed, light had already gathered.

"Yes!" she screamed and punched the air with excitement.

I told you it would be easier once the last barrier was broken, did I not?

We were made for each other. We are an extension of each other, so light responds to you as it would to me, Bhaskara told her. *The fact that you are coordinated also helps. I have had some utterly helpless hosts.* Bhaskara laughed. It was the first time Lane heard her do it or, better said, felt it. Her stomach warmed up more than usual, spreading to the rest of her body.

Lane enjoyed having Bhaskara to talk to, especially with Diana gone, Kage not talking to her and Luke away on his mission to gather information. Bhaskara understood her and didn't judge her, but was at the same time straightforward and didn't hide her thoughts from Lane. It was a welcome change.

When the warmth faded, she remembered Luke's air daggers and tried to do the same with her light. Again, even before finishing her thought, light daggers appeared before her. With a flick of a hand, they flew towards a tree, incinerating it at contact.

"Note to self: be careful. You don't want to burn down the forest."

As the afternoon progressed, she tried everything she could think of. She practised with the light daggers for hours, making them change direction with nothing but her thoughts.

She created the cutting blades Kage had used on her. The faster she swung her arms, the quicker the blades cut through the air and the farther they travelled. By squeezing her fists, she could change the thickness of the slicing objects. With an unclenched palm, the blades were so thin they were invisible to the naked eye.

She squealed with excitement.

Maintaining the body armour required a lot of energy, so she experimented with a more cost-effective defence in case she ever found herself running low. In the blink of an eye, the armour transformed into a shield that could stretch and shrink, even wrap around her to cover her back, depending on the type of protection required.

Whatever she envisioned materialised effortlessly and without a doubt. The bond between her mind and the light was extraordinary. It all appeared in the blink of an eye, without delays, making it no surprise when ninety shimmering versions of the Karazak and Gulgath that had brought her to this new life of hers surrounded her.

When Bhaskara suggested she could control the light puppets so Lane wouldn't know when and how they'd attack, Lane smiled. It would make it more interesting. And a much better training.

Bhaskara knew her all too well.

In less than five minutes, every light puppet was gone. "Again. Harder this time. Don't go easy on me." Another five minutes, and she was once more alone. "Again."

They repeated the process seven more times, and Lane felt no signs of needing to stop. A light version of the demon around her mother's neck appeared. She fought it with all she had, killing it countless times.

Only when her stomach growled and the night fell did she decide to stop and return to the Keep. If she'd brought food, she could've stayed longer.

I need to pace myself. She had to stay fresh and rested in case Diana decided to return. A headache threatened to flare up, a silent warning that she was closer to her limits than she had expected.

CHAPTER 27

Not overdoing it didn't mean Lane couldn't wake up with the sun, fill herself up with pancakes and run to the clearing. Excited about how the day would develop, she grabbed her jacket and left her room.

"What the hell?" Kage growled.

She hadn't noticed Kage leave his room, causing them to crash. "Sorry. I didn't...see you. Ho-How are you?"

"Fine," he said, cold and distant, before going his way.

"Kage..."

"I can't, Lane. Not yet. I still need to think." He didn't even turn to face her, so she let him go, feeling the crack between them widen.

It was understandable for him to be mad, to blame her for everything even. However, if that was the case, he could tell her that much and be done with it. Why drag it on? How much more time did he need? He'd known for years how his father died. He'd had years to grieve. The only difference was the person who had caused it. How hard was it to get over it?

She waited by her door long after he reached the illuminated hall halfway down the corridor. Not wanting to repeat what had just happened any time soon, she filled a backpack with a blanket, a thin mattress, and a tarp from the gear closet in the training area. Sleeping outside was nothing new. She'd done it plenty of times at the orphanage. At least inside Shuutin, she wouldn't have to worry about waking up with the teeth of a Karazak buried deep in her arm.

At the canteen, she packed food that could last a few days without going bad. She grabbed two muffins, three protein bars, a couple of apples and as much bread, cheese and jam as she could fit in the already overflowing backpack.

Sleeping and practising at the clearing would prevent her from crossing paths with Kage until he was ready to talk. He could choose not to come close, but if he did, they could speak more freely away from prying ears.

❧•●•❧

Three nights had passed, and Kage still hadn't come looking for Lane. Giving him space was becoming increasingly difficult. How much more time did he need? Sure, she had needed time too. But in her case, the information had been overwhelming and new. He'd known most of it all along. She'd broken the last barrier eight days ago. Eight. What was he waiting for?

With her last ration gone, she decided to return in the evening. She would give him a last chance to come on his own accord during the day. After, she would search every corner for him to tell him she couldn't wait any longer. She had to know if they were okay. She needed an answer, even if it wasn't what she longed to hear.

Being pushed away because of what she couldn't control brought her straight back to Stanlow. The disgusted faces of the villagers haunted her mind, mocking her at a distance for being who she was. She didn't want Kage to join the pack.

He'd told her once he would never leave her side again. Where had that promise stayed?

Kage struggled for days, not knowing what to do. Learning that his father died because of the girl he was falling for didn't change much of what he already knew. His father had died in the explosion. That much was still true, and still, the truth was now much harder to swallow.

He tried to distract himself with paperwork. It didn't work. Logic told him she wasn't to blame. She had been three at the time. Yet, it gnawed at him, holding him back from going to her. His heart ached from the loss of his father as if he were six again. The pain raw and fresh.

"How did she do it?" he whispered, walking through the streets of Caragain. He'd been six when he bonded with his spirit, and it had been painful. The spirit had almost torn his body apart. He still remembered the feeling vividly. Her surviving it at three...

"How much stronger is she?"

He had been too weak to save his dad, too weak to save Maya, too weak to save Diana and fight for Lane. Was this his curse? Was this the path meant for him? Seeing everyone he loved die because he could never become strong enough in time to defeat his next challenge? That couldn't be right. He wouldn't have it be right. That was not the future he wanted or envisioned. He wouldn't allow himself to be helpless again.

He wouldn't tremble, like when she broke the last barrier.

It was truly pathetic. The moment it went down, he sensed through his shadows just how immense her power was. A wave of energy surged over him, leaving his core cold. He had never been so afraid in his life. His shadows had flinched, and he nearly fell to his knees.

At that moment, he realised he'd been wrong about his assessment of her strength.

The main reason he'd shown her his power was for her to trust him. But also, for him to assess how powerful *she* was. His heart had skipped a beat when he felt what was inside her, immediately relieved by the barriers' presence. He had assumed the walls were stopping her from connecting to the energy pool he sensed inside her. But he had been wrong.

The reservoir he'd sensed was but a fraction of the whole. The barrier hadn't been making it harder for her to use it, but keeping whatever else was beyond it out of her reach.

When she told him about the explosion, he took the opportunity to distance himself to think of how to surpass her in strength. He had to. To protect her and those around them, he had to.

No one could ever learn to control that much energy in such a short time. She would have another outburst sooner or later, and he'd be by her side to stop her. He couldn't fail when the time came. Too much was riding on his success.

Kage. She has not had any outbursts since she broke the second barrier. She is in control.

It was true, she hadn't, but it could still happen. He couldn't take any chances. She had full access to her spirit. If, after binding, she had engulfed an area with a five-hundred-meter radius, what would happen now? Nothing else stopped her from reaching her spirit. It would be devastating.

You are being unreasonable. Paranoid even. You have to talk to her. Work it out together.

"No. I have to fight her. Assess how much stronger she has become, with and without her ability. I need to see how she manages a fight, see if she has her ability under control and if I can take her down if needed."

Kage...

"Don't bother. I'm going to fix this. I'm going to fix everything."

⟡ • ● • ⟡

The list of things Lane wanted to try was endless. Flying like Luke was probably impossible, so she'd settle for the second-best option: levitation.

Making light people, like the light demon puppets, but more agile and stronger, would be great protection against multiple opponents. And camouflaging someone by manipulating the light around them would be extremely cool.

"Or make them invisible. Or, or... Pretend they are someone else!" She got excited. Unfortunately, no one was there to train with, so she limited herself to practising levitation and making human-sized light puppets. Two things that came effortlessly.

After mastering both, she brought light daggers into the mix and fought Bhaskara's puppets again. This time, the sky was the limit. The creatures came in groups or alone, slow or fast. Bhaskara changed the pattern with every attack to make predictions impossible.

Lane would have panicked or gotten tired too fast a moon cycle ago. Now, fighting was as easy as walking, even without her ability in the mixture.

When the sun passed its highest point, she stopped to enjoy the touch of the late afternoon light on her skin. Nothing was as relaxing or satisfying.

Duck, Bhaskara screamed.

She moved without registering what was happening, just in time to see two daggers dig into the tree before her. The light armour covered her as she turned towards where the daggers had come from.

"Nice reflexes."

She recognised the voice before seeing him but remained in a fighting position. "Care to put them to the test?" she challenged.

Kage came from the shadows and smiled. "Only if we don't use our abilities. I want to see what you can do without them first."

She smiled, the armour disappearing. A shiver ran down her body as the evening air took over the area her warm light had just been.

Without warning, he attacked. And he attacked fast. Weren't it for the

266

Sight and her newly enhanced abilities, he would have landed one of his punches.

She jumped back to dodge his attack and create space between them. "I wasn't expecting you to come at me like that. Is everything all right? Don't you think we should talk first?"

But Kage wasn't listening. He was coming at her with his next attack. And the next. And the next.

Trying to understand what was happening while dodging him was difficult. Was this his way of talking things over? Maybe this was enough for other people, or perhaps it was the guardian's way of dealing with things, but it wasn't hers. She longed for days to know how he was feeling and what he was thinking. A fistfight wasn't going to cut it. She wanted answers.

After evading his attack, her body was again glowing. She'd promised him a fight without abilities, but this wasn't what she had expected from his request.

"Giving up already? I wasn't even warmed up."

"What is wrong with you?" she asked between breaths. "I don't want to fight and pretend all is fine. I want to talk."

"Why? There's nothing that can't be solved with a good fight." But he didn't charge at her. He was hesitant to keep going, his eyes filled with disgust.

What kind of answer was that? It made no sense. There was plenty that a fight couldn't solve. Sometimes, fists couldn't solve your problems.

Focus.

It was the only thing she could do. Focus. But her mind was stuck. Her eyes were glued on the disgust with which he looked at her. He had told her he didn't blame her for what had happened, but his demeanour said otherwise.

"Why are you looking at me like that?"

"Your ability," he spat. The aversion in his voice was palpable. "How much have you taken from me already? Do you want more? Is that it? I should have let the Gulgath and Karazak have you. I'd still have my sister if I had. We were fine without you."

Lane was lost. What was he talking about? How could he blame her for that? Had the days she left him alone with his thoughts only made him think everything was her fault? He couldn't be serious. She had nothing to do with Diana's behaviour, just like she had not been at fault for what happened to his father.

He knows that, right? "Have you had enough time to think about the other day?"

"I don't need more time. I know it was your fault."

Those words hurt like a dagger to the stomach. Why was he saying that? He couldn't mean it, could he?

Focus, Bhaskara resonated in her head.

Right. Thank you.

Kage didn't move, not until the light dissipated. When it did, his movements were fast and erratic. His anger made him sloppy and careless. She dodged six more blows before bringing the light layer up again.

"Seriously? You're such a coward. Fight me properly. You owe me that much!" His last words came out screaming. She'd never seen him this pissed off, never heard him scream before.

How often do I have to remind you? Keep your focus, Bhaskara said.

Often, apparently. His anger and malice kept pulling at her attention, making her doubt what she knew to be true.

Let's do this.

With the sun down, her energy would recover at a slower pace. She couldn't waste it on stupid games.

A ray of light shot into the sky. Bright and thick. Hopefully, someone at the Keep would see it in time and think to come check on her.

Kage looked up instinctively, following the trajectory of the beam. When his gaze dropped back down, she was gone.

CHAPTER 28

Druzon stared at the red lake, contemplating how his experiments were going. He was halfway through his second and already seeing promising results. Unfortunately, the downfall of going to the most southern village was the lack of traffic coming its way. He had chosen it for his seclusion but had expected more humans to come. Implementing the recorded improvements in the new batch would have to wait until he left Redwater in search of more incubators, which was dangerous.

Planning an expansion of his territory had to be done carefully. He couldn't bring the guardians' attention to Redwater. Not yet, at least. His army of demons needed to be bigger and stronger first, and he had to find a way to control the Dregma and Ezraan completely. Their independence and thinking ability made them more prone to seeing loopholes in Druzon's orders. To win the war, Druzon couldn't have demons doing as they pleased. They had to follow his orders to the letter. Not creating Dregma or Ezraan wasn't a possibility he was willing to entertain.

Less than ten kilometres out of Redwater, a pungent smell interrupted Druzon's thoughts. He would recognise it anywhere. Preparing for the unwelcome visitors, he ordered all demons to hide near the village entrance and wait for his command to attack. The closer they got, the better Druzon could smell the slight differences from each spirit engraved in the guardians riding towards Redwater.

Fifteen of them came his way, and he wanted to know why. No human had left Redwater since he arrived, and no one who came had left again either. So why were guardians here?

They couldn't possibly know of his whereabouts. They wouldn't come with such a small number if they did. Fifteen guardians wouldn't be nearly enough to lay a single scratch on him. He could quickly kill them all. So why were they here?

Druzon stood in the middle of the village's main square and waited for them to arrive. He didn't want them to know who he was immediately, so he changed to his human form. The fifteen rode into Redwater. The one at the front of the fleet, clearly in charge, said, "People of Redwater, we came from the mountains. We call ourselves the Tirich's Children and come in peace. We heard rumours of a great appearance in your village and had to see with our own eyes if it was true. Please, show yourself. We mean no harm."

"What was it you heard about a great appearance?" Druzon asked, trying to sound as human and vulnerable as possible.

"We heard about a summoning. We hope that of a Greater Demon. One who will elevate this world to a new height. One who will lead us to greatness."

"Where did you hear such things?"

"Some of us felt the world change a while back. We knew what it meant, so we searched high and low for the right location. One of our scouts mentioned that the nearby villages hadn't seen any Redwater merchants for over a moon cycle, and anyone who ventured this way never returned. We assumed the ritual took place here. We came to see if we were right."

Druzon's lips turned into a bowl-twisting grin, and the guardians backed off with their horses. "What did you intend to do if you found a Greater Demon?"

It took the man a second to answer. "W-We," he coughed. "We want to plead our loyalty to him. He's a superior being, and we want to help him reach his goals."

In response, Druzon shed his human skin. The horses bucked, letting six guardians fall off their backs before storming out of the village. With a simple hand twist, the horses were stopped by a swarm of demons. Their screeching scared another eight, leaving only the leader on his.

After a minute, the sounds of the dying horses faded.

"Is this what you were expecting?" Druzon's low voice resonated across the square as he slowly turned, allowing them all to take a good look. "Is this what you have been looking for?" The fear in the men's sweat increased. It was so strong that even Druzon got aroused by it. "You know now what you seek is true. What will you do?"

The beautiful smell of fear was so potent that it was hard to hold all the demons in place. All fifteen men were sweating like crazy. All...

No. Not all fifteen. One of the men wasn't sweating. He wasn't afraid. Druzon could smell a hint of admiration and joy. He stepped closer, and all but the leader shrank in their place. All but the leader immediately pinned their eyes to the floor.

"Is there anything you wish to say, guardian?"

"You're even more magnificent than I imagined. I'm not dignified to be in your presence. None of us is. Being allowed to witness a Greater Demon like yourself is too big of a gift for someone as insignificant as us." Realising he was staring, the man dismounted his horse, which trotted away into the village, and bowed, directing his gaze at Druzon's feet. "We apologise for being so bold and hope you can forgive such small-minded beings as ourselves. We hoped the rumours were true but didn't think about our next step if they were. At least not a plan dignified for a being as great as yourself."

Druzon smelled nothing but the truth.

This could be entertaining.

Having guardians as hosts could be an interesting experiment. He'd evolved Azrunol into Dregma in humans in about one-and-a-half moon cycles. The conditions were extreme and highly favourable, but most humans fought against the demons for as long as their feeble minds could. Having hosts willing to let the demon grow could significantly reduce the incubation time.

Druzon wouldn't waste the gift that came riding to his doorstep.

"It is indeed bold of you to dare come here without a plan and talk to me like I'm the same as you. You insult me." Druzon snarled, and the men stiffened. "You see what underestimating me leads to." He said as he gestured to the bloodied streets and caged humans.

The guardians, who hadn't bothered to scan the area at arrival and afterwards had been too scared to think about doing so, now glanced past Druzon. Their eyes nearly fell out of their sockets. One vomited.

"We truly apologise," the leader said, the only one who had remained professional until now. He fell to his knees and bowed, slamming his head to the ground. The other men snapped out of their fear-induced paralysis for a second and followed his lead.

Druzon smiled.

"It so happens to be your lucky day. I require loyal subjects and, therefore, am willing to see past your insolence." Druzon paused, letting hope build up inside them. Giving them time to believe they had a chance of leaving alive, time for their blood to fill with hope, before saying, "That is, of course, if you are willing to accept my terms."

The little amount of hope they'd built up faded. Seven men broke down crying, the fear in their tears even more potent than in their sweat. The demons let out bone-chilling sounds. A mixture of laughing and screaming, so high-pitched, it felt like your ears were about to burst. So horrifying, you almost preferred your ears *would* burst.

"Enough," Druzon roared, and the demons stopped, but the crying didn't. "My terms are quite simple. You can leave the village unarmed if each of you hosts one of my demons. They will reside in you, and you will let them grow without restrictions. You will barely notice them and can go about your daily life as if nothing has happened. Once the demons have evolved, they will leave your body, and your insolence will be forgiven. Afterwards, you can do as you please for the remainder of your life." The crying guardians now sobbed as they realised not everything was lost yet.

"If you not only allow the demons to grow but encourage them, I will grant you a place in my court," Druzon continued. "You will not be harmed in the war to come. You will be protected from demons and guardians alike and live in peace for as long as your life extends."

Hope's sweet, nauseating scent was now nearly more overpowering than fear. They would have to leave the village with just enough hope to collaborate and not betray Druzon. The fear etched in their minds would ensure they didn't.

"I will know if you suppress my demons, as I will know if you encourage them. I am connected with them. They will inform me of your doings. If you betray my trust, your insolence will not be forgiven, and I will order the demon inside of you to devour you from the inside out." Most men stopped breathing. "Those are my terms. If you accept, rise."

The leader was on his feet in a heartbeat. Four others followed him, though much slower, as if pondering whether rising was the wisest decision.

Five men in total. It wasn't enough. Druzon needed more. He'd have to sacrifice one of the other ten, make an example of him to get more to stand.

He paced forward, and two more rose. When facing the man who had puked, still bowing on the floor, Druzon said, "Rise."

The guardian didn't. Not a muscle twitched trying to do so. That was enough of a signal for Druzon to act. He grabbed the man and bit off his head, tossing the headless body to his demons, who devoured him in seconds. It happened so fast, the other men watching only realised what Druzon had done when he spat the head to the ground.

A powerful wave of fear hit Druzon's nose as three more men rose. Their bodies shook so badly that their knees buckled a few times, but eventually, they stood. From the men still kneeling, two had vomited, another had fainted, and the last one had run away.

Fool. To think he could turn his back on Druzon. With a snap of a finger, demons attacked, and the man was devoured.

Druzon paced towards the one who had fainted, and another man stood. If the other didn't do the same by the time Druzon was finished with the unconscious man, eleven would do. He couldn't have them think he was too tolerant.

The man woke up as the Greater Demon clawed his hand around the man's neck and tossed him to his demons.

Not a single cry for help left his lips. He was devoured before realisation sank in.

When silence fell, the last man hadn't risen yet. In a heartbeat, Druzon was by his side. In another, the man was flying, demons jumping and screeching for another treat.

The fear instilled in the men standing pulsed rapidly through their veins. Fear so deeply rooted, they would not dare defy Druzon. They would do anything he said, even after leaving Redwater behind.

He returned to his spot and asked them to form a line. Their leader raced to comply with Druzon's demands. "I see you are eager to fulfil your duty," Druzon noted.

"I'm honoured to be given a chance to help such a being in his plans. I'm here to serve you, to be your vessel. Do with me as you please."

Druzon smiled. "I want to handle you last." The man's shoulders sagged, so he added, "Are you questioning my judgment?"

The leader tensed for the first time. "Never."

"Master," Druzon added.

"Never, Master."

"Good, as you should." Druzon stared at the man as he marched to the end of the line. He smelled the first drops of fear pouring into the man's blood and couldn't be happier with how it was developing.

Druzon inserted an Azrunol in each guardian. When the leader's time came, Druzon inserted a Dregma in him and told him he expected great things from him. He explained he had entrusted the man with a stronger demon to control those around him. His commands would never overpower Druzon's, but the Greater Demon expected the leader to keep the other guardians in line. The man fell to the ground and kissed Druzon's feet, thanking him for being entrusted with such a task.

Before the guardians were let go, Druzon told them they could send like-minded guardians to Redwater. The same conditions would apply, but they were warned that if the wrong kind came knocking, the demons inside them would get orders to terminate the agreement. It would prevent them from preaching about Redwater in every city and village. They would need to be careful with whom they trusted and had to maintain a low profile.

When the guardians left on foot, Druzon returned to his chamber grinning. The day couldn't have developed more perfectly. He'd gained eleven new experimental subjects who would incentivise his demons to evolve. They'd been infused with the fear of what would happen if they defied him but left with enough hope of surviving in the long run that Druzon knew no other experiments would surpass the results these eleven men would generate.

He was amused at how easily he could manipulate guardians and how they so easily believed Druzon would take a second to consider saving them. He played his cards well today and could only expect more fanatics to come to Redwater to become incubators.

CHAPTER 29

The light beam surprised Kage long enough for Lane to find an opening in his defence. She sprinted to the left and jumped, hoping to get him from a blind spot. Somehow, without looking, he dodged her attack. When her feet hit the ground, she tried again and again. Every time, he dodged them blind, not bothering to turn around.

"You're not the only one with the Sight, remember? If you're not faster, you won't come close to touching me."

Light came to her. The only source in the clearing was now her and the stars. Her energy wouldn't be recharged as fast. She had to think wisely about her moves.

She studied his face. "Why are you dodging? You haven't touched me a single time. Why not use your shadows to counteract my light? You should be stronger now."

"And have our abilities touch? I would rather get hit, thank you." The look of disgust was back.

"I think there's another reason for it. Want to take a guess?" He didn't respond. "I think you're afraid. Afraid I've become stronger than you. It's better to pretend you hate me and my ability instead of facing it, isn't it?"

"Do you actually believe I'm afraid of someone who has been a guardian for a season? Don't make me laugh. You might have an ability, but that isn't enough. You must be worthy of it, and you're all but that," Kage snarled. "You're weak. So much so that you almost died. You're pathetic, thinking you can make this place your home. But you don't belong here like you didn't belong in the orphanage. No one wants you. I helped you because I was duty-bound. I couldn't have you blow up on me. Don't flatter yourself. The last thing I am afraid of is you." Her light flickered, and he laughed. "See? Even your spirit agrees with me."

Do not listen to him. You know what he is saying is not true. He is trying to hurt you to get you to fight. Do not fall for it. Focus.

I know. The light thickened around her body.

"You're right. I'm still learning, but I don't need to be the best. I've kicked a guardian's ass before, remember? Even with a fraction of my ability... Even against a guardian who trained for longer... Even with a demon inside her, making her stronger, I still beat her. The demon's salvation was that she ran away in the end," she said, standing tall.

"You seriously think that's how the fight went?" The voice came from the trees to the right. She knew it had to be Diana, but her voice was no longer hers. It was distorted, twisted, and filled with hate.

"I wondered when you'd show up. I assumed going after the demon's ego would do the trick."

Diana snarled. She was so pale and thin that a shiver ran down Lane's spine. It broke her heart to see Diana like that. She couldn't imagine what she'd been through.

Diana stopped at the edge of the clearing, raised her hand, and Kage joined her.

"Kage, what are you doing?"

"I'm choosing my sister over you. I should have done it when she almost killed you in the training area, but I crossed paths with her in the woods on my way here and thought this was as good a time as any. We talked, and I think she's right. You're the problem. We were happy before you came. We can be again if you're no longer here. The demon will leave her alone after his job is done. It's a win-win situation."

Every word Kage had thrown at her until was had been hard to swallow, but this... To side with a demon? Did he believe this was the best way to get Diana back? To sacrifice her for his sister? He couldn't possibly be blind to what the demon had done to Diana's body. She was a walking skeleton. He couldn't trust a demon's word. Not after all they went through. Not after learning Lane could save Diana with her ability.

There was no reason to sacrifice anyone. The three of them could come out of this alive. This newfound aversion to her and her ability because of his father shouldn't make him this irrational. He should understand she was the right person to side with. She was the best chance of getting Diana back safely.

You are spiralling again. Focus. You know better than to listen to what they are saying.

Right. Thank you again. I don't know why I keep falling for it.

This fight would have gone differently without Bhaskara. She would have to thank her profusely once this was done.

I will be waiting, and I will thoroughly enjoy it. Now focus. Another one is coming.

A demon jerked to Diana's other side. His pitch-black body twitched with every step as if still learning where its centre of gravity was. An Azrunol, just like Mister Kohler's book described it. Chills ran down Lane's neck.

Diana laughed, sending a second wave down the length of Lane's spine.

Lane couldn't hide her shock. "How... How can a demon be inside the barrier?"

"You underestimate me. Demons can't pass the barrier unless they are inside a guardian. Or, they can be summoned, just like I did with this one. It's a bit harder than outside the barrier, but nothing an Ezraan like myself can't accomplish." Lane's eyes widened. "What? Not what you were expecting? Don't worry. I'll give you a hint on how to win. You either kill both Diana and Kage, or you die. It's that simple. He's on my side now."

"Kage..." Lane turned to him, sorrow filling her eyes.

He laughed. "Is it so hard to believe I choose my own blood over you? Seeing how hard it was for you to get rid of an Azrunol doesn't evoke much confidence in your skills. You are weak, so I'm taking my chances with the path with the highest probability of getting my sister back."

"That's not you talking. Fight whatever is inside you. We can work together so no one has to die. We'll save Diana, I promise."

"Together? Don't be ridiculous. What are you going to do? Hug her and warm her up?" She laughed. "Do you think you'll get *that* close? Please... Be realistic. You have two options. You either kill the three of us, or you die. There's no third option," Diana said, cracking her neck. "I'm done with all the talking, so I hope you've decided because your time is up."

What was Lane supposed to do? She didn't want to hurt them, nor could she bring herself to kill anyone else ever again. What happened when she was three was enough killing for a lifetime. She couldn't do it, even if it meant she would...

Do not say that. Think of all the people who will suffer if you die. You have to fight.

How? It's three against one.

Stall them.

That was it. Time. She needed to wreck this until help arrived. Her three opponents would never make it easier for her, but she had to try.

The three bolted. Diana came straight at her, Kage from her left and the demon, surprisingly fast for what had just been struggling to take a simple step, from her right. All three came intending to kill.

She jumped.

Kage's attack hit the demon, slicing its skin open and sending it screeching. Diana halted just before colliding with the others.

Lane stood on a light platform, preventing her from falling back into her three opponents. Kage and the demon scanned the area around them, but Diana's gaze shot up. Without hesitation, she launched herself at Lane.

Lane jumped again to a platform higher in the air and out of their reach. Diana growled, but as soon as her feet hit the ground empty-handed, she grabbed the Azrunol and tossed it at her. Unprepared for such an attack, Lane stepped back, forgetting that nothing was behind her to ground her.

With a thud, she slammed into the floor, the air knocked out of her lungs. Before she could recover, Diana was on top of her. Sitting firmly on Lane's stomach, ordering Kage to pin Lane's arms to the ground and the demon to take care of the legs.

"I told my Master I would kill you, but I didn't tell him how slow. I'll enjoy every bit of this, especially since I won't be savouring your pain alone. No... I'll be savouring Diana's pain as well. I'll make her watch it. I'll make her be the one hurting you... Killing you..." Diana said, laughing hysterically.

"Finish. Druzon not happy if fail." Diana's laugh stopped at the Azrunol's remark.

"If you dare speak his name again, I'll cut you to pieces," Diana hissed at the demon before turning back to Lane. "Where would you like me to start? With your pretty face, or should I leave it for last?" Diana asked, tracing her nail along the line of the scar on Lane's left shoulder, reopening the old wound.

Lane screamed and squirmed, desperately trying to free her hands and legs, but Kage and the demon held firm.

"If I recall correctly, you're missing a few scars. Perhaps I should bring those back first. To honour how all this began, you know?"

Lane continued to struggle, causing Kage and the demon to hold tighter. Shots of pain radiated from her wrists and ankles. She attempted to summon her light, but her ability failed to answer her plea.

"Do you remember which ability your friend has?" Diana asked, squeezing Lane's jaw with her freezing hands. "Stop! You're not going anywhere, so save the energy." Lane did, and Diana loosened her grip. "As I was saying, I can use Diana's ability. And I can use it much better than she does. That's why your ability isn't working. I told you already. A fake guardian like you would never be a match for m—"

A branch snapped.

"Hurry, Gadmerad. Someone is coming," Kage said.

Annoyed for having his time with Lane cut short, Gadmerad grabbed the dagger on his belt. It looked old and rusty, making Lane shrink at the sight. He lifted the dagger above his head, leaning back to create momentum.

Fight, Bhaskara screamed, pulling Lane out of her frozen state.

Help wouldn't arrive in time. She had to do it herself. With newfound energy, she pulled her hands, but Kage's grip was still too firm around her wrists.

"It's futile. Say your last goodbyes, Light Wielder," Gadmerad said.

Still squirming, she squeezed her eyes shut to avoid knowing when the dagger would hit.

"Stop!" Kage screamed.

Even with her eyes closed, Lane saw a flash of light come and go.

Kage was too late. It had happened so quickly that she hadn't even felt the pain.

Open your eyes.

It took Lane a while to realise the voice belonged to Bhaskara.

Diana was still sitting atop her, holding the dagger millimetres away from her chest. From the clenched fists and bare teeth, it was clear it wasn't because she'd changed her mind. She was still trying to jab the rusty dagger into Lane's heart, but for some reason, couldn't move past this point.

Lane tried freeing herself, but the demon and Kage still held her in place. For a second, she forgot what she already knew. The wind blew a reminder in her direction, making her look to the right, to the edge of the clearing. "Yes! You came," she screamed.

"How?" Diana muttered between her teeth, struggling to speak. The same word popped into Lane's mind. How was she still alive? How were Diana and her demons frozen in place?

Demons... Not one, but two. Lane knew from the beginning that the Kage holding her arms wasn't the real one. The lack of warmth emanating from him was an easy giveaway. However, if it hadn't been for Bhaskara repeatedly telling her to focus, she would've still believed the demon's lies. She would've forgotten he wasn't Kage and would've crumbled from the weight of his words.

The act was *that* convincing. His face, his voice, his movements. It was all his mirrored image, except for the lack of warmth, the one thing demons couldn't replicate.

"Lane, are you okay?" the Kage at the edge of the clearing asked. "I saw your light beam and came as fast as I could."

"I can't use my ability with Diana on top of me."

"Let Lane go. Take a step away from her." Kage said, and like a puppet, Diana obeyed. The demons did too.

Lane was on her feet with her light armour around her skin and at a good distance from everyone in a heartbeat. "How?"

"I-I don't know. This white flash blinded me when I arrived, and afterwards, I sensed this connection with the three demons. I think I can..."

Kage trailed off, staring at his hands. "Lane... I'm the real Kage. I know this sounds weird, but... I think... I think I can control them." Kage said, slowly walking towards her with an extended hand. "Come to me. Please. I can protect you." His voice was soft, half broken. She had never heard that tone from him, and it broke her. She wanted to run into his arms and thank him for coming, but she couldn't until she understood what was happening.

She backed up a step, and he stopped. His hand dropped to his side, shoulders sagging. He considered his options briefly before straightening again and ordering, "You, pretending to be me. Reveal your true identity."

The Kage beside Diana shook and twisted, the skin detaching from the body and revealing a layer of black skin underneath. Two demons in their natural form now stood by Diana, one on all fours and a new one standing on his feet where the fake Kage had just been.

"Are you a Dregma?" Kage asked.

"Ye-yes," the demon answered, clearly struggling against the invisible force making it talk.

Kage turned to Lane, hopeful this was enough proof for her to come to him. Or to let him approach her. But it wasn't. She wouldn't allow him closer. Not yet. Not until she was sure he was on her side. She looked down.

"Okay, I get it. I won't step closer. Just save Diana. I'll hold them in place. You can check me after, I promise. I'm not possessed. You'll see I'm the real Kage."

He was right. There was a lot at stake. Diana needed to be saved, and those demons destroyed. Before the last barrier, she had healed Althea from a short distance. Now, with full access to her ability, it would be easy to do it from where she stood. She could probably even check Kage simultaneously.

Right?

Yes, but I do not know if it is wise. If he is the real Kage holding the demons in place, maybe our light will interfere with it. Our chance of saving Diana could be lost. Look at her. She will not survive much longer with the demon inside her.

Kage was producing warmth. She could feel it. It didn't tell her if he was on her side, but at least he wasn't a demon. It was easy to see after comparing him with the two creatures next to Diana. The two didn't have a single drop of warmth in their bodies.

Her muscles relaxed, sensing warmth emanating from Diana's body. The amount was alarmingly low, but it was present. When she first used her warmth to heal others, she believed she was the only one who could generate it. Bhaskara taught her that every living thing emanated warmth. Birds, worms, grass, guardians... As long as it lived, it had warmth, so it was interesting to see how demons not only didn't make it but also repelled it.

When Diana and Lane fought a moon cycle ago, Lane hadn't realised her friend was possessed. Her ability wasn't as developed as now, and she couldn't sense the warmth in and around others. However, she couldn't recall Diana feeling cold, which could mean one of three things. The decrease in a host's warmth production was equivalent to the demon's strength or how long they had been possessed. Or a combination of both. Figuring it out would help Lane better assess future encounters with possessed individuals.

Now, one question remained. Was Kage telling the truth? At least partially, he was. He wasn't a demon pretending to be a human. He couldn't be as far gone as Diana either, but the possibility of him being freshly possessed remained. It would explain his powers. The demon inside him could have connected with the others to get her to trust him by pretending to help her. But who would do that? Stopping a demon from killing her just to kill her later himself. It didn't seem like the greatest course of action.

Kage is controlling the demons. It is possible. I will explain later. Now, focus!

Bhaskara was right. The priority was to save Diana.

With only a thought, three balls of warmth the size of a grown man formed before her without hesitation. She didn't want to admit it, but even in a situation like that, she was excited to see how quickly her ability responded to her requests.

The demons, feeling the warmth building up, fought against the invisible hands holding them in place.

"Hurry up, I can't hold them much longer."

She tilted her face upwards, and the three balls dashed towards the demons. Each meeting its target. The two demons without a human suit to protect them dissolved into oblivion as soon as the warmth engulfed them. The one inside Diana didn't. She jerked violently as the demon attempted to free himself from the invisible hands and the host, who was now his cage instead of his ticket to freedom.

Lane guided the remaining warmth from the other two balls to enter Diana's skin and seek the demon within. As it did, Diana screamed in agony.

I know, I'm sorry. It's going to be done soon.

And it did. Silence filled the clearing. Without a demon holding Diana in place, she fell. A pair of hands made of shadow rushed to her and safely guided her to the ground.

Kage was the first to reach Diana. Dropping to his knees, his hand went straight to her neck.

"Nothing…" His body slumped.

Lane fell to her knees beside him, exhausted and speechless. He wouldn't lie, but she had to check it for herself. Slowly, she moved her hand towards Diana's neck, afraid of what her touch would tell her. She knew what to expect, yet her heart still sank when she didn't feel a pulse.

Staring at what was left of Diana ached. Her hair was thin and dull, her cheekbones protruded through her pale skin, and her eyes sank into her skull. What had she been through?

Lane didn't dare look up at Kage. Would he blame her for this?

Do not think like that, Bhaskara told her.

Her eyes filled with tears. Why not? She blamed herself for not helping Diana faster, not seeing sooner that her friend was suffering, and not acting during the fight. What she did today was nothing she couldn't have done without Kage. Why didn't she? Why waste time waiting for help to come and almost get killed in the process? All because she didn't think of using her ability to end the fight. All because she assumed she'd kill Diana while she damn well knew she could save her.

If Kage hadn't shown up, she would be dead, and Diana would've lived the rest of whatever little life she had left trapped in her own body. Her inaction almost doomed Diana. Her hesitation ended up doing exactly what she didn't want in the first place.

The demon had been right. She was weak. She still had plenty to learn. Training alone wouldn't cut it. She needed to surround herself with people better than her. She needed Kage, Luke, and Phoebe. She needed Diana.

But it was too late. She was gone, and Lane couldn't do anything to bring her back.

Who would break the news to her parents? How would Kage cope with this? Would he blame her for this outcome? The questions circled without an answer in sight. She didn't know what to do. She didn't want to lose Diana. Not this soon. Not like this. They had so many things to do, try, and experience together. It wasn't time yet. It couldn't be.

Diana gasped for air.

CHAPTER 30

Getting Diana to the canteen wasn't easy. She jumped and stiffened at every sound, stopping for minutes before proceeding. Only when Kage put a plate in front of her did she relax slightly. She hovered over the food while scanning the canteen, guarding it as if someone would take it from her.

Halfway through her meal, she said between mouthfuls, "I know you have questions... But... I don't remember much... I know I was possessed... But that's about it..." Diana glanced at Lane and Kage briefly before focusing again on eating. "Thank you for... Saving me... And not giving up... On me."

When the plate was empty, she filled it up with muffins and fruit to take. Kage and Lane escorted her to her room and asked if she wanted to be left alone for a while. She immediately nodded. Hesitant, they left her be, but not before telling her she could seek them out whenever needed.

With the door closed behind them, Lane asked Kage if they could talk. Her body wanted rest from the fight she'd just had. Her energy was depleted, but she couldn't wait any longer. She waited for him to sit with her on her bed, but he remained at the door, leaning against the frame, staring at her reflection on the window.

"Have you had time to think about the other day?" she broke the awkward silence. To hell with small talk. She had to know where he stood, where they stood. After talking with Bhaskara about her parents, she almost ran to him. She longed to speak with him, train with him, even laugh with him, for improbable as it was. She missed him and hoped he missed her too.

"I have. But after what just happened, I need more time. I have to be there for Diana." Their eyes locked. "And only for Diana. I don't want her to recover badly because of us."

Her heart tightened. The words the demon had screamed at the clearing resonated in her head. They were said to provoke her, but she couldn't shake them off. What if Kage thought like that too? The rest of the imitation had been spot-on. Why would his convictions be wrong?

"Do you blame me for what happened?" she blurted. *I need to know, to hear it from you.*

He sighed. "No. Like I said before, I don't. You were a child and didn't know what you were doing. If there's anyone to blame, it'd be your spirit." Lane frowned. "These past few days, I've wondered if I would've done the same to save you had I been in that situation. I haven't found an answer yet." Her heart tightened harder. "Saving one by sacrificing many? The answer should be a simple no, but I don't know if it's that simple, especially if one cannot foresee the consequences of their actions. I can imagine I would have saved you if I didn't know so many would die as a result. But did your spirit know what her actions would lead to? I wonder."

"She didn't. Of course she didn't. She knew I could have died from the binding and had an outburst, but she had never expected it to be as big as it was."

"That might be true, but every time I look at or think of your light now, I think of my father and how he could've still been alive."

If I were dead.

"I know it isn't fair because, at the same time, I'm grateful your spirit saved you. The outburst was also the main reason why the war ended. And, of course, I'm grateful for what you did tonight. It sounds contradictory, but that's how it is right now. I've got mixed feelings. I need time to think about it...and about us."

"Us?" was all she could muster without crying. She preferred to be back at the clearing, fighting demons rather than hearing this. She should have given him more time. She shouldn't have pressured him for answers.

He sighed again. "Yes. I don't know what to tell you, Lane. I need time to sort my thoughts out. I need time to see how Diana reacts to being back. I need time to understand my ability. There are things I need to do that need my attention more than you do. You pushing me to get there faster isn't helping."

He straightened his back. "I keep wondering if this is even a thing. Is the bond between our spirits perhaps the only reason we got pulled towards each other? Would we have felt something at all without them?"

Lane was speechless. The words hit like a blow to the stomach.

"I see you haven't been wondering as I have. We must give ourselves time apart until Diana has recovered and can tell us what she knows. Then we can decide on how to move forward."

The world she knew was shattered at the beginning of spring and replaced by a better one. One where she belonged and didn't have to hide who she was. One with Kage in it.

When her heart first skipped a beat for him on her first night in his office when he asked her if she trusted him, she didn't know what was inside her. When she did her best not to ask Diana about him and not to look for him wherever they went, she didn't know about her spirit.

She had been pinned to the ground a few too many times because she'd caught a glimpse of him passing by and lost focus. She hadn't heard parts of what Diana said when he was near or eating at the same time they were.

She fell for him before knowing she had a spirit in her.

It wasn't all a lie. But still, why would it matter even if their spirits had something to do with it? They couldn't get rid of them. They were part of them, part of their life. Their feelings would always influence the way Kage and she acted, thought or felt. Why would that be a problem in this specific situation?

She had to tell him what she thought of it all. She needed to make him understand he was wrong, but when she looked up, he was gone. Annoyed for being left alone after his insinuations, she stood up to go after him.

Wait. You need to understand something first.

What? she asked too aggressively.

Bhaskara ignored it. *Remember the flash of light and Kage making the demons do what he wanted? That was because his spirit evolved after seeing you were about to die. It was the only reaction she could produce to save us in time. It evolved, most likely to our level, which, for us, means we can heal people. For them, it means they can control demons.*

"Okay, sure. Seems logical. What does that have to do with this?" She stared at her reflection in the mirror, her eyes now completely golden like two little stars. Her hair, too, did not have a single trace of brown visible.

Changes are hard, and too much is changing around Kage right now. He learned the role we played in the death of his father. His sister is back physically but not mentally, and to top it all off, the only thing that has always been the same, his spirit, has changed too. He is overwhelmed. Let him figure out his thoughts first. Let him come to you when he is ready. Pushing for him to come to you now can do more damage to your relationship than good.

That wasn't what she wanted to hear. She wanted Bhaskara to tell her she was right and Kage was wrong, that what she felt for him was true for the right reasons and not because of their spirits.

I know, and it is. There have been plenty of soulmate spirits with guardians who were incompatible. I had this with my soulmate only three hosts ago. Hopefully, she will talk with him and make him understand we do not influence how you feel about someone, Bhaskara said. *But believe me, it is better to hear this from his spirit. He is confused and questioning everything he knows. He should hear this information from the source. Whatever you say to him right now will not be adequately received and will separate him further from you. You need to give him time.*

⋅⟫•●•⟪⋅

The minutes felt like hours. Sitting in her room doing nothing was tedious and nerve-racking. She had to move and talk to someone. Staying inside alone would make her go insane.

Before she knew what she wanted, she was in the training area, looking at Phoebe practising with Jack and hoping one day she could move as smoothly as the girl did. No wasted movements, every breath was deliberate and timed, and her focus was unwavering.

The payoff of her hard work. Beautiful.

"Hey guys, how are you?" she asked, approaching them. They stopped and greeted her back. "Phoebe, can I talk to you for a second when you're done?"

"You two can talk now," Jack answered between ragged breaths before Phoebe could.

With a grin, Phoebe added, "Let's take a little break. I'll see you in a bit, Jack."

Lane paced towards the back door to the forest without a word. Phoebe followed. Once outside, away from prying ears, she said, "Right... So... Kage talked about not being possessed anymore and how he didn't know why or how." She paused, searching for the right words. "Well... That's because of me. I can use my ability to search and kill demons inside others."

"What? Wait, that means... What? Since when? Why didn't you say it right away? Why didn't Kage? Why wait so long and keep everyone on edge?" Phoebe's mind raced, shooting question after question at Lane.

"I...have only learned to control it recently."

"This is so awesome. You're making history here, Lane. It's unheard of. How does it work?"

"I have the light." A glowing orb appeared in Lane's right hand. "But also this warmth." In her left hand, a colourless sphere formed, visible only through the subtle distortion it created in the air. "This warmth finds them and sends them back to their realm. I didn't want to risk hurting anyone before. But now I won't. I have full control." The two orbs flew around her in circles. "I thought it was time to help everyone."

"Yes, please! Do. I've been trying to keep everyone together, but some have locked themselves in their rooms and barely come out. We can ring the bell and help everyone in one go. Let's go to Kage."

Their eyes met, but Lane quickly looked away, unable to hold Phoebe's gaze. "Kage and I aren't on the best of terms right now. He's been avoiding me. That's why I was wondering if..."

"Say no more. I've got your back. We'll deal with the Keep and then inform the Capital of what you can do. This is life-changing."

"About that... Can you not send out word on this? At least not just yet." Phoebe frowned, her head tilting. "I need to ask Kage first, but...I want to go back home to get answers about my past before heading to the Capital."

"What are you talking about?"

With a deep breath, Lane told her everything. She explained about her past and what she'd been doing with Kage. She mentioned the explosion and immediately apologised if that had also affected her.

"That's a tough pill to swallow, isn't it? I get now why Kage is gone. You don't have to apologise to me. My family is fine, luckily. I did lose friends, but that was the demons' fault, not yours. I would, though, advise you to keep that for yourself. Not everyone will be so understanding. Some never put a face to the one who caused the explosion because they believed it was a suicidal attempt to help others. Learning you made it might trigger unwanted behaviour or open old wounds."

"I...I didn't know. I'm sorry."

"Like I said, don't apologise to me. Do that to those who actually suffered, but not with your words, but with your actions. Cleanse as many of those suckers as you can. Send them all back to hell. End them once and for all."

"I don't think I can do the 'once and for all' part, but for the rest, I'll give it my all."

"That's all one can hope for. Should I round up everyone without sounding the alarm? How much time do you need per person? I'd rather not end up with a line of anxious guardians waiting their turn."

"Not much. Five minutes, I think." Lane scratched the back of her head. "Can I...try with you first, just to be sure?"

"Of course. Please do. I'm dying to know if I'm infected. I don't feel different and haven't had many dark thoughts lately, but who knows?"

The warmth enveloped Phoebe, melting into her body and gently searching for any trace of demonic energy. Seconds later, it dissipated.

"Okay, that was faster than I expected," Lane said. "How do you feel?"

"The same. Was I supposed to feel different?"

"No," she smiled. "That makes sense. You weren't infected or possessed, but I wasn't expecting anything else from someone as skilled as you."

Phoebe chuckled. "Fantastic! I feel like a kid on their birthday. I can't wait to tell everyone the news. Let's check every bedroom first. The most depressed and probably infected people are there. Afterwards, we can go to the canteen and finish with the training area."

Within two hours, everyone had been checked. Most were infected, which wasn't weird for their line of work, but luckily, no one was possessed. Like snow on a sunny day, the tension building up for half a moon cycle melted away. Only now that it was gone had she realised it had been there all along. The pressure was replaced with music and chatting, with late-night fights and swims.

The last fourteen days had been stressful for everyone, not only for her and Kage. Guardians had been on edge, waiting for answers about how Kage had become unpossessed. It couldn't have been easy to be kept in the dark about a cure to a disease they thought was deadly.

Lane felt a sense of fulfilment when providing everyone with hope. This time, she had helped instead of needing assistance. She reciprocated a small portion of the support and love the others had shown her since her arrival.

Although it had felt amazing, the sense of accomplishment was short-lived. Within two hours, she was back in her room, bored and craving to go to Kage.

CHAPTER 31

After spending the night tossing and turning in bed, Lane needed to act before the temptation was too big. She'd end up knocking on Kage's door if she didn't distract herself. Without thinking further, she left her room, passed by his, knocked on Diana's door, and asked if she wanted company. To her relief, Diana nodded. She slipped inside and sat beside her on the bed. Neither wanted to talk nor be alone, so they sat together, finding comfort in the shared silence.

Enough questions roamed around in Lane's mind, but she wouldn't ask them. She would give her all the space and time and be there when she decided to talk. The questions would be answered eventually. She only had to wait and not make the same mistake as with Kage.

Hours later, Lane's stomach broke the silence.

"Can you bring me something warm? I'm starving, but I don't want to go out there. Everyone is looking funny at me."

Lane nodded and left the room, returning minutes later with a bowl of warm stew and one of tomato soup. "Which one do you want?" she asked Diana, who gestured to the soup. "Then you get a bonus," Lane added, getting a piece of bread and a spoon out of her pocket. "Not the most hygienic, but I ran out of hands, and this seemed better than my armpits."

Diana's lips twitched, almost a smile, before grabbing the bread and thanking Lane.

A few more silent hours passed until Diana spoke, "Can you make some warmth?"

"Of course."

Diana didn't have to tell her why or ask twice. Lane was grateful she was letting her stay there and help in any way possible, for as little as the request was. The room filled with warmth, and a sigh escaped Diana. Her muscles relaxed, and Lane couldn't help but smile.

"I'm fine, you know? I've just seen a lot and need to give everything a place in my head. Kage worries too much."

Lane forced a faint smile, glancing at Diana. "You don't have to be, you know? Fine. It would be perfectly normal if you weren't. Like you said, you've seen a lot." She played with her spoon. "And you went through a lot. Everyone wants to ask you how you are, but they don't want to force you to talk, so...they end up staring."

Diana slid closer to Lane, where the warmth was strongest, and melted into the mattress. As if breaking a seal within her, she began talking about how much she had missed food.

During the possession, the demon made her eat at the Keep to maintain appearances, but he stopped as soon as she fled. She went by the rest of the possession with hardly any food, apart from the occasional stolen bread on the way to the Greater Demon and the litres of human blood the demon had gulped to evolve.

A wave of nausea swept through her body, thinking about the taste, and she quickly changed the subject to how sleeping had also been as absent as meals. Her body got zero moments of rest, except again during the bath in the river. Luckily for her, the fatigue was easier to withstand than the hunger since, even though her body couldn't rest, her mind got to shut down occasionally.

Sleeping meant not knowing what the demon was up to. He got free range to do whatever he wanted. It was difficult to admit, but she'd almost considered shutting down entirely to avoid witnessing his doings. However, after the initial hesitation, she stayed awake to learn as much as possible in case she was freed. She needed a goal to keep herself hopeful and motivated to fight back. And for most of the possession, she fulfilled that goal, except during two big moments.

The first was when Diana couldn't feel her spirit any more. After less than six days, the demon had pushed hers to a dark corner somewhere inside her. To a place Diana's mind couldn't reach without fighting the demon first. While possessed, she thought she had lost her spirit, that the demon had killed her somehow. Only after being freed did Diana learn her spirit was still within her. The empty spot was filled with warmth and joy again, and for the first time, Diana heard her spirit talk.

When Kage and Lane asked her if she wanted to be alone, she immediately said yes because she wanted to check in on her spirit uninterrupted. Together, they'd been patching their memories back up, trying to reconstruct and make sense of what they'd gone through. It was a painful and slow process, but it helped Diana escape the dark corner she'd been shoved into.

The second moment that almost broke her happened not long after losing contact with her spirit when Diana thought Lane was dead. She blamed herself for not trying harder to stop the demon. For not seeing the demon had other intentions when hugging Kage, and that it was a front to insert an Azrunol in her brother in order to later control him. For not stopping the demon from going after Lane.

"Remember what I told you when you arrived at the Keep? That most demons coming after you vanished once you were inside the barrier?" Lane nodded. "Well, they didn't. Not really. They hid...inside us. Everyone in this Keep is infected except for a few. Some more than others."

"They were, not anymore. I cleansed them, just like I cleansed you."

"I'm glad to hear that." Diana forced a smile.

"What do you mean by 'some more than others'?"

"Kage and I were the first on the scene. We got the bulk of the lot. I more than he did because I'm not as skilled. But yes. Now I know why we couldn't find them."

"You mean...you can be infected with multiple demons at a time?"

"Yes and no. Yes, because you can have more than one demon enter your body, but also no, because they merge into one and sometimes evolve into a stronger version. There can only be one demon inside you, just like there can only be one spirit. The more demons infect you and merge, the quicker they evolve. It's an effective way to infect someone with a stronger demon without the struggle of inserting it in someone's body."

"Why? Isn't it easier to go for a stronger demon in one go? Wouldn't it be quicker?"

"Not really. The stronger the demon, the more the host's body resists. The best approach is to have a bunch of Gulgath jump at you. As they enter your body, they evolve into an Azrunol. If you're as lucky as I am, enough Gulgath join the party that one jealous thought is all it takes to have it cross the threshold and evolve into a Dregma."

"How?"

"See it as doing that one move you've been trying for days. You need to put in the work first. Demons have to gather a certain amount of demonic energy before evolving. That energy must come from other demons, but you can lower the threshold, just like you can reduce training time with a good coach telling you where things go wrong. Iron is one of those things, and human blood is filled with it. That's why infecting us is so desirable to them."

She sighed. "The other is negative energy. Think of bad thoughts or feelings. Jealousy or rage. With a Gulgath at the threshold to evolve, it only needs a small incentive to become a Dregma. I'm not going to lie. I had a weak moment when you left with Kage to go to the clearing without looking back. A drop of my jealousy was enough to seal the deal. The demon possessed me as soon as it evolved. That's when those mood swings started."

She grabbed a pillow and hugged it. "I should have fought harder against being possessed. I should have stopped it from hitting you. Or from letting it put another demon inside Kage and order it to kill you." She rocked slightly back and forth. "Because of me, Kage almost took your life. If I had fought harder—"

"Stop! Don't say another word. Stop." Lane put her hand on Diana's knee. "Don't ever say that again. Don't even think it, okay? It was not your fault. It was the demon's."

"Sure... You can say that again." She sniffled. "I see that now. But in the moment, that's how I felt. When I saw you hanging in the air, lifeless... I lost hope. My demon knew what you could do. He felt you destroying the ones inside Luke and Kage. You were the only one who could save me, and you were gone, so I curled up and waited for my time to come."

From then on, she stopped paying attention to what was happening around her. She numbed herself to what the demon did with her. She had no idea how long she had been stuck in the darkness, but at some point, the demon shrank so hard that Diana caught a glimpse of light.

He was so terrified that it could only mean Lane had survived. A surge of energy allowed her to push away the demon's presence the tiniest bit. He wouldn't notice the change, but it was enough to give her room to breathe and take back a drop of control.

During that time, she learned that an invisible and unbreakable bond from the Greater Demon connected all demons. It spread to all Lesser Demons in an invisible pyramid-shaped web where the Greater Demon was on top, followed by Ezraan and all the way down to Karazak. This construction allowed them to communicate telepathically with each other. It granted higher Lesser Demons control over those below them without ever being capable of disobeying the Greater Demon's orders.

But their system wasn't flawless. The Dregma and Ezraan tended to twist the Greater Demon's commands, finding loopholes in their orders to do as they pleased without technically disobeying their master. They were highly focused on how the words were used. Sentences with multiple meanings would leave room for interpretation, and they would take advantage of the situation.

Diana sighed. Talking did her good. She spoke for hours as she explained every thought that came to mind. It was as if a tap had been opened and could no longer be closed. She poured it all out, and Lane listened.

"They have a base, you know?"

She described the village deep in the south that demons had destroyed. They burned it to the ground and painted the streets red with the blood of their victims. They used it to grow an army away from the guardians' gaze and reach.

"Their evolution process... Not a fun thing to go through as a host. The demon gets bigger with each evolution. I could feel my skin stretch, even though, from the outside, I looked thinner than ever," she said, gesturing at her fragile-looking body. "It was awful. And the blood-drinking... Don't get me started on that part. It was disgusting."

Diana was slowing down and taking longer breaks between sentences. "After the demon evolved, the little control I had regained was snatched from me. I could only see or hear for about five minutes at the time, but I had to put most of my energy into it. It was exhausting and annoying."

"Do you know where the village is?"

"No, I was never awake or focusing when he mentioned it."

"We'll figure it out eventually." Lane rested her hand on Diana's knee and pinched it lightly. "I can't imagine what all that must have felt like. I'm glad we got rid of the demon. You won't have to feel it ever again. Not if it's up to me. I'll do whatever is in my power to prevent it. I promise."

Diana hugged Lane as hard as she could. Lane's heart broke slightly at how soft it was. "Thank you, and sorry for the fight. I did try to stop him."

"It was a good practice. Rough, but I learned a lot." Lane winked.

Diana let out a soft chuckle. "What happened after I left?"

"Long story. Should we talk about it over some more food? There was a stack of pancakes and a pan with hot chocolate with our name on it." A hopeful smile tugged at her lips, her eyebrows slightly raised.

Diana's lips mirrored hers, forming her first genuine smile since Lane had entered the room. "Oh...yes, please. Haven't had chocolate in ages."

"I thought you might. Chocolate makes everything better."

❦•●•❧

Lane wanted to make sure Diana ate enough. She'd felt her fragile body shiver, struggling to produce even the smallest amount of warmth to keep her toes from freezing.

Diana still needed to heal the wounds left by the demon that no one could see. Relearning to generate warmth wasn't a priority right now. If Lane could relieve some of the burden by using her ability, she would.

"What were you doing in there?" Kage asked after Lane closed the door to Diana's room, his voice sharp and demanding.

"Why do you care? I'm getting ourselves some food. She doesn't want to leave her room but still needs substance to get better."

"I told you we needed space."

"No, you told me *you* needed space, and I'm giving it. But you don't get to decide what Diana needs or wants. I asked her, and apparently, my ability helps her feel better. So, if you don't mind, I'm getting us hot chocolate, and then I'm going back in there."

She walked away, but he grabbed her arm.

"Stay away from us," he pronounced each word clearly and slowly.

Lane's gaze switched between his face and hand. "Let go of me." But he didn't. His face was stone-cold, and his grip tightened. "Kage. Let go." His eyes were greyish and distant.

What was his problem? She was helping Diana heal. That had to count for something. She took a deep breath and counted to three in her head. When he didn't let go, she made her light shine around her arm, burning his hand slightly. He wailed, letting go of her. Seeing he wasn't wounded, realisation sank in. His eyes, again green, shifted to her, shock plastered on his face.

"Lane, I'm sorry. I-I don't know... I don't know what I was thinking."

"Just leave me alone." She turned around and rushed to the canteen. *What's wrong with him?*

I do not know. I did not feel any demons inside him, so it was probably from the stress. Maybe we do have to talk to him at some point. Leaving him alone with his thoughts may not be the best approach after all. Especially without Luke here to support him.

Lane grabbed two plates, filling them with pancakes, berries and syrup, leaving only a little space for the mug overflowing with hot chocolate. On her way back, Kage stomped out of Diana's room, fuming and entering his own.

"Everything all right?" she asked Diana. "I just saw Kage leave."

"He's mad because I don't want him here. His energy is too cold and reminds me of demons. I can't handle it right now."

304

"Oh..." Lane gave Diana her plate and delicately told her about the developments involving Kage.

"I'm an idiot! I told him straight to his face that he reminded me of them. He's probably already thinking that himself, and I come with my big mouth and tell him he's right. We need to go talk to him."

"We?" Lane hesitated. "No... Thi-this is between the two of you."

"I can't stay around him for too long without your help. I need your energy to counteract his. Please..."

"But the food... It'll get cold and..." Lane sighed. "Okay... But I need to tell you what happened between us first, so you understand if it gets awkward."

Diana sat upright on her bed, intrigued. As she sipped the hot chocolate, Lane explained what happened after breaking the last barrier, how Kage had asked for space, and what he said once Diana was saved. She quickly went through the major events Diana had missed, except what had just happened in the hallway. Diana was still too weak to see that.

Maybe ever. Maybe I'll keep this one for myself. She doesn't need to see her brother like that.

"At least he said he likes you," Diana added with a nervous smile, trying to lighten the mood.

"Yeah... Sort of..." Lane's mouth twitched, incapable of summoning a full smile. "Now you know, so let's go before I change my mind."

❦●●●❧

They searched every corner of the Keep, but Kage was nowhere to be found. They even searched the lake and the clearing, but he wasn't there either. Everyone they asked gave the same answer: no one knew where he was.

"You can say no if you don't feel like it, but would you like to train with me?" Lane asked cautiously.

"You still want that after our last fight? I thought you were crazy when I saw all the Karazak and Gulgath run after you, but now, I'm sure." They both smiled, not yet ready to laugh. "But yes, please. I need to move! I need to do something other than stay in my room." But if you don't mind, I prefer to do it at the clearing," Diana said, looking around at all the people who slowed their pace the moment they saw her, clearly pondering whether they should come talk to her.

"It's as if you can read minds. I was about to say the same. I need to do something other than being in a room, and cleaning the bathroom ain't it."

For Diana, the only good thing about the possession was that she'd learned things about her ability. She could do more than she thought possible. Healing minor wounds and infusing someone with her energy was a part of it, but the opposite was also possible. She could deplete others and block their ability. It had never crossed her mind because her goal was to help, not hinder. However, learning to control all aspects of her ability could be useful in fights.

"I think that's why I can't be near Kage for too long. Since my warmth is down, I'm constantly sucking up other people's energy to compensate. With his energy, I sense it is searching within me for something it has lost. It's weird and scary."

Diana shivered. "Your energy, on the other hand, is also searching, but it's looking for stuff to get rid of. It's hard to explain, but it feels safe and warm." Diana didn't have to explain it. Lane felt it through her ability. "But anyway, let's not worry about that. Now it's time to forget about everything."

Diana needed it right now. They both did. Forgetting about what was happening, even for a minute, and focusing on what they enjoyed would do them good. It would give their minds the needed rest.

They both adopted a fighting stance and fought until the sun went down. Diana's energy reservoir had shrunken noticeably while possessed. She went through it too fast, needing lots of breaks in between. But it didn't bother Lane. She let Diana draw from her energy as much as she wanted. As long as they got to move and were away from the Keep, Lane was happy.

On their way back, Diana explained how, while they fought, she could sense the amount of energy Lane had inside her. It was as if she could assess Lane's strength. She'd have to test her new skill on others to determine if she was using it correctly, but if she was, it meant Lane was a beast. Her energy pool was enormous. Diana could only grasp sections at a time. Seeing Lane stroll so freely and lightly, knowing what she carried inside her, was mind-blowing.

"It makes me feel less remorseful about consuming it. Thank you for letting me."

"Of course. My warmth is your warmth," Lane winked.

Diana chuckled. "Thanks. And your ability... It's a brilliant idea to protect yourself with it like that. And the daggers... You don't even have to move your hands to control them. It's incredible. It makes it harder to know where they're going. And your faster response... The Sight is agreeing with you, I see." The enthusiasm brought out a sliver of the bubbly Diana Lane loved. It wasn't as energetic as when they first met, but it was good to see that side of her still resided inside her.

Lane smiled. "We're learning to work together, to control the light together to get a better response during an attack. It still needs some work, but we're getting there."

"You can say that again. I hope to get to that level with my spirit one day. I heard her for the first time seconds after being freed. We need to get to know each other first. There's a lot of catching up to do, but maybe once I'm feeling better, I might try it too. But I'm already working on something new. Did you notice?"

"You mean about the buckets of energy you stole? I did. You were fast too. I couldn't stop it, and it threw me off a few times. I had to focus extra hard not to have my light flicker."

"Really? That's great to hear." Diana's eyes sparkled. "I felt it going well, especially for the first time without the demon, but I hadn't realised it had gone *that* well."

Lane's energy still flowed inside her. Even though the demon was gone, her body still had marks of its presence everywhere. It was as if he left parts of himself hidden to torture her after he was gone. So well hidden she couldn't reach them. But Lane's light could. It found them and destroyed them with ease.

"Thank you, Lane." Diana stopped and hugged her. "For everything. Thank you for not giving up, for coming knocking on my door, and for this today. I felt a little more like myself."

Lane hugged Diana back. "That's what best friends do for each other, right? I've missed you." She pulled Diana's shoulders back to make eye contact. "Kage, Luke and Althea are fun to be around, but I missed our talks, our training and hanging out together. I'm glad you're back, and I get what you mean. I felt the same just now. It was nice to let go for a bit." Lane rested her arm on Diana's neck. "Let's keep it going a bit longer by getting ourselves a nice, warm bowl of potato and rabbit roast. I'm starving!"

CHAPTER 32

Kage didn't know what he was doing. He was lost for the first time in years and disliked the feeling. His thoughts were all over the place. He couldn't think straight. Part of him wanted to tell Lane he didn't care about their spirits being soulmates and whether they had any influence on them. But the biggest part didn't want to see her before he understood what he could do with his new ability.

The way he grabbed her in the corridor made him sick. The anger that built up inside him when she closed Diana's door made him see red. Before he realised it, his hand was wrapped around her arm, squeezing tighter and tighter, and he couldn't let go.

It was better to keep her at a distance until he understood himself again, even if it meant hurting her feelings.

He brushed the outburst off to the new spiritual energy rushing through his body. When his spirit evolved, an untamed wave of power crashed into him. He assumed it would settle in a few days, but it hadn't. It flowed through his veins like a wild animal, enticing him to use it and pushing him over the edge. It made him irritable and reactive.

More power didn't mean he was immediately stronger. On the contrary. It would kill him if he didn't learn to control it. But the possibilities... Kage could almost not contain his excitement. Reaching Lane's level, maybe even higher, was now attainable. More power meant he could protect those he loved. Nothing was as important.

Even if they end up hating me. The look on Lane's face flashed through his eyes when he told her he didn't know what to think about their feelings. It was a lie. He knew. For the first time in five years, he knew. But he had to keep his distance until he controlled his rage and was stronger.

He lost too many people because he was weak. He wouldn't let it happen again, no matter what. Understanding what his ability could do with his evolved spirit was the first step. And there was only one way to figure it out.

Signing off the last missions, creating groups of who was to go out where, he asked Phoebe to take over the following days. She didn't have to do much. Most paperwork that would arrive while he was gone could be dealt with once he returned. It was mostly a precaution in case something important came along while he was away exploring.

The Gulgath and Karazak that he felt all the way to the far end of Caragain, slithering around in sewers and waiting for the sun to go down, called at him, and he intended to listen.

How did the men I sent on patrol miss so many? There shouldn't be a single demon lurking in Caragain.

His focus turned to himself. To his relief, he didn't feel any demons inside himself. *Does that mean I'm clean?* Probably, but he still wanted to get checked by Lane to be sure. He couldn't trust his new ability if it had a blind spot.

Kage, listen to me.

"I did, Sayah. It's a lovely story about guardians not being soulmates while their spirits are. But that's not the point. I need her away from me. I need time to figure things out on my own. I can go back later and talk to her. I'll even apologise a million times if there's still anything to save between us. But not right now. So please, let it go."

Right now, he craved to reach the demons in the distance, not Lane. His ability felt like an updated report with new pages waiting to be read. He wanted nothing more than to read them, to dissect them to their core and put them into practice.

Mastering every facet of his power was crucial. It was the only path to true strength. His spirit had given him an opportunity to grow, and he refused to waste it.

While saving Lane, he felt powerful with the demons in his grasp. Even during that terrifying situation, he felt alive. He longed for that sensation again. Not what came after when the demons pushed against his invisible grip, and he almost lost control, sinking his heart to the ground. *That* could never be repeated. Neither could Diana become possessed ever again.

It was my fault. I made her susceptible. He wouldn't let it happen again. Diana would never have to see another demon near her ever again. *I'll make sure of it.*

On the outskirts of Caragain, demons lurked nearby. When the shrinking moon lit the sky, he stopped in the middle of a broad, empty street and ordered, "Come."

No more words were needed. The invisible strings tethering him to the demons in the area tightened, drawing whatever lay on the other end to him. Before long, over forty Karazak and Gulgath surrounded him, waiting for their next command.

This many?

He barked for them to follow, climb buildings and fight each other. Jump, roll over and sprint in circles. The demons obeyed without hesitation.

Sensing his energy nearing its limits and his grip weakening, he ordered the creatures to disperse and stay away until summoned again, hoping his orders would be upheld even after his grip vanished. The thrill zoomed all over his body for hours.

As the day broke in with a headache from exerting himself too much, he searched for a building with a flat rooftop to rest on. He'd told Phoebe to expect him to be gone for three days. He didn't have to return just yet.

⟨❧•●•☙⟩

Luke flew back as fast as he could, not wanting to wait a second more than necessary to tell the others what he found. He almost exploded with rage when he read the records himself. He didn't have to write it down. All the information was engraved in his mind. He couldn't think of anything else, nor dream of anything else. After Diana was safe, they would go after the Tirich's Children. Kage would agree once he heard the whole story.

Thanks to his mother's connections, he was allowed access to more restricted areas in the Capital's library, where he found a diary from the Tirich's Children. He distinguished three handwritings, with the first entries in the year 3216, around sixty years ago. In them, they documented their search for Rafael Tirich's works in the libraries of every Keep and the steps they took to create and grow their group of followers.

Rafael believed, just like Kage's book had explained, that killing one's soulmate was the last evolutionary step for a spirit: the transformation into a Greater Demon. He believed they were meant to exist and rule the world. In his eyes, Greater Demons were the perfect beings for not needing a host to be in this world, unlike spirits. They were meant to be free, while guardians were meant to be matched to create more. To Rafael, that was the true meaning of being a guardian. It was sickening.

The Tirich's Children took what he wrote to heart.

During the first three years, they wrote detailed entries about how they established the religion with a core group of fourteen fanatics. After, the entries diminished to a few each year, where the new additions to the group were mentioned. Most newcomers were infants born to two group

312

members, with only nine entries indicating adult guardians joined them independently.

About twenty-five years later, the last entry in the diary mentioned a gift a newcomer brought that would catapult the cult to new heights. It didn't specify what it was, so Luke searched for other sources, like reports and letters. In those, Luke found out there was a surge of guardians disappearing. Knowing what he now knew, he could imagine what those two pieces of information meant together.

The records of the following years mentioned the group on fewer and fewer occasions until they disappeared from the face of the world. People forgot their names and what they stood for until Tirich's Children became a name in kids' stories. People moved on and forgot the madness.

But the group didn't die off as suspected. In 3263, sixteen years ago, an unprompted reappearance of the group was recorded. For almost a year, multiple reports were written about fanatics flooding the streets of the Capital, protesting about how guardians weren't living up to their standards and how the world as they knew it was about to end. They urged people to join them as it was the only way they would survive what was coming.

In one of the later records, a member of the Tirich's Children was interviewed during one of their protests. Somehow, the author got the protester to talk about how his group knew the world would change. The protester's answer made Luke's blood boil.

"We have heard the words of the wise. The Greater Demons have spoken to us and told us what to do. Spirit soulmates are to be matched to create a new world. In seven days, you'll see we do not lie."

The author switched to an interview with the Capital higher-ups, asking them what they thought about it. Since the Tirich's Children had been protesting and saying what everyone felt was nonsense for almost a year, no one believed them. The author finished the report with a joke about hiding his spirit from the lunatics.

That report was dated two days before the war started. Luke wondered if the author had survived and put two and two together. Luckily for everyone, the Tirich's Children failed to create a Greater Demon. Instead, an army of Dregma and Ezraan flooded the streets of the Capital.

It was hard to believe they forgot or didn't know they needed to match soulmate guardians with soulmate spirits. One of the two wasn't enough. If Lane, Althea, Kage, and he had figured it out in one afternoon, it would have been highly improbable that the people obsessed with Tirich didn't reach the same conclusion. So, the question arose: Was another ingredient needed to create a Greater Demon?

If that was the case, they needed to find out what that was. Even without a Greater Demon, the number of Dregma and Ezraan summoned made it possible for them to start a war that lasted two seasons. A war that took thousands of lives with it. People wanted only to mourn and move on. Thinking how the protesting lunatics had anything to do with it was not on their list. So, the Tirich's Children felt under the radar again.

Luke still remembered that period in his life as if it were yesterday. He was nine and saw the explosion from afar. Afterwards, he waited for his father for days, even after the war was declared won.

After an entire season of hope, of his mother telling him how his father had died and of him attending his father's funeral, he gave up and accepted it for what it was. His father wasn't coming back. The war took him. The Tirich's Children took him, and nothing would bring him back.

Since every corner and street in the Capital brought up memories of his father, and the pain connected to it was unbearable, he moved to the Keep that same year. Before he left, his mother gave him a little box as a farewell gift. Afraid of what he would find inside, he never opened it. In all the years at the Keep, the negative thoughts surrounding the death of his father clouded his judgement.

But that changed just before he left for the Capital, thanks to Lane's cleansing. In the last days of spring, when he thought of his father, he remembered the good moments instead of the pain. He recalled the time spent together instead of when he wanted to talk to him but no longer could.

His mind was clear, quiet and happy. He visited his father's grave with his mother for the first time and spoke to him for hours. He opened the box his mother had given him fifteen years ago and found his father's name tag on a chain inside.

Flying back felt both satisfying and bittersweet. Leaving the place where his father was buried tugged at his heart, but he did it for a good reason. He wasn't running from his pain anymore. He found what he came for and was eager to share it with his friends. Learning what the Tirich's Children had done had reignited the fire within him. He couldn't wait to plan the next steps against them with the other.

࿇ • ● • ࿇

Time flew by as Kage wandered through the streets of Caragain. He was supposed to be back at the Keep, but the more he used his ability, the less of a headache he got and the more he wanted to feel his grip on demons. The power of holding them in place, telling them what to do, and seeing them do exactly what he ordered without hesitation was exhilarating.

His ability was limitless. He knew. He'd tried everything. Infecting or leaving any host he wanted, killing each other, killing animals, and even killing themselves.

It had been years since he felt this sense of security and strength, and still, he wanted more. He yearned for more strength, more power, more control.

CHAPTER 33

"Where the hell is he?" Diana asked after finishing their morning search for Kage.

"Not here, that's for sure," Lane answered.

"I'm starting to worry. I know I say he never has time for me, but he's still my brother. I miss him, and I can't help but think the worst. I want him to come back."

"I know, but I'm sure he's fine. Let's have lunch and continue the search later. He'll show up eventually," Lane said, sounding more defeated than optimistic.

Each morning for five days, they made the same round, looking for Kage: his room, office, canteen, training area, lake, clearing, and back to the Keep to ask everyone if anyone had seen him while they were doing the rounds. Each day, they repeated the same path after lunch, but instead of returning immediately, they trained at the clearing first to let out some steam.

But Kage was nowhere to be seen.

On the sixth day, they were headed to the canteen after checking Kage's room and office when the main door cracked open. Holding their breath, their gazes darted to the entrance. At the sight of blond hair, their shoulders dropped.

"Never mind, it's just Luke."

"Luke? Luke! You're back," Diana screamed, running to him and hugging him.

"An-and you... You're here!" He hugged her tightly and spun her around. They let go of each other, and Luke held Diana's face. "And you're you. I mean, I hope so. Or are those outbursts part of your new personality now?"

"Idiot! Of course not. I'm me again."

"Thank the spirits. I don't think I could've taken any more of those," he winked. "Jokes aside. This is fantastic. I'm so glad for you. I want to hear what happened, but I assume it concerns you." He wrapped his arm around Diana, not wanting to let go of her, and turned to Lane with raised eyebrows.

"It might have," Lane grinned. "And I hope you have new information for us too. But let's wait for Kage first. We were on our way to search for him."

Luke frowned, and Lane added, "Don't worry. It's nothing. We'll explain later. Just unpack, refresh since you must be exhausted from all the flying, and go say hi to your lovely Althea." She winked. "She's probably dying to see you. We'll meet after lunch in Kage's office to swap news."

"You don't have to suggest that twice," he said before sprinting to the infirmary.

With just the two of them again, they were about to go to the canteen when Diana suddenly felt a pull towards the clearing. Since neither of them had the slightest idea of where Kage was, it was as good a place to start.

"Where is he? I was so sure he'd be here." Diana let herself fall to the ground in the middle of the clearing after being met with nothing but birds chirping around. "This is all my fault. I should've been nicer to him. I shouldn't have said what I said."

"Don't say that. It's not your fault. He just needs time for himself.

Everyone has been through a lot, and he processes things differently than we do. We need to have someone around. He needs to be alone. Let's wait a bit longer before going back to the Keep. I'm sure he'll show up."

They lay on the ground in silence, searching for a good position to relax and stare at the clouds. The afternoon sun bathed their skin, melting them into a warm nap when they were shaken awake by the rustling leaves. Both were up in a heartbeat, ready to fight. Lane called for the light, but Diana relaxed, her hands dropping to the side, leaving Lane confused.

"We were worried sick! Where have yo—"

"Stop," Lane interrupted. "We don't know if he's the real Kage. Answer my question first: What happened when we hugged here?"

"I showed you the depth of my ability so you would trust me," Kage said, his voice flat and cold.

Lane let the light fade and joined Diana, who sprinted to Kage to hug him.

"You two did what? When did this happen?" When none of them answered, Diana went on. "Where were you? We were worried sick."

"I needed time alone. I don't want to talk about it."

The girls exchanged concerned looks but didn't push further. Lane confirmed he wasn't infected or possessed with a quick body scan.

That's a good sign.

They returned to the Keep, with Diana holding hands with Lane and Kage, doing her best to show him she could be near him, touch him even, and that his energy didn't affect her. But Lane knew better. Diana couldn't do it without consuming an enormous amount of Lane's energy to neutralise his.

To distract herself from the cold energy and feeling the awkwardness settle, Diana talked about how she was feeling better, what she'd done since returning, and that Luke was at the Keep waiting for them. When Kage replied with a simple and emotionless "Good," she stopped.

His reaction infuriated Lane. He had the right to be angry at and ignore her, but absolutely no reason to talk to Diana like that. She was trying her best for him. Couldn't he see it?

Just let it go for now. You know he can feel your energy going into Diana, do you not? Just like you can feel his do the same. He knows Diana is doing her best to make him feel welcome, but he also knows the best for her is to stay away from him. It breaks his heart.

How do you know that?

His spirit told me.

Lane had forgotten their spirits were soulmates who could communicate with one another. So, she reluctantly agreed and let it be. Kage had a spirit to speak to. He wasn't alone, and hopefully, his spirit was helping him come back to her and his senses.

❧ • ● • ❧

All five of them—Kage, Diana, Luke, Althea and Lane—sat in Kage's office. Luke sat on the couch with Althea, refusing to talk until they told him how they'd managed to save Diana.

Kage stared at Diana from behind his desk, still not daring to look Lane in the eyes. Diana, sitting on one of the red chairs, stared at her. With a sigh, Lane sat beside Diana on the remaining free chair, unamused to be designated the storyteller.

She started by explaining what she'd learned after breaking the last barrier. Luke had the right to know the truth about his father's death. As she brought up the subject, Kage tensed up. She swallowed, glancing at him, and hoped Luke wouldn't react like he had.

She regurgitated it all in one go, barely stopping to breathe. Once done, she froze, expecting the worst as she let Luke process the information. He immediately told her to continue, but nothing but an apology came out of her mouth.

"Don't. No one could have known binding to a spirit would have such repercussions, especially being so young. Even if you did, the war ended because of you. We can't deny that a lot of people died, but many more would have if the demons had been allowed to go deeper into the Capital. Think of the children, the elderly and the Hollows you saved."

He smiled so brightly it felt like a warm blanket wrapping around her, comforting her. "Besides, you didn't start the war, now did you? I've found information about who did, so again, don't apologise. I don't blame you for it. My father died, but my mother and other family members didn't. I can't say they would still have survived if you hadn't exploded, but the odds wouldn't have been in their favour. So, don't think about it for a second longer because I won't, and tell me how you saved this one over here." Luke gestured at Diana with a wink.

Lane nodded, feeling grateful for his words. She glanced again at Kage, hoping to see him agree with Luke, but instead, he was staring at her. The air around him was darker and heavier than the rest of the room.

Her gaze fell to the floor, her breath shallow. She tried to remember what she was supposed to say, but her mind could only think of the crack between them growing.

Diana grabbed her hand, grounding her. With a deep breath and a thank you mouthed to Diana, Lane's thoughts reorganised, and she turned to Althea. "And you?"

"What about me?"

"Your father also died in the war, right?"

"Oh, that. Yeah, he did, but not in the Capital. He died a few days earlier in one of the battles."

"I'm sorry."

Althea blinked slowly and smiled at Lane. An image of her mother looking at her the same way formed in Lane's mind, providing her with the courage she lacked to continue her story. As she spoke, Luke stared at Kage with his mouth open. Althea sat beside him, just as speechless.

"Is that even possible?" Luke asked after snapping out of his daze. "Spirits evolving inside guardians? I thought it only happened after the host died. That's awesome, man. How did it feel when it happened? And now? Do you feel okay? Not too much energy inside you?" Kage shook his head once. If the response phased Luke, he didn't let it show. Instead, he went on with his enthusiasm and asked, "So, controlling demons, he? That's crazy, man. How does it feel?"

Kage shrugged.

"Okay... Not the reaction I was expecting." Luke's eyes switched to Lane, who avoided it by staring at her fidgeting hands. He turned to Diana, who shook her head in response.

"Never mind, we'll talk about it at the clearing later while I'm beating your ass." Luke laughed to brighten the mood, but Kage's blank face didn't change.

Seeing Luke try so hard to keep the mood up made it clear to Lane he already knew what she'd only recently learned. Pushing Kage to talk wouldn't help. He would do it of his own accord. Forcing him would only do more damage than good.

Even after giving him multiple days to think about it. She swallowed, feeling the crack between them widening.

Aware he wouldn't pull Kage out of whatever state he was in, Luke turned to Diana, shifting everyone's attention, and said, "And I still can't believe you're here. I'm so glad you're back. You're probably not your older self yet, but you look different. A bit older, I think." Diana's eyebrows raised, and he quickly added, "In a good way. In a good way. In a wise way."

"Well, I did go through a lot, so that sounds about right. But enough about me, what did you learn in the Capital?" Diana asked as she moved closer to Lane and hugged her arm for warmth.

"Well..." Luke hesitated for a second. The air around Kage became heavier as the conversation developed. "What do you think of having a break first? I'm kinda thirsty."

"Just spit it out." Kage's words were sharp and cold. They brought shivers down Lane's spine.

Luke frowned and glanced at her. A soft and sad smile formed on her lips, hoping Kage wasn't paying attention to her.

"I'm not sure I should. Maybe we can go for a walk first, Kage. Just the two of us."

"Don't make me squeeze it out of you," Kage barked. "Spit it out. I've got enough to do. Don't waste my time."

Luke frowned. "No. I want to talk to you in private first." He stood up and turned to face the door, but before he could take a step, the walls were covered in shadows. The door was gone, as were every painting and book on the wall.

"Kage..." Lane's voice quivered. "Calm down."

"I will, once Luke tells me what he knows."

"You want to know this badly?" Luke raised his arms to the walls. "Really? You think this is the way to go? Sure, I'll tell you. But you need to give me something first. We'll trade information. If you can tell me why you're so reactive and angry, I'll tell you what I know."

Kage stared at Luke, unmoving. Even though his face was stone-cold, the shadows around him said enough about his mood as they chanced into tentacle-like structures lashing wildly in every direction.

"Nothing to say? Fine. Then I'm leaving until you calm down. Lane, open the door for me, please."

The outburst was so hard and fast that they only realised what was happening when Luke screamed. The shadow tentacle held him tightly above the ground, pressing harder and harder against his ribcage.

"Kage! What the hell? Let go of him!" Diana screamed. "Lane, help him!"

Lane didn't hesitate. She filled the room with her light, and the tentacles vanished. Once Luke was on the floor, Althea rushed to his side to see if he was hurt.

"I'm... I'm..." Kage whispered, eyes wide open.

"It's okay, Kage. Just calm down," Lane said as she approached him. His eyes flashed from Luke to her. "You're okay..." His gaze turned distant, and the shadows erupted again before she could reach him or say anything else.

A wall of light formed before her, stopping the tentacle's attack. They didn't reach her, but the force of the impact pushed her back. She grabbed the arm of the chair to maintain her balance as the crushing sound of glass shattering filled the room.

After a moment of silence, the light parted, ready to return in case the shadows came for her again. To her surprise, she was met with no tentacles, no shadows. No Kage. He was gone. In his place was a pool of broken glass from an enormous window she had no idea existed. Its curtains swayed in the warm summer breeze. Calm and quiet. A stark contrast to the chaos that had just unfolded.

The crack between them had grown so vast she could barely hold both sides together, his scent on the opposite side fading.

"What in the spirits was that?" Luke asked as he sat back down on the couch.

Lane wanted to answer the question, but she couldn't. Not only because she didn't know what was happening with Kage, but also because of the knot in her throat. She wanted to cry and scream and go after him, but her body was frozen in place, staring at the broken window, wondering where he'd gone.

"I'm going after him after I tell you what I know about the start of the war fifteen years ago," Luke said, staring at Lane's unmoving back. "I'll find him and put some sense into him, I promise. Just come sit down, Lane," his voice was soft. He, of all people, should be pissed, but he controlled his temper for her.

"You mean the Tirich's Children?" Diana asked as she nudged Lane towards a chair.

"Yes, how do you..." Luke frowned.

"The demon wasn't expecting me to be saved. He wasn't too careful about what he said or thought while possessing me, so..." Diana smiled faintly. "I suppose that was one of the benefits, if you can call it that. But I know, so go after him. Waiting will only make it harder to find him. I'll tell Lane about the fanatics."

Slowly, Lane turned to Luke. He nodded at her, a certainty sparking in his eyes, telling her everything would turn out okay.

She dragged her feet to the chair. The impact of letting her body fall onto the hard chair unleashed a waterfall of tears.

"He'll realise how he acted and be back before you know it." Diana put her hand on Lane's back to comfort her.

"He won't. I should've talked to him when I had the chance," Lane said between sobs. "I should have pushed him to let me help him. Instead, I did nothing. I let him go through all of this on his own, and it broke him. I've never seen or felt his energy like that. Have you?"

"I haven't, but he just needs to cool down. He'll be back. Luke will bring him back," Diana repeated the last words as she rubbed Lane's back.

"I broke him," Lane whispered.

⊰•●•⊱

Kage was appalled by his behaviour.

Hearing Luke speak to him as if he were a child, telling him what was best for him, had infuriated him. Before he realised it, his vision had turned red once more. He would have killed him if Lane hadn't intervened, just as he had in the corridor with her. At that moment, he felt like a bystander in his body, powerless to stop himself.

Not that I wanted to in the moment. A shiver ran down his spine at the thought. It crept into his mind without warning, yet it was true. It was precisely why he couldn't return to the Keep until his emotions were under control. He couldn't go back for his own safety and that of others. Regardless of the stakes or the situation he would eventually find himself in, he needed to be on top of it. To achieve that, he needed time alone.

ᘒ●●ᘓ

Diana attempted to give Lane some space, but early the following day, she knocked on her bedroom door and cuddled beside her. She tried to keep her distance, but couldn't relax without Lane's energy. The absence of warmth sent her spiralling back to feeling cold, lonely, and possessed.

Wandering around Shuutin hadn't distracted her. Swimming wasn't any better. Diana even attempted to use some of Luke's energy after he returned from his unsuccessful search for Kage, but his energy reservoir was minimal compared to Lane's. She couldn't consume enough to alleviate her discomfort without draining him. Besides, Lane's energy was more effective. A single drop had an instant effect. Diana would eventually have to live without it, preferably by generating her own warmth again. But she wasn't prepared to do so just yet.

ᘒ●●ᘓ

After a day spent lying in bed, sulking and waiting, Diana and Lane resumed their routine, hoping for time to pass faster. Each night, they shared Lane's bed. In the morning, they had breakfast and wandered through another part of the forest, just in case he had set up camp nearby. After lunch, they went to the clearing to ensure Kage wasn't there, practised until sundown and returned to the Keep for dinner in Lane's room. During that time, he was, as they feared, nowhere to be found. Luke even scouted Caragain but also returned empty-handed.

When the fourth night after Kage's disappearance passed, Lane gave up on the idea of him ever coming back.

"I can't stand passing by his door again or staring at the main door, hoping he walks in. He isn't coming back, at least not any time soon, so we'd better get used to it and go back to living our lives," she said after finishing the pancakes she'd served herself for breakfast.

"I didn't want to say it, but I think you're right," Diana said with her mouth full.

"I know you all want to go to the mountains and see about the Tirich's Children, but I need to go to Stanlow before I can join you."

Diana didn't ask why. "Let's go find the others." She stood, but Althea and Luke entered the canteen. Diana waved at them to come over.

"I'm leaving tomorrow for Stanlow to talk to the person who raised me. I need to ask her some questions before going to the mountains. We don't know what we might find there, and I can't do it before talking to her."

"You should," Luke said. "We don't want you dreaming about home while we fight all the lunatics, now do we? We need your full attention up there, so if you have to do this to make it happen, do it. We'll wait another moon cycle for Kage and to give you a heads-up. I'll check Caragain every other day for any signs of him."

"I can fill your place in your morning walk around the forest. I can keep Diana some company," Althea added.

"That's sweet of you, but I'll be joining Lane. It's not wise to travel alone right now."

"Di, you don't ha—" Lane started, but Diana cut her off.

"I'm going with you, and that's final. I need you as much as you need me, so don't start."

Lane smiled and nodded, relieved she didn't have to travel or face Miss Deleon alone.

"We can meet at my grandparents' house. They live in Goldcrest, a village at the foot of the mountain."

"Oh, so I'll get to meet your family? So soon? Are you sure you're ready?" Luke teased, a grin spreading across his face. Althea chuckled and tapped his arm. "Don't worry, I am. I could meet your whole family at once and still feel ready." His voice softened, becoming smoother. "Trust me."

"Idiot," she whispered, then kissed him.

Luke's fingers wrapped around her hair. Diana coughed loudly, and the two lovebirds turned to her, eyes wide and cheeks burning.

"Yeah... um... that's a brilliant idea, Althea. It'll be easier to find each other," Luke said, regaining his composure and stepping away from her. "So, it's settled. You two go to Stanlow. Once you're done, come to Goldcrest. We'll meet you there and decide our next move." His smile grew as he spoke, excited to get his plan to pursue the Tirich's Children underway.

"Hopefully, with the five of us," Lane whispered.

Diana placed a hand on Lane's shoulder. "You can say that again."

⊱•●•⊰

Kage could barely see where he was going. Shadows obscured his vision, but he didn't care. He didn't need to see. He could feel where he had to go, where the demons lurked, even those kilometres away. Controlling as many as he could at once was the best way to learn to manage his emotions. When their connection tightened, he couldn't allow himself to feel anxious, annoyed or angry, or the bond would weaken, and the demons would turn on him.

For days, he walked. It didn't matter where he was going, only whether there were demons in his path. Every Gulgath and Karazak he encountered, he connected with. Each Azrunol he sensed from afar, he summoned to abandon its host and join him. A fragile sense of stability returned with every binding, and the shadows clouding his vision began to fade.

But it never lasted.

One or two days later, the rage bubbled back to the surface, demanding more demons to hold in his grip. It was the only way to quell the feverish anger roaring inside him.

Not being at the Keep made him less fearful of those feelings. In the middle of nowhere, he couldn't harm those he loved. The rage would die down when he discovered the limits of his ability. He was certain. To achieve this and do it as quickly as possible, he needed more and stronger demons to control. It was that simple.

I need... The presence he sought pulled at him from far away.

"Druzon..."

Acknowledgements

I want to thank Thomas, my partner, for always going along with my crazy ideas. You give me space when I need it (just like when I only let you read the book once I've said for the tenth time I was done) and advice when I'm stuck. You support me every step of the way. Thank you. I love you.

I want to thank Eva, my best friend and first reader. You have been there every step of the way. You read the book when it was still 20% of what it is today. Your questions, remarks and advice shaped the story into what it is today. Without you, I would have so many plot holes that the book would be see-through.

I want to thank Ines, my sister, for drawing the awesome cover for this book, as well as all the merch I have along with it. You put up with all the weird ideas I had along the way and the incomplete explanations of what I wanted. You helped me think about promotion, got me into events to sell my book by sharing your table with me, and introduced me to Carla, whom I also must acknowledge.

Carla, you read my book when it was a few edits away from what it is now. Your enthusiasm blew me away. You saw the potential that I didn't yet know existed and have since been guiding me in this publishing journey. Your connections and knowledge of the industry made this publishing possible. Without you, I'd probably still be thinking about how to launch this into the world.

I want to thank my family and friends for their support and for keeping me accountable. I'm grateful for the people who wrote their opinions on the form after reading the first chapters, those on Instagram and TikTok who found me and supported me through the ups and downs, and the beta readers for your input.

Thank you all for the support, energy and enthusiasm you put into this book. I couldn't have done it without any of your help.

Printed in Great Britain
by Amazon

62090601R00191